Dedicated to all the CRPG fans that couldn't romance the companion of their dreams.

Damn you, Josh Sawyer!

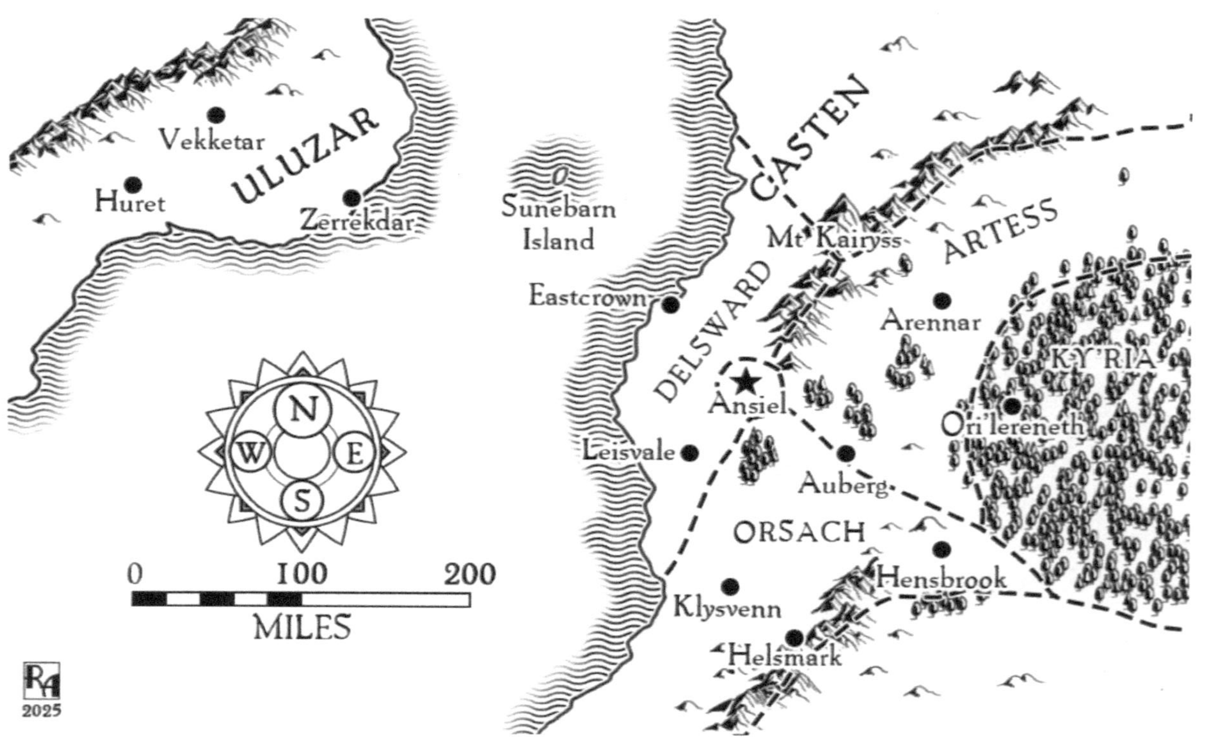

ULUZAR
Vekketar
Huret
Zerrékdar
Sunebarn Island
CASTEN
ARTESS
Mt Kairyss
DELSWARD
Eastcrown
Arennar
KY'RIA
Ansiel
Ori'lereneth
Leisvale
Auberg
ORSACH
Hensbrook
Klysvenn
Helsmark
N
E
S
W
0
100
200
MILES
RA
2025

Prologue

I couldn't help but find it a little ironic that my people fought best on calm, sunny days: an impending battle that conjured images of strong winds, clouds darkening the horizon to mirror the dark hearts of the warriors. But my eagle riders needed bright skies to see by, and steady winds to fly in—the kind of weather meant for children playing in the fields. I put those thoughts out of my mind; the gods had dealt me a hand, and it was time to play it.

Chip, my trusty giant eagle, shifted restlessly as I fitted his harness; he knew what it meant. He chirped and cawed to the other eagles in the squadron as my wingmen worked on them, everyone preparing for the fight to come.

Countess Narrisai approached. She was a tall woman with sandy blonde hair woven in artful braids and wearing a fine dress that accentuated her figure. Since she was human, and I was a halfling, she was twice my size, though I only really lamented that because she was too large to go flying with me.

She gave me a nervous smile. "Kali. I...are you sure about this?"

"A fight's never sure. What I am sure about is that the demons want you dead, and unlike the cultists, they're not going to back down with a few warm meals." I mounted Chip.

Narrisai walked to Chip's side, her hand brushing feather-light against my cheek. "Kali...be careful."

I looked at her sadly. "Were it that I could." I turned to my squadron. "Alright, let's fly!"

I gave Chip a gentle nudge, and she leapt into the sky, gathering the air under her wings. My squadron took flight, falling into formation behind me. The rocky hills of my homeland passed underneath as our eagles cleaved through the crisp mountain air, bringing us towards our target. Rookie eagle riders would be trembling from the height, but after so long on an eagle's back, flight was as natural to me as walking.

We found the demon's temple, situated on an inaccessible peak, surrounded by the less fortunate villages the demons were courting. I could see the standards of Countess Narrisai's soldiers advancing on it, and just beyond them, the handful of cultists still loyal to the demons. As I could see the distant figures form into battle lines, an unholy screech echoed through the sky. Demons, taking the shape of winged shadows, flew from the temple, slicing through the sky towards the soldier's flank. I took a few brightly coloured ribbons and waved them in a quick pattern. It was an order sent: attack.

As the demons came into range, I took out my sling and spun up. A gentle tap to my eagle's shoulder guided him to give me a clear shot, and I took it. I scored a solid hit on the demon's shoulder. It roared in rage, and it and most of its fellows turned towards the aerial threat. They flew up as my wingmen followed my shot with volleys of their own, like a lethal avalanche. The first demons fell from the sky as we closed in.

The closest demon dove down to strike Chip from above, a manoeuvre I'd seen before and knew how to counter. I tugged Chip into an abrupt turn, dodging the strike while simultaneously bleeding speed. As the demon whistled past, close enough to spit at me, I spiralled Chip downwards, following the demon. As it shifted to avoid a collision with the ground, I predicted where it'd go and guided Chip to head it off.

A blast of impossible, piercing cold dug into my back, even through my armour girded in my people's ancient magics. I could feel my spine seize up. There was one demon on my tail, no doubt lining up another shot that would without doubt finish me. Trusting Chip to attack the demon to our front, I tried to twist to see the one to our rear, but the injury to my spine slowed me. As I heard the demon start a fell incantation, I realised I had to act fast. I spun up another slingshot and fired it blindly behind me.

A bolt of unholy shadow whistled just past Chip—I hadn't connected, but I forced the demon to miss, which would be more than enough as far as I was concerned. Chip, meanwhile, had reached his target and was savaging the demon with beak and talon. The impact had slowed him, forcing the second demon to overshoot my position, flying where I could see it. With the risky situation, I decided now was as good a time as any to load a bullet laden with elemental flames, sending it at the demon. It wasn't a direct hit, but it was enough of one to ignite it, causing it to flee the battlefield, screeching.

Chip and the demon he had pinned struggled, beak against fang. Switching to my dagger, I leaned over to help. The demon, realising it had lost the advantage, tried to break free. Chip leaned into the move, using the speed to drive the demon into the mountain face, crushing it. He then pushed against it, back into the sky. With my squadron keeping the worst of the pressure from above, the soldiers could concentrate on the cultists. Being better disciplined and better equipped, they steadily pushed the cultists back.

An eerie screech emerged from the temple, and another demon appeared, this one a vaguely humanoid parody of a bat, twice the size of any humanoid. It hovered above the mountain range.

"Useless wretches! Fine! I'll do this myself!" It raised its hands, speaking a fell incantation, and the then-clear sky suddenly darkened with thunderclouds.

Realising the threat, I urged Chip towards it. The demon turned to me, grinning. He gestured towards me. I tried to tell Chip to bank, but a torrent of wind and hail came from the sky, far too wide to dodge. Chip was knocked off course. As we struggled to recover, the demon leapt at me with claws, one hitting me, the other hitting Chip. Both wounds were telling, and a large chunk was torn from Chip's wing.

We started to spiral towards the ground. Chip screeched in pain as he tried to recover. He gathered what air he could under his good wing, but we still hit the ground hard. Agonising pain shot through every part of my body as I tumbled down the mountainside, slamming hard into a mountain pass.

As I tried to move, I could faintly hear a cry of panic from nearby.

Narrisai's voice cut into my thoughts. "Oh, Etunae, please, grant me your healing power! Spare the one I love that I might finally tell her!"

For a moment, I thought it just some fantasy my mind had conjured to ease my death. But the pain faded, and the world came back into focus. Narrisai was there, her hands glowing with holy light. I blinked, barely daring to hope that what I had heard was true. "...You love me?"

Narrisai turned red. "Oh, I, uh, thought you were, um, unconscious..."

Whatever might have happened between us in that moment was interrupted by another roar from the demons. Narrisai hurried to Chip's side, invoking another prayer to her goddess. Chip's wounds closed, and he got back up, taking a moment to nuzzle Narrisai affectionately. I leapt onto Chip's back. To sate my flaming desire for just a second more, I gave Narrisai a quick peck on the cheek before flying back into battle.

The larger demon had beaten back my squadron and now turned its attention towards the advancing soldiers. Stronger than the cultists, its unholy magics battered and broke the formation. But the soldiers kept trying, loyal to their countess's cause. And that trying kept its attention for just long enough for me to come up with a new plan and rally my surviving wingmen behind me. With a shout and a series of coloured signals, I conveyed a new tactic.

My squadron started circling around the demon, keeping at range, and peppering it with sling bullets. It roared in rage, summoning a black shield of unholy force. The sling bullets bounced off but caused it to crack and fizzle. I signalled my squadron to keep up the fire. Flying out of the soldiers' reach, the demon called down more blasts of wind and rain on my squadron, but with our scattered formation, it couldn't hit more than one or two of us at a time. With the demon on the defensive, the soldiers were able to regroup, and their archers joined our barrage of fire.

Seeing that it was in a desperate situation, the demon lunged at Chip and me. It was fast and struck hard, but the battle had sapped its strength, so what could have been a lethal hit was instead a nasty cut. Still, it was enough to push us back, and my allies held their fire for fear of hitting me.

But Narrisai hadn't been idle—she'd managed to heal more of my wingmen, and they flew straight back into the fight. The first and second the demon was able to fend off, but the third eagle managed to latch on to its arm, claws digging in. As Chip tumbled away from it, he was able to recover, and I landed a straight shot with my sling. The demon recoiled, losing a chunk from his arm, just in time for the rest of my squadron to catch up. Hit after hit, our eagles tore the demon apart.

Both of us panted in exhaustion, and I flew Chip down to the ground. Narrisai smiled, her cheeks flushing just a little.

I grinned, still running on adrenaline. "Got it. Hopefully, the cultists will realise the demons aren't all that."

Narrisai approached, gently stroking Chip. "Thank you, Kali. I couldn't have done this without you."

I slid off Chip. "You gave my people something, rather than just bullying us. I should be thanking you."

"It's nothing. It's how we should all treat each other." Narrisai couldn't quite meet my gaze.

"But not everyone does. So it means something when you do this, Narrisai. It...it means a lot. To me." I could feel heat building on my cheeks.

Both of us wanted to say more but were nervous about taking that extra step. I opened my mouth to say something when one of my wingmen landed beside me.

"Kali? I think we've got the last of them. But the soldiers are asking for help getting back down the pass..."

"Figure something out. We'll make it home. I, uh, have business with the countess," I ordered.

The eagle rider gave me a flat look for a few seconds but just rolled her eyes before flying back towards the rest of the squadron. I turned back to Narrisai.

Before I could finish mustering my courage to say more, Narrisai said, "I'm afraid my men will need my aid." She turned but looked at me over her shoulder. "You know, I would like to discuss further diplomatic missions between our peoples...should you ever wish to visit my manor."

"That...that'd do. I'm sure Chip can manage the trip." I mounted again. Just before I flew off, I gave her another kiss.

Chapter 1

Someone and somewhere else, a year later

I'm sure some people would enjoy living above a raucous tavern. I would gladly trade places with any of those people. Deep into any night, there was always a crowd loudly talking at best, and loudly celebrating some game or other at worst. Then there was the constant music; my family offered its stage to anyone who had an instrument (whether they could play it apparently not being a factor). It might not have been so bad if I could have heard it clearly, but it was always obscured with a dozen other conversations, and usually a wall or two, turning a melody into an intermittent buzz. Worse were the nights when someone got rowdy. My folks ran a clean enough establishment that most such people were swiftly kicked out, but that rarely went smoothly.

That's why I frequented the farmlands outside. It was cold, unpleasant, and had its fair share of bugs. But it was quiet. Relatively speaking, at least. Most nights, it was just me, the chirping bugs, and the wind flowing through the stalks of wheat.

And the stars.

Our family's tavern was on top of a pretty big hill, so it had a commanding view of both the surrounding valley and the surrounding sky. The stars steadily wheeled overhead, countless lights illuminating the night sky. I took out my spyglass, an old family heirloom, and gazed a little closer. I watched how the patterns slowly shifted over time. A travelling astronomer had visited the tavern once, and that was one of the few times that I made a point of talking with a customer, as I eagerly listened to his words about the nature of the stars, our world, and the relations between them. She only had so much time, but my fascination with the night sky had only been fuelled, so I'd written down every word of hers that I could remember and then started writing down my own observations. My book was now filled with diagrams of constellations, planets, and dates.

As I examined one particularly bright star through my spyglass, I saw it shift and warp, rearranging itself into…a face. An eerily beautiful face, looking right at me. Awkwardly, I looked to my left and right, confirming there was no one else around, then gestured at myself with a questioning expression. Did I really just draw the attention of a creature from between the stars? I mean, I was kind of cute, being a halfling, short even by my people's standards, with neck-length messy red hair and a smattering of freckles, but I wasn't *that* beautiful, certainly nothing like the ethereal beauty gazing down at me from on high. The star looked amused. Then, it glowed brighter as a shaft of light shot down from the heavens, landing right in front of me.

It materialised into a fox: a small, fluffy thing with pure white fur and piercing blue eyes. It trotted up to me, sniffing me curiously. I cautiously stood. My curiosity and my fear were evenly matched, so I stood still, waiting to see what the fox would do, and ready to run if it was hostile. For now, the fox was examining my notebook, looking at the constellation diagrams. I looked back at the star to see it had returned to normal.

The fox yapped, and when it saw it once again had my attention, it drew a pattern in one of my constellation diagrams with a paw. I looked up at where the constellation hung in the sky. I looked at it through the lens of the pattern the fox had drawn. I reached out, tracing that pattern in the sky.

I felt something *click* in the back of my mind.

I could feel *more*.

Power.

The slightest twinkle echoed in my palm. I looked at it, then down at the fox. It wagged its tail affectionately and started rifling through my notes. Learning magic could take years of study, but this fox, sent by a star, *my* star, had shown me how to take the first step overnight. I'd heard all sorts of stories about learning magic from strange beings like these, pacts forcing nightmares on those who made them. But I always loved the stars, and the chance to know more was enthralling, let alone the chance to be given the gift of magic. I needed to know more.

I scurried back home, the fox bundled in my arms, awkwardly perched on my notebooks. I slipped through the back door, where my mother and sister Ori were cleaning up the kitchen.

Mum looked up as I entered. "Peri, you're back. Oh— you've made a friend."

I smiled, then (with difficulty, as I was also trying to hold the fox and my notebooks) I traced the same symbol in the air, focusing the magic. Again, twinkling lights appeared in my palm.

Ori was visibly surprised. "You're a witch now."

I nodded. "Witch" was the term for a mortal that had been taught magical power by the emissary of some great, otherworldly power, in my case, a star, through this fox. Reasons for this were as varied as magical patrons themselves. But a substantial number of those reasons were malevolent, so witches were treated with caution among even more accepting communities, and ostracised or even killed in those less so. Fortunately, my family proved to be in the former category.

Mum stopped cleaning and approached the fox, who sniffed her curiously. "Any idea who— or what she's from?"

"A star."

Mum laughed. "Of course. Maybe you've flattered them! Has it told you to do anything yet?"

I shook my head. Mum stroked her chin.

"Well then," she said. "Okay, you're going to be responsible for it, and that includes housebreaking it, alright? And don't let it get you into trouble!"

I nodded more enthusiastically.

So, as soon as my shift in the tavern kitchens ended every night, I scurried out to the open fields and studied the stars, Cosma at my side. She showed me new constellations and taught me the arcane signs written in the stars. I learned how to draw upon their power, and how to shape it, and through it, shape the very world. My family quickly got used to Cosma's presence, and even grew fond of her, though Dad had told her in no uncertain terms that if the star used me for anything nefarious, he'd wring the fox's neck himself.

One morning, I found Cosma very interested in the map of the local area my folks had hanging on the tavern wall. When she saw me, she yipped eagerly, tail wagging. I approached her as she continually jumped at it, trying to reach something. On a hunch, I picked her up, holding her closer to it. She pointed eagerly at a specific spot on the map, and I eventually got a rough idea of where she was referring to: a location a good few hours' march into the nearby large forest.

I whispered to her, "Want to go?" to which she yipped affirmatively.

I put her down and started to think about the logistics of the trip. I'd need some supplies from the kitchen. I was decent enough at navigation, so I was sure I could at least find the road again when it came time to come back, so that wasn't a serious problem. The biggest problems would be wild animals and any other hostile creatures that lived so far from civilisation. I'd picked up enough spells from Cosma by now that I thought I could handle some trouble, but I didn't want to rush in and get myself hurt.

To minimise the chance of having a long march through the forest in the dark, I decided to spend that day preparing and then set out first thing the next morning. Luckily, the tavern hosted enough adventurers that it was easy to get advice on what I'd need on my trip, and my mother was happy to hand me down some equipment from her younger years. I'd also picked up a pointy hat to signify my status as a spellcaster; mana was more active at high altitudes, so many spellcasters built tall structures and carried long equipment to enhance their power. (Although the benefits of a single hat were marginal, wearing one was primarily about the aesthetic, not that any spellcaster would admit that.)

The next morning, we set off. Dad decided to join me, not wanting me to run off into the forest with only a strange fox for company. He was a sailor on a warship in his youth, so I was deeply grateful for his skills, rusty as they were.

Cosma seemed to know where she was going, so we followed. We made steady progress, bar one or two short detours Cosma made to snack on some unfortunate mice. The trees grew steadily taller and the grass thicker as we marched. I was nervous, my shadow warping with mana I had unconsciously gathered.

After a couple of hours, I paused, hearing a strange rustling in the bushes. Dad and Cosma kept going ahead, but my instincts kept me frozen in place, trying to assess the situation.

Dad noticed. "Peri? What's—"

A boar charged at him. Dad rolled into the hit, quickly drawing a dagger. He had experience, but he wasn't a young man, and he could only do so much against a full-grown boar. Adrenaline forced me into motion. I hurried to cast a spell but fumbled it in my panic. I couldn't stop the boar from driving a tusk through Dad's arm.

Cosma tried to help, biting into the boar's flank and hanging on like a terrier. It bought time, as the boar whirled around, but only so much, as Cosma lost her grip. The seconds were enough for me to engage my rational mind and cast the spell properly. A bolt of searing starlight shot out from my palm, landing a direct hit. The boar screamed in pain. It then turned to its attacker.

And charged. I desperately rolled out of the way. I was full of adrenaline, but the boar was charging at me full speed and caught my leg. Pain of a level I'd never yet felt shot through my body. I pushed it down; my life was at stake. As the boar turned to finish me, I cast another spell, this one calling the darkness between the stars. It wrapped around the boar's eyes. It squealed and snorted, seeking me out. I tried to stand, to run, to escape, but I couldn't put enough weight on my foot.

But Dad was up and sprinted towards me. He barely seemed to notice the blood oozing from his arm as he picked me up and carried me away, Cosma scurrying behind. It wasn't until the snorting and grunting of the boar had fully faded that he allowed himself to set me down. He slumped to the ground, his teeth gritted in pain.

He glared at Cosma. "Smart bloody idea."

Cosma yipped and turned back up the path, looking at us, expecting us to follow.

Dad growled, "We're not going back."

Cosma whimpered.

Panting heavily, I whispered, "Hurt. Can try again another day."

Dad looked over at me. "You can't be serious."

"Not Cosma's fault."

Dad huffed. "…We'll talk about this later."

The march back home was long and painful. Dad showed me how to bind his wounds, and I'd brought a walking stick, which saved me from having to put too much weight on my injured leg, but the pain still dogged our every move. Cosma also seemed pretty dejected. I hoped the star wouldn't mind too much.

I could barely believe it when the forest gave way to farmland, and I could see home in the distance. It gave the two of us some much-needed energy. The rest of the walk proceeded much quicker. Mum and Ori were shocked to see our condition and hurried to get us some bed rest. They promised to try and find a healer—with the number of people that frequented the tavern, and Ori's way with people, we hoped for swift results.

The next day, Mum knocked at the door. "Good news! There's a cleric of the Triune here, properly blessed! He's already healed your father, and he says he has magic enough left for you. Shall I send him in?"

The Triune was a pantheon of three close goddesses, supposed to represent the best parts of people: Raiya, goddess of righteousness; Etunae, goddess of love; and Ynnelia, goddess of wonder. A rare few of of the Triune's followers had genuine power from on of the goddesses, the power to heal the innocent and smite the guilty.

After I assented, a minute passed, and the door opened to reveal a dwarven man with an immaculately braided beard and a wide smile. He wore a pendant showing the stylised embrace emblem of Etunae.

"Hail! What appears to be the problem?" When I showed him my leg, he winced. "Oof. Your father mentioned a run-in with a boar? I suppose you should be thankful that's the worst of it. Just a moment." He approached, gently laying his hands on my leg. He recited, "For love is the root of all healing!"

His hands glowed with light, and I felt a soothing power sink into my body.

I got up and gently tested my leg. Still sore, but an order of magnitude less so. I gave him a smile. "Thank you."

The priest beamed with pride. "Not a problem! 'All beings deserve love, and all beings must nurture it,', *Verses Of Etunae*, 2:3."

Mother examined my leg with relief. "Oh, that looks much better! So, how much do I owe you?"

"Oh, nothing at all, nothing at all! Such is the will of Etunae!" The priest drew himself up straight.

"Well, tonight's room and meal are on the house!" Mum said happily.

"Thank you! I suppose I could use some rest; I want to be ready when it's time for me to fulfil my destiny!"

"Ooh, you'll have to tell us all about that!" Mum led him back downstairs.

The priest explained how the Triune only granted their magic to those on great destinies; when he had developed his magic treating sick orcs in the capital of Ansiel, he earned a meeting with the Herald herself, the representative of the Triune, who sent him on a mission to bring the word of the Triune to isolationist elven conclaves far to the east.

He left the next morning with shared well-wishes. I still took it easy for the next couple of days; while the priest's magic greatly accelerated my healing, my leg was still fairly sore. Considering how close I came to getting killed, I was content with that. Cosma, however, wasn't entirely happy. She was eager to do whatever it was our patron wanted, but the boar encounter had dampened my enthusiasm, and my family's support.

Chapter 2

One night, as Cosma taught me more magic, Mum came to fetch me from the fields. "Peri? There's a woman here, says she's looking for someone who knows a bit about 'night magic.'"

It wasn't a technical term (at least not to my admittedly limited knowledge), but my study of the stars might have fit. With my curiosity piqued, I followed Mum back inside. She introduced me to a muscular mountain of an orc woman, a long mane of thick black hair bound behind her in braids. Even by orc standards, she was huge, and I didn't pass her thigh. She was dressed in patchwork hides, gaps in it showing scarred green flesh. A massive battleaxe was strapped to her back.

Mum gestured to me. "This is my daughter Peri. She's always been into astronomy, and she's been studying magic recently."

The orc gestured to the map. "Have been seeking ancient weapon. Found its resting place, but full of strange magic, stars, and night where it should be day. Need someone who knows what it is."

I wasn't the most well-read of experts, but I knew a lot about stars, and Cosma was teaching me more every day. And thinking about the matter gave me an idea. "I need help," I told her as I pointed at the map to the location Cosma wanted to go. "Cosma's looking for something. But dangerous."

I always found talking to be an effort, but fortunately, the orc seemed to realise where I was going.

"I help you. You help me. Very well! We set out at dawn."

Mum smiled. "Excellent! I'll get you a room for tonight, then, on the house. Oh, can I get your name?"

"Kurra."

The next morning, I met Kurra outside. Both of us were geared for travel, and Cosma was eager to get on the road again.

Just outside the door, Kurra looked down at me. "Hmm. Too small." She placed her pack on the ground. Then, she picked me up and put me inside. "There. Will be safe." With one fluid movement, she donned the pack, with me still inside.

It was surprisingly comfortable, even if I was wedged against her bedroll and some of her rations. The pack was large, so there was just enough room for me, with my head poking out over her shoulder. I decided to not complain, as this would save me a lot of walking.

When Kurra turned to set off, she noticed Cosma and proceeded to place her on her opposite shoulder. "There. Now, onwards!"

Kurra strode off, Cosma acting as a fluffy little compass pointing to our destination. Having much longer legs and much greater endurance than either Dad or I, she made good time. It wasn't long before she reached the site of the previous boar encounter.

I whispered, "Careful. Boar nearby."

If anything, this made Kurra eager. She took the battleaxe from her back. Her stride slowed, but it wasn't a cautious advance;

it was a predator's stalk. I kept a spell ready. I heard the rustle again. I whimpered. Kurra froze, ready to strike. The boar charged again. With impressive speed, Kurra evaded the hit, striking as the beast passed, carving a massive bloody gash into its flank. True to the reputation of its kind, the boar only got angrier.

Meanwhile, I had discovered something: Casting spells was substantially harder when one was in the pack of a raging orc woman spinning like a whirlwind. As my spell fizzled, the boar lunged at Kurra. It was faster this time, landing a solid hit, knocking her flat on her back, painfully sandwiching me between her and the ground. The boar swung wildly with its tusks, forcing Kurra on the defensive. She kicked, her immense strength striving against the boar, immense, but just shy.

I slipped out of the pack and cast the spell. Again, the boar's eyes were coated in darkness. Again, we took the chance to withdraw. But this time, it was only to attack again. Once Kurra had a pace or two between her and her enemy, she leapt to her feet, slipped to the side, and swung again. The boar squealed in pain as the axe bit in deep. It lunged at where Kurra was, but she had already moved, dancing to the side and hitting it again.

Finally, the wounds built. Finally, the boar slowed. Finally, one more strike from Kurra brought it down. Panting hard, she cheered in triumph. "Hah! Yes! We feast today! Come, Peri, prepare fire while I skin it!"

I was still pretty sore from being nearly flattened, but Kurra's enthusiasm was infectious, so I got to work. I figured she deserved a break from lugging me around, anyway. We found a couple of useful branches, and soon the boar was being roasted on a spit. It was easily enough to feed a family, but Kurra boasted that she'd probably eat the whole thing (though hurriedly adding that Cosma and I also deserved nice big bites).

An hour later, Kurra turned out unable to fulfil her boast but came close. Once we had eaten our fill, Kurra engaged in what was apparently an old orc custom of burying the rest of the carcass by a tree, to accelerate its return into the earth, which would apparently bring the blessings of nature upon those who were generous. I wasn't terribly certain about that, but there was no using all that extra meat anyway.

An hour's rest and a good meal were good for both of our conditions, so we were in high spirits as we set off again, Cosma and I once again in Kurra's pack. Eventually, we reached the overgrown ruins of what seemed to be a long-abandoned settlement. Cosma became increasingly excited, eventually leaping out of Kurra's pack, scrambling down her arm, and running off, only pausing to make sure we were following.

She led us through the undergrowth to the ruins of a small tower. It was mostly intact, with only one or two collapsed walls on the higher levels. Kurra bashed down the door with hardly any effort. The interior looked like it was richly furnished, long ago, the moth-eaten rug on the floor having an elaborate pattern, and the ruined shelves scattered around, with a wide array of books. Cosma was most interested in something on the top level. With the stairs intact, but just barely, I decided to have Kurra put me down to spread out the weight a bit. Cautiously, we headed upwards.

We made it to the top with only one occasion of nearly falling through the floor. There, I realised we were standing in the ruins of an observatory; there was a large telescope on one side. My excitement was undercut in no small way by the fact that it was heavily damaged, enough to make it useless without repairs, and I had no damn idea who'd be able to do that. Cosma, meanwhile, was sniffing around the outer wall. I looked where she was looking and found runes inscribed in many of the stones. A spell had been cast on the top of the large, sophisticated, and rugged observatory at some point. The tower falling into ruin had caused the runes to fall out of place. I figured out what Cosma wanted me to do.

I started to look around at where the bricks had fallen out of place and hauled them back. Or rather, I struggled with the weight for a few seconds before Kurra hauled them for me. I showed her where to put them. The result was something of a jigsaw puzzle, necessitating a couple of trips up and down the tower to retrieve some of the blocks that had fallen to the ground, as well as some work figuring out which blocks went where, made even more complicated by the fact that a number had been smashed into pieces.

Eventually, I managed to find all the rocks that could be salvaged and put them back in place, more or less. What followed was some work finishing the spell construct, with a few bricks salvaged from the rest of the ruins and my own spell reagents. That, in turn, required quite a bit of reverse engineering, like studying a machine to find out where to put missing cogs.

Kurra alternated between hauling the blocks, keeping an eye out for threats, and watching me work. She did so with something of a smirk. When I noticed it, I gave her a quizzical look.

She simply shrugged. "You are cute focusing on something."

I blushed and got back to work.

After a good few hours of work and no small amount of help from Cosma, we managed to finish. The last stage was to get the magic flowing through it again. This, to my surprise, Cosma managed all on her own. Sitting in the middle of the floor, she looked up at the sky. Her eyes glowed with black-purple light as she called the mana flowing around her and channelled it through the runes.

In an instant, a blanket of deep night settled around the tower.

Kurra visibly flinched, her hand seeking out her battleaxe. "What is this!?"

I reined in my anxiety, taking a moment to calmly assess the spell. Now that it was active, it was much easier to discern its function. "Mimics night. Can study stars during the day. Only for the tower. See, sun!" I pointed to a large, yellow orb in the same direction that the sun—not currently blinding to look at—was.

"Hmph. Right. Are we done?" Kurra grumbled, still on edge.

Cosma took the chance to point out some new constellations that I otherwise wouldn't be able to see for months, and she was able to show me how the position of the sun shifted their powers. As I updated my notes, Kurra stood guard. I suspected she was hoping some monster or other would jump out at us to give her an outlet for the tension. Another couple of hours later, Cosma had taught me all she wanted to for the time being.

But there was one more thing I wanted to do: investigate all the books. All were in poor repair, and large parts of most were illegible, but I did manage to find more than one with useful information. I gathered them up and presented them to Kurra.

She snorted. "Want me to carry those as well?"

I responded with my best puppy-dog eyes.

"Hmph. Very well." She put the books in her pack.

We started the long walk back. I had to walk myself, as all the books had taken up the space in Kurra's pack. She was visibly concerned for me, but the lack of walking in the first part of the day meant I had plenty of stamina for the second, and we encountered no further threats on the way back.

My folks were deeply relieved to see me back in one piece and again gave Kurra a free room. Despite my exhaustion, I was eager to peruse my little treasure haul and spent many hours studying what others had learned of the stars—and the powers within them. They were in too poor condition to keep dragging with me on adventures, so I studied all I could.

Which is why I still had my face in a book when Ori shook me awake.

"Peri? You'll want to get up. Kurra's waiting for you."

It took me a second to process the fact that I had dozed off. Once I did so, I acknowledged my sister with a nod before packing up my books.

I eventually made my way downstairs, where Kurra was waiting in front of an empty plate.

"Peri? Get ready! We have places to go!"

I whispered back, "Sorry. Sleepy. Give me time?"

Kurra didn't exactly strike me as the beacon of patience, but she managed to keep hold of her frustration. "Very well. Will train." She rose and strode outside.

I really wasn't much of an adventurer yet, so it took me another hour or two to get ready. By the time I finally scurried out of the tavern, Kurra was pacing, visibly struggling to stretch what little patience she had over the time I had taken.

She whirled around as soon as she saw me. "Hmph. Ready?"

I nodded. "Sorry, not used to this. But ready!"

Kurra again scooped Cosma and me up and put us safe and sound in her pack before turning and setting off, marching east across the fields. For a while, I poked my head out over her shoulder, watching the terrain pass by. After a while, though, a yawn reminded me that I didn't get much sleep the previous night. So, I curled up in Kurra's pack for a nap.

I was woken by a shout, and a growl from Kurra, her pack shifting suddenly. I poked my head out of her pack to find her drawing her axe, facing down a goblin with a spear. Three others were all around us. I assessed the situation just in time to notice one slinking up to go for Kurra's hamstring. I swiftly pulled my walking stick and went for his head. It was a long strike, easy to dodge, but it forced the goblin to step back, giving Kurra a valuable second—a second that she spent charging.

Ignoring the goblin behind her, she rushed forward with immense speed, a single strike of her axe shattering the first goblin's spear. She went for a strike that would have cleaved them in two but pulled it as they cowered away. She whirled around to face the other three. I was shifting to get a better view of the fight, and the total spinning left me dizzy. I wasn't given much time to reorient myself, as the other goblins pressed the attack, driving Kurra back. Kurra fought, but arrow fire from one goblin forced her to duck beneath a rise.

I shook off the disorientation and focused. Bracing myself for the jostle of Kurra's movements, holding onto a strap of her pack for stability, I prepared another spell. I blasted the archer goblin with my blinding spell. It was effective, the goblin squealing as they tried to clear their eyes. I whispered to Kurra, "Got the archer!"

Kurra trusted me, fending off the other two goblins with a wide swing before rolling to the high ground. The goblins were small and agile, but Kurra was just fast enough to match them. As one rolled underneath a high strike, Kurra lashed out with a kick, sending them flying. The other goblin took the chance to nick Kurra with a shiv, but she barely seemed to notice. She went on the offensive. Kurra hit one hard, carving deep into their flesh, blood arcing across the field. They gurgled and died. With that out of the way, she proceeded to the next goblin. They fared little better.

I looked over at the goblin archer to find the spell had worn off. It fired another shot. Too fast for me to warn Kurra. But she was already turning to face it. Not quite fast enough. The arrow dug into the pack. Thankfully, the arrow was poor and the pack thick, so what could have been a lethal shot was simply a painful sting in my side. My yelp of pain only seemed to fuel Kurra's rage, as she rushed the archer.

The archer dropped her bow, squealing and running. But her fear was little match for Kurra's anger, and her scurry was nothing compared to Kurra's stride. Kurra tackled her to the ground. She then stood, lifting the goblin into the air with a snarl.

The goblin squealed in panic. "No! No! Please! You win! You win!"

Kurra huffed. "No more robbing."

"Okay! Okay! Promise! No more robbing!" The goblin squirmed in Kurra's grip.

Kurra dropped her unceremoniously to the ground, glaring at her and the other goblins. They also slipped away. With the goblins routed, she glanced over her shoulder at me. "Are you alright?"

"Hit, but not bad. Might give it a look though."

The pair of us gave each other medical attention. When our wounds were washed and bound, Kurra took a moment to examine the dead would-be robber. She seemed deep in thought. Then, she used her axe as an improvised shovel, digging a shallow grave and burying the goblin, muttering some prayer to orc gods. I slipped out of her pack to give her a hand.

She didn't speak as we set off again across the terrain. We were heading into less-settled lands. The rows of crops gave way to grassland, which in turn grew sparse, showing the dry earth beneath. Finally, as the first slivers of the sun began to sink over the horizon, we reached a large, flat stone set in the ground. Kurra walked around to where a tunnel had been dug, leading underneath it, an old door lying ajar.

Kurra walked to the threshold before putting her pack on the ground and starting to root through it. At the quizzical look I gave her, she answered, "Torch."

With a snap of my fingers, I conjured a small, floating light.

Kurra grunted in approval. "Good. Easy. Come." She put her pack back on before pulling her axe and advancing farther.

The structure we were in was old, a mix of stone pillars and dirt walls. There was little ornamentation, clearly not a place for living. Shattered remains of golems littered the ground. Kurra reached her destination, a large chamber inscribed with runes on every wall, all circling around a plinth in the centre. Magic bounced erratically between them, leading to intermittent flickers of light. Resting on the plinth, bathed in a purple-black aura, was a large sword in a rotten sheath.

Kurra picked me up and gently placed me on the ground. "This is the place. Tell me what it means."

I studied the chamber carefully. I could tell that time had caused the walls, and thus the runes, to slide slightly out of position, leaving the spells still functional but much weaker and more erratic. The spell seemed to be a ward of some kind against the sword, or the power inside it. It still seemed to be holding the sword's power in place, meaning the wards were heavily redundant when they were first built, or else the sword's power had waned over the years as well. I also noticed a magical trap built into the plinth, ready to lash out at any attempting to touch the plinth, though it had weathered the years no better than the rest of the spells. The source of the power was familiar to me, cosmic forces similar to what empowered my own magic. But there was something different about the sword. Something dark, unbalanced. And the runes—many were warding signs.

After a while, I came to a conclusion. "Trap on the pedestal. And the sword's cursed."

"Cursed how?" asked Kurra.

"Don't know. But dangerous. All built to contain it. Weakened now. But wouldn't wield it."

Kurra huffed in frustration, folding her arms and thinking. "…Could curse be broken?"

"Maybe. Don't know how. Need someone who knows more." I shifted awkwardly; this clearly wasn't what Kurra wanted to hear.

Kurra approached the pedestal. "…Bring it with us. Not use it. But bring to one who knows more."

I considered the idea. "…Need fresh wards on the scabbard. And be careful. But could do it."

Kurra grunted in satisfaction. "Then that is what we do. Can you disarm the trap?"

"Um…probably. Stand back." As Kurra reluctantly did so, I examined the trap closer: how it worked and how the magic flowed through it. I eventually came to a solution. I drew some warding signs in front of me, then a few magic channelling runes around the trap. Then, I poked the trap with my walking stick.

Light blinded me, and I was blasted with heat and impact. I hit the ground hard.

When I came to, I was tucked into my bedroll, which, in turn, was tucked into Kurra's bedroll. It was just outside the ruin; night had fallen, and Kurra had built a fire and had a rabbit on a spit. Cosma had curled up beside me. As I stirred, she yipped happily, quickly rising and sniffing me.

Kurra turned to me with a smile. "You awaken! You alright?"

"Sore," I replied, slowly crawling out of the sleeping bag. I looked around. "Sword?"

"Left it in there. Wanted you to be around. You knew more of it than I. Please, relax. Have been hurt today." Her expression turned a touch tender. "Thank you."

I smiled awkwardly and sat by her side. We remained in companionable silence for a while.

Then, Kurra spoke again. "Uluzar plains, hard place. Where I was born. People must also be hard. Sought to join warband of Horrag. Great leader, so they say. Doubted I was strong. So, I duelled. But Horrag's champion, he had many magic weapons, magic armour. I had only my axe. Lost. Mocked. So, I sought out weapon. Magic weapon, for my own. Prove that I am just as strong when fight is fair!" Kurra sighed. "Weapon is cursed. No matter. Will break the curse. Or seek out another."

I whispered, "You are strong. Very." I delicately ran a finger over the curve of a muscle.

Kurra paused but didn't shy away from the touch. "…Thank you."

The next morning, I was feeling a bit better and returned to the underground chamber with Cosma to study the runes in more detail. Taking no small amount of inspiration from them, I came up with some more simple wards and carefully etched them into the sword's scabbard. Whatever malignant force lay inside it, it was clearly not as strong as it used to be, but I didn't want to take any unnecessary risks.

When I finished, I presented my handiwork to Kurra. "Will need new scabbard."

"Hmph. Will have one made. Thank you." She placed it in her pack, followed by me. We started the long trek home. After a while, Kurra said, "You are good with magic. Like to adventure more? Could use your magic. Split payment in half. Good money. …Think about it."

I already was. Adventuring was risky work, and I had already taken some hits. It would also involve me leaving home. But for all I loved home, there was a small part of me that would be happy to leave, even if just to enjoy the relative quiet of a campsite when I got some sleep. And I'd be able to see, to experience so much more than I would ever at home. That, and I was starting to grow fond of Kurra. She was an impressive sight, and I'd seen a caring side of her.

I weighed the dilemma all the way back home. My family were relieved to see me back in one piece and gave Kurra her room for free again. As the business in the inn started to wind down, I talked to Mum. "Kurra wants me to be her adventuring partner."

"Oh really? Is that the sort of thing you want to do?" Mum didn't exactly seem thrilled with me risking my neck in that sort of work.

"Thinking about it."

Mum looked at the ground for a moment. "Well…look, it's your choice. Whatever you decide, we'll support you. Just think carefully, alright?"

"I will."

I lay awake for a long while that night. Deep down, I knew which was the best choice for me. But actually *making* that decision, *committing* to it…I spent the whole night mustering the courage for that.

Chapter 3

The next morning, I knocked on Kurra's door. She opened it a couple of seconds later, looking at me expectantly. I took a deep breath. I had always found talking hard, and today, it took all my will to lift two words out of my throat: "I'll go."

Kurra grinned, suddenly picking me up in a tight hug. "Yes! Come, my friend! We forge a path to glory together!"

My eagerness was still very much matched by fear and the bonds of my family. I spent hours putting off the journey by packing, and taking plenty of time to say goodbye to my family. Kurra was remarkably understanding, promising my family that she wouldn't allow any harm to come to me, and, while she was visibly getting impatient as I took time to pack, she made no comment It was early afternoon before I finally gave my parents one last hug, before Kurra returned Cosma and I to her pack and set off. I looked back, watching my family, and my home, disappear over the horizon.

Evening fell, and we started keeping an eye out for shelter for the night. A little while later, we came across a sign: *Adventurers Wanted—Talk to John*. We could see a small farmstead up a dirt path. Kurra and I agreed we might be able to negotiate a night in a stable or something as part of payment, so we approached. It was a squat building, built half into the earth with a round door, as was common for halflings like me. Kurra had to kneel to knock on the door.

It was answered by a young, scrawny halfling, who immediately yelped and slammed the door shut.

I whispered to Kurra, "Maybe let me?"

Kurra seemed to understand where I was coming from, depositing me in front of the door before walking back a few paces. Just as I was about to knock, the door opened, and I was face-to-face with a loaded crossbow.

Kurra didn't like anything threatening me and drew her axe with a roar. I quickly held out a stop gestures towards both her and the crossbow-wielder, a much larger (relatively) and stockier halfling with a scarred hand. Both parties paused, sizing up the other.

Once I was confident no one was immediately about to die, I said to the other halfling, "Adventurers?"

The halfling scowled. "Odd time of night."

Kurra snapped, "Is when we arrived!"

I wanted to defuse the situation, but I just couldn't get any words out more nuanced than a hurried, "Sorry! Sorry…"

The halfling adjusted his grip on his crossbow. "Right. You're adventurers? Figure out what's messing up the south field. Got crops ripped up and dying, and the livestock are spooked. Get it done, then we'll talk more." He slammed the door shut.

Kurra huffed. "Should just leave."

I whimpered. "Scared. Need help."

"Ah, fine. Better be grateful." Kurra returned me to her pack, and we headed south.

With the waning light, investigating was a little tricky, but my magic provided what light we needed. I could never navigate between stalks of wheat with my small size, but Kurra towered over them, providing the two of us an excellent vantage point. We eventually found what looked like the scene of the crime, an area where some of the crops had been torn up, and more still had died.

Kurra knelt, examining the area. "Hmph. Tracks. Looks like undead. Halfling, I think. One, maybe two."

That would explain the dead plants; necromantic energies were generally unhealthy to any nearby, especially plants without a full soul to guard them. But that raised the question of why it was tearing up the crops, not that the undead always worked for rational reasons. (Hey, nor did the living!)

I looked to Cosma, perched on Kurra's shoulder. "Take a look?"

Cosma yipped affirmatively, scurrying down to the ground and sniffing around. She picked up a scent and followed it through the field. It was lucky she was a bright white; the little fox was hard enough to pick out through all the plants. Cosma led us back north, towards the farmstead.

About halfway there, we encountered a dead body, decayed enough to make it hard to keep my lunch down. When it started to stir, I was too busy retching to intervene—not that Kurra needed any help. She simply crushed its skull with a mighty stomp, and when that didn't stop it, she crushed its rib cage.

She asked, "Any more around?"

I managed to rein in my disgust enough to cast some basic divination spells, finding no more traces of necromantic magic. Satisfied, Kurra, Cosma, and I returned to the farmstead. Kurra knocked again at the door, which wasn't answered by a raised crossbow this time, but the farmer was still holding the weapon.

Kurra explained, "Was an undead in your crops. Smashed it. Won't be bothering you again."

The farmer blinked. "An…Where? Show me!"

We led the farmer to where the undead lay, reduced to an ordinary corpse.

The farmer simultaneously retched and sobbed. "Oh, Tenal…I told you you needed to take a break…Even when you're dead, you won't listen…"

I shifted in Kurra's pack awkwardly. A family member coming back as undead can't have been a pleasant experience, to say nothing of the body's condition, and I had absolutely no idea what to say.

After a while, the farmer fished a handful of coins out of his pockets and tossed them at Kurra. "Here. Payment. Now go. Please."

Kurra gathered up the coins before walking away. We remained silent as we walked a while up the path before making camp.

I took some time stargazing. Not the most pleasant first job as an adventurer. I had been doubting myself even before I made this decision, and the events of the day hadn't exactly encouraged me. Then, a twinkle caught my eye: the star that gave me Cosma. My star. I quickly took out my spyglass and looked at it closely. The face had returned. It gave me a warm smile. Cosma happily crawled into my lap, giving me a loving look. They liked my adventuring, perhaps the concept rather than my current progress, but it was encouragement I direly needed. I mustered my resolve, giving the star a determined nod before crawling into my bedroll.

The next morning, we were woken early by an enthusiastic yipping from Cosma, and we heard someone talking to her. We crawled out of our tent to see a middle-aged halfling woman carrying a large and delicious-smelling pie.

She looked at us with a smile, struggling to keep the pie out of Cosma's reach. "Excuse me! Sorry to wake you, but I wanted to see you before you set off."

Kurra stood. "We are here. Is about last night?"

"Yes. I just wanted to say sorry. It's been hard for us since we lost Tenal, and his coming back…" She shuddered. "Anyway, we shouldn't have been so rude to you. You helped us; if that kept up, we could have lost lots. We don't have any more money for you, but we have this." She offered us the pie.

Kurra took the pie, smiling widely. "Hah! Is forgiven! Come, let us feast!"

A couple more days passed before we reached our destination: Ansiel, the largest city on the continent of Casten. It was an immense metropolis, thousands upon thousands of buildings, most larger than any I'd ever seen. Towering above even these was the Heartshold, the greatest cathedral of the Triune and the seat of power of their mortal Herald. The streets were packed with people.

And with their chatter, it was worse than even a busy night in the tavern. Street vendors hawked wares, priests preached the value of a virtuous life, and people gossiped about minutiae. For some shred of comfort, I retreated inside Kurra's pack, plugging my ears. I didn't know how people could stand it, trying to live within that constant, painful sensory bombardment. Luckily, Kurra's pack was full of soft materials. I buried myself within her bedroll. It smelled strongly of her, which I realised I liked.

After a while, the noise quietened to bearable levels, so I poked my head back out to see where we were. We were in the middle of town, in front of the Heartshold, an immense, gleaming building of marble and stained glass.

Kurra was talking with one of the paladins that stood guard outside, tall and resplendent in shining armour, asking him, "Have cursed artefact. Weakening, but must be fully broken before it is safe. Would speak with a priest."

The paladin looked at Kurra with disapproval. "An audience with a priest is…possible, but you understand the church has a dress code. Your…equipment wouldn't do."

Kurra huffed, taking me out of her pack and depositing me at the paladin's feet. "What about her?"

The paladin clearly wasn't expecting the orc to be carrying a whole halfling in her pack but assessed me. "Hmm, better, but still, no. You need proper formal wear. One must honour Etunae with beauty."

I chirped, "We can find some."

Kurra visibly didn't like the idea of formal wear, but mumbled agreement, and the pair of us headed off to do some shopping.

A few looks at a few price tags shot a pretty big hole in our plans. My folks were pretty well off, but I'd only taken so much money with me for expenses, and Kurra was far worse off than I was. The kind of dresses the church wanted would have stretched my budget at the best of times and were simply too pricey for me now. For a church that preached charity and aiding the needy, it wasn't all that accessible.

Chapter 4

Eventually, Kurra and I agreed that we needed money, and for that, we'd need work. So, we got to digging around for those in need of some adventurers. Kurra found a notice from a local lord quickly enough. So, we headed to the lord's estate. It was a relatively slender but very tall building that shared a couple of walls with its neighbours but did find room for a small garden. After announcing our presence to a local guard, we were informed that the lord in question, one Lord Kellendair, was in a meeting, but we'd be seen to in just a few minutes. In the meantime, we were led to a well-furnished waiting room and treated to some simple refreshments. Kurra looked a little out of place surrounded by fine linens but waited with relative patience.

We weren't kept waiting too long and were soon shown into an office just as luxurious as the rest of the estate. Lord Kellendair was a large man, both in height and girth, impeccably mannered.

He examined Kurra and me for a moment. "Hmm. You certainly have the look about you. Well, I need some mercenaries for a quick job. Shouldn't be anything too difficult, just something a little…messier than I use my guards for. You see, I have something of a squatter problem: Some goblins have infested one of my rental properties. I just need someone to clear them out, someone who's willing to handle whatever dirty tricks the little buggers dream up. Can you handle that?"

Kurra rested her hands on the desk. "Will need numbers. And map. Plan a strategy."

"Fair enough." Kellendair shuffled through a few drawers before pulling out a map, detailing a small, two-story townhouse. "Last I counted, there were about a dozen of them, but only half looked like fighters of any stripe."

I had a different question. "Uh, guards?"

Kellendair didn't seem worried. "If you're talking about my guards, as mentioned, they're more traditional sorts. I need someone sharp to handle goblins. As for the city guards—well, the goblins are intruders on my property, so you're free to slaughter them. Don't count on help, though. You see, the captain of this district, we've had a…disagreement. Suffice it to say I'd rather handle this with my own resources."

Kurra examined the map. "Hmm…dozen, tight space…Peri, have you crowd control magic? Working together, we can handle them."

I squirmed nervously; it was a bigger fight than I'd even been in.

Kurra laughed and slapped me on the back. "Come! Gods favour the bold!"

Kurra's enthusiasm was infectious. I nodded. We headed to where the goblins were squatting. Kurra carefully set me down behind her, a few paces from the door.

"Be careful. Watch flanks," she said, then turned and threw open the door. "Squatters! Scum! Flee or be cut down!"

I readied a spell, glancing this way and that for goblins trying to sneak a shiv between my ribs.

But instead of the battle I expected, an older, very indignant goblin emerged, snapping, "Ours! Fair bought! Have papers and seals, see!" He showed Kurra a piece of paper.

She was bowstring tense as she examined it, prepared for trickery, but her suspicion turned to confusion. "What...?"

She eventually turned and showed it to me: a letter permitting the bearer to reside in the house, signed by Lord Kellendair, and bearing a seal with his emblem.

The goblin snatched the document back. "There! Now go!"

Kurra scratched her head. "But Kellendair sent us. Said you were squatters on his property."

The goblin screeched in anger. "Liar! We pay many shinies!"

I piped up, "Talk to him?"

"Yes, yes! Yelling at him!" The goblin stamped his feet angrily.

So, Kurra, Cosma, the elder goblin, a couple of his family members, and I returned to Kellendair's estate. The guard was much more reluctant to let us in, commanding us to wait outside while he conferred with the lord. While we waited, I briefly saw Kellendair peer at us through a window. He was scowling.

Eventually, the guard returned. "Lord Kellendair has no wish to parley with squatters." The goblins cried in objection, which the guard ignored. "As for you two, our lord assures me that this letter must be a forgery and insists you carry out your mission. Otherwise, other mercenaries will be sought out."

Kurra and I looked at each other, pondering the situation as the goblins spat and swore at the guard.

Then, something clicked in my mind. "Said he didn't want guards involved."

Kurra saw where I was going. "Because he knew! Traitor! I gut him!"

When the guards drew weapons, I interrupted. "Or sue!" All paused, looking at me. I wanted to elaborate, but my mouth decided that far too many people were looking at me to function.

Eventually, the guard laughed. "Have fun finding a lawyer that will represent these greenskins!"

I huffed, stamping my foot to announce my attention to do just that.

My morale was waning after the fifth lawyer's clerk tossed us out, laughing. An entire day had passed, with little luck for the goblins. We all stood in front of the lawyer's office, looking dejected. But I wasn't giving up so easily. "Could... go to court ourselves?" I suggested. How hard could legal research be?

The answer was *very*. While the local library had an extensive section on law, the books were numerous, elaborate, constantly referencing eachother and filled with layers of exceptions and procedures. The result was a veritable mountain of books and a forest's worth of parchment covered in notes.

This drew the attention of a lithe elven woman, dressed in an immaculate frock coat with fine spectacles. She had short cut white hair and a reservedly curious expression. "Doing your own legal research?"

Kurra grumbled "Can't find a lawyer. Think goblins are funny. Bah! So we do it ourselves."

The elf examined our notes. "Can I ask what the case is?"

The goblin held out the letter. "Sold us place! Finally! Paid many shinies! But then he calls us squatters! Forgers!"

"Well, at least you're *trying*. More than I can say for some people." She gestured to the letter. "May I?"

When the goblin handed her the letter, she examined it closely, paying attention to the signature and seal. "Hmm…it looks legitimate. And you said he called you squatters?"

Kurra answered, "Hired Peri and I to drive them out. Didn't go to guards. Getting rid of evidence, more likely."

"Did you sign a deed? Talk to the civic authority, any banks?" the elf asked. The goblins shrugged. The elf looked thoughtful for a while, then took a seat. "If I may…my name is Eledine Ducellea. I've studied and practised law in three kingdoms. And I'm interested in your case."

At midday the next day, we joined Eledine at the Kellendair estate. She was carrying a stack of documents.

She addressed the guards. "Greetings, I'm Eledine Ducellea, legal consul to the Tri-yak goblin family. I'm here to speak to Lord Kellendair about negotiating a settlement."

The look on the guard's face was priceless. "I…um…well, Lord Kellendair was clear that he didn't want to talk to the squatters."

"Sir, if you do not allow me to negotiate a settlement with Lord Kellendair, then I'll be returning with a court summons. And you don't want to try and stop one of those," Eledine said matter-of-factly.

The guard shifted awkwardly, then hurried off. Eventually, he returned. "Er, the lord is very busy right now, but he assures you he'll be able to talk in about an hour."

"About an hour" turned out to be three. It might have been longer, but the sight of a very impatient orc tended to hurry things along, and today was no exception.

We were shown into Lord Kellendair's office, where he sat, arms crossed. "Well. This ought to be good."

Eledine placed the documents on the desk. "I suppose I ought to thank you for seeing me. But you very much want to settle this case. The only reason I'm even offering this deal is because it's much quicker for both of us."

"The property is *mine*. Ask the civic administration. That's just paper," Kellendair scoffed.

"A piece of paper with your seal and signature—a perfect match to those at your bank—informing the goblins that they own the property, when they don't. Meaning it's indisputable proof that you've committed fraud." Eledine had a slight grin, one wolfish, nevertheless.

Kellendair's eyes widened, then narrowed. "You've got nothing. They're not even legal citizens!"

"Civic Law, Chapter 4, Section 2, Subsection 3 states that, quote, 'those found guilty of fraud shall compensate the damaged party equal to the damages incurred as a result of that fraud,' end quote. It doesn't say anywhere that the damaged party have to be citizens."

"And how great are those damages?" he asked.

Eledine slid a paper over to him. "Some damages for breaking down their door, the money you made selling the gems they paid you with—the golemsmith was kind enough to let me look at their accounting—money to sustain the goblins while they search for alternative accommodations, and a fee for my help."

Kellendair read the paper, his eyes bulging in rage. He stood, tossing the paper away. "This is absurd! I'll have none of it! That was a forgery, and good luck proving otherwise!"

Eledine stood. "Well. I suppose you'll be paying all that, and more. And, quite likely, losing your license to own property within the city."

Kellendair stared Eledine in the eyes as she patiently waited to see his next move. Finally, he seemed to force himself into a calmer stance. "Well. I suppose that puts us in a negotiation."

Eledine sat back down. "If you do have a counteroffer, I'd be willing to hear it."

Kellendair pulled out a bottle of wine from a nearby shelf, along with some glasses. "Come, a little wine always makes these affairs more bearable." He set a glass in front of each of us, filling each with wine.

As Kurra quickly swallowed it down, Eledine pulled out a small stick coated in some red powder. She dipped it in the wine and withdrew it, watching it carefully. It quickly changed into a blue colour. Her expression turned grave. "Attempted poisoning. Did you want to make your legal troubles worse?"

As Kurra and I spat out the drinks, Kellendair drew his sword, swearing. "Guards! Kill them! Kill them all!"

Eledine pulled a fine rapier and met Kellendair's blade. I hadn't swallowed any of the wine yet, but Kurra had, and she was staggering. Heart racing, I leapt out of my seat, casting one of the newer spells Cosma had taught me, one drawing upon the void to drain Kellendair's strength. It seemed to work, but the lord was a skilled swordsman and still was able to give Eledine a nasty slash across the cheek.

Meanwhile, a guard had charged into the room. Kurra attempted to resist him, but with her strength sapped, she didn't last long. The guard shoved her to the ground and had a killing stroke lined up, one interrupted by a goblin slipping a dagger into his hamstring. As more guards approached, I unleashed a blinding flash of light, hopefully stalling them for a few precious moments. The goblins weren't content with merely stalling, taking advantage of their blindness to attack and slip their knives into weak points.

Eledine was only barely holding Kellendair off. She was a decent swordswoman, but Kellendair was obviously much more practised. With a feint and flourish, he slashed her arm, driving her back. As she winced in pain, she pulled a vial from her belt, throwing it at him. He deftly deflected it with his sword. As it impacted a lantern, it burst into flames, igniting the nearby furniture. Kellendair certainly wasn't pleased about that, but he had Eledine on the ropes.

Until Kurra rushed him, using all her remaining strength to push him into the building fire. He swiftly kicked her away, but not before catching alight. Remarkably, he still tried to fight, but finally, the flames got to him. Eledine ended him with a swift stab through the heart.

As the flames grew, Kurra slumped to the floor. Eledine cursed, rushing to her side, wrapping one of Kurra's arms around her shoulder, and lifting her to her feet. She cursed in the elven tongue. "We need to *go*."

I concurred, but as I turned to leave, a wooden chest to the side of the room caught my eye. Well, considering Kellendair defrauded some goblins, tried to con Kurra and me into covering his tracks, and then tried to kill us, I felt at least a little entitled to his wealth. The key was most likely in the fire, but one of the perks of being a bookworm was that I had read a lot about how locks worked and how to bypass them. I knelt and got to work. Luckily, my small size meant it would be some time before I had to worry about the smoke, and it made working with fine details easier.

As she struggled to carry Kurra out, Eledine shouted, "Are you sure we have time for that?"

I kept at it. The fire was spreading, but I had the lock open a second later. I threw the chest open, revealing a massive stack of papers. I might have been disappointed, but I could read quickly and found that they were all banking documents; Lord Kellendair seemed to have a number of assets, including some residences. I took the stack and scurried away. The goblins seemed to have dispatched the last of Kellendair's guards, and the rest of his staff decided to not stick their necks out for him, making haste out of the building just ahead of us.

Eledine said, "Come on. I'd rather not go out the front door, but there's got to be a servant's entrance somewhere around here."

She was quickly proven right, with the lot of us slipping out the back as a fire—and a crowd—built around the front.

Once we were far enough away for plausible deniability, Eledine sat Kurra down, panting in exhaustion. "Alright, hold on…" She quickly mixed a series of substances in a vial before offering it to Kurra. "Here, this will purge your gullet. By causing you to throw up, so please aim for the gutter."

I took a couple of steps back at that last part. Kurra seemed reluctant, but she shakily downed the tincture. There was a pause. Then, she demonstrated just how much an orc's stomach could hold, filling the gutter.

Eledine adjusted her glasses. "Alchemy. Not a science for the squeamish."

Kurra panted, slowly standing. "Would have preferred proper healing magic."

"Well, no-one with healing magic is around, so you'll have to make do with someone who's spent decades studying bodies, and how they interact with all sorts of substances." Eledine folded her arms behind her back, looking pleased with herself.

The goblin elder asked, "Um…do we have our house now?"

Eledine sighed. "Well, that's tricky. The property will likely go to his next of kin. As to money, well, it's a little tricky to sue a dead man. Possible, actually, but tricky."

Meanwhile, I was rifling through the documents I'd swiped from Kellendair's office. I found one particularly interesting: the deed to the goblin's house.

I held it up to Eledine, who took it with raised eyebrows, and said, "Well…everyone would assume this was destroyed in the fire. Which means if it turned up…" She tapped her chin. "How many documents do you have there?"

I handed her the rest of the stack.

She thumbed through them. "Hmm…this might have been worth risking a fiery death for after all. Let's get somewhere more private."

The lot of us returned to a tavern. We were then engaged in a rather dull discussion about laws and bureaucracy.

Eledine explained, "Contrary to what you might hope, simply holding the deed doesn't give you legal possession of the property."

Kurra sighed, resting her head on her hands. "…Again. Nothing. Should have…urgh…" At the quizzical looks the rest of us gave her, she explained, "Happens every time. See the weak, see all they have. Could take it, but…"

"But you have basic decency?"

"Hmph. Not decency in Uluzar. Failure. Strong take what they will, and that is how they rise. But I can't…don't…take. So I don't rise." Kurra sighed.

I shifted my chair a little closer to her. "You do good things. That's better than ruling."

Eledine nodded. "For obvious reasons, most people prefer rulers to *not* be ruthless raiders. But, for what it's worth, some of those documents you've recovered will help us, ahem, *withdraw* some money from Kellendair's accounts, and with the confusion caused by his death and the fire, most won't be able to trace the money." She turned to the goblins. "For the same reasons, I have a plan to get you that property permanently. It will take a few well-chosen lies and a few visits to the right offices, but it should work, especially with that letter promising you the estate."

Chapter 5

The next day mostly involved running between those various offices and letting Eledine do the talking. Kurra didn't exactly enjoy it, but as previously mentioned, the presence of a large, impatient, heavily armed orc tended to grease wheels.

As we walked between offices, Eledine asked Kurra, "So you…carry a halfling in your pack?"

"Yes. She is friend. Helping me break curse on this sword. Very clever, knows magic," Kurra said.

I slightly grinned at the praise.

Eledine looked between me and her. "But you carry her in your pack?"

"Is too small. World is dangerous, and she has very short legs. Much safer in there."

Eledine turned to me. "And you're okay with this arrangement?" I nodded enthusiastically, and Eledine shrugged. "Very well."

As we took a shortcut behind a cobbler's store, a haggard woman with a missing finger and a dozen missing teeth stumbled up to Eledine, grabbing her and drooling all over her coat. "Ayyy, got a snack?"

Eledine recoiled in disgust. "Th-that is hardly hygienic!"

The woman scoffed, spraying a torrent of spit all over her. "Just askin'."

At another cry in disgust from Eledine, a pair of guards wandered up.

"Is there a problem, ma'am?"

"A Bryden Root addict, I'd guess from the symptoms." Eledine removed and carefully folded her coat, frowning all the while.

The guards grabbed the woman. "Bryden Root? Banned by church decree."

As the woman squirmed, Eledine added, "For what it's worth, it's highly addictive. Part of the reason for the ban. I'd recommend medical attention before anything else."

The woman struggled. "I'm just hungry! And on medicine! Medicine!"

The senior of the two guards frowned. "Needs something a bit more than a hospital—poor woman probably can't afford one. The Reborn Colonies should help."

Kurra cocked her head. "Reborn Colonies?"

"For poor wretches like her, too poor to live anywhere else, don't know how to take care of themselves. Somewhere safe and monitored, where they can heal," the guard explained. "Don't worry about it, ma'am. We'll take this from here."

They dragged the protesting woman off.

Kurra frowned. "…I hope she'll be alright."

Eledine shifted awkwardly. After a moment, she asked, "On to a subject we can more directly address: You mentioned a curse?"

"Need magic weapons, armour. Need fair fight against orc champions. Only one I could find was cursed. Peri says curse is weakening, so we might break it. Trying to find priest in the city. Need dress code. So, need money," Kurra explained.

Eledine sounded doubtful. "Hmm…even if you did speak with a priest, finding one with true power…the Herald considers those a valuable resource. You'd be better served seeking a wizard of Ansiel University, which I'm currently working for."

That got Kurra more enthusiastic. "Could you break curse?"

"Myself? No, my speciality is alchemy, something of a new field. But one doesn't get far in academia without connections. I could point you in the right direction. Of course, curse-breaking isn't cheap, but if you provided a service to the university…suffice it to say, the university staff would be happy to explore ways of reducing the strain on their budget." Eledine gave the two of us a knowing look.

Kurra sounded cautiously interested. "Have something in mind?"

"Yes. But we have paperwork to take care of. Let's speak more on that tomorrow, shall we?"

"The blueren fern; a particularly rare plant, commonly used by nobles as a cosmetic. It's believed that it has more sophisticated alchemical properties, but due to the high demand, most sources have been overexploited," Eledine explained, gesturing to a number of sketches and maps on the table before us. "However, a student of the university has pointed out that a valley in this forest here is the perfect environment for the fern, and as far as we know, it's never been harvested. The objective of the expedition is to scour the area for any samples of the fern. If some are found, we will take samples for experimentation; hopefully, we'll be able to grow them in a more controlled setting."

Kurra leaned back in her chair. "Sounds okay. But why you need us?"

"The reason the area hasn't been exploited until now is because it's kobold territory. We don't want to pick any fights, but one might be inevitable. Though we certainly won't be engaging dragons."

Kurra snorted derisively, but I, for one, was perfectly happy to not have to face any. Kurra asked, "So, guard you while you look for fern? That is all?"

"Any expertise on wilderness or arcane matters would also be asked, but that is the sum." Eledine rested her hands in front of her. "Not only will the university pay for all supplies, plus a fair payment for the two of you, but I've found a wizard in the university who will see about breaking that curse. Do we have a deal?"

Kurra looked at me. "Sounds good. Thoughts?"

I looked through the maps, thinking about the logistics and difficulty of the job. Being satisfied with my conclusions, I gave Kurra a nod.

A couple of days later, the expedition of around a dozen, including Eledine, Kurra, and me, set off. Eledine had exchanged her fine coat for a suit of leather armour that hinted at a lithe, athletic frame. The rest of the party were varied in terms of their preparedness for an adventure: a few academics who had spent their lives inside of an office, a couple more that weren't strangers to fieldwork, one or two hirelings brought along for muscle, and a weather-beaten halfling named Kel who was apparently an experienced survivalist hired as a guide. There were also a couple of pack animals to carry the expedition's numerous supplies.

We set off on the long march towards the forest. I had a growing gratitude for the fact that Kurra seemed wholly content to carry me in her pack, an occasion where my stature was a blessing instead of a curse. I'd figured out how to slightly adjust her belongings for maximum comfort. Cosma was generally by my side, though once in a while she'd pop out in pursuit of a mouse or other critter that was unlucky enough to pass us. Eledine, for her part, seemed to be slightly out of her element but bore the situation with a cool head and collected demeanour.

A couple of days into the trip, we stopped at a village at the edge of the forest. It was larger than we expected, having recently turned into a major exporter of lumber. We headed to an inn on the edge of town. Having had my fill of the interior of inns as a child, I headed outside as soon as I finished dinner. As Kurra caroused, I took my nightly magic lessons from Cosma.

As I worked on shaping runes in the earth, I saw an orc with cropped hair run at me. With no one else around, I decided to slip behind a crate. I was pretty sneaky. Unfortunately, the orc was pretty sharp.

He immediately ripped into my hiding place and held a sword to my throat. "Money. Now."

As I hesitated, trembling, I heard Eledine's voice. "Drop it." She had emerged from the inn's back door and had a rapier pointed at the orc's throat.

The orc cursed, dropped me, and fled. As Eledine helped me up, I heard a commotion from the dirt streets. Eledine and I poked our heads around the corner to see a few guards wearing the emblem of the merchant's guild mercenaries rushing in pursuit of the orc, while another approached us.

"Is everything alright?" he asked.

Eledine explained, "Just a simple mugging; he ran off when I got the drop on him."

The guard gripped his spear. "Not to worry, ma'am! We'll handle that hooligan!" He hurried off to follow his comrades.

Eledine turned back to me. "Perhaps you need someone more than a fox for company." She gestured to the inn.

I clutched one of my books tightly. "Loud."

"Ah. Not the best environment for study, is it? On that note, I have to agree. Well, perhaps I could study beside you?" She sat down, pulling out a manual full of alchemical diagrams.

I smiled widely. "Thank you." Just as I turned to resume my work, I noticed her adjusting her position, trying to find a good balance between light to read by and distance from the sound. I pulled a little starlight from the sky and set it to hover beside her.

She smiled. "Much appreciated."

The pair of us studied together for a while, until I figured it was time for me to get some sleep.

The next day, the expedition headed through the village towards the forest proper. On the way past the more respectable houses, we encountered a shanty town. Despite the abundant lumber, all the buildings were cobbled together from what looked like scrap wood. A few orcs lay around, getting what looked like a rare moment of rest. I felt a bit more sympathetic to the orc that tried to mug me last night.

We heard shouting and the cracking of a whip and quickly changed course to investigate. In the middle of the street, a number of merchant guild's guards were publicly whipping an orc with long braids. When they saw us, they waved us over with a sick smile. "Got the bastard!"

I blinked. "Not him."

The guard looked offended. "What? I got a confession out of him!"

Eledine stepped forward. "It wasn't him! I saw the mugger. I know you humans struggle a bit in the dark, but I saw the mugger well enough to know for a fact that you have the wrong man! Did you just grab some random fool off the street and start beating him?"

"I don't like your tone, miss." The guard's eyes flared with anger. They stepped closer, gripping their weapons.

Kurra stepped in front of Eledine. "I don't like you."

The guards looked like they were about to escalate the situation before they realised they were badly outnumbered. After a tense second, one spat at the whipped orc, "Don't do it again!" before the band scurried off.

Once the guards were out of sight, Eledine knelt beside the orc. "Hold still." She pulled out some balms from her alchemy kit and began to tend his wounds.

The orc flinched. "What the hell's that?"

"Agar fruit extract. Properly prepared, it eases pretty much any wound." She moved to apply it to the orc.

"Couldn't bring a druid or something?" he grumbled.

Eledine frowned. "I've spent twenty years studying how humanoid bodies work and how they interact with alchemical substances. But fine, bleed for all I care." She stood and turned to storm off.

I whispered, "Eledine…"

She froze, sighed, and turned back to the orc. "Fine. But keep your mouth shut."

The orc was still visibly sceptical but remained silent as Eledine tended his wounds. When she finished, she stood.

"There. You should feel better in a few minutes. Now, I really must be off."

We entered the forest proper. Mountainous trees grew all around us, and it took Kel no small amount of work to find routes for our pack animals. The grass was thick and tall, to the point where the other halfling occasionally vanished into it, only visible with his sling staff poking up from the green sea. I kept to the safety of Kurra's pack.

Midway through the day, Kel abruptly called a halt. When the other members of the expedition asked him what was going on, he simply hushed them. He crept forward. He knelt. An arrow passed where his head just was.

The expedition quickly drew weapons. Just ahead of us were the small, reptilian forms of kobolds, about ten, crouching in the underbrush, all levelling weapons at us.

Kurra charged into the fray as Kel called, "Tripwire! Tripwire!"

Kurra simply leapt over the area where Kel was crouching before continuing her charge. Unfortunately, she was in too much of a rush to notice the second tripwire, recklessness which earned her a flurry of darts. She simply kept charging, quickly slicing one enemy into ribbons.

I'd started to get used to the cadence of Kurra in a fight, well enough that I managed to cast a spell, directing a blinding blast of light at the kobolds. As they ducked for cover, Eledine pressed the advantage, flinging a few vials of fire at the enemy. It wasn't long before we had the advantage. The kobolds realised this and quickly fled, vanishing between the trees.

That was lucky, as it was right around then that the poison on the darts began to set in, causing Kurra to collapse. Eledine rushed over to her, hurrying to administer medicine. Meanwhile, Kel was binding the wounds of one of the kobolds, as well as its arms, though that might have been redundant as the reptile was frozen in fright.

"Alright, scales. Know common?" Kel asked. The kobold showed no signs of understanding, so Kel turned to the rest of the expedition. "Anyone know the kobold language? We might be able to tell them to leave us alone."

Eledine finished tending to Kurra. "Most speak Dracolic. Just give me a moment…" She packed up her equipment and then turned to the kobold. Dracolic's harsh and sibilant sounds sounded odd coming from Eledine, but the kobold seemed to get the message, as it nodded nervously. After a little back and forth, Eledine switched back to common. "She'll report back to her clan. Let her go."

Kel did so, and the kobold scurried off in the same direction as its kin. Kurra, for her part, was back on her feet, though seemingly embarrassed about having been beaten so easily. I was torn between reassuring her that she looked very heroic and chastising her for her recklessness against an enemy with a reputation for traps, so I did neither.

The expedition eventually finished licking its wounds and so set off again. By this time, we were getting deeper into the forest and slowed down yet more; not just because of the difficult terrain, but because we were looking for the ferns, and that required a slow, careful search pattern.

Early the next day, we found ourselves having to hack through a thick patch of brambles, making everyone glad that Kurra had brought a massive axe.

As she hacked a path through, her muscles rippling with every easy motion, I whispered to her, "Thank you."

"For what?" She seemed surprised at the sudden praise.

"Carrying me." The threat of brambles had brought the idea into sharp focus, but really, the entire time Kurra had been carrying me had made my life much easier.

Kurra shrugged, causing the pack to bob. "Not a problem. You very small. Not much space. And need to be protected." Kurra grew more serious. "I am warrior. Must protect the weak. Horrag, he says that if you are warrior, others should serve you. Strive to be you. Do not agree. Not all skills are on battlefield. You prove that. You are good woman. Smart. And…" Kurra stumbled over her words for a moment. "You should be protected. You are a good thing."

I really didn't know how to handle the innumerable emotions swelling inside me, so I slipped back into the safety of her pack.

Chapter 6

The following day, I was woken from a midday nap (safely in Kurra's pack, as usual) by a cheer from one of the expedition members. I poked my head up to see what the fuss was. The expedition had gathered around a rock. Just beside that was a blueren fern.

Eledine was faintly smiling. "Just one, but that means there could easily be more. Let's leave this here and sweep the area closer. Once we know how rich the area is, we'll know how many we can safely take."

The expedition split into two parties and began to comb the area. When evening drew near, we regrouped, a little disappointed since our party had only turned up a single other fern. The other party was happy to dispel our disappointment; they'd found a grove filled with them and had taken a few samples. Eledine was more than a little pleased and started running some experiments right away. I was glad to see her so happy, but. I was significantly less happy to try and get some sleep amidst the innumerable strange smells she unleashed.

The next morning, breakfast was interrupted by an alarmed Kel. "Someone's stolen our maps." The expedition glanced at each other. Kel continued, "I found dirty handprints on the chest. Halfling size. Which means it's either me, or Peri, or someone else who's followed us. I could have swiped the maps later, and Peri…"

I quickly pulled out my pack and held it wide open so the others could look inside.

Kel inspected it, and me. "…Doesn't look like it. And you'd want to clear out quickly. No, this is someone else."

I had a brainwave. I beckoned Cosma over to the chest. "Track."

It took Cosma a bit to distinguish the various scents of the party, but then she picked up one of particular interest, leading away from the camp. The rest of the expedition hurriedly packed up and followed her. She led us through some particularly rough terrain, forcing Kurra and me to focus on following the fox while the rest of the expedition explored other routes.

Eventually, we found signs of another campsite, one recently inhabited. Cosma kept following the scent. Soon enough, we could hear conversation.

I tapped Kurra on the shoulder. "Could scout?"

A little reluctantly, Kurra placed me on the ground, and I slunk into the underbrush. A bit closer, I saw what appeared to be a large party, at least twenty, taking a lunch break. Many were armed, and most had the merchant's guild insignia. I slipped behind a tree, using a root to give me a little extra height, and scanned the camp with my spyglass. I saw another halfling discussing something about my expedition's maps with what looked like the party leader, a hirsute dwarf with a constant sneer. After the party leader was satisfied, the other halfling rolled them up and stuffed them in the side of his pack.

I was a little miffed at my expedition's hard work being stolen, so I decided to get the maps back. And I figured out how to do it. My bond with Cosma had grown enough for some kind of short-range empathy and the ability to communicate moderately complex concepts. So, as I snuck around behind where the halfling was sitting, I had Cosma slink around to the opposite side. When I was ready, I gave Cosma a signal. She leapt out of the brush, stealing a chunk of a guard's lunch. The guard cursed, turning and running after a giggling Cosma as the rest of the party laughed at his misfortune. With my rivals distracted, I quickly swiped the maps from the halfling's pack before slinking back into the woods.

Cosma quickly shook her pursuer, and we regrouped where the expedition waited. I presented them with our maps, beaming with pride.

Kurra grinned, patting me on the back (nearly knocking me over with her strength). "Hah, well done!"

Kel took the maps. "Hmm. They annotated it. And"—he shuffled through the maps— "these aren't ours." He held out a few papers that had been bundled up with the maps. It looked like some financial calculations involving the merchant's expedition.

Eledine reviewed them and the annotations they'd made on our maps. "…They're planning on stripping the entire grove. Because apparently having a few extra gold coins is entirely worth making an entire plant extinct."

Kurra hissed. "Can we stop them? I will fight!"

"Setting aside the legal ramifications, their party is significantly larger. Even in this terrain, I'm not fond of our odds." Eledine stroked her chin.

I piped up. "Kobolds?" The rest of the expedition looked at me. I elaborated, "Ask them for help?"

Kurra frowned. "We fought them. Will they help?"

Kel hummed as he worked through the idea. "Well, they do know the terrain far better than we do, and El can talk to them. But motivating them will be the problem."

I could see a light flash behind Eledine's eyes as she said, "Unless the ferns become a trade good. We could set up a regular trade with the kobolds. At that point, the grove becomes a resource for them. A resource the merchant's guild is going to over-exploit."

I smiled. "Brilliant!"

Kel stretched. "Well, time to track down a kobold lair in a forest. This will be interesting."

It probably was, but Kel was doing most of the work in that regard, leaving me to simply scan the area for anything unusual and occasionally second Cosma to the ranger. The expedition was a lot more tense from that point forward, facing not only the threat of territorial kobolds but also the merchant's guild. It would only be a matter of time before they noticed I stole our maps back. I wasn't sure how they'd react to that. I could take some comfort in the fact that, since their party was much larger, it would also be slower and less subtle. Still, I wasn't looking forward to our next meeting.

It was early evening when Kel called a halt. "Hold up! I think we've got company."

His suspicions were confirmed when a flurry of projectiles was fired from the trees. Eledine called out in Dracolic as Kurra charged. I tugged slightly on her pack straps to remind her we were on a diplomatic mission. This was at least somewhat effective, as she dove for cover rather than at the throat of a nearby kobold.

After a heart-racing few seconds, the kobolds began sending words rather than missiles. Eledine spent some time explaining the situation. After a few exchanges, she turned to us. "They're willing to allow a small party in to speak with their chieftain. It'll just be Kurra, Peri, and me. The rest of you, stay here, and on guard."

Kel said, "It might be safer to move slightly and cover our tracks. We don't want the merchants following us."

"Not a bad point. Very well. We'll be back as soon as possible. Assuming the kobolds don't stab us in the back, but hopefully Kurra will dissuade them." Eledine checked her gear quickly before giving Kurra and me a nod.

We nodded back, and alongside her, followed the kobolds. They led us through a steep ravine and from there into a cave. We were instructed to walk the entryway carefully to avoid stepping on the innumerable traps they had set up. From there, the cave was surprisingly worked, the kobolds having carved out a decent living space out of the rock. In the depths of the cave, a throne room had been formed, and a kobold-sized throne hewn out of the rock. Atop it sat a wiry red kobold that reminded me a little of a salamander, bedecked in various shiny rocks.

Eledine bowed and gave what I was pretty sure was an introduction. She and the chief spoke for a while. Eventually, the chief stood and turned to leave. Eledine said something else, more quickly. The chief considered for a moment and then nodded.

As we were escorted deeper into the cave, Eledine explained, "Chief Sektul says he wishes to commune with his dragon. I convinced him to allow us to join him so we could pay our respects. If the dragon is awake and in charge, we might make our case to it instead."

I had to stop myself from curling up in Kurra's pack. Kobolds were dangerous, but their small size meant that they would at least fold quickly if you could get them in a straight-up fight, as Kurra had shown. A full dragon was another matter entirely. They were avatars of material power; even the smallest could defeat a company of soldiers, and the largest were demigods.

We headed deeper into the cave, through a tunnel that was much less worked. It was covered in works of art and symbols of devotion. We reached a much larger chamber, outfitted much like a temple, in the centre of which slept a massive dragon, torchlight glinting off its silver scales. Chief Sektul approached it and knelt in prayer. The other kobolds, while they kept some distance, also knelt. I ransacked my head for everything I knew about dragons. They could sleep for years, decades, even centuries if they were large enough, and they did so to conserve their power. Their power they drew from their hoard; their hoard being whatever form of material granted them their form. I climbed out of Kurra's pack and carefully approached the dragon, examining it carefully (and keeping just out of arm's reach, lest the kobolds take offence).

I returned to Eledine. "Metal dragon. I think. Wants more metal."

Eledine gave me a smile and a nod. "And metal isn't too hard to trade."

She waited a moment longer. When the chief stood, she addressed him again. There was some more back and forth, Sektul initially sceptical of Eledine's words but warming up to them. He then discussed with some of the older kobolds. Finally, he made an announcement. Eledine smiled and bowed once more.

She looked at us. "We have some scaly new friends."

The next morning, Eledine, Kurra, and I walked into the blueren grove. The merchant's guild had set up camp, and a band of workers were stripping the grove of every plant they could get their dirty hands on. Upon seeing us, the guards gathered around us.

The expedition's leader directed his sneer at us. "So, a slip, a knife-ear, and a greenskin." Derogatory terms for halflings, elves, and orcs. "Got some gall, showing up here. Taking those notes was just a pain in our ass."

Eledine adjusted her gloves. "Angry at us for thievery? Rich. Regardless, you need to stop this operation. Blueren ferns are rare enough without you seeing to it that every single one is smeared across some noble's face. Or do I have to explain to you how plants reproduce?"

The leader laughed. "Making 'em rare is the point! Then we can charge more!"

"I'd point out how that's utterly callous, selfish, and short-sighted, but you obviously don't care. So I'll give you a more rational reason." A grin slowly began to bloom on Eledine's face. "This is kobold territory. And the academy has just agreed to a trade route with the local tribe; it promises to be quite beneficial—and sustainable—for both parties."

"Then we'll slaughter the fucking lizards!" The leader laughed.

Eledine's grin grew larger. "Will you now?" She snapped her fingers.

A second later, the guards surrounding us found themselves surrounded in turn by kobolds. A few more kobolds pointed weapons at the workers. The guards drew their weapons but hesitated; in addition to being surrounded, they were outnumbered at least four to one.

Eledine drew her rapier. "You're all going to leave your weapons, tools, and money—oh, and any plants you've already gathered. Then you're going to leave and tell your superiors that by the time they manage to take the grove, costs in equipment and personnel will far outweigh any possible profit from the blueren ferns here."

The leader was breathing heavily. "You…I…they…You'll regret this! The lizards, too!"

"Noted. Now—what's the common phrase? Ah, yes: Fuck off." Eledine gestured to the path the caravan came down.

There was a long pause. Finally, the leader spat at us. "A pox on you. Fine." He dropped his weapon, and the guards followed suit.

We kept our guard up as the caravan took a minute to divest itself of pretty much everything not essential. They then started back up the path, glaring at us all the while. We waited until the sounds of their footsteps had receded into the distance.

A bit suddenly, all the kobolds started cheering, quickly gathering all the guild left behind. More than a few raced off, eager to give offerings to their dragons.

After watching them with contained amusement, Eledine examined the grove and what the guild had harvested from it. "Hmm…They've taken almost all the ferns. But at least some of the seeds should still be viable. A little care and the grove should be self-replenishing again."

One of the kobolds apparently overheard and understood, rushing over to fetch a different kobold, this one an older one with mottled black scales. They spoke to Eledine in Dracolic for a moment, and Eledine seemed impressed.

"Hmm," she said. "They have a druid. That should make things easier."

It did, and it also turned out that the druid knew a thing or two about the blueren fern, just not about its uses in alchemy or cosmetics. With a little work and a little magic, healthy sprouts littered the grove. We happily called the expedition a success.

Chapter 7

The trip back to the city was a pleasant one, especially since it lacked kobold ambushes. Eledine and I kept spending our nights side by side, studying our respective arts in quiet company. In time enough, we were back on the plains, giving me a clearer view of the night sky. On one such night, Eledine watched Cosma teach me a spell to shield against a greater variety of attacks.

As we finished, she slid over next to me. "If you don't mind my asking, how does your magic work, to your knowledge?"

I was eager to share my knowledge. "Okay, so stars, void, earth between them. Power flows from one to the other. Groups of stars make constellations, emitting power in patterns…" I spent the next half an hour explaining all I'd learned about the fundamentals of cosmic power.

When I ran out of things to talk about, Eledine looked mildly surprised. "…I admit I haven't exactly known you that long, but you've said more words in the last ten minutes than I've ever heard you say previously." When I awkwardly shrugged, she laughed. "You're saving your breath for conversations about stars. Understood. Come to think of it, I have found words come easier to me on the subject of alchemy." She stood. "Well, I won't try to coax any more from you. Good night, Peri."

The next day, we returned to Ansiel. It was nice to be back at a bastion of civilisation after so long in the wilderness, even if the innumerable sounds of the bustling city got to me. Eledine's superiors had reservations about the conflict with the merchant guild and the trade route with the kobolds, but acknowledged that, given the situation, things could have been a lot messier. As for Kurra, the university kept its word and found us an expert on void magic.

That expert was Professor Emrodar, an elf slender enough to slip between floorboards. After we explained the situation, he spent some time studying the sword, casting runes about it as Kurra and I watched.

Eventually, he said, "Well, I can break the curse. Unfortunately, doing that would also undo all the enchantments on it, reducing it to a relatively ordinary sword. If you want to keep it, you'll want to invert its power. For that, you'll need a strong source of stellar energy, enough to overwhelm and replace the void energy. During the process, you can rearrange the bindings on it to keep its power. Unfortunately, that's where my ability to aid you ends; I simply can't think of any possible sources of the power you need."

Kurra looked at me. "You know much about stars. What you think?"

"…Will need to research."

Kurra picked me up. "To library, then!"

What followed was about a week of burying my nose in countless books. Despite being in a university, progress was slow. According to the none-too-pleased librarian, the Heartshold kept the most interesting texts within their own libraries, only open to the church's agents. Still, there was information of note in the university's works, just not quite enough for us to find what we were looking for. It was also a very pleasant change from camping in the middle of nowhere. Kurra didn't entirely agree, but she didn't have much to do other than reach for books on the higher shelves.

One morning, as I researched, Eledine approached Kurra and me. "Peri. Kurra. It's good to see you well. Did you have any luck with that curse business?"

Kurra grunted. "Some. Not enough. Peri is looking for solution. Is in one of these books. Don't know which."

Eledine chuckled. "I'm familiar with the feeling. Anyway, considering how well you handled those kobold ambushes, I thought I'd mention another job. The Heartshold is planning an expedition to investigate an ancient temple, supposedly where Saint Eldrey of the Triune first brought the Triune's light to the orcs. The tricky part is it's in what's now Uluzar; warband territory. They're not exactly friendly to outsiders, so we need the option for diplomacy and combat. Your dress and accent are from the region. Am I correct in guessing you're from the area?"

Kurra sighed. "Yes. But…others see me as weak. Weakness isn't tolerated."

"Considering how fast I've seen you move with an entire halfling on your back, you'll forgive me for not being entirely convinced." Eledine rested her hands on the table. "At any rate, we could use someone trustworthy who knows the region and culture. Rest assured, you'll be paid well. Would you be interested?"

Kurra looked at me for approval. I nodded. She looked back at Eledine. "We are interested. Getting bored here anyway."

A couple of days later, Kurra and I joined a group in one of the university's halls. It was a large group, around forty, and reasonably diverse, with priests standing alongside rangers and scholars alongside mercenaries. Eledine introduced us to the expedition's leader, Sir Renedarl. He was an older man, bearing the star sigil of the goddess Ynnelia.

He appraised Kurra with a frown. "Hmm. You're the guide to the area?"

"More than guide. Warrior," Kurra stated.

Renedarl snorted. "Of course you are." He looked at Eledine. "She can come, if you're really certain. I trust you'll keep her under control?"

Eledine coolly replied, "I'm her friend, not her master. If you want a person's skills, you should offer a person's respect."

"And a person's standards." Renedarl turned back to Kurra, poking her firm in the chest. "Understood?"

Kurra growled, stepping forward. I gave a slight tug on her pack to remind her that now really wasn't the time for confrontations. She looked at me, then back at Renedarl.

She stepped back and fixed Renedarl with a vicious glare, saying, "Want peace, do not ask for war."

Renedarl sneered. "Is the very existence of authority a challenge to you greenskins?"

At this moment, another woman stepped forward. She was clad in gleaming golden armour and had the dusky complexion of the northern, sun-swept islands. Her wavy hair was cut chin-length on one side, with an undercut on the other. On her chest was the shield emblem of Raiya, Triune goddess of righteousness. "Captain, it was your decision to hire a guide to the region. Antagonising her gains us nothing and risks everything."

Renedarl turned his focus to the newcomer. "You're out of line, Xeldia. 'Knowledge of evil is better than ignorance,' *Verses of Ynnelia*, 2:13."

"'To have a heart is to be able to choose to be something more than you are, judge ye not by who one was,' *Verses of Raiya*, 5:10-11." Xeldia retorted. "So she doesn't like being talked down to; no-one does."

"That's enough!" Renedarl snapped. He then sighed. "She can come. So long as she stays in line. If she betrays us, I'll be the first to gut her." He turned and marched off, continuing to prepare for the expedition.

Xeldia took a deep breath. "I am told Ynnelia teaches us to embrace what is different. Were it that more people listened."

Eledine said, "I don't expect many will. I'm nearing my first century, and I've never seen ignorance go out of style."

Xeldia laughed bitterly. "That would be too much to hope for." She offered Eledine a hand. "Xeldia, paladin of Raiya."

Eledine shook it. "Eledine, school of alchemy."

Xeldia offered her hand to Kurra, who clasped it firmly. "Kurra."

I held out my hand, pushing myself above Kurra's shoulder. "Peri."

Xeldia looked mildly surprised but shook my hand firmly. "Well met. If I may…" She gestured between me and Kurra.

Kurra shrugged. "Is too small for dangerous world. Must be protected. And can move much faster not worrying about little legs."

When Xeldia looked at me, I smiled warmly, doing my best to convey that I was perfectly happy with this arrangement. Xeldia looked at Eledine, who shrugged.

"They both seem perfectly content. So who are we to judge?" Eledine said.

"Judging is supposed to be most of my duty. Though I would much rather judge murderers than orcs." Xeldia looked over the rest of the caravan. "Anyway, the captain is calling a meeting soon. There is much to be done."

It turned out that, for Kurra and me at least, there wasn't *that* much to be done; the church and the university were handling most of the logistics. The expedition had paid us a decent sum up front and, combined with the money we'd been paid for our previous adventure, we had enough to invest in some better gear. At a magic shop, I paid for a wand inlaid with moon-bound pearls that would improve my magic. Kurra outfitted herself with armour made from the hides of dire bears.

Once all was sorted, we set out on a trip to the nearby port town of Eastcrown, in the kingdom of Delsward, to catch a vessel to our destination. The trip was a mostly pleasant one, with the bulk of the expedition leaving Kurra and me alone. Eledine, of course, remained often by our side, and she seemed to have struck up something of a rapport with Xeldia.

The next morning, just before we were due to arrive, I saw Kurra staring at Eledine as she prepared her alchemical equipment for the day. (You never knew when you were about to run into some opportunistic bandits.)

Kurra was sitting some distance away, focused intensely on the sight. I walked up beside her and asked, "Problem?"

Kurra watched as Eledine carefully measured a vial of fluid. "...Eledine. Knows things. Power within all things. Can draw it out. Kill and mend. She scares me..."

She said "scare" in a way that wondered whether she (this language being a second for her) had confused it with the word "aroused." I decided not to ask.

The expedition arrived at Eastcrown on schedule. The church had already arranged for a ship. Thankfully, it wasn't my first time on a ship; Dad had taken me on one or two boat trips when I was little, reliving his glory days, so it wasn't completely unfamiliar to me. It still wasn't exactly *pleasant* getting crammed onto a swaying ship with forty other people.

We were shown our berths and found...a few too few. Eledine counted the hammocks before turning to the ship's captain with a frown. "Captain, were you not informed our expedition had forty?"

The captain, a tall and brawny man, shrugged. "Couple of 'em are slips, right? Hammock fits two."

I wanted to confront him, both for the slur and for the lack of consideration, but I always hated confrontations, and I couldn't find the courage within myself.

Thankfully, Xeldia did so for me, opening by slapping him. "First, you refer to those doing the Triune's work with a slur, and then you insist on packing them in like livestock? You will give the halflings an apology. Then, we will discuss finding more beds."

Despite being nearly twice Xeldia's size, the captain was well and truly cowed. "I-I'm sorry! I didn't mean nothing! Just—just thought it was practical, is all! But look, I can't do nothing about the beds! We're full to bursting, and the slips—halflings, halflings! My crew are already doubling up. We just plain ain't got no more beds!"

Xeldia sighed in frustration. "Idiot. Fine, I'll talk with Renedarl to see if we can hire another ship." She left. She returned a minute later, with a frown that told us all we needed to know. "No luck, I'm afraid. I'm afraid some of us will have to share. Do we have any volunteers?"

A pair of lovers on the expedition quickly put their hands up, but there was still one bed too few. The others on the expedition looked at each other, sizing each other up, trying to determine who would be the least awkward to share a hammock with. I entertained the idea of sharing a bed with Kurra; I already pretty much lived in her pack, so sharing a berth wasn't much worse, was it? But the beds were small and Kurra huge. Even with my small size, there was no way I could fit comfortably beside her. I looked around before my gaze settled on Eledine. She was slender and not too tall, and she and I had already spent plenty of time studying side by side. Besides, she *was* attractive.

I mustered my courage. "Eledine?"

It took a second for Eledine to parse what I was asking. "You and me? Well, I suppose you don't take up too much space. And you're pleasant enough company. Very well."

Sighs of relief were audible from the rest of the expedition. Everyone started to get settled. Eledine and I approached our berth. It was the largest and most convenient of the hammocks, some small reward for taking a bullet for the rest of the expedition. We stuffed our belongings underneath. Eledine's pack smelled subtly of the innumerable alchemical reagents and concoctions within, all neatly arranged to take up minimal space despite the volume inside. Her longbow didn't seem as out of place as most such weapons would, being slender, carefully carved from fine wood.

After conducting our pre-voyage checks, we got underway. We watched from the top decks as the ship turned towards the sea, careful to keep out of the way of the dozens of crew rushing to and fro as the captain barked orders from the forecastle. We headed out to the great blue beyond.

Night fell, and the passengers returned to their bunks to get some rest. I stayed up a little longer, and the crew even allowed Cosma and me into the crow's nest to get a better view of the stars for our studies. I saw the face in that star again, and she looked pleased.

My lessons ended, and I scurried back down to my berth. I arrived to find Eledine cleaning up a spill.

She looked up with a mildly apologetic expression. "Alchemy on a ship in open water presents some…unique challenges. I assure you, I'll be more prepared in the future."

I shrugged; the spill wasn't evidently dangerous, and only a few droplets had landed on any of my belongings. I simply grabbed my sleepwear, ducked into a hidden corner to change, and dropped in the middle of the hammock. Remembering the situation, I shuffled over to one side before curling up to take up as little space as possible (which was a very small amount).

Not long after, I felt Eledine sit on the hammock beside me. A pause, then she lay down. Her back brushed mine. I could feel her sleepwear, very light. She tried to give me as much space as possible, but it was little use, as the slope of the hammock drew us towards each other. I could feel how warm she was. I could smell her own scent, mixed amidst the innumerable alchemical brews she was always working on.

When I awoke, I was nestled closely into her, her arm gently lying across me. My head jerked up in surprise. Eledine quickly sat up as well. I remembered that elves didn't sleep in quite the same way as humans; it was closer to a meditative state than outright unconsciousness. As such, they remained at least somewhat aware of their surroundings and woke quickly. Eledine and I looked at each other for a moment. In my drowsy state, I found it difficult to process much other than the fact that Eledine looked just a little odd without her glasses.

Eledine cleared her throat before standing up. "Good morning. Did you sleep well?"

I nodded. The pair of us started our usual morning routines, along with the ship's passengers and crew. I noticed Eledine seemed a little lethargic, apparently not having slept well the previous night, despite her status as an elf. I figured it was, at least in part, due to the amount of time she spent studying. I had a different problem to address: There was really not all that much to do on the ship. Keeping up my magic studies eased the boredom a little, but there was only so much such information that my mind was allowing me to cram into it at any given point.

Cosma also seemed bored, so she found a way to entertain herself: stealing the belongings of the various passengers and crew and stashing them under my bunk. At least the task of finding her stashes and returning the various objects to their rightful owners gave me *something* to do.

Kurra was handling the wait even worse. I was in the middle of returning the (very nice) undergarments that Cosma had stolen from Xeldia when Kurra came stomping up to the paladin. "Xeldia. You are warrior? Spar. Am bored."

Despite Kurra's abruptness, Xeldia remained perfectly composed. "Assertive, aren't you? But I'm not exactly finding this voyage thrilling either. Hopefully the captain won't mind us taking up a little of the deck."

The pair got permission from the ship's boatswain, found a pair of sturdy sticks for practice weapons, and got into their armour. A small crowd gathered; there wasn't any other entertainment on the boat. The pair circled each other for a moment before Kurra made a move.

The two were both skilled warriors. Kurra was tall, fast, and strong, and knew it. She struck fast and often, constantly moving, constantly on the offensive, her massive muscles powering every blow. Xeldia, meanwhile, was focused and disciplined. She knew a dozen manoeuvres, and had drilled with them, each called to the fore when they were needed and executed perfectly, almost as if the fight was an art form.

The pair had more than a few bouts. Each was closely fought, the pair drawing no small amount of exertion from each other. Kurra won the greater number of bouts, but not by a great margin; Xeldia proved herself a worthy match. After a while, the pair were satisfied. The ship smelled heavily of their sweat.

That night and the following morning passed much like the previous. Eledine still wasn't sleeping well, though she declined to discuss the matter.

A little after breakfast, Kurra approached me. "Peri. Have been thinking. You have not trained much in battle, have you?" I shook my head. Kurra handed me a practice stick. "Need to practise. Just in case."

She made a good point, and it wasn't like I had anything better to do. So, we sparred. This started with me getting a few hard whacks to the face. Fortunately, Kurra had no interest in disparaging my lack of skill, simply correcting my technique after my head cleared. I didn't win a single bout, but Kurra commented that my skill was already improving, so I took that to be something of a victory. I spent the rest of the day sleeping off the innumerable bruises.

I was in better condition when the stars came out, to Cosma's relief. As Cosma and I studied in the crow's nest, a shadow on the water caught my eye. I turned my spyglass towards it. It was a sail poking out over the horizon, soon followed by the rest of a ship. I poked the night watchman on the nest beside me. "Ship."

The watchman followed my gaze, peering into the distance. He looked deeply concerned. "That…is heading to intercept. At night."

He scurried down the rigging and headed straight for the captain's quarters. I followed him. With my smaller size and less practice, I was much slower, so by the time I reached the deck, the captain was already up and examining the approaching ship through the spyglass. He immediately headed to the ship's bell and rang it loudly.

There was a great commotion as the rest of the ship stirred, more than a few of the passengers none too pleased about being woken.

Any frustration at the captain was set aside when he called, "Pirates! All hands, prepare to repel boarders!"

I headed down to the crew berths to get my wargear. Many of the other passengers were also hurriedly arming themselves.

Xeldia called, "Someone help me with my armour!"

Being already dressed, I did so. Despite the threat of pirates, a small part of my mind found time to appreciate her firm, athletic figure as I girded it in armour plates. My small hands made quick work of the buckles and straps, and soon Xeldia was clad in shining armour.

She stood with a smile. "Thank you." She headed to the top deck, where Kurra was already eagerly bounding.

The captain was already there with most of the crew. The pirate ship pulled alongside. It was an orc galley, low to the water and armoured. A large crew of orcs, half-dressed in leather armour, jeered at us, eyes glinting in the low lantern light.

Their captain, a large brute with broken tusks, snarled, "Right, then. Each and every one of you is going to drop their weapons, or we'll have fun decorating our ship with your hides."

The captain was about to respond, but Xeldia stepped forward. "Quite the opposite! I am Paladin Xeldia of Raiya, charged with holy duty, as are my companions. I will no longer allow your piracy. You will yield to us your weapons and wargear or be sent to your gods!"

The orc captain hesitated; this was clearly much more of a challenge than he expected. But I could see him force away his fear with anger. He barked an order to his crew. They grabbed ropes and swung over to our ship. Battle was joined.

Some of the crew stepped back, not wanting to be on the receiving end of an orc's momentum. Kurra, for her part, simply turned that momentum to her advantage, using it to drive a pirate onto her axe. Xeldia stepped back, but only to allow a pirate to overreach himself before she killed him with a counterattack. I opened with a few magic blasts, but as the second wave readied themselves, a wicked idea stirred in my mind. As they swung, I cast blindness at a few on the flank. A couple started gripping their ropes desperately, not attempting to board, while another leapt, only to misjudge and slam painfully into the railing before falling into the water.

Those efforts weren't enough to prevent boarding, and so the fight started in earnest. They pressed forward, driving the crew back. Eledine rushed around the deck, alternating between flinging some sort of alchemical muck at pirates and providing the crew direly needed medical attention. That only slowed their advances to the fore and aft of the boat, leading to Kurra and Xeldia being surrounded as a third wave approached.

They held the line. Kurra roared as she swung her axe around like a whirlwind, blood flying across the deck. Xeldia put herself between the enemy and a few nervous crewmen, holding firm as a shining example of courage. Lantern light glinted off her armour plates as she stood tall. The pirate captain roared in anger and approached her, his scimitar levelled at her.

Xeldia gladly accepted the challenge. The two leapt at each other, blades clashing. The captain immediately followed up with a punch to the gullet that left a dent in Xeldia's armour. She staggered back, teeth gritted. The orc pressed the advantage, but Xeldia evaded the strike, nicking his arm as he overextended himself. The orc barely seemed to notice, forcing Xeldia back farther.

I could see Xeldia was outmatched, so I decided to tip the scales. Invoking the power of the cold void, I sapped the strength from the orc's bones. He roared in anger, looking at me, but there was no way he could get at me without leaving himself open to Xeldia.

He snapped, "Someone kill the witch!"

I suddenly found myself the focus of attention of more than a few pirates, and there weren't nearly enough crewmen between them and me. Worse still, my magic was stretched thin. As a couple pressed through the scattered crew to charge me, I decided that I was much more useful alive than dead and ran for cover. A trio of orcs pursued. Absent places to run, I headed below decks, the orcs hot on my heels. I had no chance of outrunning them, so I decided to use my small size to my advantage, slipping between some crates and into the shadows as I rounded a corner. The orcs came around a split second afterwards and looked around briefly. Not immediately seeing me, they huffed, then turned and headed back above deck.

I realised that while they were looking for me, they weren't part of the wider fight. So, I conjured a bolt of cold and sent it at the ankle of the orc in the rear. He screamed in pain, dropping to his knees. The other orcs took the challenge. They charged back down as I slunk behind a pillar. I waited a second, then fired another blast. Again, they charged. Again, I slipped away.

I kept up the game of cat-and-mouse, slipping between bunks and barrels as the pirates tried to outmanoeuvre me, a task made more difficult by their mounting injuries. But, in a brief lapse of my attention, I failed to notice one recover and move towards where I was retreating. With a kick, he sent me sprawling. I just barely managed to evade a follow-up stab with a scimitar. I tried to move away, but the other two orcs moved to corner me. I tried to weave between his legs, but he kicked me to the side as another stuck a spear in my leg. I screamed.

The orcs suddenly stopped. I forced my awareness through the cloud of pain to see why: The pirate captain's head had just landed between the three.

Xeldia approached, face covered in blood, sword pointed at the pirates. The rest of the crew were fanning out behind her. "The battle is over. Yield or die," she said.

They might have fought to the end, but there was a fire in Xeldia's eyes that cowed them. They dropped their weapons.

As the crew disarmed and bound the pirates, Eledine rushed from behind Xeldia to tend my wounds. I wasn't remotely used to pain, but I held myself still as best I could. Luckily, one of Eledine's alchemical concoctions managed to ease the pain quickly, and soon I was stable. Meanwhile, Xeldia was sorting out the surviving pirates. She stripped them of their weapons and valuables, then returned them to their ship and let them loose.

As the crew picked up the pieces, the ship's captain approached me. "Ahoy, witch? You like the night, right? Well, Jerrem, my night watchman, didn't make it. If you want to spot the next batch of pirates before they're on us, I was thinking you could take his spot for the rest of the trip."

I was pretty tired after the night's events, but he had a point, so I accepted. Curling up in a hammock with twice the recommended number of occupants wasn't exactly comfortable anyway. Eledine had patched my leg up enough to manage the climb back to the crow's nest, so I headed there and kept watch as best I could. Which wasn't that well, as I was pretty tired, but the rest of the night was uneventful.

I was still conscious by the time the sun rose, but only barely. By some miracle, I managed to make it back to the deck without slipping off the rigging and arrived for breakfast. I sat down and waited to be served. It was about that point that my consciousness decided it had been working far too much overtime.

When I awoke, I'd been carefully laid in my berth, the heavier of my clothes neatly folded and placed beside my other things, and Cosma lying atop me, providing some welcome warmth. A grumble in my stomach informed me that I hadn't had breakfast. I wasn't looking forward to negotiating with the cook for a meal, but

I found some leftovers neatly wrapped in paper and left atop my belongings for me. I ate them happily. I had been missing Mum's doting affections, but this was a very welcome taste of them.

A little after I finished, Eledine came down from above deck and started working through her alchemical supplies.

After a minute of working past my deeply ingrained shyness, I asked, "Eledine? Who…" I gestured to the discarded paper, to myself, and to my berth.

After Eledine parsed what I was asking, she said, "Xeldia. She seemed surprisingly…I don't think *concerned* is the right word. Caring, perhaps. Regardless, when one or two of the crew started suggesting pranks, she silenced them." At my cocked head, she added, "Her precise words were, if I recall, 'Touch her and I'll kick you in the balls so hard you'll cough up your own spine.' On the subject," she said, as if that threat was something entirely mundane, "she remarked that she owed you thanks for your help against the pirate captain."

Chapter 8

We reached the ship's destination, the orc port town of Zerrekdar. While not exactly a metropolis, it was a lot larger than the tiny shanty towns I'd heard of in rumour. The infrastructure was actually kind of impressive, the port having a large wall and plenty of docks. The port's maintenance, however, left something to be desired; the docks were half-rotten and covered in refuse of all sorts. Despite the heat of the savanna, the streets were constantly busy. Oxen and slaves pulled cartloads of goods here and there, orc warriors marched to and fro, and merchants bartered haphazard collections of goods.

We found a tavern on the edge of town where we could get some rest while the expedition resupplied. While eating, we heard a commotion outside, so we left to see what all the fuss was about. We found a large crowd gathered around a pair of orcs, one heavily armed and armoured, the other dressed in rags and with a rock. They were locked in single combat. The crowd around them cheered, some placing bets.

Seeing our concerned expressions, Kurra explained, "A challenge. By the ancient traditions, a slave may challenge their master to single combat for their freedom, so only the weak remain enslaved."

As the heavily armoured orc ran the other through, Eledine remarked, "And I suppose not being permitted any wargear is a weakness, hmm?"

I saw a sour look on Kurra's face, but she didn't comment further on the subject.

We set out across the plains the next day. The terrain was more varied than we expected, savannas often abruptly slipping into rocky gorges or thorny scrub. Despite that, we managed to keep a steady pace. The heat was a bother, and to my surprise, so was the cold; when the sun set, the temperature dropped quite sharply.

On our first night out on the plains, Cosma and I huddled close in our bedroll. I overheard Kurra, resting next to me, mutter something in her native tongue.

Then, she said, "Is too cold. Need to share warmth. Peri, Cosma, come." She opened her bedroll.

This was something of a shock to my thought processes. It wasn't like it was from a stranger; Kurra and I had grown into good friends, and it wasn't like we weren't reasonably comfortable around each other, especially with the whole her-carrying-me-in-her-pack thing. But this was a step further.

A step that I realised I very much wanted to take. I crawled out of my bedroll and into Kurra's, Cosma following behind. I was wrapped completely in Kurra's warmth and scent. She held me tight. I could feel her firm muscles against me, shielding me from everything outside. It wasn't long before she dozed off. It took me a while longer.

We reached our destination a couple of days later, only for scouts to report it had been turned into something of a fort for a local orc warband. Renedarl convened a council to decide what should be done.

The scout leader, a delicate-looking elven woman named Juniper, explained the situation. "There's about fifty in there total, about half combat-ready. It's been heavily fortified. Multiple siege engines on the walls, and I think I heard some angry-sounding animals in there."

As Juniper sketched a diagram in the sand, Renedarl observed with a frown. "I doubt they'll just let us in."

I squeaked, "Why not?"

"Because who opens their doors to every possible holy mission? Especially orcs!" Renedarl sounded like he was stating the obvious.

But Kurra, a little unexpectedly, supported me. "*Could* talk. Maybe. Who do they serve?"

Juniper shrugged. "No sign of their leader, must be holed up towards the centre of the fort."

"Banners? Markings?" Kurra asked.

"Well, yes…" Juniper sketched the insignia in the sand, though it was heavily abstract and really looked like a series of jagged lines.

They meant something to Kurra, though. "Hmph. Mark of Kelarak. But are far from his territory. Why here?"

"Perhaps he's expanded his territory?" Eledine suggested. "I understand the orc warlords are constantly vying for dominance."

Kurra shook her head. "Does not happen that often. Warlords more interested in keeping lessors in line. Besides, Kelarak focused on keeping own lands. Why plant flag here?"

Renedarl stroked his chin. "If he's made advances into another warlord's territory, we might be able to use that situation to our advantage. What happens when the locals find out?"

"There would be an entire army here, and that makes our job much harder," Xeldia pointed out. "But that might provide some incentive for them to leave. So perhaps we *could* go the diplomatic approach."

"Are you insane? These are barbarians sitting on a sacred site! Wasn't your ship attacked by these people just a few nights ago?" Renedarl exclaimed.

Kurra said, "Pirates were of the eastern shores, different groups from those inland."

Xeldia added, "And the fact of the matter remains that this isn't a military expedition. We're outnumbered and likely out-armed. If we can talk to them, that could save us a bloodbath."

Renedarl sighed. "Fine. But only a small party goes out for diplomacy, and the rest of the expedition gets ready for a fight."

The diplomats chosen were me, Kurra, Eledine, and Xeldia. When morning came, we approached openly, the rest of the expedition taking cover behind the dunes. It was clear that the church was of familiar architecture, but the orcs had more recently added to it, covering it in fortifications like sandstone barricades and pikes. We approached the large pair of double doors at the front of the church. A commotion could be heard from behind the walls. Kurra called out a greeting in the orc language.

An orc woman with a half-burned face emerged on a balcony overlooking the church's fore. She hefted a crossbow. She shouted something at Kurra, both parties visibly on guard. But when Kurra responded, the woman's expression suddenly shifted to astonishment—and hope. She switched to the Casten tongue. "Are you truly agents of the Triune? From Heartshold itself?"

Xeldia stepped forward, bowing politely. "It is so. I am Paladin Xeldia, servant of Raiya. I am under the command of Captain Renedarl of Ynnelia."

"A moment!" the orc woman called, before hurrying back inside.

The party shifted anxiously. It was certainly a hopeful sign but could also be the precursor to an ambush. I scanned the walls carefully, watching for any sign of activity.

A few minutes later, the double doors opened, revealing a large crowd of orcs, but not in a combat formation. They were looking at us with…excitement?

Another orc woman stepped forward, this one with a paler green hue and wearing long robes. "Hail, fellow servants of the Triune! I am Orreke, priestess of Etunae. We've long hoped we'd be able to reach out to the rest of our faith!"

Xeldia approached carefully. "Worshippers of the Triune? Here?"

Orreke smiled warmly. "Of course you are surprised. But my mentor, rest her soul, found this place many years ago. Deep within, she encountered the teachings of the Triune. She learned of beauty, of wonder, of honour. After ten thousand wars, our people finally found a place where warm hearts were not hated! So, she built a sect of our faith here, in secret. Raiya, forgive us, but we have not the strength to stand openly, not yet. But please, come in! We have much to discuss!"

"Let us just gather the rest of our expedition," Xeldia said before bowing and returning to where Renedarl was observing the exchange from behind a rock.

He had a very sceptical look. "What in the hells did you say?"

"Captain, these people are also faithful to the Triune. Apparently, they found our teachings here and saw their worth," Xeldia explained.

"I have a hard time believing these savages could be bothered to read." Renedarl scowled.

Eledine said, "Have you seen their iconography? Most of it dates back to the time of Saint Eldrey and predates the Ioran Heresy. This could be exactly what we're looking for, and they're outright welcoming us."

"Or leading us right into a trap. How do you know we can trust these people?" Renedarl asked.

Xeldia looked at him sternly. "What would you propose, then? Slaughter them? Decline staying the night if we must, but you call them savages when you're the one pushing for battle!"

Renedarl swiftly stood. "Don't give me that! This is my expedition, not yours! You're on thin ice with the commander already!"

"And what about you? You risk throwing away the lives of good people, and for what? Because you'd rather risk a definite battle over a phantom of treachery?" Xeldia snapped.

"I am an agent of Ynnelia! It is my duty to seek the truth, no matter what it may be! And you—"

"You're not even entertaining the notion that these people are just who they seem!" Xeldia interrupted. "You say you seek truth, but you're not even looking!"

Renedarl poked Xeldia hard in the chest. "Xeldia, if I hear one more piece of lip from you, I'll have you excommunicated!"

The two paladins stared at each other. Renedarl's anger was fully borne on his face; Xeldia's only hinted in the subtle shaking of the deep breaths she took.

Eledine spoke up. "If you're not willing to dedicate the entire expedition, then perhaps we could continue with our 'small party' tactic. Xeldia, Kurra, Peri and I seem to be getting along with the locals well enough. And if they do betray us, well, that solves your insubordination problem, doesn't it?"

Renedarl sized Eledine up for a moment, trying to discern if there was any mockery in her words and to what extent. Finally, he said, "Very well. But I'm sending Kay with you. Hold a moment." He left.

He returned a few minutes later with another halfling from the expedition, a brunette who had somehow remained looking neat and tidy this far into the desert. She looked eager for the assignment.

"Hi! I'm Kay! Xeldia, right? I think we met back in a first-year theology course."

"Perhaps we did. Well met, regardless," Xeldia said politely.

Kay turned to the rest of us with a smile and a polite nod. "And well met to the rest of you! Anyway, archaeology, right? Come on!" She happily headed down to the church, the rest of us following close behind.

Some of the excitement had died down in the church, but Orreke was still there, looking hopeful. Kurra said something to her in orcish; I guessed she was updating her on the arrangement, but I could tell from her tone that Kurra didn't think terribly highly of Renedarl (not that I did). Orreke, for her part, frowned, but nodded in understanding.

The mood was lightened when Kay spoke. "Hi! So, you're a follower of Etunae, too? Wow! Didn't expect to see you guys all the way out here!"

Orreke's smile returned. "Yes! If you wish, we can show you the lower chambers. That is where our people first found your teachings!"

We gladly accepted, and Orreke led us farther into the temple, and through what would have been a secret passage in a wall were it not left wide open. We headed down a flight of steps into an underground chamber. Orreke muttered a prayer, and an orb of light appeared in her hand.

Kay's eyes widened. "You—the Triune granted you magic?"

"Yes! It took a few years of deep devotion and learning, but I feel a true connection to Etunae, and she grants me these small blessings whenever I need them," Orreke explained.

Kay was amazed. "That's—wow! The Triune only grants their magics to those with great destinies! Maybe it's leading the other orcs to the Triune's light?"

Orreke looked just a touch bashful. "Please, I am no chosen one. I simply work with compassion in my heart. A few of my students have also been granted power."

"No way! That's amazing! Look, you should really talk to the Herald. She definitely will want to meet you! She can even help you work out what your destiny is!" The words raced out of Kay's mouth.

"That's a bit of a journey. But I would like to meet more of our faith…" Orreke turned to the rest of the chamber we found ourselves in, walls lined with detailed carvings and some half-faded murals. "…Anyway, this is where my mentor uncovered the words of the Triune all those years ago. The upper levels had been ransacked many times over, but this place was guarded by a cunning puzzle—only those genuinely curious would bother to open it. Here, the priests who originally inhabited this temple stored their most valuable works and relics, among them a number of writings, from which we learned of the Triune and their values."

Orreke showed us several old books, nearly falling apart from age, but what was left was carefully preserved by her and her followers. We all examined them carefully. Kurra didn't seem to understand much about what was going on but was impressed, nonetheless. The rest of us examined the various murals and texts with fascination.

Eledine, in particular, was nearly awed. "Fascinating! These appear to be records of the Ioran Heresy!"

I managed to whisper, "You mentioned it before…"

"Don't you know? Around five hundred years ago, the kingdom of Ioran turned against the Triune, betraying it to demons. The result was a bloody war, one large enough to almost entirely redraw the political map. Apparently, that's what caused the Triune to turn away from mortals, and consequently, why they only give powers to those with great destinies." In a more casual tone, she added, "My grandfather still tells a number of stories about the time period, though I've grown to doubt them mainly because I haven't found a source that backs a single one up. Either his memory has failed, or his honesty."

As we studied the chamber, Kurra asked, "You fly Kelarak's flag. Does he share faith?"

Orreke shook her head, her mood a touch dampened. "No. It's a deception; Kelarak is known for brutal retaliation against any who threatens his claims. We're hoping no one near is willing to test him. It's worked so far."

We spent the rest of the day enthusiastically taking notes on all we had discovered and talking with those in the church. They were friendly and outright enthusiastic hosts. While their knowledge of the Triune's canon was limited, their belief in the underlying principles of care, courage, and curiosity was undeniable. Xeldia was happy to talk about their shared faith and was curious to hear the orc's perspective on theology. Kurra grew to like the group, describing them as having all the strength of her people with none of the stupidity.

When evening drew near, we returned to the expedition's camp and told the others all about our talks. Most were very much curious, though Renedarl was as sceptical as ever. When the rest of us returned to our bedrolls, he and Kay stayed up talking.

The next day, we returned with more of the expedition. Kay was eager to talk Orreke and her blessed acolytes into returning with us to Heartshold. Meanwhile, Eledine and I got to work translating some of the ancient texts we'd found.

Some of the work had Eledine scratching her head. "Odd… there's a letter here, detailing who's taking which side during the Heresy. But it's completely different from what we know. Either we're missing far more of this letter than I expected, or someone's gravely mistaken."

It wasn't the only sample. Granted, we only had fragments, but those fragments created a picture that simply couldn't be lined up with what we knew. The outcome of a battle here, an alliance drawn there.

After a while, I whispered, "Could…Heartshold be wrong?"

Eledine frowned. "Never a comfortable notion to entertain. But admitting you're wrong is the first step to being right. This might not *prove* anything, but we should take every note we can back. If nothing else, a future scholar might find it useful to know there was another perspective."

It took the rest of the day and a lot of ink, but we assembled a large collection of notes on the Heresy and the events leading up to it. The reactions of the rest of the expedition were mixed. Some were just as fascinated as we were with our discoveries, others didn't really see what the fuss was about, and others were just eager to get out of the desert. For Orreke's part, she and one of her acolytes decided to join us heading back to Heartshold but insisted on leaving the others to guide the rest of the remaining orcs.

The march back was in reasonably high spirits, considering the terrain and locals. Eledine and Xeldia spent a lot of the trip discussing geopolitics, both apparently having a significant amount of knowledge and interest in the subject. I, for one, spent a lot of time cleaning sand out of Kurra's pack, a small task for which the big orc was very much grateful.

Chapter 9

One morning, not far out from Zerrekdar, Juniper reported an orc warband moving to intercept us. Renedarl quickly convened a council.

Juniper explained, "There are at least fifty of them, mostly fighters, moving to intercept us. They've got a number of scouts as well, ran into one just a minute ago. Whatever we're going to do, we have to do it quickly."

Renedarl looked grim. "I doubt they're coming to ask the time. We need a defensive position, and fast."

Another paladin, a servant of Etunae named Andrea, said, "Captain, are you sure? Barely half of us have even rudimentary combat training. We can't win a fight."

"We certainly won't if we don't get into a better position! There was a ridge a few minutes back; that'll cover our flanks at least. March!" Renedarl barked the last word, and the whole expedition scrambled to move.

As we marched, Kurra said to him, "Might be able to avoid mass battle. Can challenge them to single combat. Will need a valuable wager. I will gladly be champion."

"Well, it's the best idea I've heard yet. What kind of wager will suffice?" Renedarl asked.

Kurra sounded grim. "Slaves are best. Don't want them slain in battle."

"And since we have none, we'll have to offer members of our expedition," Renedarl added.

"Yes."

Renedarl sighed. "Dammit. Fine. Probably better than death, at any rate."

We reached the ridge a little after the orc warband appeared on the horizon. A large number of orcs carried heavy weapons, while a handful of slaves were laden with massive sacks. They approached as the expedition quickly assembled into a formation.

Eledine discreetly handed Kurra a vial of fluid. "Here. It'll improve your strength for a short while. You can't lose."

Kurra hesitated but took it and swiftly drank the vial's contents with a wince. She then turned back to the incoming warband as it fanned out. She called out in orcish. One orc, a large brute covered head to toe in bronze armour, answered. After a brief exchange, Kurra unslung her pack, with me still inside, placing it on the ground before she moved a few paces towards the enemy. The armoured orc moved in kind.

After sharing what I'm pretty sure were taunts, the two drew weapons. They circled each other, sneering. Then, they charged. Kurra's axe dented her challenger's shield even as a sword strike forced her to step to the side. The orc warlord pressed the advantage, forcing Kurra back. She grimaced. Then, she locked the orc's sword with the haft of her axe and pushed back.

The duel was closely fought. I ached to do something. If Kurra failed, the consequences... But I wasn't a subtle enough spellcaster to be able to cast spells without obviously cheating. Though that gave me an idea: At the very least, I could stop others from cheating. I scanned the orc warband. It wasn't long before I saw, crouching behind a wall of their comrades, an orc preparing a spell. I couldn't get a good enough look at the runes surrounding their hands to figure out what or how to counter it. Instead, I gave

Cosma an order. She sprinted across the dune and chomped hard on the spellcaster's fingers. The runes collapsed in a flash as the orc swore, swatting at Cosma as she scurried away behind friendly lines before the other orcs could react.

Kurra, meanwhile, had her opponent locked in a contest of brute strength—a contest she was winning, pushing the warlord back, bit by bit. Many fighters in this position would have disengaged and changed their approach. Most, but not this one. Perhaps the option didn't occur to him, or perhaps he couldn't accept he was losing a contest of strength. After a moment, he fell on his back. Kurra raised her axe for a lethal blow. The warlord went for a quick chest stab. Kurra parried the strike, knocking his sword away before shifting and decapitating him.

My reaction was a mix of elation, relief, and disgust. Kurra roared in triumph. She glared at the orc warband; some met her eyes with a glare, while others turned away. One brought forth a number of orcs and a couple of humans, all dressed in rags, with collars around their necks. He handed Kurra some keys before turning and leaving, the other orcs following.

Xeldia approached Kurra. "Well fought, friend. These..." She gestured at the collared people who had remained behind.

"We bet lives. We won. They are now ours," Kurra explained, examining the dead orc's armour.

Xeldia scoffed. "No one belongs to anyone." She took the keys from Kurra, who showed no objection, and unlocked the slave collars. "You are free people now. Do what you will. If you wish, you may accompany us to Zerrekdar."

Renedarl added, "You'll be hauling supplies if you're taking from them, though. Only fair."

One of the ex-slaves spoke to some others in orcish. All were astonished at the development. Another slave fell to her knees. "Thank you! Thank you!"

Orreke stepped forward, smiling. "Such is the will of the Triune! You cannot love what you seek to control, and all beings are worthy of love!" Orreke happily continued to preach the Triune's word as the caravan got itself sorted out again.

The ex-slaves didn't mind hauling some of our supplies—in fact, their previous owners had them hauling far more. They were happy to hear about the Triune. Apparently, the local god, Arragrun, patron of war and conquest, wasn't terribly popular among slaves. The Triune priests and paladins, along with the expedition, certainly didn't mind Orreke doing missionary work.

Meanwhile, Kurra had stripped her opponent of his armour. After examining it for a while, she offered it to Xeldia. "Don't like heavy armour. What about you? Looks enchanted."

Xeldia looked flattered. "Truly? This is not a small gift. I'll have to have it resized, and maybe adjust the iconography…still, thank you. Truly."

Kurra grasped Xeldia's shoulder. "You are good warrior, and good friend."

Renedarl huffed. "You'll have to hand that to the quartermaster—"

"It is hers! *I* claimed it in duel, and gifted it to *her*. Not you," Kurra roared.

Even the normally stubborn Renedarl paused. "…I see."

On the sea part of the voyage home, the clouds started to gather and darken. The rain started to beat down.

The captain addressed the passengers. "Alright, we've been clipped by a storm. Not a big one, nothing our crew hasn't handled before, but things are going to get a little rough for a while. Should be through by tomorrow."

The passengers mostly nodded; if nothing else, the captain sounded like he knew what he was talking about. I figured I might as well have faith in the crew; after all, it wasn't like I could do anything about the situation. But as the sky darkened, the rain beat down, thunder roared, and the waves tossed the ship, faith proved to be a very difficult thing to keep.

I'd always hated storms. They were immense, powerful, unstoppable. There was never a damn thing I could do about them, and their power could be felt all around you. The tossing of the waves only made it worse. I tried to carry on as normal, but a deep, animal part of me begged for me to flee, to find cover, and I found it impossible to ignore. The best cover I could find was curling up in a corner, braced against the ship's walls. I remained there for a long time, whimpering.

Then, Xeldia approached. "Not fond of storms?"

I managed to shake my head.

"Me neither, truth be told. Still, I have trained for many years to learn to set aside my fear. Not an easy task."

At that moment, thunder boomed right outside the ship. I whimpered.

Xeldia softly sighed. "That was pretty close…" She was quiet for a while. Then, she gently wrapped me in her cape, picking me up and carrying me to her bunk. She sat down with me in her lap, holding me close. "There, there. It's going to be alright."

While her words did little, her warmth did much. I calmed a little. I only needed a little; my body was so exhausted from being so tense that I dozed off.

When I awoke, it was Kurra who was gently holding me. After processing this, I gave her a quizzical look.

In response, she said, "Xeldia said she needed to stand. Took over for her."

I relaxed again, content. Quite impressively, Kurra was even more comforting than Xeldia, being even larger with even greater muscles. I still very much didn't like being on a ship in the middle of a storm, but the presence of close friends made things much easier to deal with.

We returned to Ansiel without further incident. Orreke was astonished at the sights and sounds of the big city and insisted on spending some time browsing the exotic goods at the local market before we headed to the university to debrief. A few local priests were there, whom Orreke was eager to meet. After some enthusiastic introductions, Renedarl explained all that had transpired.

When he got to the part about my party speaking further with Orreke's followers, Eledine presented the priests with her notes. "There were a number of records of the Ioran Heresy. They were in poor condition, but from what I was able to salvage, there were a number of significant inconsistencies with current histories. To the extent that I'm not content merely writing them off as miscommunications."

A priest took the notes, flicking through them with a frown. "Hmm…I see. This is probably nothing. Between the distance of the church from the events of the Heresy—"

"You may not have heard me.   already considered factors like distance and damage to the records,. Eledine said, quite emphatically.

Renedarl snapped, "Eledine! Listen to the priests! Do you think them fools?"

"I'll listen to them when they listen to me and think them fools when they say foolish things." Eledine managed to keep her voice level.

Renedarl didn't. He stood angrily. "Are you disrespecting the most trusted agents of the Triune?"

The priest calmly rested a hand on Renedarl's shoulder. "Now, now, captain, I'm sure she didn't mean any insult. You know how competitive academics can get. I'll compare this to our more complete records in the Heartshold. Perhaps we can work out where our brethren got confused."

Eledine nodded assent. Renedarl sat down, visibly still annoyed at Eledine, but he resumed the story.

After the meeting, people began to file out. I was looking forward to sitting down with Kurra for a meal and taking our time for once.

But Kurra looked like she had something on her mind. She approached Eledine. "Eledine, Think priests were acting odd?"

Eledine paused, stroking her chin. "Hmm…nothing in particular stuck out to me. I suppose they did seem somewhat dismissive of my notes."

“Too dismissive. Warrior trusts her instincts. Mine says something wrong.” Kurra shifted her weight anxiously.

“Perhaps. Though I’m not sure what exactly can be done…” Eledine thought about the problem.

“Investigate ourselves! See what the Heartshold records really say!” Kurra’s voice rose with enthusiasm.

Drawing Xeldia’s attention. “You can’t exactly walk into the Heartshold libraries. Unless you had my help.”

Chapter 10

Xeldia insisted on us all getting better clothes to visit her workplace, which we could now do thanks to our significantly fatter purses. Eledine still had some very fine clothes from her previous career as a lawyer, and I managed to find a store that stocked enough halfling-sized clothes to include something that fit me. Kurra, however, needed something custom-tailored for her massive bulk. She seemed simultaneously annoyed by and proud of that fact.

It took a couple of days, but Xeldia was eventually satisfied and showed us inside. The interior of the Heartshold was every bit as grand as I had imagined. The halls were tall and grand, and I could see half a dozen stories above us, walkways framing the tall roof, artfully painted with tales from Triune scripture. Lifelike statues were carved from the fine marble pillars. The library itself was no less impressive, with countless books stacked on shelves so tall that the walkways were built around them.

Xeldia left to try and retrieve Eledine's notes from the priests, while the rest of us got some suggestions for records from one of the librarians. With a note in hand, we started looking through the maze of shelves.

Eledine had a mildly disgruntled look. "We need to standardise library organisation. This would be so much easier if—ah, here we are." She looked up at the shelves, eyes fixed on one of the books we were looking for, at the very top of the shelf. Eledine looked around. "There's got to be a ladder—"

Kurra grabbed her by the waist and lifted her up. "Can you reach now?"

It took Eledine a second to process her abrupt change in altitude, but then she was able to reach the book. After Kurra lowered her back to the floor, she adjusted her coat. "Well. That's one way to do it."

We collected our books, Kurra lifting Eledine up more than once, and gathered them at a desk.

As we did so, we were approached by one of the librarians, a scrawny elf woman. "Excuse me, but you're disturbing the others."

The three of us looked at each other, confused.

Eledine said, "We've barely talked."

"Yes, but there are some concerns about your, ah, servant." The librarian glanced at Kurra.

She snarled. "I am not servant! And am here on invitation!"

The librarian took a step back. "Please, please, there's no need for that. I'm just going to have to ask you to leave."

Eledine fixed the librarian with a stern look. "We're here on business with Paladin Xeldia, at her invitation. And we have broken no rules."

"Ladies, I'm afraid that if you don't leave, I'll have to call the guards."

Kurra sounded like she was about to start making threats, but Eledine laid a hand on her shoulder. "Very well. But please, keep these books for Xeldia. And inform her when she arrives that we'll be waiting outside."

The three of us left, taking our time. Just as we reached the main doors, we heard Xeldia yelling from the library. We paused, looked at each other, then turned and headed back.

We heard Xeldia's words long before she arrived. "…service to the Triune! And you kick her out because some simpering idiots see an orc and get scared? Do these same fools call for the guards every time they walk outside? I am going to retrieve my friends, and when I return, you will give each of them an apology, the orc most of all! And next time someone is being 'disturbing,' ask yourself whether they are the ones making a fuss over someone being green, you whelp!"

We reached the door of the library just as Xeldia threw it open. She paused as she saw us. "Ah. There you are."

Eledine smiled. "We had almost left, but we could hear you yelling from the other side of the building. I take it the librarians will be more cooperative now?"

"They best be." Xeldia turned and led us back inside. "No luck with your notes. The priests insist they've misplaced them."

Eledine sighed. "No matter. I have a very good memory."

The librarians were profusely apologetic as we returned, just as Xeldia had commanded. We got back to work studying the history of the Ioran Heresy. An hour or two of reading only confirmed that the history recorded by Heartshold was drastically different from those records in the church of Saint Eldrey.

After a while, I noticed something strange. I called the attention of my friends. "Here. Says Iorans massacred humans at Auberg. But halflings at Auberg don't mention that many humans."

Eledine adjusted her glasses as she pored over the pages. "A good catch. Perhaps we should see what their records say."

I smiled eagerly: Auberg was just off my home.

Eledine continued, "On the subject, I've been thinking of visiting my grandfather again, and my hometown is in that direction. Perhaps we could make it a trip?"

"Could visit my family, too!" I chirped

Kurra smiled. "Then it is quest! Dive deeper into history!"

Xeldia simply nodded, deep in thought.

I quietly asked, "Xeldia?"

"Hmm? Sorry, I was…I am worried. At first, I thought this was just some historian's mistake, but"—she lowered her voice to a mere whisper—"what if this is conspiracy?"

Eledine's eyes flashed with resolve. "All the more reason to bring it to light."

We started plotting our journey using an atlas we found. As we did, Cosma leapt on the table and started pawing at the pages.

Xeldia glanced at me. "New orders?"

It took us flipping through the atlas a bit, but eventually we managed to figure out roughly where Cosma wanted us to go: a patch of plains a day or two's detour from our planned route. I examined the maps of the area, trying to figure out what it could be that drew my star's attention.

Kurra said, "Some druidic orders around there. Were, at least. Focus on the weather. Something to do with sun? Could break sword's curse while we're there."

A couple of days later, I could see my family's inn on the horizon, just like it had always been. I peeked out from Kurra's pack, shifting with excitement.

Kurra glanced over her shoulder at me. "Glad to be home?"

I nodded eagerly. Kurra grinned and picked up the pace.

The four of us opened the door to see the tavern in the middle of its lunch rush. Kurra approached the bar with a wide smile.

Dad was working the bar as usual. "Welcome, Peri! You're back! With more friends!"

Xeldia bowed politely. "Hail. I am Xeldia, paladin of Raiya. Peri has proven herself a woman of cunning, and no small magical power."

Eledine followed suit. "Eledine, research alchemist, and I concur with Xeldia. I'm glad to be able to call Peri a colleague and a friend."

Dad beamed. "Well, you lot find yourselves a table, and we'll have you served right away!"

We were all treated to a veritable feast by my family. When the lunch rush died down, Mum and Dad quickly sat down with us, eager to hear the story of my journeys. I was happy to tell them, though, since I wasn't much of a talker, I let my companions fill in a good deal of the details. Once they'd been filled in, we set out for Auberg, with a promise to be back in time for dinner.

Auberg was only an hour or two away, though it was a little longer with all of us weighed down with Mum's cooking. It was, strictly speaking, part of the eastern kingdom of Sellen, but the village chose its own leaders, and the king of Sellen generally left my people be so long as we paid tribute when needed. It was the very model of a halfling village, finely appointed houses half-dug into the hillsides scattered with colourful gardens. Unfortunately, that meant a lack of an actual library (much to my chagrin), but literature was popular enough among the well-to-do in halfling society that I was still confident we could find some records. Of course, that meant quite possibly the chore I hated most: making polite conversation with the gentlefolk. Thankfully, I now had a paladin with diplomatic training and a former lawyer to handle that problem for me.

At my direction, the party headed to the home of Radan, a local wizard who sold his flashier magic for parties. Xeldia politely knocked on the door.

Radan, a portly halfling with a great appetite, even by our people's standards, answered. "Oh, hello there! Radan, spellcaster extraordinaire, at your service!" He gave a deep bow.

Xeldia bowed in turn. "Xeldia, paladin of Raiya. A pleasure to meet you. These are my companions: Eledine, Kurra, and Peri."

Radan looked up at where I poked out from over Kurra's shoulder. "Peri! It's been a long time. How is the family business? Must be slowing down a bit for the planting season."

Radan had a head for all the gossip in Auberg, but apparently none for the fact that I *hated* small talk. I simply gave him a thumbs up. Radan's mouth pressed into a line.

Rather than wait for Radan to press, Xeldia asked, "We're researching the history of the region. Peri tells us you're something of a scholar."

"Well, she told you the truth! Come in, come in, I'll make some tea." Radan stepped aside, beckoning us in with open arms.

Kurra examined the door frame, watching as Xeldia and Eledine had to crouch to fit through. "…Will remain outside." She set me back on the ground.

Radan busied himself in the kitchen and started chatting about everything except what we were there for. I had much better things to do than hear about who in the village had said what about whom to whoever, so I got to browsing his bookshelves. While historical accounts weren't exactly in abundance, there was a detailed record of Auberg's genealogy. (My kin were almost as bad as nobles when it came to using bloodlines for bragging rights.) Flicking through, I did find one or two records of humans residing in the town during the period of the Heresy, but in nowhere near the numbers that would make sense for them to be massacred as happened in the Heartshold records, nor were there any gaps in the genealogies that such killing would have to have caused.

Xeldia, meanwhile, had managed to manoeuvre the conversation to something relevant, remarkably quickly for one talking with a gentile halfling. "You mentioned she taught students about history; does that include Auberg's involvement in the Ioran Heresy?"

"Involvement? From what I understand, there wasn't all that much. I know some of the Hainfolgers. They live on the other side of the hill. A couple of their ancestors went off to fight. Real proud of that. Pious, too. You'd like them. Couple of their kids went for paladin training just last year," Radan explained.

After a little more conversation, and after I managed to search a few more books for a distinct lack of involvement with the Heresy, we said our goodbyes and left. We then headed to the other side of the hill, where the Hainfolgers maintained a small chapel of the Triune (though big enough for Kurra to fit in, albeit just barely). We met their current patriarch, a lanky fellow named Terral and engaged in much the same pattern of pleasantries. Xeldia managed to turn down the offer of yet more tea without causing offence. I was anticipating yet another bout of complex social strategy to bring the conversation on topic, but I had forgotten the fact that the villagers of Auberg needed little prompting to brag about the achievements of their families.

"…You see, Kai Allanbrook had married into the family, and since she was Lord Oritar's most faithful servant, he allowed Rini and Kal Hainfolger, along with Kai herself, into his personal guard. That's how they fought alongside him in the Second Battle of Whitemarsh," Terral happily explained.

Eledine frowned. "Hang on—I remember reading that the Greater Auberg region was heretic-controlled until the later battles of the Heresy. And you're saying the local lord was Orthodox? Surely, then, the region would have to be considered at least contested territory?"

"Well, your books must have been wrong," Terral stated confidently. "Lord Oritar was famous for his faith!"

Xeldia suggested, "Perhaps he remained Orthodox when the populace of the region was heretical?"

Kurra said, "He raised army? Had to have territory. Lots of it. Not just people; need farmland, weapons, medicine. Hard to have army without base. Very hard. Greater Auberg must have been Orthodox. Some, at least."

Terral immediately steered the conversation back to his fine lineage until enough time passed that wanting to get home for dinner was a good enough excuse to leave.

As we started back on the road, Xeldia was deep in thought. "…If it was just for these facts alone, I doubt I would have even remembered the matter of Greater Auberg."

Eledine finished, "But it's not just a single battle. I'm used to records not being perfectly accurate, especially for something as chaotic as war. But this? I'm no longer doubting my grandfather's memory."

We made it home by the end of the dinner rush, and I got to introduce my sister to all the others. Everyone got along well, and our rooms were free for the night. It wasn't for long, but I was deeply refreshed by even a single night in familiar environs. I even got the chance to further study some of the old tomes I'd recovered from the observatory, much to Cosma's delight.

When morning came, none of us were in a hurry to leave, especially after Mum filled us all up with her speciality pancakes.

Chapter 11

The next stop of our journey, Eledine's hometown, was in the elven kingdom of Ky'ira. While there was local ongoing friction in the kingdom between followers of the Triune and the older elven religions, its relations with the other kingdoms in Casten were generally peaceful. We joined a small trading caravan on the middle leg of the journey, hoping to exchange fresh halfling produce for rare elven lumber. We were travelling through a tight gully when the caravan was accosted by a cluster of poorly washed bandits.

Their leader, a big orc covered in tattoos, called out, "Sorry for the trouble! But I'll be taking all your silver now. And your copper. And your gold!"

Kurra growled, pulling out her axe.

The bandit leader laughed. "Oh? Up for some fun, are you?"

Xeldia stepped forward, fixing him with a fierce gaze. Barely seeming to notice the array of weapons pointed at her, she poked the orc in the chest. "This is what is going to happen. You are going to hand over all your weapons and all your stolen goods. Then, you are going to run. And you're going to do that to save me the effort of cleaning your blood off my armour."

Kurra may have been the larger woman, but Xeldia had an unmatched fire in her eyes that caused something to bloom in my heart. The bandits hesitated. Xeldia drew her sword. The bandits dropped their weapons, turned tail, and ran.

Xeldia snorted, turning to the rest of the caravan. "You, gather their weapons. We can sell them afterwards. Kurra, Eledine, Peri, let's track down their camp and their ill-got gains."

Between Kurra and Cosma, finding the bandit's camp was easy. Between all of us, cowing the one bandit left to guard their camp was even easier. The tricky part was getting the several barrels of trade goods back to the caravan, but an old, abandoned cart and some of Eledine's strength-enhancing elixirs solved that particular problem. Even knowing the feat of strength was, in part, thanks to Eledine's work, it was still very appealing watching Kurra and Xeldia pull the cart with ease across the terrain. I wondered if either of them had a thing for small, timid witches.

It was another few days before we reached Eledine's homeland. It was a heavily forested region, the trees reaching far into the sky, the sunlight casting rays through the leaves, and birds fluttering between the branches. The paved road turned to a dirt track, little more than a game trail weaving between the trees.

We arrived at the settlement of Ori'lereneth. It was built into the trees, buildings and bridges woven between them like spiderwebs. As a consequence, I discovered that I hated heights, rope bridges, and rope bridges over heights, leading me to spend much of the trip curled up in Kurra's pack. Thankfully, none of my companions deigned to comment.

It was quite a bit of climbing and walking to get to the home of Eledine's grandparents. (I needed to find some way to thank Kurra for all the carrying!) Eledine led us to a small abode in the highest levels of the town. As she knocked, I popped my head out of Kurra's pack, careful not to look at the deadly drop that was no doubt behind me. The door was answered by a willowy elven woman. The elves didn't age in the same way humans did; they decayed more like trees than animals, their flesh greying and cracking. I could see the earliest stages of the process in Eledine's grandmother, but she still seemed active.

"Eledine! Oh, it's been so long! How's your law—no, you're studying alchemy now! How's that going?"

Eledine smiled warmly. "It's been going well, thank you. But my friend Xeldia here is working on studying the history of the Ioran Heresy. I was hoping to talk to Grandpa. Is he here?"

Her grandma's face fell. "Oh dear, he's become sick. Some affliction of the mind. Happened all of a sudden just the other day. Can barely string two words together. I guess it had to happen sooner or later."

"All of a sudden?" Eledine replied. "Odd…can I see him?"

I could see the cogs of Eledine's razor-sharp mind turning.

We were led into the house and into a smaller bedroom. Another older elf, thin and gangly, lay on the bed. He opened one bleary eye. "Merelen, is that you? Oh, dear, I'm afraid I'm still having problems with that snake. And here I was, hoping to go to the dance…"

Eledine sat down beside his bed, taking out her alchemy kit. "It's Eledine. You're sick. Please, let me examine you."

"Eledine? Oh, but you're gone far away. Far away. You're not taking me on those ships, are you?" He seemed to be growing in alarm.

"No, no ships, just poking you with a few alchemical instruments. A little uncomfortable at worst, I promise." Eledine did her best to show calmness.

It wasn't working. "The thorns? No, not the thorns! They're everywhere!" The old man tried to stand.

Luckily, I had a spell prepared for a non-lethal takedown, and now was as good a time as any for it. Calling upon the power of night and the stories woven within it, I conjured a wave of somnolent power and sent it at him.

His panic stopped, and he slumped back, Eledine catching him before he collided with the wall and setting him back down. She gave me a thankful smile."Thank you. Now, for something most spellcasters *won't* know how to do." Eledine said.

She poked him in various places with various sticks and cloths, and stuck those sticks and cloths in various fluids, watching as they changed colour. Finally, she said, "As I suspected. Poison."

Her grandmother's eyes widened. "What? Who? Why? How!?"

"All good questions, none of which will be easy to answer." Eledine stood. "I'll do my best to develop an antidote, but at his age, I can't promise anything. We'll also have to investigate who poisoned him and why. At least I can say that the poison was ingested. Whoever did this must have had access to his food. Who would that be, other than you?"

Eledine's grandmother took a shaky breath. "Well…uh, about a week ago, we went to dinner with Kelerai of Oni'dir. And there was the Thousand Stars Festival a week before that. And—oh! There's the kitchen window! I have it open all the time when I'm cooking! Anyone could have snuck something in!"

Xeldia had settled into a confident, business-like parade rest. "Can you think of any motive?"

As the older elf racked her brain, coming up with nothing, I held up Cosma. "Track?"

A touch of enthusiasm, just a touch, entered Eledine's voice. "Now *that* is a promising route. If we can find—or even *make*—a small sample, we can have your furry friend identify anything or anyone that's been in contact."

Kurra said, "Will examine outside kitchen. If lucky, killer spilled some." She left, Xeldia following behind her.

After a minute, Kurra called, "Here!"

Eledine and I left and found the others crouched over a particular place on the walkway. Kurra pointed to a place on the ground. Eledine and I crouched beside them. Kurra was pointing at a small, dry droplet on the ground that had slightly discoloured the wood.

Eledine scraped at it with a stick, examining the residue with a frown. "Hmm…it's something. But not enough for me to identify what it is. Do you think it'll be enough for Cosma?"

I gently took the stick from Eledine and presented it to Cosma. "Track?"

Cosma sniffed it thoroughly, then wagged her tail enthusiastically. She sniffed around the area a while before returning to my side. Somehow, I managed to understand, at least vaguely, what she was thinking. "Can't follow it. But she remembers the scent!"

Eledine stood. "Then we need to try to find where the attacker is or has been. My grandmother is fairly familiar with most of the town, so she'd probably know if the attacker was somewhere local. My guess is they're from out of town, which means they'll be staying at an inn. I know every inn in town, so let's start checking them."

Xeldia said, "While you and Peri do that, Kurra and I will start talking with the neighbours."

The local innkeepers were a little bemused to see a whole party of heavily armed adventurers focusing on a fox sniffing around their common rooms, but I managed to keep Cosma from causing any trouble, so they didn't raise a fuss. The main problem was that the amount of traffic meant that most scents over the past few days had already been covered up. I was pondering solutions to this problem as Eledine and I moved between inns when Xeldia and Kurra met up with us.

"Good news. A neighbour saw a stranger about the time of the poisoning. We're looking for a blonde halfling woman," said Xeldia.

So, at the next inn we visited, Xeldia asked for any blonde halflings. The innkeeper didn't recall any, so we headed to the next.

There, the innkeeper said, "Been a couple here recently. One left just yesterday, heading back west. Other's still around."

Xeldia asked, "Could we see her? She fits the description of someone connected to a poisoning. Our furry friend here should be able to ascertain if she's the culprit." She gestured to Cosma.

"Well, I'm afraid she's not in right now. Probably won't be until dinner time. You could wait," the innkeeper suggested.

Xeldia shifted impatiently. "We need to identify the poisoner before they escape. Could we examine their rooms? I am only interested in their guilt; Raiya as my witness, we will not disturb them any more than absolutely necessary."

Eledine added, "And that will, hopefully, merely consist of Cosma here quickly sniffing around."

The innkeeper seemed a touch reluctant, but led us to the rooms, opening the first with a master key. We first entered the room of the suspect still present. Cosma sniffed around for a while, finding nothing. So, the innkeeper opened the door of the other. This time, when Cosma sniffed, she spent a lot of time investigating underneath the bed, getting increasingly excited. She emerged with a wagging tail. We all looked at each other with nods.

Xeldia turned to the innkeeper and asked, "You said she was heading west?"

The innkeeper nodded. "Sure. Started asking around for caravans heading that way. Think she was going to Ansiel."

Eledine adjusted the straps on her pack. "If she is travelling with a caravan, she'll be slower. If we hurry, we might be able to catch up. Thank you. We'd better get moving."

With the heavily forested terrain of Ky'ira, there weren't many paths for caravans, which made following our quarry easy. What was less easy was catching up to a whole day's lead; even with only four of us chasing a caravan, we needed to make a hurried pace. I entertained the idea of walking to save Kurra the strain, but her legs were two or three times the length of mine, and she seemed to handle my weight without much issue, so I figured trying to walk would slow us down more than anything. The big orc was striding forward with ease, and Xeldia was keeping pace.

Eledine, however, started faltering after an hour or two. It showed first through her gritted teeth, then her lagging, before she finally stopped. "I...ugh...I am not built for these long marches. And no, this isn't a problem that I have a convenient elixir recipe to solve. Ugh..."

Kurra scanned the horizon. "Still a long march to go."

Xeldia sighed. "If the caravan reaches a large town, our target vanishes. Eledine, you need to find more strength."

Eledine shook her head. "Another few minutes, maybe. But I'm a scholar, not a paladin or warrior. I'm afraid hauling books between lecture halls hasn't been training enough."

That stirred an idea in my mind. I tapped Kurra on the shoulder. "Could carry her? Instead of me?"

Eledine laughed between pants. "I'm afraid I won't exactly fit in her pack!"

Kurra was unperturbed, sweeping Eledine into a bridal carry. "Hmm…could go for a while more like this."

"Romantic. Well, I'm hardly in a position to complain, despite the fact that my hamstrings have been protesting brutal working conditions for the last hour."

Kurra crouched and let Cosma and me out of her pack. What followed was me discovering the hard way that spending long marches curled up in an orc's pack was not a great way to stay in shape. Still, I wasn't about to let my friends down. I did my utmost to keep pace with the rest of the party. My utmost wasn't all that much, as I found myself faltering faster than even Eledine.

Xeldia noticed, pausing briefly to kneel in front of me. "Come on, Peri. You can do this. I *know* you can do this."

Xeldia's gentle but firm tone did something to my heart, sending it racing and giving me a rush of butterflies that shifted my attention away from my aching limbs. I managed to put on an extra burst of speed, pushing past my fatigue for a little longer.

Unfortunately, Xeldia's unforgettable charisma could only fuel my body for so long.

After I started lagging once again, Eledine said, "I think I've had enough of a rest, if you want to carry Peri for a while."

Xeldia gave an amused grunt. "And when is it my turn to be carried?"

Kurra set Eledine down. Then, she swept up an unsuspecting Xeldia. Kurra looked briefly thoughtful. "Hmm. Too much armour. Bit too heavy. Eledine, how long do strength elixirs last?"

Eledine snickered. "Not long enough, I'm afraid. It's quite an image."

Xeldia cleared her throat. "Regardless, I have strength for a while yet. I think it's Peri that requires your, ahem, assistance more."

Eledine and I continued to swap being carried by Kurra at regular intervals. If Kurra minded, she gave no sign. As night fell, however, even Kurra and Eledine began to strain. Eventually, we had to camp for the night. Xeldia pointed out that Eledine and I should perform most of the tasks required in setting up camp, and neither of us could argue the point.

As we sat down around the campfire, resting our aching legs, Eledine held an empty flask towards Kurra. "Could I trouble you for a shot of that orc tonic you carry around?"

Kurra snorted in amusement before pouring her a little. "Interesting alchemical properties?"

"It's my grandfather…the idea of losing him is one that had been becoming clearer, at his age. I *was* becoming more prepared for it, but to suffer so suddenly…" She sighed. "I'll be alright. I just…" She took a sip of the tonic, then winced and coughed. "Oh. Strong."

Xeldia slid closer to her. "A great shame, but he still had a long, fulfilling life, did he not? And we will extract justice for what he has lost."

I slid closer as well, gently taking Eledine's hand in mine.

She sadly smiled at each of us in turn. "Thank you. All of you."

Chapter 12

The next day, I decided it was as good a time as any to start getting back in shape, so I forwent Kurra's pack for the first part of our march. Both Eledine and I were still in noticeably poorer shape than our more martial companions, but we managed to ease the strain on Kurra at least a little. Though after a few hours, we resumed taking turns being carried by that mountain of muscle.

It was mid-afternoon when a cluster of people and carts appeared on the horizon. The sight of our quarry gave us all a much-needed boost of energy. Kurra set Eledine down, and we approached. The caravan slowed as we did so, one or two guards moving towards us, cautiously sizing us up.

Xeldia held up a hand in greeting. "Hail! I am Xeldia, paladin of Raiya. How goes your journey?"

One of the guards shrugged. "Well enough. What brings a paladin all the way out here?"

"We are tracking a fugitive, a poisoner. We believe they have hidden themselves among this caravan. A blonde halfling woman who joined in Ori'lereneth."

The caravanners were understandably alarmed.

The guard said, "Well. Uh, there's Sall. She ain't blonde, but she's a halfling that joined us there."

A couple of the caravanners shifted away from a freckled brunette halfling.

She shifted nervously. "Me? I've never…I would never…"

I sent Cosma forward, who sniffed at Sall curiously. She started getting more enthusiastic, her tail wagging as she got closer to Sall's pack.

Xeldia frowned, advancing. "If you had nothing to do with it, then why does Cosma recognise the scent of the poison?"

Sall fidgeted awkwardly before seeming to realise something. "Oh! Maybe she's just interested in my rations." She reached into her pack and pulled out a few rashers of bacon.

Cosma did indeed seem interested, but she then slipped into Sall's pack, emerging with a vial of suspiciously coloured fluid between her jaws.

The rest of the caravan took a few paces back as Xeldia stepped forward. "By my authority as a paladin of Raiya, I am taking you into custody for grievous poisoning of an innocent man."

Sall stepped back. "Hang on now, hang on. Look, I have something here that should clear everything up…" Sall grabbed something in her pack.

Xeldia was already drawing her sword. With a sudden movement, Sall flung something tiny at Xeldia. She cursed, knocking Sall down with a pommel strike before holding her sword to the halfling's throat.

The rest of us approached as Xeldia pressed a boot down and said, "You are going to…to…" She suddenly staggered back, doubling over in pain.

My eyes widened. "Xeldia?"

As she writhed, with the caravanners watching in horror, thick black hair began to grow all over her body. Her body warped and shifted, her mouth elongating into a snout, gritted teeth turning to fangs, claws bursting forth from her gauntlets. Her cries of pain shifted into a guttural whine.

One of the caravanners cried, "Beastman! Beastman!"

I'd heard legends of the beastmen: ordinary people who would turn into berserk person-animal hybrids without warning and go on destructive rampages. That didn't at all make me okay with the way the caravanners immediately drew weapons on Xeldia. I cast darkness at the first guard to attack her, the sudden blindness reason enough for him to back off. The second and third found an angry Kurra between them and their target. I could see Eledine trying to line up a shot at Sall, but she slipped behind the gathering mob.

A few more caravanners rushed Xeldia, who had fully transformed into some kind of wolfwoman. She ducked behind her shield as they swung with spears and hatchets. I felt a stab of rage. With a whistle, I called Cosma to my side. Together, we called the power of the stars and unleashed it with a flash and a bang. The mob screamed, scattering like roaches. The few that stood firm met a bloody end at Kurra's axe.

Eledine took a few steps towards where Sall had slipped off to before she turned and returned to where Xeldia, now a wolfwoman, crouched, groaning in intense pain.

None of us were entirely sure what to do, but Eledine was obviously resolved to do *something*. "Xeldia? Can you still understand me?"

Xeldia moaned something unintelligible before nodding desperately. She whimpered.

Eledine gently took Xeldia's head. "Did she poison you?"

Xeldia lay on her back, as flat as she could while still writhing. She bore her neck, gesturing with a claw to where a small, metal needle was stuck.

Eledine took out her more complex alchemical tools. "Alright, I'll try to help you. Kurra, I'll need you to hold her still."

Kurra obliged. Xeldia made no effort to resist.

Eledine removed and carefully examined the needle before cutting away some of the fur to get a closer look at the flesh around the wound. "Hmm…okay, I can make an antidote. Peri, come here. This will be a bit quicker with two pairs of hands."

I hurried to Eledine's side and followed her instructions to the letter, mashing up various plants and mixing them in carefully measured amounts.

Finally, Eledine dipped a dart in it and stuck it into Xeldia. "Alright, it should take effect in just a few seconds."

It was a gut-wrenching few seconds, but Xeldia started to calm. Breathing heavily, she stood. With her canine eyes, she looked at us.

I managed to find something to say. "Feeling better?"

Xeldia nodded. Then, she crouched on the ground and started sniffing.

I asked, "Sall?"

She nodded again. She seemed to pick up a scent and started to follow it, the rest of us following behind.

After an hour, Xeldia slowly started to revert to her original form. As her snout retreated, she said, "It's getting difficult to keep following the scent; Kurra, can you find anything?"

Kurra paused for a moment, trying to process what had just happened, but then knelt where Xeldia was sniffing. "Hmm…yes, tracks. This way."

As Kurra resumed following the trail, Eledine asked, "So, I believe we're due for a discussion about what just happened."

Xeldia didn't look at her. "Perhaps. Not now. Let us first deal with this 'Sall,' if that's even her real name."

"Very well. But one pertinent question: Do you remember what happened when you transformed?"

Xeldia seemed a touch irritated but answered. "Yes. As much as I'd rather not, the poison that woman used was *very* painful."

Evening was starting to fall when we followed the tracks to a small village, really just a place for nearby farmers to gather and trade supplies, back within Sellen's borders. It was so small that it didn't even have an inn, so the first place we looked was the local church of the Triune.

There, we found Sall talking to the priest and a few villagers. As we entered, she turned to us with a shriek. "It's them! It's them!"

The villagers formed a protective wall between us and them.

Xeldia held up a hand, the other resting on her sword. "Hold! I am a paladin of Raiya, and this woman is a wanted fugitive. She grievously poisoned an innocent man."

One of the villagers snarled, "What kind of paladin travels with an orc?"

"She's proven trustworthy time and time again. I say again: That woman is a wanted fugitive. Examine her pack, and you'll find a number of dangerous poisons."

That turned the villagers' suspicions onto Sall.

She whimpered. "She's lying! She has to be! Look!" She opened her pack. Then, she threw a vial at the ground, which burst into a cloud of yellow gas.

The villagers staggered back, coughing and wheezing, and Sall made a burst for the door. She slipped between Xeldia and Kurra, and my desire to help the villagers gave me the split-second pause Sall needed to get past me.

Eledine rushed forward. "I'll help them! Don't let her get away!"

We all trusted her, so we turned and pursued Sall in the dirt streets. She ducked and weaved through fences and alleys. Kurra leapt over any obstacles with ease, quickly gaining ground, Xeldia and I lagging. Kurra eventually caught up in a nearby barn. Sall suddenly whirled around, flinging darts at her. They got caught on Kurra's armour. She answered with a swing of the axe, Sall slipping underneath and between her legs. Xeldia and I caught up, the former running forward to try and trap Sall in the melee. With the whirlwind of movement, I couldn't pick out a target, so I prepared another blast of darkness and held it ready for a clear shot. One came as Sall moved to slip away. The blast connected. Blinded, the fleeing Sall ran headlong into the wall before Kurra tackled her against it.

Sall was quickly bound, and Kurra carried her back to the church. Eledine was outside, along with most of the villagers, apparently having been dragged out and laid on the ground.

The air was filled with some floral scent, as Eledine attempted to apply some gaseous medicine. She looked grim, saying, "I was able to save about half of them. A potent poison, I'm afraid. And some of these bumpkins decided to risk the poison's effect alone rather than turn to me for help."

Apparently deciding we had more important things to worry about than the "bumpkins" remark, Xeldia glared at Sall. "Yet more you have to answer for."

Not wanting to cause more of a fuss, we decided to strike camp outside of the village.

As we carried Sall there, slung over Kurra's shoulder like a sack of potatoes, Sall said, "This isn't going to end well for you, Xel."

Xeldia paused. "How do you know me?"

"Not in front of your goons."

Xeldia glared at Sall for a moment before taking her from Kurra.

"I will keep this brief," Xeldia said. She moved a few paces away, close enough that we could all clearly see the pair as they exchanged whispers.

Whatever Sall opened with shocked and angered Xeldia, who initially expressed disbelief. She glanced at us before the pair exchanged some more whispers, Xeldia visibly furious.

Xeldia returned soon after. "She claims to be an inquisitor. On a mission."

Sall chuckled. "So much for faith. You're not supposed to say that."

"She claims she poisoned the elf on orders. More than that, she won't say." Xeldia handed Sall back to Kurra. "We get a little more distance in, then we make camp. Search her for weapons. Then…" Xeldia looked like she wanted to say a dozen different things.

I chirped, "Decide in the morning?"

"Yes. Thank you." Xeldia was audibly relieved.

Night had fallen by the time we were all gathered around the campfire, Sall tied up to the side. I was wondering how to broach the subject of the whole "beastwoman" thing.

Thankfully, Xeldia did it herself. She was sitting by the fire, staring deeply into the flames, voice low, gaze distant when she spoke. "I was thirteen the first time I transformed. It was my first year of training. Well, it was doing chores for the paladins, mostly. Anyway, I was debating theology with a friend, Cairae, and the debate got heated. I remember how callous her words sounded, how they sparked anger inside me. And that anger grew. I didn't notice the transformation until it was already complete. Cairae screamed and fled. I was standing there, alone, and everything felt different. I could smell more, see more, and feel my claws. I was stunned. I didn't know what to think. After a few moments, I reverted. Just in time for half a dozen paladins to rush into the room. Luckily, they just guessed that Cairae was being hysterical. But she never trusted me again. Whispered behind my back, said I was just waiting for the moment to strike.

"A week later, I saw a few of the other cadets play a wicked prank on an old man. Before I could intervene, I could feel the fur starting to return. I panicked and hid in an alley. I missed two classes before I reverted. I couldn't think of a lie to tell my teachers about what I was doing. Over time, I came to realise that the beast form came in moments of heightened emotion. So, I held my emotions tight. Those who follow Etunae say we all deserve to feel our emotions, to savour them, to connect with them, but that was a luxury forever denied to me. I remember the day I was finally knighted. In the middle of a sermon, I felt such pride that I nearly triggered the transformation. I'd learned how to slow the transformation by that point, enough that I was able to escape by feigning illness, Raiya forgive me. I fled to the privy. There, I wept, for even joy was denied to me."

There was a long silence. Eledine, as usual, turned analytical. "The stories say that beastmen are mindless ragers. But you were able to communicate when transformed, even let me close enough to tend to you. Animals wouldn't do that."

"I cannot speak for all beastmen; I've never met another. But, as far as I can tell, I don't think any differently when transformed, save for whatever emotions trigger the transformation."

Kurra scoffed. "So what? You get angry. I get angry all the time!"

Xeldia's expression darkened. "Beastmen are animals. A dangerous animal is put down."

The only sound that could be heard was the crackling of the campfire. Xeldia, an animal to be put down? I couldn't stomach the thought. After a moment, I shifted so I was sitting next to her. I gently took her hand in mine, smiling up at her. Words were always a lot for me, but I hoped an expression, an action, would be enough to say *I accept you. You're my friend.* Xeldia's smile told me at least a little of that got through. I could feel a bit of fur manifest on her hand.

Chapter 13

The next morning, we had a lengthy talk about our plan for the next leg of the journey. We wanted to visit the site that Cosma was interested in, but Xeldia wanted to bring Sall to the church to face justice and to investigate her claims of being an inquisitor. After some deliberation, we planned to first head to the town of Hensbrook, which had a paladin base large enough for our purposes and wasn't too far from our next destination.

When we resumed our march, I made a point of not spending the whole time in Kurra's pack. A big part of it was wanting to be ready the next time we needed to hustle, but it was also that spring was starting to turn to summer, and Kurra's pack got awfully warm. Cosma certainly wasn't enjoying the heat and was leaving a trail of white fur.

The guards were understandably suspicious when we showed up with a prisoner in tow, but they escorted us to the paladin's base, a large castle in the middle of the city. Xeldia left the rest of us in the courtyard while she took Sall in to interrogate. We stood around anxiously.

It wasn't long before Xeldia returned, a sour look on her face. "The paladin commander took her aside and won't speak to me anymore on the matter." She sighed. "Come. It has been a long march. Let us enjoy some shade."

As we left, I gently tapped Xeldia on her side (her shoulder being out of my reach). When she crouched down, I whispered, "I could sneak in?"

I could see Xeldia draw a breath for a quick denial, but she paused. "We need to discuss this somewhere quieter," she said.

We headed to a nearby tavern, a low-end joint, but not an outright dive. We rented a room and huddled around a table.

"I could sneak in," I repeated. "Figure out what's happening."

Xeldia looked grave. "To infiltrate my own order…I want to say this is outright treason. But there is a conspiracy here. We must investigate. And you're our best chance at doing that."

Kurra wasn't her usual daring self. "Just you, against whole fortress? Bold raid needs cunning plan."

Eledine took out a piece of parchment and an inkwell. "Xeldia, what do you know about the castle's defences?"

Over the next few minutes, we hashed out a plan. Xeldia would (reluctantly) smuggle me inside her pack, and I could slip out and make my way to the commander's office. Cosma had recently taught me how to turn invisible for brief periods, and combined with my tiny size, I was confident I could slip between the patrols, and my skill at lockpicking would hopefully get me access to any useful documents. Eledine handed me a few vials of alchemical fire in case I needed a distraction on the way out, and Kurra promised to be nearby in case things got messy.

Xeldia's pack, being smaller, was a much tighter fit, especially since I was doing my best to make it look like there wasn't, in fact, a halfling crammed in there. Xeldia got me outside without too much trouble, by virtue of the fact that no one really wanted to interrupt a determined Xeldia. She slung her pack underneath a bench and went to talk to a comrade about Sall, and as expected, found out little more of use.

I cast my invisibility, stashed Cosma under my robes, and slunk out. I scanned the area, seeing the door I was aiming for. With the nearest guard distracted, I crept out and slipped through the door. I briefly thought I'd already blown the mission when the guard turned towards the noise, but he simply muttered annoyance at someone having not closed it properly. I slipped through without him noticing.

My heart was racing throughout the whole infiltration. Sure, I was invisible, but that didn't mean undetectable; I could knock something over, bump into someone, hells, a *sneeze* could blow my cover. And my invisibility only lasted a few minutes, putting me on a timer. I did my best to control my nerves, slipping under benches, dashing through briefly open doors, and crawling through windows. It was late afternoon by this point, late enough for many to be leaving their duties for the day, but not so late as for the sentries to be prepared for infiltrators.

Halfway through the infiltration, I saw Sall being escorted through the castle by a paladin. But it wasn't a "bringing a prisoner to the dungeon" escort; it was "bringing an honoured guest to their quarters" escort, and that drew my attention. I tailed her closely. As we reached a set of guest rooms, Sall abruptly stopped, looking around suspiciously. Realising she must suspect my presence, I quickly slipped behind a nearby potted plant.

The paladin frowned. "Is something wrong?"

Sall drew a dagger. "I heard something. But I didn't see anything. And that means someone's sneaking around."

"You're sure? I didn't hear anything."

"Because they're trying to be sneaky, you idiot!" Sall snapped. She pulled out a bag of powder.

I crammed myself into the gap between the potted plant and the wall as best I could. Sall threw the powder into the air. It seemed to just be chalk, white dust settling over the area, but I realised that for detecting the invisible, it would work well. But very little of the chalk landed in the cranny I'd jammed myself into.

Sall paused. "… Must have slipped off. Be careful on your patrol. They could still be lurking. Keep an eye out for an elf with white hair and glasses—had a run-in with her earlier. And is Paladin Xeldia still around? I think she might hold a grudge."

The paladin said, "I'll check, ma'am. In the meantime, your quarters are here." He opened the door to one of the guest chambers wide—wide enough for me to slip in beside Sall.

I slunk under the bed (human-sized, thankfully) as Sall entered.

"Thank you. That will be all," she said. She sat down at a desk and started writing a letter.

It had been enough time now that the invisibility spell had worn off, but she didn't at any point think to check under the bed, so I was safe. What followed was some uncomfortable, tense waiting. After a few minutes and a few sheets of paper, she finished. With alarm, I noticed her burn one with a candle. I realised that I needed to make my move now.

I cast darkness at her. She whirled around at the incantation, but she was a split second too late to stop the powers of the void clinging to her eyes. She swore loudly, flinging a dagger that got stuck on the bed frame. I rushed forward to grab the letters, only to find that she had foreseen that move and swung a short sword at me. I tried to parry with my staff, but only half succeeded, ending up with a serious cut across my arm.

Despite her blindness, she was able to force me back, screaming, "Guards! Guards!"

I needed to cut off reinforcements. I did so by throwing the alchemical fire at the door. But I still couldn't grab the letters. I called, "Cosma! The paper, grab it!"

Sall couldn't stop both me and Cosma while blinded. Her lack of opposable thumbs gave Cosma a bit of a challenge, but she managed to scoop up the paper in her jaws. Sall, meanwhile, managed to give me another deep cut. It was well past time to leave. I backed up to the window as the furniture in the room began to catch fire, and I quickly opened the window before backflipping out of it.

I landed in an awfully thorny bush. With no time to lose, I caught a leaping Cosma before rolling out of the bush and rushing for the cover of a nearby shed. I could hear alarm bells ringing behind me. The afternoon was turning to evening, the lengthening shadows giving me just cover enough to evade the paladins scrambling to figure out what was going on. Keeping low, taking cover behind plants and decorations, I made my way towards the castle's gate.

The bad news was that the portcullis was closed. The good news was that the gaps in it were just wide enough that I could slip through. After a moment of waiting for the guards to be looking somewhere else, I scurried into cover by the outer wall. I conjured a burst of sparkly lights across the yard to draw their attention, then slipped through the portcullis, disappearing into where a crowd was gathering.

Kurra and Xeldia, both looking concerned, were waiting nearby. As soon as I approached, Kurra swept Cosma and me into her pack and hurried off. We returned to our inn room.

As soon as Kurra sat me down, Eledine looked at me in concern. "That evidently didn't go entirely to plan. Hold still." She started to tend my wounds.

Meanwhile, Xeldia took the letters from Cosma. She frowned. "I do hope these have more significance than is immediately apparent."

I said, "Sall wrote them. Haven't looked at them." I explained all that had happened during my infiltration.

Xeldia sighed. "There's a very good chance Sall recognised you. Which means we'll need to leave town as soon as possible. And I'm afraid these letters are either encoded or are an incredibly dull description of a trip to a local play."

Eledine was just finishing up my stitches. "Xeldia, can you access your wolf scent?"

"I can't muster enough emotion right now. Why?"

"There are certain alchemical substances that turn invisible until exposed to the proper conditions, like heat or certain light sources. I was hoping you could check if it smells unusual," Eledine explained.

I could see Xeldia concentrate for a moment, and the tip of her nose turned black. But just the tip. "Hmm…no luck, I'm afraid."

Kurra kissed Xeldia full on the lips.

A mixture of surprise, jealousy, and desire collided in my mind, exploding in a mess that took a second of stunned silence for me to clean up. Xeldia had a similar reaction, simply stunned even as she shifted into her wolf form.

Eledine looked over the rims of her glasses. "…You know, I was planning on simply checking anyway."

Kurra shrugged and sat down. Xeldia gave the orc an unreadable look before taking the letters, sniffing them thoroughly.

Eledine asked, "So, do they smell strange?"

Xeldia nodded.

Eledine turned back to me. "I see. I'll look at them closer in just a moment. Peri picked up more than a few cuts."

Kurra sat down on the bed, chuckling. "Anyway, meant as much as you want. But, I wonder: You understand humanoid tongues but cannot speak them? In beast form, I mean."

Xeldia responded with a series of growls and utterances which sounded more than a little like speech but didn't quite get there.

I said, "Mouth's a different shape?" to which Xeldia nodded.

Eledine finished tending me and then turned to the letters. "While I work on these, the rest of you should come up with a plan to get out of the city. I have, so far, evaded seeing the interior of a dungeon cell, and I have no intention to see one tonight."

The other three of us bounced around a few ideas, including disguises (Kurra was too big for that to work), Xeldia's authority (what if the other paladins turned against her?), and fighting through (would be bloody even in the best-case scenario). But it wasn't long before Eledine got results, and soon the letter was covered in much more interesting text.

Ennerat,

Mission accomplished, but not without complications. I drew the attention of the paladin of Raiya, Xeldia. She's friends with an academic type, possibly related to that business with Yettrian? If they're starting to suspect us, we'll need to do something about them. Anyway, she tracked me down and captured me. She grew angry when I told her I was an inquisitor. Called me a heretic. I have a feeling she might continue to be a problem for our work; we might need to send her to the Reborn Colonies. We can probably use the fact that she's a beastwoman as an excuse. Took me to the Hensbrook garrison. Luckily I managed to talk to the captain there.

Anyway, the old man won't be talking anymore. He did seem pretty spry, though. Might be too many for us to wait out or take out. Regardless, I'll get comfortable, wait for more orders. See if there's anything else I can dig up on Xeldia.

Serren

I frowned; if what I'd heard of the colonies was true, they weren't fortresses—why use one as a prison?

Eledine, meanwhile, said, "Yettrian was one of the foremost linguists in the world; he suddenly vanished last year. The implication that the inquisition is involved is…deeply concerning. And what did my grandfather know that caused the inquisition to get personally involved to conceal?"

Kurra casually said, "History? Is why we were there."

The other three of us were nowhere near as casual. We were silent.

Xeldia finally spoke. "Is the inquisition…are they engaged in conspiracy to rewrite history? The church is supposed to stand for truth! This is…" She paced around the room, unable to find any more words.

Eledine stood. "When we get back to Ansiel, I'll look more into Yettrian. If we're lucky, we can figure out what the inquisition's interest in him was. In the meantime, we need to appease whatever force is giving Peri her magic, and to do that, we need to get out of the city. Any new ideas?"

I slowly raised my hand, not terribly keen on my idea. "Sewers?"

There were a lot of things that vexed me about being small: difficulty reaching things, never being taken seriously, and being easily overpowered. Being able to crouch in Kurra's pack while we marched through sewers bathed in an indescribable scent made up for all of them. Granted, there were walkways above the filth itself, but they weren't exactly stellar examples of hygiene, and there was still that *reeking* scent. Poor Eledine threw up twice, and Kurra was half-crouching the entire way, unable to stand in the tight environs. The place was pitch-black, illuminated only by a mote of starlight I called to my staff. Xeldia had reverted to her human form, thankfully. I dreaded to think what it might have smelled like to canine senses.

While I ducked for cover at first, I realised that the team deserved more from me, safe and sound as I was, so I poked my head out and did my best to keep watch, pushing against the ever-present damn *smell*. So I was the first to notice a suspicious bright green sludge starting to pool on the walls of a larger junction, and I pointed it out.

Eledine was eager for something to occupy her mind. She slipped around Kurra to get a closer look. "Hmm…yes, this is the residue of a green slime. There must be some living off the city's trash. Weapons ready."

Xeldia's attention was behind us. "Green slimes like that?"

Indeed, behind us, emerging from the sewer water, was a steadily moving blob of green goo, the size of a pig. It latched onto the side of the walkway and climbed up. We drew weapons. Xeldia stepped forward and thrust her sword. The creature slushed to the side, but Xeldia quickly swung her sword to the side, cutting through the slime. The top of it rolled off, only to re-cohere in the water and move back to the walkway.

Eledine called, "Xeldia! It's a slime! You need to stick to thrusting attacks!"

"Understood!" Xeldia gave a little ground to the slime's bottom half before stepping forward and managing to pierce it deep.

Meanwhile, I was able to burn the top half away with starlight.

Kurra roared, "More!"

She was right; there were at least a dozen slimes converging on us, ranging in size from rats to bulls. Kurra moved to swing her axe at an approaching slime before stopping herself, instead kicking it. While that did send it flying, it wasn't before Kurra got some of the acidic goop on her boot. She switched to her own longbow; thankfully, slimes weren't terribly fast.

Fighting slimes on a tight walkway with one of us limited to a ranged weapon was a tactical nightmare. Worse, most of my crowd control spells relied on light or darkness, and the slimes didn't have eyes. I did my best to stay cool, blasting the slimes with starlight as they came in. But Kurra hadn't been keeping up her archery, and one of the bigger ones got closer.

Eledine got my attention. "Peri! Cover that flank!" She handed me a vial of alchemical fire.

I grabbed it and flung it over Kurra's shoulder at the slime. It got sucked inside.

"You had to aim for —" she stuck an advancing slime with her rapier—"for the walkway!" Eledine said.

That would have made more sense. Instead, the slime was advancing on Kurra, lunging at her, coating her in the disgusting, corrosive goo. I just barely managed to use the flaps of Kurra's pack as a shield. Then, I had an idea. I blasted starlight right at the vial of fire. It connected, and the whole thing exploded, scattering the slime everywhere. Kurra, now coated with goop and soot, still stood firm. Eledine handed me another fire vial, and I aimed this one at the walkway. The slimes advancing on us from that direction were too stupid to avoid the fire, simply burning up. With one flank safe and some of the slimes schlooping to their own deaths, we were able to stand our ground against the rest.

When the last was burned to ash, we paused, panting hard. We slowly lowered our weapons.

Eledine pulled one of her arrows from one of the slimes, examined it a moment, then tossed it away in disgust. "I think that's the last of them. That alchemical fire should burn itself out promptly."

As we watched the flames dwindle over the course of about ten seconds, Kurra crouched, watching the water. "...Slime is pooling."

At the looks the rest of us gave her, she gestured with the tip of her bow, pointing to where the remnants of the slimes were flowing into a pile of refuse at the edge of the junction.

Eledine rubbed her chin. "Hmm, unusual. Probably just seeking a smaller food source. Unless all those small bits noticed each other and are re-forming, in which case…"

The pile of refuse shook. It slowly rose up, reaching the sewer roof with ease, all suspended in a wave of green muck.

Even Kurra retched. "Ugh! Worse than warlord's privy!"

Xeldia slipped past the rest of us. "Let me take point. Words I will no doubt regret."

The mountainous trash slime lunged at her. We all gave ground. Xeldia was able to skewer it as it advanced, but it didn't amount to much. The rest of us bombarded it with arrows and starlight. The slime slowed, but not much, and it just kept flowing forward, pushing us farther and farther back.

Kurra felt around in her quiver. "Three arrows left! Have you more alchemical fire?"

"One vial left! We have to make it count!" Eledine called back.

Kurra switched to her axe. "Throw it into centre, when I say! Xeldia, pull back!"

Xeldia didn't need any further motivation to put distance between her and the disgusting morass.

As she withdrew and the slime advanced, Kurra carved a deep slash into the centre of the slime and yelled, "Now!"

Eledine threw and hit her mark, the vial landing right in the middle of the mass. I already had a bolt of starlight ready, and with one straight shot, I ignited the vial. A wall of flame took root inside the slime and spread. It bulged. I ducked for cover just as it exploded, scattering a whole mess of substances I did not want to think about all over the other three.

Despite being covered in I-didn't-want-to-know-what, Kurra cheered. "Ha! Masterful! True warriors, all of us!"

Eledine threw up a third time.

We managed to escape the sewers without further incident, coming out at a river. We followed it a while more before reaching a small, clear pool.

Eledine said, "Alright, we're having a bath. Then I'm replacing the contents of my stomach." She slung her pack to the side, then started disrobing, her desperation overriding any sense of privacy.

From the cut of her clothes and armour, I knew her figure was slender and lithe, but now I could see its elegance in full, long limbs with an archer's muscles, faint burns decorating her fingers. She slowly slid into the water, sighing in relief. She slid in deep, until she was fully submerged before slowly surfacing, flicking droplets of water from her hair, glistening in the evening light.

Kurra deposited her pack beside Eledine's (carefully, as I was still in it) and started casting aside her own armour, showing off her immense musculature built over a lifetime of war, a dozen scars recording her greatest battles. She leapt into the water with a splash. She stretched out, smiling happily.

Xeldia thought a moment before saying, "Peri, help me with my armour. You've been hiding in Kurra's pack this whole trip. If anyone doesn't need to worry about a bath, it's you."

I couldn't fault that logic, so I helped Xeldia out of her armour. Her dusky complexion was marked with her fair share of scars, and I got a look at finely sculpted, athletic abs.

She slid into the water. "Peri, can you get the soap from my pack?"

Eledine added, "And there's a bottle of white fluid in mine; that's for healing skin irritation. We'll need that as well."

I did so without complaint. I was about to start getting undressed for a bath myself when Kurra asked, "Peri, can you get my back? Think splinter of something stuck in there."

For most people, I would've pointed out that I was neither bathhouse attendant nor massage therapist nor medic. A large, muscular, friendly orc woman with epic battle scars wasn't most people. So, I got to work.

I spent a while helping my companions bathe and tend their wounds. They insisted it was me making up for not being nearly as filthy as the rest of them, but honestly, I needed very little incentive to get close to this group of athletic, mostly undressed women. Eventually, they ran out of things for me to do, and I got a chance to quickly wash myself as well.

After a while, Kurra lifted herself out of the pool and lay down on a nearby rock. "I've got a knot in my back from all of that. Peri, could you get it for me?"

Getting hands-on with Kurra? I was glad to! I quickly pulled myself out of the pool and dried off the worst of the water before getting to work on massaging Kurra's immense muscles. The woman was so tense, and my hands so small that I ended up just literally walking on her. Surprisingly, it seemed to work.

Kurra chuckled lazily. "Feels nice to have halfling walking on you. You should try."

Xeldia stretched. "I think I might. My shoulders aren't thanking me for that fight."

Oh, Kurra, I could kiss you.

Chapter 14

We set out to the plains that Cosma and the star were interested in. There was a level of anxiety; a respected agent of the Triune had reason to want us dead, and she just might have had the authority to have us outlawed. Xeldia's paladin status came with it a level of authority, but that could only go so far, especially if the fact that she was a beastman became public. For now, at least, we had a long march over open fields, and our jaunt through the sewers would have made us harder to track.

As we got closer to our destination, Cosma pointed out some astrological signs for me to follow, saving the party from fussing over a map. Our destination turned out to be a ring of standing stones, inscribed with stellar runes.

Kurra carefully ran a hand across them. "Hmm…druidic construction, I think.. Sun brings life, growth, night brings rest, space. This place honoured that cycle."

Cosma started digging at the base of one of the stones. I started digging, too. A few minutes of digging revealed that the stones were much larger than anticipated, so I called over the others. We got to work planning a larger excavation. Kurra cut a few branches from a small nearby tree, and with a little work, Eledine was able to fashion them into something that would serve as a shovel.

It took a good few hours of work to fully excavate the site, which we did either side of a night's rest. The ruins were a bit more elaborate than it first seemed; there was a stone floor and a large bowl of inscribed bronze in the centre. Once the worst of the dirt was cleared off, and the bowl now exposed to the sunlight, I could sense power was flowing through the site once more.

I looked up at Kurra with a smile. "Can break the curse!"

Kurra tossed me the cursed sword, then lounged back, sweating from the exertion. "Go ahead."

I started plotting out the ritual. After realising how involved it would be, I decided I would need a bit of rest before starting, and the ritual would work best at midday anyway. Once I was ready, I laid the sword on the altar, undid the bindings, and started channelling the stellar powers. It was a complex ritual that I had mostly developed myself, but I'd been planning it for a while, and Cosma was a great help. The runes all around me glowed brightly as I started purging the hostile void magics from the sword.

Then, darkness enveloped the site, light vanishing from the sky.

Eledine sat up and asked, "Was that supposed to happen?"

I quickly realised what had happened: The forces inside the sword had been driven out, but they were none too happy about their eviction. I quickly called a magical light to illuminate the area. Suddenly, Xeldia, in her wolf form (what had driven her to transform?), rushed past me, a tendril of shadow dissipating as she passed. I looked and could see shapes of darkness emerging from beyond the runes, advancing towards me. Xeldia raised her sword, baring her teeth at them in warning. Eledine and Kurra were beside her swiftly. They swung weapons at the shadows. They retreated but quickly reformed.

I blasted them with starlight. An eldritch screech came from them as they burned, writhing as they flashed and died.

Eledine called, "Only Peri's attacks are effective! We need to defend her!"

The other three formed a defensive ring around me, swinging at the shadow creatures as they advanced with claws of nothingness. I took a deep breath, trusting in my friends and focusing on taking out the shadows.

I made progress, the creatures falling back to my power. But while Kurra and Xeldia were skilled front-line combatants, Eledine wasn't quite so skilled. She missed a parry, and a shadowy, clawed hand slashed her, then grabbed her, claws digging into her flesh. I yelped, trying to aim a shot at the strange, gangly parody of a humanoid that grabbed her, but its slender and insubstantial nature meant I couldn't get a clear shot, not without risking hitting Eledine. She didn't give up; she pulled a vial of fire and poured it on the creature. It shrieked, fleeing as it burned.

"So that also works," Eledine said and wheezed as she threw the rest of the vial at another of the shadow creatures.

Another tried attacking as her back was turned but was driven back by a countercharge from a furious Xeldia before I blasted it with more starlight. Another volley of fire, both stellar and alchemical, drove the last of the creatures off, and the sunlight returned.

Eledine slumped against a standing stone, panting hard, fumbling with the straps of her armour. "Peri, I could use an extra pair of hands for my wounds."

As curious as I was about the sword, Eledine's condition was certainly more urgent. While her wounds were serious, luckily Eledine's quality medicine and my swift attention had them patched up quickly.

Kurra, meanwhile, was examining the sword. It glowed now with an inner fire. She gave it a few test swings, watching flames dance in its wake. She grinned. "Now, this is weapon! Hah, could have used it just now!"

After I finished tending to Eledine, I turned to examine the sword, confirming that it was no longer dangerous, at least not to anyone who stuck to the hilt side. With that done, we got to planning our next move.

Eledine started, "So, we have to assume that Sall—or perhaps more properly, Serren—was able to put together that Peri stole her letters, which has to mean she's after her, and by extension, after us. I must say, this wasn't exactly what I expected when I signed up for an archaeological expedition, but between what happened to my grandfather and the fact that I might be a wanted criminal, I am somewhat invested."

Kurra hefted her new sword. "Well, you helped me make new sword. Happy to help unravel evil plot!"

Xeldia was pacing up and down the camp. "Our best lead is Yettrian, but to investigate him, we'll have to return to Ansiel. We need to no longer be wanted before we can do that. I have been thinking, and our best chance is one of my mentors, Captain Drenn, paladin of Etunae. She is a good woman; one of the few who know I am a beastwoman and does not judge me."

Eledine rubbed some of her stitches. "You're assuming that she's not part of the conspiracy herself. A risk I'd be willing to take, but a risk, nonetheless."

I see no other way to so much as get close to Ansiel without help, and the thought she would betray me -" Xeldia shuddered "- No. We will simply need to send her a message."

I squeaked "My folks?"

Between Kurra's skill at fieldcraft and my stellar power, charting a course straight to my family's inn while avoiding major towns was actually not that hard. Kurra was also huntress enough to easily keep the four of us fed. With the exception of a run-in with a none-too-happy bear, which ended up being turned into a rug for my folks, we managed to make our way there without serious incident. In the meantime, at Eledine's suggestion, Xeldia started practising to see if she could learn to talk in her beast form; she was figuring out how to shape sounds with her canine mouth, but she had yet to produce any intelligible words.

We came in through the back entrance this time, to the surprise of my parents. We hurriedly explained to them the whole situation. They were shocked to hear of such a grave conspiracy and bewildered that I'd somehow got caught up in it, but happy to help. They agreed to keep the four of us hidden for now, and with the traffic the inn saw, it wasn't long before they were able to find someone to send a message to Captain Drenn.

To minimise the rooms occupied, and thus suspicion, Xeldia started sleeping on a bedroll in my room while Kurra and Eledine shared another room. Xeldia was an incredibly polite guest, careful not to disturb my belongings too much. She occasionally asked about the books I was reading—the astronomy manuals I salvaged from the abandoned tower—and I was happy to talk about them.

After a few days, we received a reply from Captain Drenn (who had remarkably neat handwriting).

Xeldia,

I understand what you're trying to do, but it's not for us to interfere with the work of the inquisition. I'm sure they have good reasons for doing what they're doing; it is for them to work in the shadows, to do those dark things for reasons not for us to understand.

I've been talking to command, and I've managed to convince them that you earnestly thought there was a conspiracy. But sending an agent to rob an inquisitor was overstepping, severely. You and your companions won't be arrested, but Captain Korran wants a word with you regarding your next posting.

I know it's low for the inquisitor to have threatened to use your secret against you like that. But you need to trust in the will of the Triune. You've got a bright career ahead of you, so please don't jeopardise it by questioning orders.

Drenn

Xeldia sighed deeply, pacing around the room. "A word regarding my next posting…fancy words for receiving a punishment posting."

Kurra scoffed. "Sit down, listen to orders, do nothing. Words of coward."

For a moment, Xeldia looked like she was going to argue the point. But she simply sat down, burying her face in her hands. I really wasn't very good at the whole "comfort" thing, so I did the first thing I could think of and deposited Cosma in her lap. The ball of white fluffiness worked, at least a little.

Eledine was in her usual analytical mode. "Well, at least we're able to reach Ansiel now. We can start looking into what really happened to Yettrian. If we make haste, we can conduct at least some of the investigation before you're expected to receive your next posting."

"What then?" Xeldia stroked Cosma.

"Something we'll have to figure out. Worst case scenario, we keep pursuing this without you." Eledine started packing her alchemy kit.

Kurra laughed bitterly. "Worst case, indeed!"

We started on the road to Ansiel straight away. The journey was quiet, all of us weighed down by questions we didn't know the answers to, dreading whatever they might be. When we reached the city, we headed straight to the university. Eledine managed to find an urgent meeting with one of Yettrian's former colleagues, a dwarf alchemist named Olar.

His office was sparse and immaculately organised. The same couldn't be said for his beard. Olar gave us a half-curious look as we entered his office. "A paladin, a wizard, and an orc. What kind of experimenting are you doing now, Eledine?"

Eledine wasn't in the mood for humour. "Olar, I need to know everything you do about Yettrian's disappearance. I have reason to believe the inquisition is trying to rewrite history and that they had something to do with his disappearance."

This, understandably, took Olar a second to process. "Well… hmm. Much as I'd like to call you crazy, he was acting pretty odd before he disappeared. Said something about leaving town but didn't say where he was going. And now I think about it, his assistant, Russal, was sent to the colonies the next day. Hysteria, they say. I believed it at the time, way he was acting. But if there really is a conspiracy…you won't mind if I try not to get too involved, will you?"

Xeldia had an expression of determination. "Which colony?"

"No idea. His mother might know, Lady Berrisen. Real bigwig, they say she bankrolls half of the church's shipping."

So, we headed straight for Lady Berrisen's estate. We were planning a dozen ways we could persuade her to grant us an audience, but apparently being interested in her son was all we needed. We were welcomed into her office (an awfully gaudy affair) within the hour.

Xeldia made introductions, being the one of us the most accustomed to dealing with nobility. "Thank you for your time, Lady Berrisen. I am Paladin Xeldia of Raiya. I apologise if I am bringing up bad memories, but I have reason to suspect that your son is the victim of conspiracy."

Berrisen looked aghast. "Conspiracy? Why? He was always so sweet! A bit rambunctious at times, but truly the kindest soul to ever grace this world!"

"He was the assistant to Professor Yettrian, correct?" Xeldia showed her the inquisitor's letter. "And he was sent to the colonies shortly after Yettrian's disappearance."

"Oh, yes, I could tell something was bothering him greatly. Turned white as a ghost when the guards turned up! I begged them to help them, but they said the colonies were the best they could do! And he promised to write, but I never heard anything back! And the colony hasn't sent word about him, and gods, it's just left me to wonder!"

Eledine's tone was matter-of-fact. "Your son, more than likely, knew something the inquisition didn't want him telling anyone. I'm afraid you'll have to prepare yourself for the eventuality that he's dead."

Berrisen shuddered. "Oh, my boy, my boy…Xeldia, please. I have given everything to the church! I need your help now. Find out what happened to my boy!"

Xeldia frowned. "I am interested in further investigating this conspiracy, but I'm about to receive a new posting. My…superiors believe I am overstepping."

A spiteful smirk suddenly appeared on Berrisen's face. "A punishment posting? Well, they're going to post you to Kessedarn, the same colony as my son. With the amount of money those parchment-pushers owe me, I'll make sure it happens! Then you can find out yourself!"

"A cunning plan, Lady Berrisen. But my agents and I may need resources to conduct the investigation, especially so long after the fact—"

"Of course, of course." Berrisen reached into a chest and pulled out a fistful of platinum coins, handing them to us.

Xeldia accepted them with a smile and a bow. "I promise, if there is anything to find out about your son's fate, I will inform you as soon as I can."

Chapter 15

We gave it another day for Berrisen to pull the strings that would see Xeldia sent where we needed to go. We took the time to turn the platinum coins into better equipment, Eledine purchasing some of the latest alchemical tools, and me getting some new robes woven with protective spells. Xeldia was understandably anxious the entire time.

The next day came both too slowly and too quickly. Xeldia said she had to enter the meeting alone, so we waited outside the Heartshold for news. Now it was our turn to be anxious. We paced around awkwardly.

After what could have been a minute or an hour, Xeldia returned, holding a letter. She gave us all a solemn nod. "It worked."

We started preparing for our trip to Kessedarn; the colony was far to the south, in the kingdom of Orsarch. Its southern regions were infamous for the cold, even in the summer months. I often struggled with the cold, so I made sure to invest in plenty of cold-weather gear. I found a place that did halfling sizes and soon was wrapped in the warmest furs.

When I stepped out to show Kurra, she laughed heartily, immediately picking me up and pulling me into a hug. "Ha! Small and fluffy! Like bear cub!"

We joined a caravan heading south. My magic had grown overt enough that some gave me distrustful looks, but helping the caravan in a skirmish with some rampaging elementals earned their trust quickly enough. With the heat of the summer starting to build up north, the south's cooler climes were something of a relief, particularly for Cosma, laden with fur as she was.

We reached the town of Helmsmark, as far south as most went. Kessedarn itself was nestled high in some treacherous mountains; the only way up was a thin mountain pass, directly controlled by the church. To prevent the risks of travelling with such a small party, we joined a supply cart heading up the trail. The fact that this place was a punishment posting was one evidently not lost on any of the guards there; each had a perpetual dour look.

We approached an imposing stone wall, a large gatehouse leading into the "colony," a designation I was starting to doubt, with the wall's imposing nature.

When we entered, the guard saluted Xeldia. "New posting? Gate to your left." To Kurra, he said, "You, gate to the right." He then looked at Eledine. "And what's your business?"

Xeldia said, "They're with me. Including Kurra here." She gestured to Kurra.

"Oh. Alright, but she needs to stay with you at all times. Captain Periet will be expecting you."

The gate led to a large stone fort, in which we got directions to the captain's office, on the upper levels. We were led into a furnished room, where Periet was examining the colony from a small window. She was an elven woman with raven black hair and a perpetual scowl. It lessened just a little as we entered.

"You must be Xeldia. Welcome to this frigid pit," Periet said.."Stand up and shut up, and I'll keep your posting short. And the hells is with the greenskin?"

Kurra snarled. "Name is Kurra!"

"I wasn't talking to you, retch! Now keep your tusks—"

Xeldia interrupted. "She is doing the Triune's work, and you will give her due respect!"

Periet's scowl returned to full intensity. "I don't tolerate back-talk. You're here to follow orders."

Eledine politely coughed. "To turn the conversation to a less volatile topic, we're here to aid in an investigation. Do you have a man named Russal Berrisen in the colony?"

"Not one of my men." Periet sounded entirely disinterested.

"He was a colonist, not a guard."

Periet scoffed. "Since when do I care about the colonists? We give them numbers and tell them to work."

Eyes widened around the room. Xeldia was, on this rare occasion, at a loss for words. "What…?"

Periet shrugged. "Maybe you can beat something out of one of these dregs. Anyway, I better give you lot the tour. Come on."

The tour started off normally enough, being shown barracks and armouries and a chapel. The four of us looked at each other, all of us unsure of what to say. Then, we were led out towards the colony proper.

As we approached another gatehouse, Periet summoned another guard before turning to us. "Never go out in groups of less than three. These wretches get antsy if they think they can overpower you."

I quietly asked, "Aren't you trying to help them?"

Periet laughed. "Help? These scum don't deserve help. We're here to keep them contained and keep them productive."

I could see a tickle of fur on Xeldia's neck.

She snarled "We tell those in the city that this is a place of healing, of learning! And you've been lying to them?"

"I'm not in charge of preaching. Talk to the priests when you're back if you want. In the meantime, keep your trap shut and follow me, if you don't want me to flog you for insubordination." Periet opened the door and led us into the colony.

A series of ill-maintained wooden shacks dotted a pit dug into the mountain, surrounded by mud tracks trodden into the sparse grass. Inside the first of the shacks were dozens of rows of hammocks, with a scattering of blankets.

"This is the bunkhouse," Periet said. "Everyone's working the mines or smelter right now."

Eledine frowned. "You don't have enough blankets in here, when winter comes—"

Periet snapped. "What part of 'shut up' do you lot not understand! This is what they're given. They deal with it."

She remained at the fore, leading us towards the next stop on the tour. Luckily, Xeldia was dedicating every ounce of will towards resisting her transformation, and even then, her teeth had turned to fangs and her eyes had turned canine.

We arrived at a massive forge. Hundreds of people, most sickly, were smelting ore into ingots. Right now, the focus was on a goblin, face streaked with tears, being flogged by a guard.

The guard was shouting, "…And I don't want any more carelessness! Now back to work!"

The goblin cried, "I-I can't stand! I can't!"

"Stop whining and—"

Xeldia roared in anger, her transformation completing. She stepped between the goblin and the guard, snarling. The rest of us were at her side without a moment's hesitation, hands on our weapons.

The guards drew their weapons, and one of them shouted, "Beastman!"

Xeldia drew her sword.

A bright, golden light filled the room.

Everyone froze, stunned. Xeldia was glowing with a divine aura, the emblem of Raiya on her chest shining with golden light. She pointed her sword at the guard. She didn't need to speak to issue a terrifying threat.

Periet shouted, "Kill her! Kill all of them!"

When guards moved to Xeldia's flanks, Kurra roared, her blade igniting with solar fire as she cut them down. As Periet moved to attack, I blasted her with starlight. She deflected the hit with her pauldron, but it gave her the second of pause needed for a pair of prisoners to lunge at her with hammers. She cut them down, but four more took their place, driving her back. Eledine quickly moved to start patching up the wounded even as more guards rushed in. Xeldia howled, raising her sword as a rallying cry.

As Periet tried to fall back behind reinforcements, Xeldia charged, the prisoners behind her, the riot well and truly underway.

Xeldia caught the guard's spears on a field of holy light, forcing them back, leaving critical openings for the rioters to exploit. More guards appeared through other entrances, but Kurra and I had Xeldia's back; those I couldn't keep at bay with my magics were swiftly cut down by Kurra.

Periet and Xeldia crossed blades. Both were skilled warriors, well equipped, with both training and experience. Periet fought aggressively, with quick, hard strikes. Xeldia's newfound holy defences held. Periet managed a feint that shifted Xeldia's shield out of position, and followed up with a desperate lunge that, even with a last moment parry, hit Xeldia hard in the shoulder. But the lunge left Periet's neck exposed, and Xeldia bit down hard with lupine fangs. The side of her snout found a gap in Periet's chain mail and reached flesh. Periet staggered back, her armour stained with bright blood. She kept fighting, but it was only a matter of time before the lost blood cost her strength, and a single missed parry gave Xeldia the opening to land a lethal blow to the head.

With their captain dead and the centre of their line broken, the guards fell back towards the fort. The colonists cheered as they pressed the advantage, a massive throng surging out from the forge and spreading throughout the colony, more colonists emerging from the nearby mines to join them. The burgeoning riot hit a snag when a hail of arrows came from the walls. Xeldia barked to get the rioters' attention, then circled her sword above her in a signal to rally. She led the rioters back into cover.

She hurried up to Eledine, who was focusing on treating the numerous wounded prisoners.

Eledine said breathlessly, "I do hope you weren't planning this and just forgot to tell me?"

Xeldia made a series of hand signals that none of us could understand.

Instead, Kurra hurriedly explained, "Archers on walls. Direct assault would be bloody."

"Then it's time for a new recipe I've been working on." Eledine drew some strange, black balls from her pack. "Throw these hard enough, they'll kick up a massive cloud of smoke. Should keep you covered."

Xeldia mimed climbing a ladder to Kurra, then gestured towards the wall, cocking her head in an inquisitive gesture.

Kurra didn't seem to understand, but I thought I could translate. "She's asking if you can scale the wall."

Xeldia nodded.

Kurra glanced outside at the wall. "Hmm…Need one of those strength elixirs. But then, yes. And then I drop ropes!"

Meanwhile, one of the colonists shouted, "Ladders! The mines have ladders! We'll get them!"

As some of the prisoners hurried off, Xeldia took the black balls from Eledine. As Kurra downed another of Eledine's elixirs, Xeldia threw one towards the nearest section of the wall, and another towards the centre of the colony; a diversion, I realised. Still with me in her pack, Kurra headed out into the smoke. With a mighty bound, she leapt onto the roof of the forge. She took a few steps back, then rushed forward, leaping towards the wall. She was short of the top but managed to find purchase in the pitted masonry. The guards cried in alarm at her sudden appearance. I cast a shield of arcane force around her, holding off the arrows they fired. One got past, hitting me, but Kurra's pack and my robe's warding absorbed the hit. Kurra started to climb. Bracing herself between the wall and an adjacent tower, she made swift progress. She propelled herself over the rampart, fending off a guard with a swift punch as she did so. As he staggered back, she followed up with a kick that sent him tumbling over the wall.

The guards on the rampart turned towards Kurra. She roared, drawing her sword and charging into the melee, keeping the guards between her and their comrades.

I leapt out of Kurra's pack. "I'll get the rope!" I quickly pulled out some rope, tied it around the rampart as tight as I could, and cast the rope down.

Kurra made sure the guards didn't get close enough to stop me. When I was finished, I signalled the colonists with a few flashes of light before turning to blind the guards on Kurra's rear with starlight.

The battle on the wall was fierce; the guards realised that if the colonists were able to take the wall, they would lose their best chance at containing the riot. The cacophony of the riot bombarded my ears. I gritted my teeth and focused as best I could; I was in pain, but lives were depending on me. A large force of guards advanced from the fort. The narrow wall meant they were close enough for me to catch a good deal with one magic blast, so when I dedicated my full power, I was able to keep them at bay.

Things grew more complicated when a battlemage turned up. Fortunately, my small size made me hard to target, especially in the chaos of battle, but Kurra had no such protections. The battlemage sent an icy blast at Kurra and landed a direct hit. But she just roared in rage and kept fighting. Another blast of ice, and she noticeably slowed. Enough for a guard to land a hard hit.

But she'd held long enough for the first of the prisoners to finish climbing to the top of the wall. Every guard that fell was another prisoner armed, and they had deep-seated rage and little to lose. They quickly moved to Kurra's side. With her flanks covered, she was able to keep fighting just a while longer. The battlemage turned his attention to the ever-increasing number of prisoners climbing up the walls and managed to slow them, but they kept coming.

Meanwhile, Xeldia was leading an assault on the fort's gate. A number of prisoners had taken the guards' shields and were keeping them held high as they moved on the fort with a large rock that would serve as a battering ram. Despite her current inability to speak, Xeldia managed to keep them coordinated, and a field of holy protection supplemented the stolen shields, giving the prisoners enough cover to reach the gate. It was solidly built but not prepared for such a large-scale attack.

With the walls taken, the fort breached, and the captain dead, the battle had swung well and truly in the prisoners' favour. Those few guards still remaining fell back to the fort. The prisoners swarmed towards the entrance on the wall, but guards were managing to hold them at the chokepoint. Slipping between the tall legs of the prisoners, I managed to evade detection until I was right beside the door. Crouching as low as I could, I aimed a blinding blast from an angle they weren't expecting. That little bit was enough to turn the tide. The guards buckled, and the horde of prisoners stormed in.

My magic and my energy were mostly spent at that point, and I figured that with the fort's walls breached, the few remaining guards had little chance. So, I left them to it and moved back to check on Kurra. She was leaning heavily on the parapet, teeth gritted. A couple of blows had found her; her dire bear-hide armour had prevented any from becoming lethal, but she was in poor condition. Still, she was heading to the fight.

I gently lay a hand on her thigh to stop her. "See Eledine?"

Kurra snorted. "Will have a long line. Can still fight."

I pressed a little more firmly and gave her my best puppy-dog eyes. Kurra laughed.

"Oh, alright," she said, then stood.

Exhausted, I slipped back into Kurra's pack before she was on the rope, curling up in its relative safety and quiet. Once I had recovered from all the noise, I took a moment to examine the shot I'd taken earlier; it had turned into a slight cut and nasty bruise, but nothing immediately threatening, something I could trouble Eledine with after she dealt with the no doubt innumerable more serious wounds the prisoners had suffered in the fight.

After a minute of catching my breath, I heard the sounds of battle die down. I saw a commotion on the fort's roof. There was a band of prisoners on the roof, and they were dragging some unarmed guards to the edge. I could hear the guards begging for mercy. The prisoners seemed to be enjoying it, holding them right at the edge, revelling in the guards' terror and their newfound power.

Then, there was a growl that could only be Xeldia. I couldn't see her from my position, but I could see her holy glow. I briefly saw the prisoners argue with her. But when Xeldia said not to do something, that thing was very rarely done, and I had no doubt that being shifted would make her even more intimidating. The prisoners dragged the guards away from the roof's edge.

The battle was over. The roles of prisoner and guard had been reversed, and the newly freed colonists locked the surviving guards in the dungeons below the castle while they decided what to do about them. Xeldia sternly observed the whole process, ensuring that no colonists took the chance to torture their former tormentors. Eledine, meanwhile, was swamped with wounded, and when I arrived to check on her, she immediately sent me to sweep the fort for more medical supplies. Kurra was low on the priority list, but I was fairly certain the wait was bothering her more than her wounds.

Now that no lives were in immediate danger, I was able to process what had just happened. We came here to investigate a lead on a conspiracy and ended up sparking a successful prison riot. Furthermore, I had been under the impression that colonies were supposed to be places of healing, not just containment, but that illusion had been well and truly shattered. Worse, Eledine and I had allowed guards to drag a woman into one of these nightmares; I hoped the gods would consider my liberating of this place to be redemption for that crime.

I eventually decided it was past time to get to the reason we came here in the first place. Figuring that it would be the place with the highest concentration of people, I headed to Eledine's impromptu clinic. Strangely, when I arrived, I noticed two large groups: one lined up near the clinic, the other huddled in an adjacent building. Uncertain what was happening, I headed to see Eledine, who was busy binding a broken leg.

She glanced at me as I approached. "If you're looking to get your wounds treated, the other prisoners will be furious if you don't wait in line."

I gestured in the direction of the other group.

She understood my meaning. "Oh, those idiots? They thought I was 'scary' or 'doing things mortals weren't meant to.' I told the fools that if they wanted healing, they could cooperate or leave. I think a few of the morons are busy praying to a demon lord for healing."

I gulped; the demon lords were definitely bad news, but after all the abuse these people had suffered in the name of the Triune, I couldn't really blame them. Sneaking back towards the second group, I indeed found a priest of one of the demon lords holding service, using unholy magics to heal their followers, but there didn't seem to be any outright sacrifices or torture going on right that moment. With a gulp, I let them be; they needed healing, and while the demon cults could mean bad news in the long term, we didn't have any alternative sources of healing, and I didn't have much faith in my ability to convince people of Eledine's methods.

At least my investigation gave me a problem I *could* solve. I walked around Eledine's clinic, questioning the colonists about Russal.

The first two knew nothing, but a third was a bit more talkative. "Haven't heard the name before…when did he come?"

"A year ago. About."

The colonist hummed. "Hmm…well, Grenki showed up about that time as well. She might know him."

It took a bit of asking around, but I managed to find Grenki, a hunchbacked goblin woman. She gave me a wicked smile. "Saw that magic. Vicious stuff, that. I like you."

I decided not to comment on the dubious compliment. "Russal Berrisen?"

"Oh, him? Poor wretch was shanked a couple of days after he arrived." My shoulders slumped. But then she said, "But he told me a secret. Call it payment for busting me out of here. He said that he knew a guy, a guy that could prove the Herald ain't the Herald at all."

My eyes bulged, my jaw dropping. If the *Herald* was an impostor, that called literally the *entire church of the Triune* into question.

Grenki snorted in amusement. "Faithful woman, are you? Hah. Anyway, he said that the proof is stashed in his professor's old house, where was it…? Ah, can't remember, been too long. Yettrian, that was the professor's name! Anyway, normally I don't believe legends about hidden treasure, but him turning up dead right after? Something good is in that stash. Well, so long as no one's got to it first. Said something about a loose brick in the hearth."

I gulped; I wasn't looking forward to sharing this with Xeldia. But it wasn't something I could delay for long. I thanked Grenki and went off to find Xeldia. I found her standing on the fort's roof. Her divine aura was no longer present, but I could see a faint glow on her breastplate, embers of power waiting for the time to be fanned into an inferno. She was still in her wolf form, talking with one of the freed colonists, a heavily scarred woman. The woman was gently gesturing to parts of Xeldia's snout, talking about shaping sounds. They noticed me approaching.

"Alright, why don't you try greeting your friend?" the woman said to Xeldia.

I could see Xeldia concentrating. Slowly, careful with each syllable, she uttered a guttural "Hello."

I smiled. "Hello!"

The woman gave Xeldia a friendly pat on the back. "There you go! You'll be holding conversations in no time. The real trick is to practise. True about pretty much everything about being one of us."

I gave her a quizzical look. Xeldia gestured to her and tried to say something else but struggled to speak.

The woman explained, "I'm a beastwoman, too. That's what landed me in this shithole. Teaching her how to talk in her beast form. Would've been handy in that mess."

I asked, "Which animal?"

"Badger. Anyway…" The woman got back to teaching Xeldia while I watched, having nothing better to do at this instant.

After a few more minutes, Xeldia dismissed her. "Enough. T-tired. Th-th-think."

The woman nodded and left. Xeldia turned towards the colony, looking out over it, deep in thought. She clearly had a lot on her mind. I couldn't quite bring myself to add something more to it just now. Instead, I walked up beside her and took her hand (even if it was more of a paw right now). We remained like that for a few minutes.

After a while, she let me know some of what was on her mind. "Blesssthing. For mosstht fa-fa-faithful. I rebel. Blessthed. For thhhat."

Well, it naturally led to what I was here to tell her. "Talked to someone who knew Russal. Said he said the Herald is an impostor." Xeldia's mouth fell agape. "Proof, apparently, in Yettrian's old house. Something about a loose brick near the hearth."

"…Herrrrrald. Lllllreader…" Xeldia sat down, leaning against the parapet, burying her head in her hands.

I sat down next to her. I searched for something to say, but what was there? I wasn't the most eloquent at the best of times, and Xeldia's entire faith had just been turned upside down. What could I say? What could anyone say?

But much to my own surprise, I did manage to think of something. "You're a hero." She shifted her head just enough to look at me. I gestured up and over the parapet. "Look! You freed everyone!"

She didn't look but did seem to relax a little. A few minutes later, she was able to shift back to normal with a moment of concentration. She stood. "Come. There is much to be done."

Chapter 16

We spent the next night and day helping the freed colonists get organised. Most had nowhere else to go, but the mountains, while inhospitable, were rich in metal and highly defensible, so the church would have a hard time trying to retake it. The colonists established a new government, a simple elected council, and arranged plans to begin trade with foreigners to the east. The colony's former staff were put to work in its mines, a poetic punishment for the abuse they inflicted on their captives.

The next morning, the colonists were treating themselves to a breakfast of the guard's rations. Kurra was happy to boast about her feats in the battle, leading some of the colonists to try to one-up her, leading to a contest of boasts that future historians would no doubt rue. Eledine did correct one or two of the more outlandish claims; while she didn't see much of the fighting herself, she saw most of the wounds and could extrapolate an impressive amount from that.

Xeldia, for her part, was uncharacteristically quiet, especially since the Triune took a dim view of lies. The rest of us noticed. She even left breakfast early, saying something about checking Periet's office for any useful information. I finished quickly, following her. I found her there, looking at a stack of papers, but not reading them.

While I wondered what to say, Kurra arrived behind me. "Xeldia?"

Xeldia set down the papers with a sigh. "...When we complete our training and become full-fledged paladins, we take oaths. To serve the church and its Herald. I swore my entire life to them."

Kurra strode forward. "They lied to you, so oath is nothing. You are your own woman, Xeldia, make your own choices. Besides, Raiya sees your value. Hah, even if not, I do!" She clasped Xeldia on the shoulder. "You saw injustice, you fought! Pox on church, and Herald, and—well, not Triune, they helped. But church doesn't deserve you! Fight for what *you* believe!"

Xeldia paused, looking out the window. "The Triune, they are supposed to represent the best of us. Our courage, our curiosity, our love. The church has never supported any of this. Damn it, they *repress* it!" Her hands balled into fists, and she strode out.

We followed her as she headed out into the colony and into its chapel. Of all the buildings in the colony proper, it was the sturdiest, made out of stone bricks and with metal windows. Graffiti in the nooks and crannies showed the colonists never cared much for it.

Xeldia strode towards the altar, dedicated to the Triune as a whole. She knelt. "Raiya, I swore myself to your church once, before I saw just how far away from your will they had fallen. But it was always in you I believed. In your cause. Not because it was right to serve you, but because you represent what is right. I am no longer an agent of the church, so now, I forge new oaths. Raiya, I swear to you, here, that I will carry forward the light of courage and righteousness. I will allow no lie to pass my lips nor injustice to pass my blade. I shall be a shield to the downtrodden and a sword to the unrepentant. I am Xeldia, and I shall be your paladin!"

She drew her sword and held it high. It glowed with a golden light, filling the chapel. She smiled, even as she shifted.

Once we had tied up loose ends in the colony, we set off back down the mountain. Eledine was certain she could dig up Yettrian's address from her contacts in the university. The tricky part would be getting into Ansiel; there was a very real chance that the inquisition knew of Xeldia's desertion or would learn of it by the time we arrived. Captain Drenn could perhaps arrange a pardon for a scuffle with an inquisitor, but an outright prison riot straight afterwards was no doubt beyond her ability to cover up. After some debate, we settled on sending a letter to Eledine's contacts and hoped Yettrian's house would turn out to be somewhere not easily guarded. We also sent word to Lady Berrisen, informing her of her son's fate; with luck, she'd gain a vendetta against the church that we could use to our advantage.

In the meantime, we set out in the city's direction. One of the colonists, a scrawny orc named Hulbred, told us of a former contact, a woman named Sandrae, who would help people hole up, no questions asked. So, we set out for a rural town named Klysvenn. We kept our distance from the well-travelled roads. It wasn't so bad, having some time with just the four of us.

As we camped one night, Kurra remarked to Xeldia, "You smile. Feeling better?"

"Yes." She leaned closer to the fire. "All my life, I have been trying to balance my belief in justice with my duty—no, my obligation—to the church. I didn't realise just how difficult it was for me until now, when I no longer have to do it."

Eledine snorted. "Come to think of it, that should have been a warning sign that perhaps the church isn't as loyal to the Triune as they think."

"When all around you say that the church is the agent of all that is good, it's easy to believe. It's easier to believe than to believe that you can see something that no one else can." Xeldia examined a tuft of fur starting to materialise on her hand.

I considered the idea. "Maybe…maybe a lot of people have doubts. But they never talk about them."

"Because they all think they're the only ones." Xeldia nodded. "Perhaps if I show them all my power, show them my blessings…"

Eledine frowned. "I'd suggest making that a longer-term goal. I expect the church's priests would simply argue you're using illusion magic. You'd want to have support before openly moving against the church. Preferably more support than a mob of former prisoners."

"Hopefully, whatever Yettrian hid will allow us to garner that support."

We arrived at Klysvenn late the next day. Eledine, who was surprisingly quite a hand with needle and thread, quickly arranged a tabard for Xeldia to better hide her status as a paladin, which she reluctantly donned. After a bit of digging and Kurra scaring off a band of muggers, we managed to find someone who was probably Sandrae in an inn in the seedier part of town.

The interior was cleaner than I expected. What I didn't expect, but perhaps should have, was that the "inn" was clearly a brothel. Eyes were on the four of us as we entered. We approached someone who was apparently Sandrae, an older woman with pepper brown hair and a little too much make-up.

Xeldia took point. "Hail. We're looking for Sandrae. Hulbred sent us."

The probable Sandrae's expression turned from suspicion to surprise. "Hulbred? He was sent to the colonies a year ago. But yes, I am Sandrae. What news of Hulbred?"

"He's well, circumstances considered. But the story is quite complicated. Do you have somewhere we can talk without your… clients listening?"

Sandrae led us into an office in the back.

Once there, Xeldia explained our story, starting with our investigations into history and our uncovering of the conspiracy. "…we realised we'd need a place to lie low while we awaited a reply. Hulbred, very happy with his newfound freedom, told us of this place, and here we are."

Sandrae paused, taking some understandable time to process all we'd just told her. "Well. Well. Well. I can't say I have much interest in ancient conspiracies, but if you want to hide, that I can arrange. It *will* cost you, I'm afraid, and not a small amount."

Eledine drew a stack of papers and handed them to Sandrae. "Here, funding forms from the colony, allowing it to requisition additional funds from banks whenever needed. A woman as silver-tongued as any of your staff could use it to siphon funds from the church."

Sandrae flicked through the papers. "Hmm…yes, I could. Very well, this will buy you shelter for a week or two. This way."

She led us into one of the guest rooms, then moved the bed aside to reveal a secret passage, leading into an underground chamber. Inside was a pair of cots, a lantern, a crate pressed into service as a table, and little else. "Here you are. Not the most comfortable accommodations, but I can guarantee you won't be found. It's even warded against divination magic. My staff will check on you regularly to get anything you need and to empty the chamber pots."

Kurra dropped her pack on the ground. "Hmph. Well, dry, at least."

With little other recourse, we all settled in. Which presented a problem: Two beds, four people.

Kurra said, "Well. Biggest sleeps with smallest, two middles sleep together."

There was a silence, and everyone looked at each other. The rational part of my brain offered the solution of taking turns sleeping in our bedrolls, but the rest of my brain proceeded to tell that part to shut its damn trap.

Thus began a long few days of waiting. Sandrae had, at least, furnished our hideout with a deck of cards, which Kurra proved to be quite adept with. Still, there were only so many games we could play before getting bored. Eledine passed a little more time with a quick lecture on alchemical principles, which were actually somewhat interesting, even if there wasn't much else to hold our attention.

Night came, and I found myself sharing a small bed with a big orc. We'd shared a bedroll on our march through the desert, and that alone was a memory seared into my mind. This was just a bit more. Mainly because, due to the bed's small size and Kurra's immense muscular bulk, there wasn't enough room for me to sleep beside her, so I had to sleep on top of her. She didn't seem to mind the fact that I used her chest as a (*very* nice) pillow.

With nothing else to occupy my mind, I couldn't stop thinking about that night. Kurra was so warm, so strong, and yet able to hold me so gently…part of me wanted to say something. But

I was due to share a bed with her another night, and I didn't want to risk making things awkward. Instead, I remained quiet.

Eledine decided to entertain us with a few lectures on alchemy. Not the most exciting subject, but it was better than simply sitting and doing nothing. While she was explaining the effect of various vial sizes on things like temperature and reaction rates, she noticed a quizzical expression on Kurra. "Kurra? Are you following?"

Kurra frowned. "I...do not know what you mean by 'multiply.'"

Eledine gave Kurra a flat look. "You cannot be serious."

"Not a word I've heard before!" Kurra raised her hands defensively.

Eledine scoffed. "It's basic mathematics. Did you pay *any* attention in school?"

"Did not go to school. Parents didn't have money," Kurra whispered, her gaze dropping to the ground.

"You didn't—Kurra, basic maths like this—" Eledine started.

Xeldia interrupted. "Eledine, that's enough. Even in Casten, with the church's support, it can be hard to find a proper school, and most people are too busy to teach their own children. Do you think it would be any easier in Uluzar? Kurra's education is lacking. That isn't her fault."

Eledine opened her mouth and closed it a few times before sitting on the bed with a sigh.

I sat down next to her. "Frustrating. I get it." After an awkward pause, I added, "Could teach Kurra some maths?"

Eledine nodded. "Yes. I'm sure she'll find it useful."

The three of us worked together to help catch Kurra up on her education. She wasn't the sharpest student, but she was eager, and we all found the time productive.

The next night started much like the previous. The tension with Kurra kept me awake. Which was why I was up quickly when Eledine suddenly stood.

"Something's wrong," she said.

The rest of us were just as quick to rouse ourselves, grabbing our weapons. I was about to ask Eledine what was wrong before I heard the cracking of wood near the entrance to the hideout. The entrance was forced aside. A burly dwarf with a warhammer charged down the stairs. Kurra leapt to answer him. They both swung wide, evading each other's hits, but were quick to recommit.

I turned to curse the dwarf with magic, but an incantation from up the stairs summoned an arcane shield around him. The rest of us drew weapons to help, but Kurra and the dwarf were locked in combat on the stairs; none of us could line up a shot on the dwarf. But we weren't out of options.

Xeldia quickly grabbed a symbol of Raiya from her pack, holding it high. "Raiya shall shield the righteous, that we may bring forth light together!" Her aura of divine light returned, encompassing her.

When the dwarf's hammer got too close, it slowed, not greatly, but enough, by that crucial split-second, for Kurra to parry or evade. The dwarf's allies tried aiding with spells of their own, so I turned my power to unravelling their magics.

The fight was evenly matched, both sides skilled warriors with no small amount of raw muscle behind their strikes. But the dwarf overextended himself just a bit, leaving an opening that Eledine had been waiting for. With a flick of the wrist, Eledine sent a dagger into his arm. He swore loudly and went up the stairs. Kurra pressed the advantage. She landed another cut as he stumbled on a stair but was then blasted back with arcane ice. Roaring in rage, she resumed her advance, Xeldia close behind her.

The problem was, there were at least four attackers atop the stairs, including the dwarf and the wizard. Not just random thugs, either; these were experienced and well equipped. On top of that, the open positioning of the top of the stairs made advancing up them a tactical nightmare. Even Kurra could see that, as a dagger cutting deep into her shoulder drove her back downstairs.

Time to do something clever. I cast my invisibility spell. I whispered to Xeldia, "Get their attention!"

She trusted me enough to advance, guarded by her shields of steel and faith. They held enough to hold our attacker's attention. I headed upstairs, deftly slipping between the legs of Xeldia and our attackers. Then, I turned and blasted them all with all the starlight I could muster. They screamed in pain, covering their eyes.

But one, a woman with a shortbow, wasn't hit quite hard enough, guarded by some combination of a dark hood, looking in the wrong direction, and perhaps some sheer grit. And casting the spell had dismissed my invisibility. The woman's attention—as well as her aim—immediately turned to me. As I quickly summoned a shield of force around me, but she landed a straight shot what penetrated. The shield stopped the hit from being lethal, but I was still hit firmly in the chest, hard enough to cut deep.

I heard Kurra roar in rage. As Xeldia advanced, capitalising on the chance I had created, Kurra outright leapt up to the upper level, swinging at the archer. She barely evaded. Kurra kept up her momentum, swinging into another strike that bit deep. Xeldia, meanwhile, had pushed our attackers off the top of the stairs, had cut down the enemy wizard, and wasn't having too much trouble holding off the other wounded attackers.

As Eledine ganged up on the archer with Xeldia, the dwarf managed to lock Xeldia's sword, forcing her to drop it. With gritted teeth, she shifted and sank her claws into his neck, tearing into it with a spray of blood. A shield bash and a harsh bite kept the third attacker busy long enough for me to finish him with a blast of stellar fire, while Eledine and Kurra were able to quickly finish the archer.

We paused, panting.

Eledine flicked some blood off her blade. "What the hell happened? Did Sandrae betray us?"

I shook my head. "Forced the door."

Xeldia retrieved her sword and moved out into the hallway. What she saw stopped her in her tracks. "Dead...Arrllll dead..."

I squeaked "What?" and slipped out into the hallway with her.

Blood.

So damn much blood.

And bodies, too. Scanning the rest of the building showed that the attackers had killed *everyone* inside, save us (and not for a lack of trying).

Eledine emerged from the room. After taking a second to process the carnage, she said, "The inquisition must have found us. They had our descriptions." She held up a piece of paper. "I expect we have nothing to gain by remaining here. We need to leave and hopefully find a moment for me to patch all of you up."

Kurra called, "One moment!" and emerged that moment later carrying the head of the archer.

I was growing worryingly used to death, but still, the sight was uncomfortably gory. Which was why I flinched when Kurra offered it to me with a beaming smile.

"I have slain your enemies in your honour!" she said.

I had absolutely no idea what I was expected to do with a severed head. I also wasn't exactly keen on people being killed in my honour; in this case, it was definitely self-defence, but that didn't mean it was a *good* thing. On top of the dead civilians, this really wasn't something I was ready to deal with. I turned away, focusing on keeping my dinner down.

Chapter 17

We left the brothel. We decided on an ordinary inn (if the inquisition could find us in a specialised hideout, why bother with anything more elaborate?), and Eledine got to treating our wounds. We set up our usual watch in case the inquisition had any more men and got what sleep we could.

Thankfully, the rest of the night passed without incident, and Eledine received a message from her contacts late that morning. "A villa outside Leisvale. Closer to Ansiel than I'd like, but at least it's not walled off."

Xeldia quickly started packing. "We need to stay on the move anyway. Let's get going."

Kurra took us on a longer, winding route to Leisvale, with the hope of shaking any inquisitors on our tail. She seemed unusually quiet over the first leg of the trip, something evidently bothering her. But I lacked the confidence to ask her about it, and the others didn't seem to notice, not that there weren't plenty of other things on their minds.

We managed to reach Leisvale without major incident. We found the manor, a large affair surrounded by an immaculately maintained hedge.

Eledine frowned when she saw it. "Obviously inhabited. Which will make it difficult to search."

Xeldia said, "Then we get permission."

"I do hope you've considered the possibility that they are allies of the inquisition? Or otherwise have been informed that we are traitors?" Eledine rested a hand on her rapier.

"Both are possible, but unlikely. Even the inquisition isn't omnipresent. And I doubt the inquisition will publicly advertise that I am a traitor; to do that, they would have to admit such a thing is even possible. I carry Raiya's blessing; that will open most doors." Xeldia strode forward.

The rest of us fell in behind her. We all kept our weapons in easy reach, even Xeldia.

Xeldia approached the door and knocked. A servant answered, a well-mannered halfling. "Oh, hello. I'm afraid Sir Peraworth isn't expecting any guests."

Xeldia bowed. "I apologise for not sending word of my arrival; I am a paladin of Raiya, on a holy mission. I believe this manor is, or was, the residence of an academic named Yettrian?"

"Erm, I'm not sure, but Sir Peraworth *was* granted this land only recently. I could ask him about this, ah, Yettrian, was it?" The servant shifted nervously.

"We believe he came into possession of a valuable document and hid it somewhere in the estate. We simply wish to look for it. You have my word. We will do our utmost to ensure the rest of your master's possessions are undisturbed."

"I see. Let me talk to Sir Peraworth." The servant bowed and left. We scanned the area for any ambushes while we waited for the servant to return.

When the door opened again, it was a young man with an impressive battle scar. "Hail, paladin! Allow me to introduce myself. Sir Roden Peraworth, at your service." He bowed.

Xeldia politely bowed in turn. "A pleasure to meet you. I simply require access to your estate to search for the hidden documents. In particular, we believe it was hidden in a hearth."

This got Peraworth's attention. "The hearth…? Now you mention it, shortly after I moved in, the servants discovered some loose bricks in the drawing room's hearth, and one had a strange design on the back. I simply had the area re-mortared."

Xeldia sighed. "Well. I'm afraid we'll have to undo your worker's hard work. Rest assured, I'll see to it you're properly reimbursed."

Peraworth didn't exactly seem keen either, but he said, "Very well. This way."

He led us to the hearth and pointed us at some particular bricks. Kurra got to work with hammer and chisel. Soon enough, the bricks came loose.

Kurra pulled one in particular out. "Hmm. This diagram, like ones of stars. Peri?"

I took the brick, examining the diagram. It seemed to display the planets in orbit, some of the constellations, a date, and some magical runes. It looked absolutely nonsensical to me, until something clicked. "A puzzle." I quickly got out a sheet of parchment and started working out maths, figuring out where the planets would have been on that date and recreating the diagram. After a while, I managed to write out a series of runes and a place to cast them. A little more magical arithmetic revealed that the runes would access an extradimensional space; hopefully, containing whatever Yettrian had hidden. I walked over to the location (a few steps in front of the hearth) and cast the runes. A small portal opened.

I reached in and pulled out a scroll. A gilded affair, written on fine vellum. I immediately opened it, my companions gathering around in excitement.

We, the Triune, wardens of this land by will of its people, hereby strip the post of our Herald from Violae Senredia, and with it all blessing and authority, due to her direct opposition to the principles of courage, love, and discovery. We denounce her words and actions as harmful to our cause. Should she continue to spread fear, hatred, and ignorance, she is to be thwarted, detained, and tried. Furthermore, we apologise for the harm she has wrought with our authority and seek to make restitution to the people of this land.

Beneath was a symbol of the Triune, gleaming with an impossible light. Beneath that, a date in the current calendar: 500 years ago.

Peraworth paled. "Is this—Herald Senredia herself? The very woman who has ruled for the last five hundred years? It's not possible! It's an illusion!"

Xeldia tried to speak, but at that moment, she shifted.

Peraworth, already not in the best of moods, outright screamed. "Guards! Guards!"

Eledine sighed. "I suppose that's our cue to leave."

The four of us were able to put plenty of distance between us and the manor without being accosted; none of the servants wanted to stop a heavily armed beastwoman and orc, and the guards happened to be on the other side of the building at the time. We kept the document.

Once we weren't concerned about being chased, Eledine said, "Alright, I believe this warrants a review of the facts. So, we know for certain that the Herald, Violae Senredia, was, ahem, *pointedly fired* by the Triune, for…as of yet unknown transgressions against their doctrine."

I squeaked, "*The* Herald? Isn't there only one?"

Xeldia, still struggling to shape words with her bestial snout, answered, "Imorrtal. Firrrve hunndread years. Saarme."

Eledine deadpanned. "So, for a lifetime, even by *my* people's standards, the religion of the Triune has been controlled by a woman the Triune fired. An entirely usual and stable affair."

Kurra hummed. "How? Is human, and priests say she can work miracles. Must have power. Not blessings, maybe, but power."

"A wizard, perhaps?" Eledine suggested.

I said, "Maybe? Would be really hard."

"Speculation, anyway. A more interesting question: How was it so difficult to find that document? Surely the Triune would be smart enough to be public with firing their second-in-command."

Kurra stated, "Ioran Heresy." The rest of us looked at her. She continued, "Happened five hundred years ago. About as long as Herald has been reigning."

This piqued Eledine's interest. "So you're suggesting that the Ioran Heresy was the Herald trying to hide the fact that she was fired?"

Xeldia's tail twitched anxiously. "Rrrforms. Alfthter Heresy."

Eledine started flicking through a large book of notes. "That would explain why we've had such a difficult time keeping track of who was on which side! *Senredia* was the heretic, and she's been rewriting history to make everyone think she was loyal!"

Kurra grinned. "Well, time for her rule to end. Let's start showing this!"

"As much as I'd like that, I doubt that the Herald will simply allow us to do that," said Eledine. "Even discounting the immense magical power she must have, she still has the assets of the *entire church* at her beck and call. Certainly, some will believe us, but in the short term, at least, we're immensely outgunned and outnumbered. And I'm sure that the Herald or her agents will destroy this document the second they get their hands on it."

I squeaked, "Xeldia knew it was legitimate."

"Bleshing. Cen *feeel* it. Mosht worn't." Xeldia shifted anxiously.

Kurra asked, "Find others blessed by the Triune? Xeldia isn't only one. Like Orreke and her acolytes!"

Even with her bestial face, I could tell Xeldia was in a dark mood. "Arll sent arway. Ssracred queshts. Rarrrely ret-return."

"Dammit, enough despair!" Kurra roared, standing. "Yes, will be difficult. Yes, we must work with cunning. But we can bring down entire church! Together!"

Eledine chuckled bitterly. "To think all of this started with a simple archaeological expedition…but you're right, at least in that we need to look at this problem from a different angle. So, we want to topple the church, or at least the Herald. To do that, we're going to need a movement. To do that, we're going to need supporters. To do that, we're going to need to find people who can recognise the authenticity of this document. To do that, we need to find someone blessed, that the church hasn't yet sent to their deaths."

"Like Orreke's acolytes! At least one blessed remained. We return there and start building our forces!" Kurra grinned.

"That's quite a distance, but at least it gets us out of the church's territory, and I don't see any other options. Unless one of you has ideas?" Eledine looked at Xeldia and me. We shook our heads.

We started the long march to Eastcrown. We pressed ourselves; if Peraworth reported what he had seen, then the inquisition would be right on our tail; though, if we were lucky, they wouldn't guess our next move, so as long as we kept moving, we could be on a ship before the Herald's agents tracked us down.

After a couple of days of marching, we reached a small town called Uranalf. Eledine and I managed to work out disguises for us, though we weren't sure how far it would go—Kurra being an orc was something we couldn't disguise, combined with the fact that she was huge even by her people's standards, and she was worryingly distinctive. Still, we could only spend so much time in the wilderness, so once in a while, we had to risk visiting town to resupply (and occasionally sleep in an actual bed).

Kurra had taken the chance to sample some of the local brews—quite a few of them. While she was a large woman, it was just enough to loosen up some of the things that were weighing on her heart. "…Ever feel bad for those you kill?"

Xeldia whispered, "Every night."

Eledine nodded. "Perhaps not *that* often, myself, but I'm not proud of some of the things we have to do."

I nodded as well, more emphatically.

Kurra sighed in relief. "Am not alone, then."

Xeldia snorted bitterly. "I guess killing is another matter in which you disagree with your people?"

"Such is life in Uluzar. The strong kill the weak. I do not fear the rush of battle, but the taking of a life…" Kurra's shoulders slumped.

I gently rested a hand on her thigh. "That means you're kind. Like we should all be."

The rest of the night (our inn room guarded by an alchemical trap of Eledine's design) passed without incident. When we prepared to leave, we noticed Xeldia donning her paladin's armour, something she'd been doing less to attract less attention.

Eledine raised an eyebrow. "You're moving out in the open?"

"I'm familiar with the local priest of Ynnelia," Xeldia explained. "Before we leave, I want to show her what we've found. I know it's a risk, but we can start spreading the word now. Hopefully, she will choose truth over doctrine."

Eledine tightened the straps on her armour. "Well, I hope you're not expecting to go alone."

Xeldia wasn't. The local church of the Triune was a fairly standard affair, a stone building with some stained-glass windows and three altars, one for each of the Triune. It was very early in the morning, so a congregation was just starting to gather. Xeldia walked in, purposefully, but not deliberately drawing attention. The congregation parted quickly for the paladin, bowing respectfully. She quickly led us to a tanned woman in night-blue robes.

Xeldia greeted her with a polite bow. "Cerra, it has been some time."

Cerra's eyes widened. "Xeldia? I heard you were excommunicated!"

"Conspiracy. There is something we must discuss in private. Quickly." Xeldia's tone was enough to convey the gravity of the situation, and Cerra led us into a back room. As soon as the door was closed, Xeldia showed Cerra the document.

Cerra's face paled. "What…Xeldia, you can't be serious!"

"I wish I wasn't. But this is the truth, I know by Raiya's blessing." The emblem on Xeldia's breastplate gleamed with holy light.

Cerra stumbled onto a nearby seat. "And— and you've been blessed…"

"It happened when I saw the conditions in the Reborn Colonies. The church has been lying; they are places of containment and abuse, nothing more. I earned Raiya's blessing by fighting against that evil. As for this scroll, it was hidden by an academic, who vanished shortly afterwards," Xeldia explained.

Cerra peered closely at the scroll, examining each and every part of it with the utmost care, trying to find some kind of evidence that it was in error. Finally, she sat back. "We have to tell everyone."

Eledine said, "I'd be delighted if we could shout this from the rooftops, but I doubt the Herald will simply let us do that. I should remind you that she's had the last five hundred years to fill the upper echelons of the church with those more interested in power than truth, the inquisition, at least, that we've observed doing her dirty work."

Xeldia returned the scroll to her pack. "But that does not mean we have to be idle. Start sowing the seeds of doubt. Start building support. I'm afraid I cannot tell you my plans. I cannot risk an inquisitor overhearing. But I'm building support. We will cleanse the church, in the Triune's name."

Cerra was silent for a long while. "…Ynnelia light your way, Xeldia."

"Raiya guard you, Cerra."

Chapter 18

We managed to reach Eastcrown without incident, and from there, even managed to find a ship that took passengers. It was a much dingier affair than our last trip to Uluzar; not many people sailed to orc territory, especially without the church's wealth to motivate them. But at least this time there were enough hammocks.

In a stroke of bad luck, this trip was also clipped by a storm. I still absolutely hated every second of it, but I had built enough courage to not spend the entire time crammed into a corner. Still, I spent every second close to my companions.

We reached Zerrekdar and from there, set out across the savanna. It was deep summer, and the land was painfully hot. Kurra had been smart enough to prepare accordingly, having bought loose robes of light material for all of us to shield us from the sun. I wasn't nearly as eager to leap into the warmth of Kurra's pack.

We kept up a steady pace, long into the afternoon. Soon, all our clothes were drenched in sweat.

Finally, Eledine said, "Might I make a suggestion? We have a longer break in the afternoon, when the day's the hottest. We can make up the lost time by marching longer into the mornings and evenings."

Kurra grunted. "The warbands, they don't care for time of day. They march and let the weak sweat."

"Then they're fools. If nothing else, marching in the afternoon will drain our supply of water much faster." Eledine's tone was entirely matter-of-fact.

I wiped some sweat from my brow, grateful that my witch hat already came with a nice wide brim. "Agreed."

Xeldia thought for a moment. "I could keep going, but if Eledine and Peri can't say the same, then I will allow us to rest."

Eledine sat on a nearby rock. "I *could* keep going, but that's not my point. My point is that it will be more efficient—and more pleasant—to not march in the hottest parts of the day. I don't know if the orcs consider cooking themselves to have innate virtue, but I don't."

Kurra shifted uncomfortably. "I do not wish to allow sun to win."

Eledine gave Kurra a flat look. "Are you seriously trying to directly fight the sun?"

Xeldia chuckled. "When you put it like that, the choice does become quite clear. I think I can see a large tree up ahead; we'll head there for some shade and rest for an hour or two."

Kurra didn't exactly seem keen, but when she settled down for a nap, she dozed off quickly. We gave the day a couple of hours to cool before setting back out. We made more progress and kept up our march even after the sun set. After so long under the baking heat, the cold of the night was an outright relief. It also gave me chance aplenty to study the stars. I saw the face in the star again, looking down on me, pleased.

That night, Cosma taught me a new spell. This one allowed me to call upon the cold of the space between the stars. A power with offensive applications, but Cosma was obviously teaching me this spell for more of a utility purpose. Not that I wasn't deeply grateful.

When the next day came, and the sun started to beat down once again, I put the spell through its paces, cooling the air around us. The other three looked at me like I had saved their lives.

We returned to the church to find rotting bodies hanging from its walls and a different flag flying.

Kurra examined the scene through my spyglass. "Hmm. Common, as warning to attackers. But unusual for Triune.'"

Xeldia frowned. "Very unusual. Something is wrong."

Eledine took the spyglass from Xeldia and examined the fort herself. "Damn. I recognise that one—one of Orreke's followers. That one there, too. It appears the church has had a change of hands."

Xeldia buried her head in her hands. "Damn it…they were peaceful! Healers! And now…"

Kurra grunted, "Peace is a weakness. Here, one must always be willing to fight."

Just as I saw some fur beginning to build on Xeldia, Eledine said, "Calm down; there's still every chance that some survived and escaped. I'm only counting ten, maybe twenty bodies. Less than half. It will simply be harder to find them."

"Hmm…only so many places to go. Cannot go far without water. And the insignia, the symbol of Horrag, he lives west of here. Must have headed east. Did not encounter them, so headed northeast. Closest settlement that way is Vekketar. About a day's march." Kurra sketched a map in the dirt.

Lacking other leads, we headed to Vekketar, arriving early the next morning. Much like Zerrekdar, the town's architects clearly were more interested in construction than maintenance, from the tall, crumbling walls to the extensive roads, riddled with potholes. We scanned the city, looking for any sign of the Triune's agents.

What we found was a public execution. A number of people, mostly orcs but also a human and a couple of halflings, were being dragged towards a stage in the middle of a crowd. Atop the stage was a large orc, clad head to toe in sable armour, bellowing in orcish.

Kurra looked surprised, hurriedly translating, "They were harbouring escaped slaves. Triune worshippers."

Xeldia already had a hand on her sword. "We need to get them away. And quickly."

Eledine scanned the urban terrain. "One of my smoke pellets should obscure our escape if we hit the alleys. Getting to that point, though…"

I took a deep breath, mustering my courage. "I'll distract."

Xeldia gripped her sword. "Kurra and I will be ready. Eledine, get a vantage on that building to the south. We'll flee in that direction."

We all gave each other an affirmative nod before we made our move. Kurra, Xeldia, and I started moving towards the stage; I found it just a bit easier, as I could slip between people's legs, while Xeldia and Kurra couldn't use their usual forceful personalities without drawing attention to themselves. I managed to slip underneath the stage unnoticed, but by the time I managed that, I lost sight of the others, and the first of the prisoners was on the chopping block. I was out of time.

Through a gap in the stage's floor, I blasted the orc warlord in the face with starlight. He screamed and recoiled. I could hear blades being drawn and finding their targets, as Kurra and Xeldia made their move. Using the stage and its supports for cover, I ducked in and out, blasting the guards with light and void. The hits weren't lethal, but they didn't need to be—the guards were flung into disarray, long enough for Kurra and Xeldia to cut their way on top of the stage and free the prisoners. The warlord had cleared his eyes by this point, but Kurra attacked him with all her might, striking with speed and strength, breaking down his guard with raw rage.

An arrow found its way into my leg. I screamed in pain, dropping to the ground. A large, green hand grabbed me. Kurra's, I hoped. I was wrong. It was a guard, snarling at me.

Xeldia roared, "Perr-ragh!" She shifted mid-yell, turning towards me.

Another guard stepped into her path. She ripped his throat out with her fangs, but a barrage of arrows forced her to duck behind her shield, while Kurra was too busy engaging the warlord. Panic pushed me past my pain, and I cast a spell to sap the strength from the guard's arm before smacking him in the face with my staff, forcing him to drop me.

The other guards had noticed me and weren't happy. I fended off one with more starfire, but the others quickly surrounded me. I froze. Then, Cosma slipped out of my pack. She yipped, and beneath it, I could hear an occult secret, a glimpse into the bindings that tied the universe together. Could things truly be that easy? I tugged on cosmic strings. The force that pulled me to earth vanished. I pushed against the ground and flew.

The guards were understandably surprised at this development, too stunned to stop me. Cosma was less surprised but was still scrambling to get back into my pack before I flew out of reach. Unfortunately, while I was out of reach of melee attacks, archers still had a bead on me, and I quickly had to muster what magic I had left to avoid being turned into a pincushion.

My new vantage let me easily see Xeldia lead the prisoners through the crowd. None of the civilians wanted to get in the way of a beastwoman in gleaming armour, glowing with holy light, so she faced little opposition. A priest of the orc's war god, Kornar, healed and rallied the wounded guards, but Kurra was holding the rear against them. She had taken a few deep cuts but barely seemed to notice in her battle rage. Eledine was perched on a roof, supporting us with longbow fire. Arranging the forces of gravity like reefing a sail, I propelled myself towards her.

Another arrow struck me in the chest, the warding spells on my robes just barely enough to stop the shot from being lethal. The impact knocked me off course. I gritted my teeth, struggling to breathe. I needed help. I allowed gravity to return to me, trying to land near Eledine. But, in my panic, I misjudged how far the arrow had knocked me, and I stumbled off the side of the building. I managed to roll into the landing, but it was still enough to daze me.

As I struggled to get up, I felt life magics flow into me, clearing my head and easing my wounds. I looked up, expecting to see Xeldia, but it was one of the prisoners, channelling blessed magics. Surprising, but hardly unwelcome. As I got to my feet, Xeldia, Kurra, and the prisoners reached the alley. Eledine dropped her smoke bomb. Xeldia quickly started leading the procession through the winding alleys. We hadn't had the time to plan a route, but simply started taking turns, hoping to lose the guards in the maze.

Eventually, we found ourselves between some warehouses and some crates. We all took cover, trying to catch our breath as silently as we could, trying to hear over the thundering of our hearts for approaching guards. As seconds turned to minutes, we finally seemed to have lost them.

The prisoner who had healed me, a relatively short orc woman, beamed at Xeldia with delight. "It's you! Oh, Raiya be praised!"

"You know me?"

"You might not remember; I was at the temple when you first visited, when Orreke led us. That was just before I was granted my powers. My name's Kellet," she explained.

Xeldia asked, "What happened in the temple?"

"Karnor's warband attacked us, entirely without warning. It…it was a massacre. Half of us managed to escape, only because Orlar held them off, but gave his own life doing so. We headed south and stumbled on a small village named Huret. They had a disease, but Hora was able to cure it with Ynnelia's power, so they accepted us. We settled there and decided to start spreading again. I came here to help those I could with my blessing. As you can see, the local warlord took exception to that. But what of Orreke? She spoke with the Herald herself, didn't she?"

Xeldia sighed. "She did. But that was before we discovered…" She handed Kellet the scroll detailing the Herald's dismissal. As Kellet read it, Xeldia explained, "We think *she* caused the Ioran Heresy to cover up the fact that she was dismissed. She's gained immortality through some other means, and she's spent the last five hundred years covering her tracks. It's been months; Orreke is no doubt dead by now. But we were hoping to find you and her other followers. We can't allow the Herald to maintain her control, but removing her will be no small feat. We had hoped we could start gathering support with you."

"That's…I'll take you back to Huret, where the rest of us are. Hora should know about all this," replied Kellet.

Getting out of the city proved to be something of a challenge, considering that our party consisted of over a dozen fugitives. Eledine, Cosma, and I scouted the city for exits. We eventually found a rusted grate that covered the river that flowed through the city. The river was full of trash, but we didn't have any other options. After some debate, we planned to move during the night, hoping that we wouldn't run into any guard patrols. Supply was also a difficult problem, but Xeldia realised that she'd be much more difficult to recognise without her heavy armour, and her skin tone was relatively common for humans in the region, so she was able to go shopping.

When the time came to move, Cosma was able to scout ahead for guard patrols and moved us easily around them. We reached the grate without trouble. The grate was easily ripped off in what was an impressive feat of strength by Kurra (my desire to fawn over the feat very much muted by the trash floating around her), and one by one, we slipped through, then slipped into the night.

Chapter 19

We reached Huret a couple of days later. It was a small, squat hamlet, but there seemed to be relative prosperity, the buildings in good condition, and the crops well-tended. Kellet led us to a building that seemed to have been freshly converted into a church of the Triune. She happily greeted an orc that I recognised from our first trip to the region, one of Orreke's acolytes.

She greeted us in turn. "Paladin Xeldia! What brings you all the way back here?"

Xeldia's expression was grave. "Grim news, and high stakes. We have much to discuss."

The orc, Hora, sat down with us, and we explained everything that had happened since we last met. Her eyes were wide the entire time. When we finished, there was a long silence.

Hora was clearly struggling to process everything. "You… seek to topple the entire church? I'm not sure how much help I can be."

Xeldia nodded. "A great task, but we need not do it alone. None need to work alone. That is why the Triune stand together—as a reminder for all of us to do the same. The first step will be to start spreading the truth to the faithful; when they know that the Herald does not truly serve the Triune, they will abandon her."

"How much help will that be? If she's got the kind of power you say she does, she won't need their support—or rather, any support she needs, she can force." Hora sighed, looking out the window.

Eledine looked thoughtful. "I'm not so certain about that second part. Certainly, if even half the stories about the Herald and her most trusted agents are true, no one can match them one-on-one. But who says we have to fight on their terms? At Kessedarn, we only had half-starved prisoners, but that was enough, when we outnumbered them five to one. Not that building an army is going to be simple, but it's an achievable goal."

"An army…" Hora thought for a while. "Do you really think you can do that?"

"Well, we have a fully trained and blessed paladin, a veteran orc warrior, some occult powers, scattered supporters, and some gold." Eledine counted the items off on her fingers. "Not an army, yet. But assets. We just need to start growing them."

Kurra added, "And we start that here. Church can't reach you here; can speak openly. Start spreading the word. And start building resources."

Hora frowned. "We're speaking of a war, here. I…listen, I need time to think. And to plan. And I think you could use some time to rest."

"Hmph. Doubt the Herald will rest." Kurra scoffed.

Xeldia said, "You'd be surprised. I understand the whole point of high rank is avoiding doing work. And we're well and truly out of the inquisition's sphere of influence, now. It's past time we're not marching or constantly on guard."

Eledine sighed in relief. "I have to concur. Frankly, I'm surprised anyone can fight in this heat. Perhaps once we've had some time to relax, we'll be better able to come up with a plan."

As evening started to fall, I stood on a nearby ridge, gazing at the stars with my telescope, occasionally taking notes as I watched the constellations shift. The other three casually walked up.

Eledine followed my gaze. "Stars doing anything interesting tonight?"

I nodded enthusiastically. "Stars are in slightly different positions in different places! Look!" I held up my books full of astronomy knowledge and quickly launched into an explanation of the movements of planets and stars. The others sat and listened. How much of my explanation they understood and would retain wasn't something I was sure about, but I enjoyed giving the explanation, and they enjoyed listening.

Midway through, I scanned the stars and found my star again. The face had returned and was looking at me, happy. I squealed in delight. "It's her! The star!" I held the spyglass in position, stepping aside so my companions could look.

Eledine approached. "The star that gave you your powers, and our furry friend?" She knelt to look through the spyglass. Her eyebrows rose. "Well. Hello there."

After looking for a moment, she stepped aside so Kurra could have a look. No one was exactly sure how to address a star, so she and Xeldia looked, expressed some combination of surprise, awe, and respect, before stepping aside.

Xeldia looked up at the sky with relative awkwardness. "Good star, I'm not sure if you can even hear us from all the way over there, but thank you for your help."

The next morning, we met up with Hora for something like a war council. She was examining some maps when we entered. "I have been thinking," she said. "There's only so much I can do without drawing the ire of Kornar's followers, but it is perhaps more than I first thought. There is little love for the god of war among those who cannot fight."

Eledine sat down at the planning table. "Honestly, I wasn't expecting to engage in direct battle for a long while yet, so we don't need warriors."

"And that got me thinking—you also can start with those already disillusioned by the church. Like those in the Reborn Colonies. They are all in places difficult to reach; if you can stage more rebellions, you will have defensible positions." Hora gestured to the colonies' locations on the map.

Xeldia leaned over the map, thinking. "It will not be easy. Our first rebellion succeeded, in no small part, because we had caught the garrison completely off guard. Further rebellions will not be so easy."

Kurra laughed. "None of this will be easy. Will succeed anyway!"

"There is also the matter of spreading word of the Herald's treason to the rest of the faithful. The colonies will not help us there —colonists have reputations as madmen," Xeldia said.

Hora's eyes flashed with resolve. "My followers and I can do that. A number of us have been blessed; we can see the power in the pronouncement's seal, and we can start spreading word."

Eledine nodded, but her expression was grim. "The inquisition won't like that. I suggest spreading out and staying on the move. Hopefully, pockets of resistance will start to grow faster than the church can stamp them out. But the fact of the matter is, more than one of your agents will have to pay the price."

Hora gently touched her symbol of Ynnelia. "Then may the Triune keep our souls."

Kurra scanned the map. "So, we have strategy. Turn that into our next move. Begin deploying your agents—need to choose a colony to liberate. What about this one? Sunebarn Island?"

Xeldia paced around the room. "A plantation colony mainly grows food to be sent back to the mainland. Not much of a fortress."

Eledine raised her eyebrows. "Xeldia, you may have forgotten that an army marches on its stomach. Having a plantation like that will be a significant asset. Though that does raise the question of how to defend it; we don't exactly have a navy."

Kurra gestured to a nearby Uluzar port town. "Know a man —Captain Drekker of the Blue Fang. Pirate, but man of his word. If plantation gives him tribute, he'll keep church away."

"I can't say I'm entirely keen on dealing with a pirate, but we don't have an abundance of options. Very well. But before we go farther, we need a plan to liberate the place. Xeldia, do you know anything about their defences?" Eledine asked.

I could see Xeldia doing some mental arithmetic before she responded.."A sizeable garrison, and at least one combat-capable ship. I had a friend tho served in a similar plantation –the only docks on the island were heavily fortified, but not the rest of the island. The waters kept the colonists in. There will be watchtowers scattered around the island, however."

"Well, an attack plan can wait until we've actually seen the place. Let's start on a higher level. We need to get an army of prisoners to turn on their guards and make sure as few as possible die in the fighting. To do that, we'll need to coordinate and ideally arm them without raising suspicion from the garrison. How do we do that?"

Everyone was silent for a minute, trying to think of ideas. I already had one, but it took me that minute to muster my courage. "I could do it." Everyone looked at me. "I can turn invisible. Help the prisoners. Spread word. I'm sneaky."

Xeldia shifted uncomfortably. "I'm not eager to see you off on your own."

Eledine took a deep breath. "I'm not eager either, Xeldia, but while she's a halfling, she's an adult. And we've all seen what she's capable of. She's, quite simply, the best infiltrator we have."

The first step of our plan was meeting with Captain Drekker. That involved heading to a seedy Uluzar port town and talking with some seedy people. Fortunately, Kurra and Xeldia were, between them, more than intimidating enough to stop anyone from trying to take advantage of us. We learned that Drekker was out sailing but was expected to return soon. We occupied ourselves with helping Hora recruit more followers among those dissatisfied with the status quo. It was easier than one might expect—among those who couldn't count on those in power, agreements to count on one another were appealing. Then, we received worrying word: Another captain was boasting about sabotaging Drekker's ship and leaving him as bait for the Delsward navy.

We were a couple of days into gathering intelligence for a rescue mission when we learned that Drekker managed to escape on a captured Delsward ship, along with the bulk of his crew. He arrived in town the next day, and we eventually managed to find him in the least seedy of the town's bars. He was short by orc standards, but with a layer of scarred muscle. He was shirtless, wearing only light pants and a leather bandoleer containing some flintlock pistols.

Xeldia, as usual, was the face of the party. "Captain Drekker?"

Drekker glared at us suspiciously. "Whadd'ya want?"

"We've heard you're a man of integrity. I—"

"Don't even think about rubbing it in, pinkskin!" Drekker snarled.

Xeldia held up her hands in a placating gesture. "My apologies, I did not mean offence. I'm afraid I don't know the details regarding your recent betrayal, but I won't pry."

Drekker sighed. "Three ships, loot split three ways. It was my crew that found the ship's hold. But I kept my word—three ships, loot split evenly three ways. And what did I get for doing the right thing? Making backstabbing me easier."

"I am sorry to hear that. But I am an agent of Raiya, and you have my word. I have no intention of betraying you," Xeldia said coolly.

Drekker's eyes narrowed. "And what does Heartshold want with me?"

"I am no longer serving the church. It is a lengthy tale, but I have discovered that the church does not truly serve the Triune's interests. And so, I am working against them."

Drekker leaned forward. "Alright, my curiosity has overpowered my desire to tell you to fuck off. What *do* you want?"

Xeldia leaned forward and whispered, "You help us take and keep control of the reborn colony of Sunebarn Island. In exchange, we will ensure it gives you regular tribute."

Drekker thought for a minute. Finally, he whispered back, "I'm interested. But the price will be a bit more than tribute."

Xeldia gestured for him to continue.

"Revenge," he said.

Chapter 20

Captain Bledd, of the Sandshard, was the captain who had planned the betrayal, and after he learned that Captain Drekker had survived, had gone to ground. Fortunately, Uluzar streets were littered with the downtrodden, and a little charity loosened tongues quickly. We managed to locate the Sandshard, and from there, a vagrant was happy to point out a member of Bledd's crew. Cosma was able to tail that crewman to another, and that one to a camp outside town.

Night fell, and the four of us approached, along with Drekker and a pair of his most trusted marines. We slipped into some shrubbery just far away enough that we could see the campfire. From there, I went ahead to scout, my magic shielding me from sight. There were at least a dozen orc pirates in the camp. Bledd was pretty easy to recognise, his face covered in intricate tattoos and a stressed expression. I slipped past the sentries to where he was talking with some of his men.

One was saying, "…and I've seen him snooping around the ship. He's coming after us, alright."

Another added, "And I've seen him talking with his crew. He's going to track us down, sooner or later."

Bledd snarled. "Alright. Then we count on that. Here's what we do." He started sketching a map in the dirt.

I crept closer, hoping my invisibility would hold for long enough.

"If he wants to come at us, he'll have to come through—" He suddenly stopped, looking at my feet. As he drew his sword, I suddenly realised that the invisibility spell didn't extend to my footprints.

He swung at me. Thankfully, he was counting on a human-sized opponent, so the strike did nothing but knock my hat off. I quickly grabbed it, turned, and ran.

Bledd shouted, "Invisible spy! Get it!"

The sentries quickly surrounded me. But between my small size and my invisibility, they weren't able to contain me, and I managed to slip between them.

I heard one nearby utter a prayer in the orc tongue. A wave of divine power flowed over the camp. My spell construct warped and failed. I was visible and in sight of a dozen angry orcs. Thinking quickly, I blasted the closest ones with blinding light, doubly effective in the darkness. But they were spread out enough that there were still half a dozen pirates coming for me. I turned and fled as fast as my little legs could carry me. Which wasn't remotely fast enough, and I was quickly tackled by one of the sentries. I slipped out from underneath him, but the delay had given the other orcs time enough to catch up.

With no other way to flee, I cast my flight spell again, inverting gravity, so I was propelled upwards. Bledd managed to give me a nasty cut to the face as I flew, and a crossbow bolt sank deep into my leg. Gritting my teeth against the pain, I kept flying. Once I was at long range for the bolts, I turned and flew back to where my party was waiting.

It turned out that either someone had gotten bored of waiting or had seen that I was in danger, and the rest of my party was sprinting to intervene. Bledd's crew saw them and quickly regrouped to face them. Kurra was the first into the fray, leaping into the middle in a storm of steel. Some pirates tried to flank her, but Xeldia was quick to her side, the pair fighting back-to-back. As Drekker and his crew moved into the fight, an orc wizard emerged from a tent and turned his magic against them. Frost built on their limbs, slowing their movement and strikes.

I landed beside Eledine, who was struggling to pick targets in the melee. Seeing me, she quickly handed me a vial. "Here, this will keep you going until I can get a closer look." As I skulled it down, she handed me a second vial. "And, while you're flying, drop this on that spellcaster in the rear."

I happily did just that. It took a bit of manoeuvring, and another bolt came terrifyingly close to hitting me, but the darkness of night was just enough cover for me to fly above the enemy wizard and drop Eledine's vial. I was a little off target, but some of the fluid landed on his robes, which caused them to ignite. He quickly turned his attention to putting them out. It would be a short distraction, but hopefully enough.

In the meantime, Xeldia and Kurra were fighting hard against the pirates, Xeldia in a fierce duel with Bledd himself. They were badly outnumbered, so I turned my magic to their aid. A blast of light here and some ice-cold darkness there took one or two of the warriors out of the fight, giving Kurra just enough of an advantage to press, cutting down the pirates.

But Bledd was a different story. He was lightning-fast with a pair of cutlasses of such fine steel that even Xeldia's holy protections couldn't keep up. I turned the power of the void into sapping his strength, but my magic glanced off his warding tattoos. Kurra was busy with the pirates, too busy to intervene, when a sudden flick of the blade carved a deep gash into Xeldia's arm, forcing her to drop her sword.

Xeldia persisted, fighting with just her shield. She went back on the offensive with a hard shield bash. The unexpected move pushed Bledd back a few steps, but he quickly recovered, moving to slip under Xeldia's guard. She quickly fended him off with a kick, moving to slam down the shield on him. He evaded at the last second, using one hand to keep the shield locked to the ground, the other coming down on Xeldia.

Then Drekker pushed past the cold that had bound him, pulling a pistol and landing a shot right in Bledd's exposed belly. As the other captain staggered back, Drekker pulled another pistol, firing another shot, this one knocking Bledd down. Drekker rushed over to him, standing over him with a knife. He taunted in the orc tongue, taking his time as he repeatedly stabbed the man who betrayed him.

Whatever loyalty Bledd's crew had wasn't enough to keep them in a fight that they had clearly lost. Those who still could fled. Those that could surrendered, begging for mercy. Drekker's crew looked at their captain for orders, which weren't fast in coming, as he was busy ensuring Bledd died a painful death. Meanwhile, the rest of us queued up in front of Eledine, all eager for some medical attention.

Once Drekker had the survivors of Bledd's crew captured for slaves, he approached the rest of us. "That's your end of the bargain. Now for mine."

The Blue Fang had been sunk, but Drekker had commandeered a small Delsward carrack called the Will of St. Raiden. This proved to be a blessing, as it would allow us to get closer to Sunebarn Island with less alarm than a ship of orc construction. After stealing Bledd's belongings (after Xeldia talked him into giving us a cut), Drekker was quickly able to replace casualties in his crew, and the Will made good time.

When the island appeared on the horizon, Drekker turned the Will about and sailed right to its edge before dropping anchor. When night fell, we took a skiff towards the island. As predicted, watchtowers dotted the coastline, but cloudy weather and Drekker's keen eyes spying a blind spot allowed us to reach the shore with reasonable confidence that we hadn't been spotted.

As I hopped off, with plans to rendezvous the next night, Xeldia whispered, "Be careful, my friend. I…this mission will be dangerous."

I mustered my resolve, gave her a nod, and slipped off into the night.

The island was mostly covered by plantations of exotic trees planted in thick rows. I picked my way through, slowly and carefully, with only the tiniest shred of starlight I could risk to see by. The walk itself wasn't too hard; the marches of the last few months had proven to be great practice. But what strained me was the tension—a guard could come walking from any direction, to say nothing of island wildlife, and how much warning would I have? Nevertheless, I pressed on.

After far too long, or perhaps just too long for me, I reached the compound that housed the colony's prisoners. Guards patrolled the perimeter, but they didn't even look in my direction, expecting any trouble to come from within. Slowly and carefully, I scouted. I took note of guard patrols, shift changes, and the layout of the compound. Once I had all the information I felt like I could get, I slipped back into the night, finding a sheltered nook to hide in while I got a little sleep.

Dawn arrived, and it was time to get to work, both for the prisoners and me. I watched from the shadows as they were marched off to work, hundreds digging into the earth, pulling at weeds, carefully pruning the trees, gathering their fruit, all the while having whips at their back. I ached at the sight. I forced myself to focus—I'd be able to help them all, with just a little patience.

I watched as one unfortunate prisoner stumbled, dropping a full box of fruit. The nearest guard snapped, "Useless wretch!" before grabbing the prisoner and pushing him up against a nearby rock. The guard pulled out a sap and started to viciously beat the prisoner.

I had an idea and whispered it to Cosma. The fox snickered in approval before slipping off. I slunk behind the rock. As the guard yelled abuse at the prisoner, Cosma bit into his heel. The guard swore in anger, quickly turning to get himself a fur coat, but Cosma was already disappearing into the underbrush.

As the guard pursued, I peered over the rock and whispered to the prisoner, "Riot when the wolf howls; it will be bringing weapons. Tell those you trust."

We had planned ahead of time to use Xeldia's beast howl as a signal to start the riot; a specific time would be too easy to disrupt if someone snitched. The prisoner looked at me with surprise. I gave him a nod before slipping back into cover.

Cosma quickly regrouped with me, tail wagging from the mischief. By the time the guard gave up the chase and returned to his post, he'd entirely forgotten about the prisoner's mistake, and it was back to business as usual for the colony.

I kept subtly helping the prisoners where I could. A distracted guard here, a cooling spell there, and when I did, I whispered those words to the prisoners I helped. By the time night fell, guards were starting to gossip about the spooky goings on in the colony. Meanwhile, I sent Cosma to the rendezvous with a report on my progress. I took the chance to get a closer look at the interior of the colony's fort. Not an easy task, but between my invisibility spells, my skill at picking locks, and my small size, none of the guards saw anything they couldn't explain with the wind and a few rats.

As I got some rest that night, it occurred to me just how much I'd grown to rely on having the others around me. I always felt that much safer, knowing that I could always count on Kurra's brawn, Eledine's genius, or Xeldia's faith to protect me when things got complicated. And more than that, they were good company. They were always happy to listen to me ramble about stars, and they never pressed me for more talking than I wished. I was comfortable around them. Now, I was alone.

Chapter 21

The second day dawned, and I kept up the work. I shared my rations with a few starving prisoners and gave some of Eledine's elixirs to the sick and injured. I also kept up my notes on the guard's patrols and defences and managed to see a blind spot or three, inevitable with all the trees blocking sight and prisoners to control. Our little revolution was shaping up nicely.

In the afternoon, I overheard a courier who'd approached one of the guard's lieutenants. "Sir? Captain Sidren's calling a meeting in the evening, just before dinner. Her office. High priority."

That raised my interest—and my concern. Had I been detected already?

As the day wore on, I slipped into the fort. It was straightforward enough to find the captain's office, and I managed to find a nearby cupboard in which I could hide until the meeting. The hour was easy to identify, but I had to wait for the sudden burst of traffic to die down before I could listen in.

The first voice, whom I presumed was Captain Sidren, addressed the assembled. "Alright, listen up. We have word that the colonists are preparing a riot. According to our sources, the signal is a wolf's howl, and the 'wolf' will be bringing weapons. Now, I'm not sure if it's a literal wolf's howl, Ynnelia only knows how they'd get one up here, but that's what we're hearing. What's interesting is who's organising it—I'm hearing of a red-haired halfling woman snooping around the area and not in a prisoner's uniform. I'm also hearing rumours of hauntings and random curses on guards. I can't say for certain what it is, but until I hear more information, we're going to assume there's a hostile halfling spellcaster here. Sergeant Venns, anyone missing from the roll?"

A second voice: "No, ma'am. No one who fits the description has been to the colony in months. She must have slipped in on a supply boat."

A third: "If I may, ma'am? I've heard reports of a Delsward carrack lurking around the northwest. I don't know whether it's related, but it showed up around the same time all this happened."

The captain: "That doesn't strike me as a coincidence. Get a patrol ship to take a closer look. In the meantime, I want everyone to be prepared for a riot. As soon as we hear a wolf's howl, we lock down and go on full alert. When that happens, the central garrison will immediately deploy to where the signal came from to secure any arms stashes. Everyone else will focus on keeping these wretches in line. In the meantime, Lieutenant Hans, you're in charge of finding this halfling. I'm granting you all non-critical personnel at your disposal. I want this woman found, understood?"

A fourth: "Yes, ma'am."

Ill news, but at least I was forewarned. I slipped away and headed back to the rendezvous. I reached it with time to spare and was able to watch the faint shadow of the skiff as it arrived on shore. Kurra, Eledine, and Xeldia were all there, plus some of Drekker's crew. I hurriedly briefed them on the situation.

Kurra growled. "Someone snitched."

Eledine's expression was as analytical as always. "That was almost inevitable. At least we know what their response will be. Excellent work, Peri."

This caused something to click in Kurra's mind. "Hmm…we do know…" She grabbed a lantern and used it to illuminate a crude diagram she drew in the sand. "Plan: Xeldia, you give signal, then fall back. Draw out garrison. Then, Drekker and crew take fort while it's vulnerable. Leave them out in open."

Xeldia rubbed her chin. "That kind of manoeuvring will be difficult to coordinate with the prisoners."

"You did as much without speaking at Kessedarn! Will be easy!" Kurra gave Xeldia a firm pat on the back.

"I suppose I did. Very well. But that also leaves the question of what we will do about the Will. We need to be prepared to handle the incoming patrol. I don't doubt we could fight them, but that would raise too much suspicion." Xeldia's gaze wandered aimlessly across the dark shadow of the sea.

Eledine leaned forward. "How much authority does a paladin have in the church? You have a captain's armour, and you've always had one's demeanour. Could you simply tell them to —what's the military phrase? Fuck off?"

"I do not like lying, but I don't see any alternative. Very well. And Peri, if you"—Xeldia, uncharacteristically, choked—"if you get captured, remain calm. We *will* rescue you."

It was reassuring. I kept up with my part of the plan, from here on out replacing "tell those you trust" with "spread the word," since the plan had already been leaked to the guards. I made my own moves more cautiously; with the guards now actively looking for me, I had to choose my targets carefully, keeping to only the most isolated prisoners and guards.

That was until I saw one of the prisoners being beaten by a pair of guards, apparently for "challenging their authority," which, from what I overheard, meant pointing out that prisoners couldn't work infinitely fast. There were more around than I was planning to risk, but I couldn't ignore the prisoner's cries for mercy. Peering out from behind a rock, I blasted their eyes with darkness. Their screams of alarm were hilarious. I whispered to a nearby prisoner who had seen the beating, "Riot when the wolf howls; it will be—"

"There!" One of the guards shouted.

I was made. I turned and dashed through the trees. I considered taking flight, but there wouldn't be much cover there. I could hear at least a dozen guards pursuing me and gaining ground. I had my invisibility spell, but I had learned the hard way that those weren't perfect. I needed some greater cover.

I had an idea. I doubled back, heading back towards the compound. This proved to be not quite as clever as I initially thought, as another guard patrol was advancing towards me. A blinding blast of starlight managed to get me out of that particular mistake, and I managed to weave between their legs into a large crowd of prisoners.

The pursuing guards obviously started to break up the crowd, but that took time, time extended by one or two prisoners deciding to make a fuss. Ducking through the crowd, I managed to slip into a nearby crate. Obvious cover, but it bought me enough time for me to cast an invisibility spell. With that achieved, I headed back into the crowd.

It was then that I discovered just how much of moving through crowds depended on other people being able to see you. I ended up being jostled around more than a little. Still, my plan worked—with so many people around covering my tracks, the guards had little chance of finding me.

One of the guard's lieutenants called out, "Alright, we're locking down! Everyone, back to your bunks!"

The prisoners grumbled, but obeyed, the guards corralling them back towards a large, stone shed. I considered trying to break away, but as I planned my route, I saw some wizards starting to scan the area with magic-detecting spells. They were scanning the areas where the prisoners had left, so staying in the heavy cover of the crowd was the safest option for me.

In my panic, I hadn't thought far enough ahead to consider where the prisoners were being herded *to*, and by the time I did that, everyone was packed tight enough that, even with my small size, I had no hope of manoeuvring. So, I found myself thrown into the bunkhouse with the prisoners.

At least the thick crowd, innumerable pillars, and countless hammocks gave me a decent amount of cover. But I heard the door locked and barred behind me—getting out again wasn't going to be easy, if it was possible at all. And I had to assume the bunks would also be searched, and my invisibility spell wasn't going to last much longer. I needed a place I could properly hole up, and I needed it fast.

Off to the side, I recognised one of the prisoners I'd helped and was currently not being observed by many: a disfigured orc man whom I'd helped by hiding some treats from the guards. A gamble, but so was any approach in this situation. Sneaking up behind a pillar, I dismissed my invisibility. I poked my head out from behind the pillar, offered a strip of jerky, and whispered, "Hide me!"

The orc was surprised but quickly regained his composure. After looking around to check that no one was watching, he stood, picked me up, and tossed me onto a rafter. It was tight, and I had to share it with quite a bit of contraband (including some shivs!), but at least it was hidden. I dropped the jerky to him, which he happily gobbled up. I'd seen the slop the prisoners were fed; my trail rations were a delicacy in comparison.

I did my best to get comfortable. After fifteen minutes, I managed to find a position where I wasn't at risk of accidentally impaling myself on a shiv, so I called that a victory. What followed was a long and unpleasant wait as the guards scoured the area for me. In that moment, the bunkhouse itself was the worst, by a long shot, but the hiding spot held. Once the guards had left, I left a little more jerky on the prisoner's bunk.

That's how I spent the bulk of the following night. I probed the area for an escape route, but the bunkhouse was locked tight, and the guards were on high alert. I didn't even want to risk Cosma by sending her to the rendezvous. I knew that when I failed to arrive, the others would start the riot the following day. I had to hope enough of the prisoners were prepared to make this a success.

After a long and painful night, dawn came. The guards lifted the lockdown, and the prisoners filed out for another long day of labour. They had seemed to have decided they'd lost my trail, so I was able to restore my invisibility and slip out. Yesterday's close call wasn't terribly good for my morale, but I was determined to make sure the prisoners were as prepared as possible for the impending fight.

I had a plan to help the prisoners get a little more breakfast, but the guards were still on high alert, and one of the wizards was patrolling the area, regularly casting divination spells. I spent breakfast hiding under a table.

The prisoners were halfway through leaving when Xeldia's howl resounded across the island.

The guards called, "Lockdown! Lockdown! Everyone back to the bunkhouse!"

Some of the prisoners looked like they were obeying, but a large mob rushed the guards, managing to overpower one or two before the others had time to react. In a stroke of luck, a number of the prisoners were right on top of the cutlery; not exactly proper weapons, but in this situation, that little bit was better than nothing.

The guards, having expected this, quickly rallied, a squad swiftly forming a shield wall by the exit to the guest house. The tight formation held well against the mob. But it left them wide open to a blast of starlight, which blinded the lot of them. The rioting mob was happy to capitalise on the advantage, swiftly overwhelming the formation, stealing their weapons, and fighting their way out. I continued to help the fight; the time for stealth was over.

The riot spilled out of the mess hall, and the prisoners rushed to where Xeldia was calling. I followed them. Looking back, I could see the garrison marching out of the fort. I picked up the pace, hoping the plan would work.

We reached the plantations, but the guards were gaining ground rapidly. Deciding it wasn't helpful for me to try outrunning them, I changed my tactic, taking flight and harrying the vanguard with magic as I wove between the trees. It had the desired effect, forcing them into a more defensive formation, giving the prisoners that extra time. It also had the effect of causing them to fire a few volleys of crossbow bolts at me, but my magical shielding and the cover of the trees saved me from taking any serious hits.

I continued to skirmish with the guards through the plantation, the thick trees denying them the chance to form a strong formation. It wasn't long before I found Xeldia standing amidst a collection of swords, shields, crossbows, and bolts, gleaming with holy light.

She held her sword high. "Free men, to me!"

The sight of weapons gave the prisoners that last burst of energy, and they sprinted towards their prizes. Each grabbed whatever was closest before turning and facing their captors. Xeldia immediately started directing them, ordering the prisoners here and there, drawing the guards out farther. Her voice was clear and commanding, and few of the prisoners doubted her.

Of course, that made her an obvious target. The guards charged forward, led by a woman who could only be Captain Sidren, a large woman with a banner on her back and swinging a warhammer. She was the tip of the spear, driving the prisoners back. It was only a matter of time before Xeldia had given all the ground she could afford to. So, she stood her ground and faced Sidren.

Sidren was fast and quickly landed a hit that sent Xeldia flying and might have killed her were it not for her divine shield. I wasn't about to simply let Sidren do as she would, quickly drawing upon my power to drain her strength.

She swore as she faltered with her hammer. "Someone kill that damn witch!"

I narrowly avoided another flurry of bolts. Things might have gotten complicated, but I managed to position a solid tree between myself and the guards. With the riot going on all around us, none of them could reposition to get a shot at me. So, I was safe to cast darkness at Sidren's eyes.

For all I'd sapped her strength, Sidren held on well, managing to fight with hearing and instinct. But Xeldia was a skilled warrior, and with Sidren weakened, it was only a matter of time until she brought her down. When she did, Xeldia immediately rallied the prisoners around her and launched a counterattack, driving a wedge through the guards' ranks. Split up and scattered, they fell back to the fort.

I was concerned when the gates to the fort opened for the guards. Much less so when Kurra leapt down from on high, catching her enemies completely off guard and slaughtering them with terrifying speed, Drekker's pirates alongside her. When they realised what had happened, the remaining guards threw their weapons on the ground in surrender.

The second the fight was over, Kurra rushed up to me, scooping me up in a tight hug. "Peri! You're alright!"

I wanted to explain why I hadn't made the rendezvous, but Kurra had crushed all the air out of my lungs, so I simply hugged back. Eledine had also arrived. She was busy treating the innumerable wounded, but I could see from her expression that she was also deeply relieved to see that I was alright.

Xeldia got to work assembling the former prisoners and making sure they didn't get carried away with their revenge. I didn't envy her; the prisoners had been badly abused and were understandably angry and mistrustful of authority. After establishing something that would hopefully serve as a government, Xeldia helped them make an arrangement with Captain Drekker for his protection. The colony would still have to export food as a trade resource, but not to the absurd degree that the church had been demanding of them.

This time, Eledine proved to be a bit more patient with those scared of her strange alchemy, taking time to explain the mechanisms behind her elixirs, and a few words from Xeldia calmed many of those left. There were still one or two who were too scared to approach Eledine, but most were able to swallow their fears enough to get their wounds tended.

While the others settled all that, I took some much-needed time to relax. Being in enemy territory for days straight was tiresome, and a nap curled up in the safety of Kurra's pack was exactly what I needed. I didn't realise just how tense I'd become until I finally had a chance to rest.

By the time Xeldia was confident that the newly liberated colonists wouldn't immediately rip themselves apart in infighting, night had fallen, and everyone was much too tired to begin planning another move. Since I'd already caught up on my sleep, I could spend plenty of time studying the stars. Cosma insisted I spend some time painting some stellar diagrams on the fort's roof, and her tail proved to be a surprisingly effective brush.

Chapter 22

We were interrupted by a bright light streaming in through the window. I peered out to see an enormous, multicoloured column of light in the distant northeast, shooting up from somewhere across the horizon. I peered through my spyglass, trying to make heads or tails of it.

It wasn't long before I was joined by Xeldia, which was surprising, as I expected her to be sleeping after a lengthy battle and even lengthier talks. "Peri. That light, is it something you're familiar with?"

I shook my head. I could tell that it meant at least a *little* more to her than it did to me, but she didn't elaborate.

She looked at it for another moment before saying, "I need a map."

She headed down to the fort's command centre, Cosma and I following her, and started rifling through the fort's paperwork, eventually finding a map. She laid it on a table, and I illuminated it with my magic. She placed a finger on Sunebarn Island. "We're here, yes? Which direction is that light in? As precisely as you can, please."

I scurried up to the roof, comparing the columns' location to that of the various celestial phenomena and doing some maths. I returned to the command centre to find Xeldia talking to Drekker's navigator, who was also curious as to the nature of the light and was happy to break out his compass.

From that, Xeldia had drawn a line on the map in the direction of the light and had circled somewhere it had crossed. She looked up at me as I entered and said, "Mount Kairyss."

The navigator blinked. "You're getting that just from the direction?"

"Not just from the direction. It is holy in nature; I can feel it. And Mount Kairyss is said to be the very place the Triune first came down," Xeldia explained.

Cosma suddenly jumped on top of the map, giggling excitedly, tail wagging.

Xeldia raised her eyebrows. "You want to see Mount Kairyss, too?" Cosma yapped affirmatively. "Then we prepare to move first thing in the morning."

By the time day broke, the light had faded, but word of it had spread like wildfire. Everyone was speculating as to its meaning, coming up with very little of substance. As soon as breakfast was finished, Xeldia called Eledine, Kurra, Drekker, and me to a meeting in the command centre.

When we arrived, she was standing over the map, her eyes glimmering with holy light. "The Triune placed that light, and it came from Mount Kairyss. I am certain we are being called there. I can feel the Triune speaking to my soul."

Eledine said, "Well, we previously took a days-long detour on the insistence of a fox, and that actually turned out rather interesting. I suppose we could follow this…'lead.'"

I added, "Cosma also wants to go."

"Well, there we have it. Anyway, what do you know of Mount Kairyss?"

Xeldia explained, "It is a barred place; the Herald claims it is to protect the sanctity of the site. There is a small garrison surrounding the base. Beyond that? No one knows for certain; only that it is the most holy site in the world."

Kurra scowled. "Garrison will have seen the light. The Herald herself, possibly. Will be there before us. But...the mountain. Is it big?"

"Uh, yes, I believe so. It can be seen from a great distance, and it is said that the highest peaks are dusted with snow all year."

Kurra calmed a little. "Very hard to move large forces up a mountain. Very hard to move up a mountain at all. Very breath can betray you, to say nothing of the nightmare of maintaining supplies. At least we will only have to fight small parties. Will need to prepare."

Kurra turned out to have some mountaineering experience and knew what kind of things we'd need. She also hired a few extra hands from the liberated colonists—apparently, the logistics of mountaineering demanded a supply train, even for a party as small as ours.

Drekker was understandably sceptical of our plans, but since we'd scored him a stable source of income (something very rare for a pirate), he was willing to at least give us transport back to the mainland, from where we could launch our expedition. Once there, we did our best to keep a low profile, not that that was easy with a woman as tall as Kurra around. Xeldia did manage to check on some of her church contacts, which told her the Herald was mustering a large expedition to the mountain.

Gathering supplies and travel took about a week. The deepest part of summer had waned by that point, the weather warm but no longer oppressively so, especially now that we were out of the tropical deserts of Uluzar. Meanwhile, Cosma started teaching me deeper occult secrets, such as how the power of the stars could bend space and time itself.

We saw Mount Kairyss long before we reached it. The closer we got, the less keen I was about climbing it; it was *immense*, its upper reaches seeming to stretch past the clouds themselves. Truly, the Kurra of mountains. When we approached the base, the others agreed that it was time for a scouting mission, especially with a larger party, and that Cosma and I had spent plenty of time in Kurra's pack. So, I headed out, sticking to the tightly packed trees dotting the sides of the path.

It was good that I did because it wasn't long before I had eyes on half an army. Around a small watchtower, clearly the small permanent garrison, hundreds of soldiers were camped. There was a large mix of insignia; the force seemed to have been pulled from a large array of sources. Curious, I slipped closer, my invisibility easily getting me past the outer layer of sentries.

I headed to the watchtower, guessing that whoever was in charge would use it as a command centre. I was either right or close to it, as I discovered dozens of sentries patrolling the area, including wizards casting magic detection spells and war dogs that wouldn't be fooled by my invisibility. After briefly deliberating, I figured it wasn't worth the risk to move farther, at least at this stage.

Then I saw one of the soldiers, a high-ranking knight, I judged from the enchantments on his armour, leave the command post, looking frustrated. Hoping to get *something*, I followed. The knight headed to a section of the camp where a few dozen soldiers flying the same colours milled around. They offered salutes as he approached.

One, a lieutenant I guessed, asked, "Any news?"

"Not a bit. Command's lips are shut tight. A whole bunch of inquisitors have shown up, and they're the only ones allowed up. But apparently the Herald is sending an Anointed to take over the whole operation, so whatever this is, it's important." The knight sounded frustrated.

Another soldier stood. "No one's going after the scouts?"

"The inquisitor mentioned they'll keep an eye out. So, no."

I hurried back to my waiting companions and explained what I'd found out.

Xeldia grimaced. "The Anointed are the Herald's most trusted lieutenants, each hand-picked by and answering only to her."

Eledine simply said, "Well, at least we know we're in the right place."

Kurra's attention was on the mountain itself. "Cannot surround entire mountain. Will find a way up."

Xeldia took our hirelings and led them into cover, while the other three of us started scouting the mountain itself. Kurra was right, and I quickly found a hidden path a decent distance from any sentries. It didn't have sentries because it was horrifically inconvenient, involving more than a bit of rock climbing and a few thick bushes of brambles. Between Kurra's experience and Eledine proving to be a surprisingly canny engineer, we managed to move ourselves and our supplies up to the mountain with the church none the wiser.

We started the long climb up the mountain, scouting routes and establishing supply depots. Kurra found tracks of more than one scouting party, so we made sure to keep alert. Things grew concerning when we found evidence of skirmishes—who were the church's operatives fighting?

My spyglass allowed me to keep half an eye on events around the mountain's base. Which was why I was the first to notice an array of orc banners approaching the mountain. I called to the others, "Orc banners! There!"

None of us was expecting that. Everyone looked to Kurra, who took the spyglass from me. What she saw made her scowl.

"Horrag," she said, "Rotten slave driver. Brutal. Countless slaves. Can move fast. And is girded in ancient magics. Armour from dragonbone, blade of primal metal."

Eledine peered out to the horizon, picking out what few details she could from the great distance. "Well, at least he'll have to go through the church's forces before he reaches us. You have the best view of his forces; what do you think of his chances?"

"Very good. Horrag is greatest of Uluzar warlords. Will gladly sacrifice thousands for what he seeks." Kurra handed me back the spyglass.

Xeldia said, "I am not so certain. The church has a large force, and if an Anointed arrives, even dragonbone won't save him."

Eledine turned to the rest of us. "Regardless, there's not much for us to do about it. We keep a steady pace, and if we encounter Horrag, we'll deal with him then."

We kept climbing. It was long, hard, and slow, involving a lot of coordination with our hirelings, especially since the need for stealth denied us the easiest routes. Hard as it was, it was at least a pleasant change from marching through the Uluzar heat. My ability to fly made it much easier to navigate some of the tighter ridges that formed the long and winding path up, and Cosma's small size let her scout out less stable areas.

The second morning of our expedition, Cosma returned from a scouting trip with alarm. I gently stroked her. "I'll check it out. Wait here."

I kept to cover as Cosma led me near a rise. Peering up and over, I caught sight of a band of church agents. Their equipment and manner varied, clearly a carefully picked party—a couple of heavily armoured knights, a couple of scouts, and a spellcaster or two. I abruptly realised that I had left my tall, pointy hat on when one turned to me, pointing me out. I turned tail.

Luckily, my small size meant that tight ridges weren't quite so tight for me, and I had a decent head start on the other party, so I managed to reach my friends before my pursuers reached me. I managed to squeak out, "Church scouts!" just in time for the first arrow to take the hat off my head.

The two parties leapt into battle. Xeldia charged forward, catching a volley of projectiles on her shield, Kurra right behind her. Eledine and I dived into cover before returning fire with arrows and spells. Kurra was clearly going for a quick victory, fighting fast and aggressively, but her tactics didn't pay off; her enemies quickly outmanoeuvred her and scored a few hits that I was sure Eledine would have some trouble with. Xeldia and Kurra were swiftly surrounded, and while they held their own, their opponents were starting to wear them down.

It was time to give some of my new magics a field test. Calling upon the power of the stars, I felt the currents of space and time. I felt where they flowed around my companions. And, invoking the runes that Cosma taught me, I propelled them forward. Not greatly forward, perhaps, but enough.

Kurra and Xeldia moved faster, quickly outmanoeuvring their foes and overwhelming them with a barrage of blows. Eledine's arrows turned into a one-woman volley, swiftly killing a wizard and driving the enemy archers into cover. Of course, the enemy didn't simply sit there and accept defeat, and I had to hurriedly duck behind a rock to avoid enemy arrows taking my head off.

The others were skilled enough that the small boost to their speed was all they needed to shift the tide of battle. When I next poked my head out from behind the rock, Kurra was charging up the hill with impossible speed. The surviving church scouts wisely surrendered. They were quickly disarmed and bound.

While Eledine tended to Kurra's wounds, Xeldia started interrogating them. "Now, who are you?"

One of the scouts answered, "Corporal Ellian, Third Hyren Scouts. This is Corporal Sel. And that's all we're keen on telling you."

Xeldia reached into her pack and showed them the scroll of the Herald's denouncement. "The Herald has been opposing the Triune's will for centuries. Are you faithful men, good men, or simply obedient?"

The scouts looked at each other, uncertain. After a long pause, Sel said, "Look, neither of us has the faintest idea what's going on. We got our orders, and we carried them out. The inquisitor knew something, but you just killed her. So you're wasting your time with us."

Meanwhile, I had started rifling through the belongings of their fallen comrades. They had detailed maps of the paths up the mountain and church camps, which I happily took. Little more information was forthcoming; what appeared to be the scout's leader had what I guessed were written orders, but they were encoded. I took them anyway, in case I could figure out how to crack it.

Xeldia snorted and returned to where Eledine and Kurra were sitting. We gathered close.

Xeldia said, "They may be right with that last point. The church has never been terribly open with information at the best of times. Which these are not."

Kurra glared briefly at her before returning her focus to the rest of them. "Then what do we do? Don't want them reporting back, but only coward kills unarmed man."

There was a brief silence as everyone pondered the dilemma. Then, I had an idea. "Throw their stuff down a ravine! Then they have to go get it. Will slow them a lot, at least!"

The others thought for a moment, then nodded in agreement one by one. After Kurra did just that, Eledine tended Xeldia's wounds, and I retrieved my hat, we let the scouts go and resumed our march up the mountain.

That evening, I managed to catch with my spyglass sight of a battle between Horrag and church forces. I was too distant to pick out details, but I could see the shifting of battle lines, how banners and signals advanced and retreated. It seemed that Horrag's forces took significant casualties but were ultimately victorious.

With the dangers of the mountain, even Kurra recommended a cautious pace. Raiding church camps did ease our logistical problems, but only so much, and we had to take pains to cover our tracks. Another cause of anxiety was the movement of soldiers at the mountain's base—it was getting hard to see, but I knew that

Horrag had at least briefly camped at the mountain's base and that the church had received yet more reinforcements.

The higher we climbed, the easier our breath was spent. Eledine tested out a medicine of her own invention that helped our lungs; Kurra was impressed and promised that even a little help in that regard could allow us to outpace church scouts.

As the air shifted from "cool" to "cold," our march was interrupted by the sounds of battle up ahead. I hurried forward, keeping to the shadows, hoping to figure out what was going on before we had to commit to a fight. My companions were right behind me.

I peered around a bend to see the fight. On one side was another party of church scouts, much like the ones we fought. On the other side were glowing humanoids with feathered wings, clad in resplendent armour, eyes orbs of holy light, bearing the Triune's symbols. Unsure of what to do, I waved Xeldia forward.

When she saw the fight, her eyes widened. "Angels! Hurry to their aid!"

Xeldia immediately charged, shifting into her wolf form as she did so. Kurra was immediately behind her. It was a little abrupt for Eledine and me, but we didn't doubt our friend, joining the battle. The good news was that we had the enemy off guard and outflanked, allowing us to quickly cut down their rearguard and advance on their heavier warriors. The bad was that we were just a little too late to save the angels. By the time the loyalist knights realised they had lost, and surrendered, the angels had all been cut down, slowly dissolving into silvery light.

One remained but was obviously dying. Eledine rushed to his side but hesitated. "Alright, Xeldia, what do the holy texts say about angel physiology?"

Xeldia managed to growl out, "Nothing!"

The angel clutched Eledine's hand. "Listen…the…faithful…are…deceived…the gate…south…of the…peak…"

The angel died. Eledine sighed as its body dissolved in her arms. "Damn…"

I asked, "The gate?"

Xeldia explained, "Gate to celestial realm. Sealed."

Kurra was finishing binding our enemies. "Not anymore, I'd guess. Best get there before too many church agents do. Which reminds me…" She pushed one of the knights to the ground and pressed a boot to his chest. "You attacked angels. Why?"

"The inquisitor said they were demons! And in case you don't know, inquisitors tend to execute people who don't obey them!" the knight said hurriedly. "They had the entire plan. We were just following orders. Honest!"

Kurra scoffed. "Again, ruthless leading mindless."

I was looking through the enemy party's belongings, finding more encrypted notes, a map annotated with unexplained markings, and some rations that could replenish our own supplies. Eledine was busy examining the strange, metallic residue left by the dissolving angels. She hurriedly scooped all she could into vials. Xeldia looked uncomfortable but said nothing.

Chapter 23

Another couple of days passed. The air grew even thinner, and even with Eledine's medicine, we needed to take more frequent rests. Eledine's attention was torn a million different ways, eager to study the alchemical properties of all sorts of herbs and rocks on the mountain that were apparently rare or non-existent elsewhere in the world, to say nothing of the angel residue. It was honestly a little amusing watching her try and fail to maintain her usual organisation and composure.

One day, something in the sky caught Kurra's attention. She cursed loudly, "Horrag's dragon."

We all whirled around to face her, before looking in the direction she was. I managed to pick out the sight—indeed, a dragon, far away, but massive, circling the area.

Eledine had a hand on her bow. "You could have mentioned this earlier!"

"Horrag doesn't do much personally, and dragon is bound to him. Must be desperate. And farther from horde than usual," Kurra explained.

I whispered, "Can we beat him?"

"…If necessary, we will try." Kurra turned and resumed the march.

That night, as we camped, the shape of a dragon interrupted my stargazing. I cried out in alarm, and my party ran for weapons. As the dragon circled our camp, I saw a large party of at least twenty orcs approach. Most were slaves, dressed in rags not remotely appropriate for the cold, and near skeletal with starvation. Just shy of half were better-equipped warriors, most with an enchantment or two on their wargear.

As we hurried back into our wargear, the dragon landed right in front of us: a large, sky-blue beast, wrapped in rune-inscribed chains. An orc slid off its back. He was huge, eye-to-eye with Kurra, but with twice as much fat barely crammed into dragonbone plates. I didn't envy the dragon having to carry him.

He stomped over, and while his face was obscured with a fanged helmet, I could hear a triumphant grin in his tone as he faced a snarling Kurra. "I remember you! Some idiot who's only alive because my champion couldn't be bothered to finish you off."

Kurra wanted to retort, but Xeldia stepped in front of her, armour glinting in the firelight. "I don't remember you, warlord. You aren't worth remembering."

Whatever the orc had expected her to say, that wasn't it.

"What? I am Horrag! Lord of the Western Plains! Dragonmaster! The blood of ten thousand runs over my hands!"

"On others' hands, maybe. You are nothing but that which was given to you. I am more interested in knowing your slaves than you." Xeldia examined some mud on her boot.

Horrag roared in rage, drawing a massive spear. "Then you'll know them! You'll join them! I'll have you—"

"Have me?" Xeldia said. "Of course. Because you can't do anything yourself."

"You think I'm not a warrior! Face me then!" Horrag stomped towards her.

Xeldia looked him up and down. "Clad in the armour of your fathers? If that's how you fight, why not dig them out of their graves? They'd probably stand a better chance."

It was then that I realised what Xeldia was doing, as Horrag started undoing the buckles on his armour. "I won't take this from you! You and me, one on one! I'll tear you apart with my bare hands!"

"Single combat, no armour or weapons. Very well." Xeldia set her weapon aside and got out of her armour herself.

Horrag's followers approached. There was a brief exchange in the orcish tongue.

Kurra quickly translated, "Telling them about single combat. Also insulting Xeldia. Will not repeat."

Out of his armour, Horrag looked noticeably less threatening. Sure, he was still a massive, full-blown orc, but he was also hairy and smelly, and a good deal of his size was fat. Xeldia, meanwhile, had shifted into her wolf form, bearing fangs and claws. Beneath her fur, I could see her athletic build. If this gave Horrag doubts, he didn't let it show. Kurra, Eledine, and I looked at each other. I was aching for something to do. I was honestly considering cheating, even knowing that would give the other orcs and the dragon the only excuse they needed to overrun us.

The two fighters circled each other. Everyone else took a few steps back, giving them space. Xeldia was the first to attack, rushing forward in a change, before side-stepping to dodge Horrag's counterattack. Horrag proved to be faster than expected, swiftly whirling around to land a solid punch. Xeldia staggered back but kept fighting. Horrag tried to press the advantage, but Xeldia deftly stepped just out of reach of his strikes, landing a few cuts on his arm as he struck.

Horrag switched tactics. He grabbed Xeldia's arm as she attacked, drawing her close. Xeldia was smart enough to not attempt to match his strength. Instead, she used the proximity to land a bite on his shoulder. Horrag roared in pain, responding with a solid headbutt. It knocked Xeldia back, but she took a large, bloody chunk of Horrag's shoulder with her. Driven by sheer pain and rage, he pushed her into a pin, repeatedly punching her as he did so. Eledine gripped her longbow. Kurra lay a hand on her shoulder.

But Horrag had forgotten Xeldia's legs. She stuck a sudden knee strike to his crotch. His warriors all visibly cringed as Horrag shouted, recoiling. The brief hesitation was the only opening Xeldia needed to sink her claws into Horrag's neck. He moved to grab her arm, a move which she leveraged to pull her mouth into biting range, taking another bloody chunk out of the warlord.

Horrag screamed again, twisting Xeldia's arm with a sickening crack. Xeldia grimaced but kept up the fight with her remaining good arm. She shifted to a more defensive tactic, evading and blocking Horrag's strikes as best she could. Despite her position, she managed it to no small degree.

It proved to be all she needed to do. Horrag was losing a lot of blood from his wounds, his strikes steadily slowing. In a last, desperate effort, he went for Xeldia's neck. But he overreached, and Xeldia was able to bite his hand clean off. Horrag died a painful, gory, but at least somewhat quick death.

Xeldia slowly stood, spitting out the hand in disgust. She was battered and bruised but glared at Horrag's followers with fire in her eyes.

Kurra laughed in elation, hurrying up behind her, ducking down to scoop Xeldia onto her shoulders. She chanted, "Xeldia! Xeldia! Xeldia!" She gave the other orcs an expectant look.

After a moment's calculation, they joined in, one by one. "Xeldia! Xeldia! Xeldia!"

The dragon slowly approached. With a deep, guttural voice, it intoned, "By the laws of my bindings, I am yours, slayer of Horrag."

Xeldia took a deep breath and reverted to her human form. "I will not be a slaver. I free you of your bindings, dragon."

The dragon's eyes widened as the chain's runes glowed. They opened, clattering to the ground. "I—I'm free! Yes! Hah!" Without another word, the dragon leapt off into the sky, gathering wind under its wings and flying northward.

Eledine adjusted her spectacles. "Perhaps that's draconic for 'thank you'?"

The slaves, meanwhile, were looking at Xeldia with hope in their eyes. Xeldia slipped off Kurra's shoulders and approached them. "The same goes for all of you. Have you enough provisions to make it down the mountain?"

One of Horrag's warriors stepped forward. "Hold on! Some of those are ours. Throw Horrag's off a cliff for all I care, but this wretch—"

"Will be set free, unless you want Kurra here to test her new axe on your flesh?" Xeldia interrupted.

Kurra's face lit up at the implication that *she* was the new owner of Horrag's axe, forged from black metal and gleaming with an inner fire. She hurriedly picked it up and stared down the orc, grinning maniacally. I stepped beside Kurra, conjuring some lights to demonstrate I had magical power to back her up.

The other orc warriors looked at each other, uncertain. They muttered to each other quietly before turning and leaving, some taking large packs from the slaves as they did so. Kurra growled at them in orc tongue, and they shouted back.

After a brief exchange, Kurra turned to Xeldia. "Deserting. Cowards."

"Fine." Xeldia sighed before adding, much more loudly, "But they will leave enough provisions for the *former* slaves to make their way back down the mountain!"

Horrag's former warriors glared at her before unceremoniously dumping a collection of breads and jerky onto the ground. There was a minute of awkward silence as they stomped back down the mountain, grumbling. Then, the slaves leapt at the abandoned food, gobbling it up in desperation.

Eledine said, "Can I suggest leaving *some* for the trip back down?"

Their eating slowed, and they looked at each other sheepishly.

Xeldia examined the chains around their necks. "The orcs probably took the keys. Peri, can you get the chains off?"

I nodded, and the freed slaves quickly gathered around me as I took out my tools. The locks were cheap, and I managed to get all of them open pretty quickly.

Meanwhile, Xeldia addressed the crowd. "To all of you, I offer you a choice. You are free now; if you wish to leave, then go. But if you wish to stay closer for protection, I promise to take you with us on our task and protect you until we are finished and safely away from the mountain. In exchange, I will ask for aid in carrying our supplies."

They muttered to each other; it seemed that half of them didn't speak our language. But they reached a consensus quickly.

One stepped forward. "Don't like our chances on our own. We'll stick around."

Our party, suddenly gaining another dozen members, did make something of a logistical challenge, especially since our followers had been pushed up the mountain dangerously quickly. We decided to send our new followers back down to our nearest supply stash to get a few meals into them, and we'd count on raiding church supplies to feed ourselves. A risky strategy, but between Eledine, Kurra, Cosma, and me, we had a decent capacity to see any church patrols before they saw us, and it gave the ex-slaves the best chance of survival. It was a fight Kurra was eager for; Xeldia had given her all Horrag's wargear, and the delighted orc was chomping at the bit to find an enemy on which to test it. Our new pack of hirelings did have one benefit in that they were content to carry large amounts of supplies for us, in part because Horrag's orcs had been burdening them with far more.

A couple more days passed on the climb. The work strained our muscles, the ever-present cold strained our resolve, and tight rationing strained our stomachs. News from the base of the mountain dried up, as by now it was too distant for me to pick out useful details, and our suppliers were too busy keeping their heads down to risk gathering information on enemy movements.

As we neared the peak, we started investigating some of the markings on the scout's maps. We guessed that at least some of them indicated locations of skirmishes. Looking at the maps strategically, Eledine guessed they were defending the gate, and from the patterns, made a few guesses as to its location.

Chapter 24

One day, we noticed Xeldia growing increasingly restless. It took us a while; we weren't exactly in the most relaxing of situations, but it finally occurred to us that Xeldia simply couldn't sit still.

Kurra was the first to say something. "Xeldia. Something wrong? You walk like there's a sand wyrm on our back."

"I-I suppose I have. My apologies. But we are getting close; I can feel it. Raiya is calling me." She paced anxiously. "Come. We are nearing the end of our journey."

That evening, Cosma picked up a scent that had her excited. We followed; there was a good chance it was a mouse or some such creature that Cosma was hoping to snack on, but even that much would save precious rations. But when we crested a rise, we came upon angels.

These ones were much more lightly armed and armoured than the ones we'd encountered earlier; from their leather armour and cloaks, they could have been foresters were it not for the wings and halos. They were gathered around a patch of grass, in the middle of tracking. When she saw them, Xeldia eagerly rushed over the rise.

Perhaps a bit too eagerly, as the angels drew their weapons. But they promptly relaxed when Xeldia knelt before them.

Xeldia said, "Most holy, I am but a faithful agent of Raiya, hoping to know how best to bring justice to these lands."

The leader of the angels, resembling a lithe human woman, returned her weapon to its sheath. "Ah, my apologies. Many have been carrying our banners without loyalty."

Xeldia hurriedly reached into her pack, pulling out the scroll that had driven us so far. "I know. I uncovered this, something the church has been striving to hide."

The angel examined it briefly before smiling. "Ah, it's you! The Triune have taken a great interest in you. They wish to speak to you in person. Head up that right to the right and follow it until it bends east. Then, climb the cliff. A few dozen meters up, you'll find a cave. The gate to their realm is a short way inside."

For the first time since I'd met her, Xeldia was utterly speechless. She shifted involuntarily. She flinched away from the angels, but they barely reacted.

Kurra walked up beside her. "May we join? Is our friend. We have spilled and shed blood beside each other."

The angel nodded. "So long as you're not church agents. But I must bid you make haste—the enemy advances higher up the mountain every day. It's only a matter of time before the celestial realm itself is compromised."

Xeldia was on her feet in an instant. "Then we go now!"

Our collection of followers didn't seem to know exactly what was going on, but the angels had made an impression, so they didn't complain when Xeldia picked up the pace. Cosma also seemed excited to reach the celestial realm, enough so that I suspected that the star had an interest in it as well.

The remainder of the march took less than an hour, and a good deal of that was the climb up the final ridge. Xeldia was so eager that she nearly started scaling the cliff face by hand, and Eledine had to point out that we'd be much less useful to the Triune if, in our haste, we fell to our deaths. The others waited with varying degrees of patience as I flew up to the cave that was our destination.

I peered inside, illuminating the area with magical light, mana primed and ready for whatever was inside. I saw a large double door, wrought from silvery metals with intricate curved patterns, guarded on each side by a titanic angel, each the size of an ogre, covered head to toe in a celestial plate inscribed with the Triune's emblem. Their heads turned towards me. I floated inside, waving awkwardly.

One of them spoke. "Hail, star-marked. What is your purpose?"

"Brought friends," I said quietly. "Xeldia, a paladin."

The other angel asked, "A paladin? Of the church?"

"No. She found the scroll that fired the Herald."

The angel nodded. "I see. And your star, what is its purpose here?"

An excellent question. I looked at Cosma, who was perched on my shoulder. She yipped.

The first angel addressed her, "Emissary. Approach."

Cosma leapt off my shoulder and scurried to the angel, then giggled and yapped a few times.

The angel seemed to understand. "Hmm. I see. I will bring word of your presence to the Triune." The angel turned back to me.

"In the meantime, feel free to bring your paladin ally up, and any in her party."

I carefully hammered some pitons into place, affixing some rope before flying back down with it to where Kurra was preparing to secure the other end. I told them, "Angels are expecting us."

The climb wasn't easy, but Xeldia wasn't being stopped so close, and she was as inspirational as ever. The climb was made much easier by my flying a few packs of our supplies up and casting a shield to protect our followers from the biting winds.

When Xeldia finally reached the top, I could tell she was putting all her focus into controlling her shift, and even then, I could see patches of fur starting to manifest on her neck.

As she approached, one of the angels spoke. "Ah, hail, Paladin of Raiya. You've been expected. Please, enter. Your party is welcome as well." Then, the angel turned to Cosma and me. "Star-marked, you and the emissary are welcome, but remember you are guests in the realm of the Triune."

I nodded; I wasn't really sure what Cosma and the star had in mind, but I was willing to bet that, at the very least, they wouldn't try anything stupid in the realm of gods. The angels stepped to either side, and the doors to the celestial realm slowly opened. Beyond it, I could see stars glimmer and auroras dance.

Xeldia bowed to the angels. "Thank you." She then started hurriedly stepping towards the door. Halfway there, she looked like she realised she should probably wait for the others to catch up.

She was as tense as a bowstring as, one by one, our party climbed into the cave. When the last of us finally clambered up the mountain, her patience finally faded. "Come! I won't keep my goddess waiting!" She half-ran through the gate.

Eledine snorted. "I would think the immortal wouldn't be concerned over a few minutes." Regardless, she followed, with me right behind her.

When I crossed the threshold of the gate, I felt like I had stepped into a constellation. Stars twinkled in every direction, and clouds of colour floated amidst a night sky. We stood upon an aurora, light itself having formed a bridge for us. I took a moment to observe the breathtaking sight. Xeldia had, too, her efforts to hold back her shift failed or were abandoned. There was a brief traffic jam as everyone who had stepped through was awestruck by the sight.

Our reverie was interrupted by an angel hovering nearby. "Welcome, esteemed guests! The Triune are expecting you. This way, please."

We followed, most of us sticking to the middle of the path due to the lack of guardrails. We were led up the bridge, which snaked between floating, pearlescent platforms, towards what looked like a grand floating pavilion. It was surrounded by a rainbow aura, like the most breathtaking sunset. We reached steps forged of fine white marble.

The angel took a step ahead. "My ladies? Your guests have arrived."

A melodious voice responded, the mesmerising quality ensuring it could not be misheard. "Excellent. Come."

Xeldia, to my surprise, hesitated. But then she rushed forward. I was right behind her. I crested the steps.

What awaited me was warmth.

The warmth of a bright spring day, calm but full of promise. Three breathtakingly beautiful women reclined nearby, not the distant, alien beauty of my star, but something familiar, brought forth in a way for my mortal eyes to see.

The first was like seeing a magnificent citadel, clad in a resplendent golden plate. She was tall, with statuesque features and short, fire-red hair. The second was a lithe woman, clothed in a shimmering cloak that glittered with the promise of far horizons. Her long and voluminous hair fell in dark waves around a slender, elegant face. The third was an endowed figure, with long hair dyed every colour of the rainbow. Her dress was impossibly elaborate, elegantly patterned in multicoloured pastels.

Raiya, Ynnelia, and Etunae. The Triune themselves.

The implications of what I was seeing were uncountable, primarily because my mind was too focused on pretty women to count. Xeldia had fallen to her knees, trembling. The rest of us had simply frozen in awe.

Raiya smiled. "Xeldia. It's good to finally see you, face-to-face." When Xeldia only spluttered and squirmed from the attention, Raiya lightly chuckled. "At ease, all of you. Now is not the time for formalities. Please, relax."

That was kind of hard when faced with three goddesses, but those assembled awkwardly shuffled around, sitting on assorted benches and rises. The one present who seemed to know exactly what they wanted to do was Cosma, who ran up to the Triune, giggling.

Ynnelia gave her an appraising look. "Ah, the emissary of a star. We are interested in hearing what your mistress has to say, but there are other matters that must be addressed first."

Cosma seemed to understand this and returned to my side, curling up by my feet, though she remained excited.

Xeldia had stood, but her gaze was fixed firmly on the ground.

Etunae said, "Xeldia. I feel shame in your heart. From where does it come?"

Xeldia swallowed hard, speaking slowly, careful to shape each sound with her canine snout. "Can't control my beast form."

"And why is that something to be ashamed of? It is no more than a sign that your heart is rich and full. The fear of the beast form is simply rooted in ignorance, nothing more."

Ynnelia added, "Being a beastwoman makes you delightfully unique. And has it not aided you and your friends, time and time again?"

Xeldia's tail wagged, even as she squirmed from the attention. "…Thank you."

Raiya leaned forward. "But let us begin business. We've called you here for a reason. As you know, the woman who now leads our faithful stands against the very values we incarnate."

Eledine spoke up. "If I may, this sounds like a…complicated situation. Perhaps we should start this story from the beginning."

Etunae sat straighter. "Perhaps so. Very well. The story of Viola Senredia begins centuries ago, a lifetime even for elves. It was a couple of centuries after we had first arrived to guide mortals, and we had made great gains spreading our message across the nearby lands, but had much work left to do. We had conflicts with Urrak, the god of war at the time, diplomatic friction with other pantheons, and the rise of the demon queen, Cussendra. Viola was one of the most faithful of our followers. She was an inspirational speaker and, time and time again, rallied our faithful against those opposing us. Of course, we granted her power, and in return, she granted us countless victories. It was in no small part thanks to her will and charisma that the lands entered a golden age, making peace with foreign powers and beating back the demon hordes. It was because of this that when our previous Herald, Selene Ioreth, fell, we granted her that position.

"When we had seen our peoples were content and growing, we believed it time for the next stage of a plan millennia in the making—to start to withdraw from this world, for does not every parent await the day that their children can stand on their own? We are old and wise beings, but alas, we are not perfect. If we were, perhaps we might have seen that Viola's loyalty was to us, not our cause. We might have seen that she would take our withdrawal for abandonment, and treason.

"As our Herald, she was the first to know of our plan. We had taken her to the depths of this realm and showed her the divine engines—the bedrock upon which we build our power. We told her secrets of great power and gave her her final mission—to prepare the world to start taking steps without us.

"But Viola had a very particular vision for the world. A vision she fought to impose on it. It was a peaceful, prosperous vision, but it was stagnant, absolute. Being asked to grow, to develop, to advance, to become something more, would destroy it. So, she turned against us. She took the divine engines and used them to sustain her power without us. Then, she moved to seal the gates of the celestial realm, to keep us from communicating directly with our followers.

"Her success was only partial, and in what was then the kingdom of Ioran, we found those who still believed in goodness, not just the appearance thereof. We cast out Viola from our order.

But we underestimated her support—there were many that shared her vision of a so-called utopia, and many more that were simply loyal to her, not us or our cause. Thus began the terrible war that is now called the Ioran Heresy.

"Simply put, we lost. Viola had empowered her followers with the divine engines, and the siren song of normalcy was just too tempting for too many. She managed to take the celestial gates, and we were forced to close them to prevent her from attacking us directly. She took control of our church and rewrote history, building a masquerade of us to take our places in her utopia.

"We have spent the centuries since maintaining a close watch for those who believe in righteousness, love, and curiosity, not just faith for its own sake. We have sought to guide people like you to the truth. Finally, we succeeded. When we saw your rebellion starting to take form, we reopened the celestial gates and called for the faithful. Viola, obviously, has already deployed every sword she could muster into sealing the gate again, but thanks to your skill and trust in each other, you managed to reach us before her agents could overrun ours. Now, we can start anew."

Raiya stood. "We have a great charge for the four of you. To defeat Viola, we must deny her the divine engines. You must infiltrate Heartshold and reach its depths, where she has secreted them. Then, you must seal them away, deny them to our enemies. Destroy them if necessary."

Kurra laughed. "Quest for ages! To battle, against Herald herself!"

Xeldia shifted uncomfortably. "That...I know not if that is even possible. Only the chosen ones may enter Heartshold's depths, and every babe in the Casten, and beyond, is checked for the mark of the chosen."

Ynnelia seemed confused, a strange look on the divine. "Hold, why the babes?"

"The excuse the Herald gives is that they must be trained for their destiny. Looking at it now, I suspect the Herald wishes to kill them before they can threaten her." Xeldia's tail drooped, not understanding the source of the goddess's confusion.

Raiya asked, "But why babes? Why would we give a child the mark? With the responsibility that entails, it would be tantamount to child abuse."

"…We assumed it was something one was born with. Something innate." Xeldia shifted awkwardly.

Ynnelia raised an eyebrow. "Hardly *chosen*, then, is it?"

Eledine leaned forward. "If I'm understanding you correctly, then you can choose anyone, at any point?"

"Not *anyone* at *any point*, but those the bulk of our power can reach, and then align with the values we incarnate," Ynnelia explained. "In short, it is something we can arrange. You're much better concerning yourselves with the Heartshold's more mundane defences. Viola will no doubt anticipate us coming for the engines and will have prepared accordingly. Expect defences of her most loyal agents, at least some empowered by the engines themselves."

I whispered, "The Anointed."

"Indeed."

Eledine frowned. "That may be a problem. At least one has arrived at the base of the mountain."

Raiya seemed unperturbed. "Yes, we can sense their presence at this distance. A cause for concern, but we have time before they strike. Time enough to plan a counterattack."

Kurra stood, pacing the garden. "Will not be quest. Will be war."

Raiya's gaze turned grim. "Sadly, yes. But you are keenly aware of the church's crimes, of the price the innocent pay to maintain Viola's false utopia. It cannot be tolerated. The blood of the righteous is the price of justice."

Eledine muttered, "No pressure..." She took a deep breath. "...The logistics of a war are hardly straightforward. We need armies, and those armies will need supplies."

"Fear not, we have not spent these last centuries entirely idle," added Raiya. "There are pockets of resistance here and there. The church's forces have crushed them as they have found them, but many have slipped through their fingers. And there are the colonies you have freed, as well as those faithful on the fringes of the church's influence. Our assets are far greater than you may think. Yes, we are outnumbered, but we have enough to make a stand. Enough to win you the chance to infiltrate the Heartshold. Enough for victory."

Etunae smiled warmly. "But that can wait. You've had a long, hard journey here. Time may be precious, but so is rest, so I say you can afford a single night. A well-rested mind makes fewer mistakes, and we must be at our best to plan a war."

There were audible sighs of relief from those assembled.

Etunae gestured to a nearby angel. "I've already had rooms prepared for all of you. Celenriel will show you to them whenever you're ready."

When Cosma yapped, Ynnelia smiled. "Of course. Come."

Cosma scampered up to Ynnelia, who gently scooped her up before taking her aside.

Celenriel gathered our party and started leading them out of the garden. Just as we left, it occurred to me that if, as the scripture dictated, Etunae knew the hearts of all things and could see how they fit together, then she'd be able to solve the dilemma I'd been having. Careful not to draw attention to myself, I turned and slipped back to the gardens.

Etunae smiled politely as I scurried up to her. "Yes?"

She patiently waited as I wrestled my wild heart under control enough for me to tease out the question I wanted to ask. "Um…I was thinking…my friends…they're all so…you know?"

Thankfully, Etunae was communicating with a being that knew all hearts didn't actually require that many words. Etunae chuckled lightly. "They are indeed."

"So, um, if you don't mind, um…which do I pick?"

Etunae laughed. "A most terrible choice! You have such a warm and full heart. A heart that might just have room for more than one love. But the tangle of hearts can be a maze, and while I can offer advice, you must traverse it yourself. Go to those you love. Tell them how you feel. What happens next? Well, you'll just have to see."

I nodded. "Okay." I shuffled off, my heart racing. Confessing your feelings to one person was nerve-wracking enough —admitting to my three closest friends that I was smitten with each of them? I'd rather be shot at.

My crushes gave me quizzical looks as I approached. I avoided their gaze, simply falling in behind them as we were escorted to our quarters:;fine, palace-like rooms built of fine marble. One room was given to the four of us. As the rest of our followers were taken to their own rooms, we were left alone.

We all set down our packs, glad for a moment to rest. I sat awkwardly on the foot of my bed as the others undid their gear. I realised that now was the best time I was ever going to get to say what I needed to say. The problem was mustering the courage to do that.

Kurra noticed. "Peri? Are you alright?"

I took a few deep breaths, trying to muster the courage. I squirmed awkwardly. The others looked at me, worried and confused. I realised that this was only going to get worse. I forced the words out, one by one. "I'm…smitten…with…all of you!"

Whatever they expected me to say, it clearly wasn't that. They looked at me, stunned. With the die cast, the drought of words turned into a flood.

"You're all so amazing!" I continued. "And powerful! And beautiful! And smart! And nice! And interesting! And…" I squirmed awkwardly. "If—if none of you like me, I understand…"

Kurra was the first to find her voice. "Had slain enemies in your honour, you turned away…I thought…"

Eledine answered, "I believe Peri isn't all that familiar with Uluzar culture. To be fair, I think the region is unique in that offering the heads of one's enemies is considered a form of courtship."

Xeldia rubbed the back of her neck. "And…you are wondering which one of us to choose?"

I squirmed awkwardly. "…Not like I want to choose…"

Kurra took out her axe. "Single combat, then? For Peri's hand?"

Eledine had an ever-so-slight blush. "Don't Uluzar warriors sometimes have multiple wives?"

"Privilege reserved for the greatest of warriors. Though…" Kurra chuckled nervously. "Having known the three of you? Would slay a dragon—no, a dozen dragons— to be worthy of that honour!"

Xeldia shifted her weight back and forth. "And here, I thought I was strange for having my heart pulled so many different ways…" She abruptly laughed. "A dozen campaigns for the church, and a rebellion against it, fighting to the death countless times, and now this has me nervous!"

Eledine snorted. "That *does* put this conversation into perspective. We're all adults here. Though I must admit, if Kurra wants to have all three of us as wives, then, well, I don't intend to put a dragon in her way. The three of you do make *excellent* company."

I giggled. "So…all four of us? Together?"

Xeldia smiled, shifting again involuntarily. "Yes, if you all will it."

Kurra grinned, re-equipping herself. "Then is settled. There is but one thing to do!" She strode out of the room. The rest of us followed behind, confused. We trailed Kurra to the garden where the Triune still lay. She brandished her axe. "Raiya! I challenge you to single combat!"

As the rest of us blinked, bemused, Etunae laughed musically. "Oh dear! Darling, I'm sure your lovers are quite content with a relationship—you've already proven your might a thousand times over! You don't have to challenge anyone to a fight you don't want to."

Kurra lowered her axe, disappointed. "To have many lovers is a privilege. I must prove myself worthy!"

"Winning their hearts is proof enough of your worth, Kurra. Love is something found as much as earned, and you have had a stroke of great fortune." Etunae smiled widely.

Ynnelia added, "But if you really wish to settle your heart's doubts, know that your battle against the false Herald will be the stuff of legend. Even working together, defeating her will be proof beyond all doubt of your might."

Kurra hummed, stroking her chin. "Hmm, perhaps…but I still need to find an offering to make…"

Eledine snorted in amusement. "I'm happy to wait on that regard. I'm sure we'll find some dragon or giant or something in time."

"Very well!" Kurra turned and kissed Eledine full on the lips.

As Eledine blinked, processing what had just happened, Kurra kissed Xeldia as well. I scurried up to her feet eagerly. I didn't have to wait long. Kurra picked me up and gave me a kiss I'd remember for the rest of my life.

The four of us returned to our quarters and proceeded to ensure that the bedsheets would need changing before the Triune hosted other guests.

Chapter 25

I woke up the next morning surrounded by the warmth of my companions. Not the first time this had happened, but this time there was no tension, no questions about boundaries or feelings. It was also different in a way: I was being flattened underneath the weight of all three of my companions, but I actually didn't mind. I simply lay there, enjoying the heat and pressure.

Xeldia was still in her wolf form and had remained so all night. She was gently stroking my hair with a paw, and Kurra's with another, while she had Eledine's head tucked into the crook of her neck. I nestled into the affection. Eledine and Kurra awoke one by one. Neither moved.

After a while, but far too soon, there was a knock at the door. "My ladies? Breakfast is being served. After which the Triune is arranging a war council, and they expect your presence."

There was a collective groan.

Xeldia managed to shift into her human form before answering, "We'll be out promptly!" She looked down at the rest of us. "…We do have to get up."

Eledine sighed deeply before reluctantly slipping out of the embrace. One by one, we followed her, picking up our clothes where we had hastily discarded them the night before. We then exited our room, barely presentable.

As another angel guided us through the celestial realm, Ynnelia approached, Cosma bundled in her arms. When she saw me, Cosma leapt down, scurrying up to my shoulder, giggling happily.

Ynnelia gestured to another aurora path. "Peri? A few minutes, if you please. Your patron and I would like a word with you."

I nodded and followed Ynnelia down the path to what looked like a balcony. She extended her hand to me. Hesitating a moment, I took it. I felt the sudden lightness of gravity loosening its grip on me. Ynnelia leapt into the open sky, taking me with her, and a second later, the entire universe was shooting past. I caught brief glimpses of wonders beyond imagination, spaces I'd never seen before.

And then, we came to rest on a small cloud of blue dust. We were floating around my star, gleaming bright. Ynnelia whistled musically, and a wisp of starstuff flew from it, landing on the cloud and shaping itself into a stylised humanoid form, one with a familiar face.

"Hello, clever one. Your people call you Peri, yes?"

Entirely unsure of how to react, I nodded awkwardly. As I did so, Cosma happily leapt off my shoulder, wagging her tail at the feet of the star's avatar.

The avatar gently stroked Cosma. "You've done very well, my emissary." She turned back to me. "You've both done well."

Ynnelia explained, "Drawing upon cosmic power can allow the star to gain terrestrial influence. That's why she's been eager for you to spread knowledge of the wider cosmos. I also appreciate those who look to the horizons, so she and I have worked out something of a deal regarding education."

The avatar added, "And you'll be facing one who attempts to suppress the truth. Ynnelia wishes me to grant you more power. Here." She gestured to me, and a mote of starstuff floated from her into me.

I felt it flow into my body, becoming part of it. Cosma had taught me much about channelling and shaping the power of stars, but now that power was within me, and it came to me so much easier. I held out my hand, watching starlight dance between my fingers. I smiled at my star with gratitude.

She said, "Good luck, clever one."

Ynnelia took my hand again. "Anyway, animals like you need to eat. Back to breakfast, shall we?" She leapt, pulling me back to the celestial realm.

When we returned, Ynnelia led me to a fine dining hall, open to the starry sky. My companions were there, along with the rest of the Triune and a host of angels. My companions were happy to see me.

As I sat down next to them, Xeldia remarked, "Peri! Those, er, decorations suit you."

At the quizzical look I gave them, Etunae conjured a mirror with a wave of the hand. Examining my reflection, it seemed that my cheeks and arms had been lightly dusted with motes of starlight, like sparkly freckles.

Kurra peered over my shoulder. "I agree. You look even prettier!" She punctuated the remark with a kiss on the cheek.

Breakfast was quite a feast, with food only seen on the celestial plane. Ynnelia cast a translating charm that allowed us to speak with our more recent followers, and we told them the story of our journeys. They had been cast pretty far out of their depths, but so far, we'd been treating them orders of magnitude better than their former masters, so they said they'd be happy to haul whatever it was we needed hauled so long as we kept their bellies full and other warriors away.

When breakfast was finished, we were led to the war room. It was no less beautiful than the rest of the realm, but the atmosphere was much more sombre.

Raiya addressed us as we assembled around the central table. "Today, we must engage in the most terrible of crafts—the craft of war. The blood of the righteous is the price of justice, and soon, many of us will be forced to pay it."

Xeldia saluted her goddess. "As I have sworn to you before, so I swear to you now: I will gladly be the first."

"Your courage is beyond reproach, Xeldia. Thus, I have no doubt in my decision to make you my chosen. Please, give me your hand."

"I—" Xeldia started, Raiya's recognition enough to once again trigger her shift. But she stopped doubting her deity, or perhaps herself, and extended her hand.

Raiya clasped it firmly, and the pair glowed with a bright golden light. When Raiya released Xeldia, the paladin's hand glowed with the shield emblem. The glow faded after a few seconds, but the emblem remained, marked in black fur. Xeldia reverently ran a paw across it.

Ynnelia smiled, saying, "I have also made my choice. Eledine."

"…What?" Whatever Eledine was expecting, it certainly wasn't this.

"You're inquisitive and happy to shed your own biases. You look over the horizon, eager to see the truth, whatever it is. I ask nothing more."

Eledine blinked. "I'm not exactly a religious woman."

"Your faith would be ideal, but it isn't necessary. You believe in everything I incarnate. If anything, it's more remarkable that you came to these beliefs wholly on your own. I choose you, and I do so happily."

Eledine thought for a moment, then stepped forward, slowly extending her hand. Ynnelia took it, and the pair glowed with silvery light. Eledine shuddered, stepping away, staring at the glowing star mark of Ynnelia on her hand. "Well, that was…hmm."

Etunae was the next to speak. "I could only choose the most passionate among you. Kurra."

Kurra lit up. "Me? I am honoured!" She stepped forward, and Etunae took her hand. The pair glowed with rainbow light. Kurra grinned, flexing. "Yes! Divine power! I feel it! Fear not, I will return the favour!"

"I know you will." Etunae smiled.

Raiya gestured to the map. "To business. I will not lie: Our assets are currently scattered. A direct, conventional war is not one we will win; we discovered that five hundred years ago, even when we had the armies to fight that war. The engines simply give Viola too much power. But one thing is different this time: Viola has had her 'utopia' for five hundred years. And to maintain the illusion of perfection, she has pushed every problem out of sight."

I whispered, "The Reborn Colonies."

Ynnelia nodded. "Among other crimes, yes."

Raiya paced around the room. "But a problem out of sight is a problem, nonetheless. And while Viola's strategy has made a number of people very comfortable, it has made a far greater number of people very angry. It is that anger we will harness!"

Eledine adjusted her glasses. "So…Xeldia starts more riots?"

"There are more to our plans than that, but that will be the central part, yes."

Kurra had the expression of someone who just had an idea. "Wait! Let them *think* we march on traditional war! Then, when their armies take the field, cities riot!"

"My thoughts exactly!" Raiya gave Kurra an appreciative nod. "Of course, for that plan, we will need at least the appearance of an army, but that is not beyond us. Many of the church's own warriors believe in the cause, not the banner. We need only rally them, calling them to our side."

Ynnelia gestured to Mount Kairyss on the map. "But we're getting ahead of ourselves. Your first task will be to break the tip of the spear that Viola levels at our realm. You must defeat the Anointed. No easy task, but the mountain has demanded they advance with only a small party, so with your newfound powers, you have hope."

"Once that is done, you'll have to sabotage the enemy camp," Raiya continued. "Defeat their commanders and destroy their supplies, enough to delay the assault while we assemble our own forces."

Eledine examined the map. "What about Horrag's former warband? If I'm familiar with Uluzar custom, by defeating their leader in single combat, Xeldia has inherited it."

"Gone, I'm afraid. Between a renewed assault from the church's forces and a lack of loyalty, the remainder of Horrag's forces have been routed. We have more reliable sources of new recruits," Raiya explained. She gestured to a different part of the map. "Specifically, here, in the reborn colony of Ealshaver, and here, in the town of Avvenar."

Xeldia nodded. "I expect our plans in Ealshaver will be the same as in the other colonies?" At the affirmative nods in the room, Xeldia continued, "Then what of Avvenar?"

Etunae's voice warmed. "There, you'll meet Countess Narrisai. While she never received formal training, her faith, artistry, and genuine love I found enough to grant blessings to. Too high profile to have killed, Viola ordered her to defeat the demon cults in the region, with the hope that Narrisai's lack of combat training would ensure her demise. What she didn't anticipate was that Narrisai would take an economic approach to defeating the demon cults, establishing a number of aid centres for the vulnerable people whom demons prey upon. Thus, she still lives and will recognise the authenticity of the document you bear. With her authority, she will be able to rally an army to our cause. Furthermore, her lover is Chieftain Kali, of the Orani people. They trust each other deeply, and Kali will follow Narrisai into war, bringing her people with her."

We spent a while longer discussing the wider strategy for the oncoming campaign: which settlements to incite revolts in, where to manoeuvre armies, and, crucially, how to manage supplies. The gods and their angelic advisers had already figured out the bulk of the plan prior to our arrival, so most of the discussion was for our sake. Eventually, we had everything we needed ironed out, so it was time for us to stop making plans and start implementing them.

The Triune loaded us with some fresh, celestial equipment, including a staff of stellar metals for me and a celestial shield for Xeldia. Ynnelia gifted Eledine with a whole stack of new recipes for ever more exotic elixirs, as well as a longbow formed from the aurora that supported the celestial realm. Kurra didn't get anything, but that was because Horrag's wargear was quality enough that the Triune couldn't spare anything that surpassed it. We were also restocked on supplies, something we were greatly thankful for so far up a mountain.

We said our goodbyes and left the celestial realm, heading to where the angelic scouts had last seen the Anointed. The climb down was easier than the climb up, but still far from easy, doubly so as we were obligated to *look* down at some of the seemingly bottomless crevasses. (Luckily, our visit to the celestial realm was good for morale.)

The next day, we started approaching the Anointed's expected location. I cast my invisibility and scouted ahead. Cosma managed to pick up a scent. We followed it to another party, church agents, all carrying heavily enchanted equipment. A small, eclectic party (not unlike my own in that way): an arcanist, a heavily armoured warrior, a woman in priest's robes, and a cloaked survivalist. After observing them for a second, I slunk back to my party and reported their location. We moved to intercept.

A little cunning mountaineering on Kurra's part allowed us to position ourselves on the high ground. As the church's party approached, everyone took a few shots of Eledine's elixirs to give us strength that would be needed in the fight to come. Xeldia stood in the open, while the rest of us got into position behind scattered rocks.

The Anointed's party came into view over a ridge. They paused as they saw Xeldia. They looked to the priestess for orders, who gestured for them to cautiously advance. The survivalist slipped out of sight, while the others approached, hands on weapons.

The priestess called, "You must be Xeldia."

Xeldia's cape flapped in the wind. "I am. You must be one of the Anointed."

"I am. And I'm ordering you to stand down."

"I have spoken with the Triune themselves. They have told me the truth of the woman you dare to call 'Herald.' It is you who must stand down."

The Anointed scoffed, but I could notice her tension, ready for a fight. "Are you seriously siding with greenskins?"

"I believe in justice, and justice is for *all*. That is why Raiya has granted me her strength." Xeldia slowly drew her sword.

"Well. That makes you in the way." The Anointed held up a hand.

Fire streaked from it, and Xeldia ducked behind her shield just in time to absorb the hit. Xeldia charged, shifting. I called upon my stellar magics to grant us speed as Eledine opened fire on the priestess, her arrows deflected by a magical shield.

As Kurra leapt into the fray, the survivalist fired a volley from out behind a rock. Even through Kurra's new dragonbone plate, she took some serious hits, arrows finding weak points in the armour, one slipping into the vision slit and another into the heel. The shots should have taken her out of the fight. But Kurra's raw rage propelled her forward. The enemy arcanist saw the rampaging orc just barely quickly enough to take flight on a summoned typhoon, seeking to escape Kurra's reach. It didn't work; she simply leapt up with a mighty bound, her mighty axe crashing through his arcane defences and spraying his blood across the mountainside.

Xeldia, meanwhile, was fighting for her life against the Anointed and her heavily armoured companion. The terrain allowed Xeldia to stop herself from being completely flanked, but fighting two experienced combatants at once was no mean feat, even for one of Xeldia's blessings. Eledine and I concentrated our fire, trying to punch through the shield around the Anointed. We seemed to be making progress, as a few shots forced her back to re-channel her power. Eyes burning with rage, she turned her power against Eledine.

A beam of holy light shattered the rock Eledine was hiding behind with a massive eruption. Eledine was hit hard, sending her toppling over a ledge. I screamed in panic. I rushed towards her, taking flight. Then, I heard an eagle's screech, and a sharp, digging pain in my ear. I rolled across the sky, the bird slashing at me.

I pushed my panic to the side, focusing on my magic. The power of the stars flowed through me, and I channelled it into another bright flash. That's all that I needed to send the eagle flying off, screeching. I turned my attention back to where Xeldia was fighting for her life. Her canine snout, poking out from her helm, had a deep, bloody gash in it, and her armour was sundered in three places.

The Anointed's holy protections were too strong. So, I changed my tactics, cursing the soldier, sapping his strength. His flagging sword arm bought Xeldia precious time, but she was still outnumbered two to one. I didn't give up, piling on curses of burning starlight and icy void, hoping to take the soldier out of the fight.

The Anointed glared at me, turning her blasts of divine fire at me. I caught the volleys of divine fire on my magical shields. She suddenly switched tactics, turning to unravel the threads of magic around me. The powers shielding me from gravity vanished. I fell, feet first, but hard enough that I was certain I'd broken something.

Xeldia put all her effort into a shield bash that managed to knock the Anointed back. She stumbled into a pile of strange, sticky goo that I hadn't noticed before. The soldier moved to stop Xeldia pressing the advantage, but my curses slowed him, leaving him open for a kick from Xeldia that sent him tumbling down the mountain. Xeldia bore down on the Anointed with her blade. She summoned her divine fields, but a volley of arrows strained them to breaking point. Eledine had returned, emerging from behind a ridge, blood staining her face but still ready to fight.

I gritted my teeth through the pain. I gathered my power and sent it through in one powerful, concentrated blast, scoring a direct hit on her neck. She dropped. Xeldia finished her with a stomp.

It was then that Kurra staggered back into view, covered in blood and peppered with arrows. "Got the archer."

Eledine slowly crawled up the ridge. "And I don't think that heavily armoured fellow will be foolish enough to give us any more problems. Not alone."

Xeldia shifted back to human. "It's done. One of the Anointed, slain."

One of our followers, a scrawny half-orc named Jann, scurried up to us. "Healing elixirs, m'ladies?"

There was a collective sigh of relief.

Chapter 26

When we returned to the mountain's base, we found that the church's camp had only grown since we'd last seen it.

Eledine's gaze slowly swept over the area. "We have to stop *all of them* from attacking. I do hope one of you has a very clever idea."

Kurra snorted. "Army marches on its stomach. This many? Wouldn't want to be managing supplies."

"That still leaves an army or two we have to get through to get to those supplies. And I would rather be able to get back *out* again. At least one of those things is going to have to involve doing something creative." Eledine sat down behind a rock.

Something clicked in my mind. "I could drop alchemical fire!" The others looked at me. I elaborated. "I can fly. High! Drop it."

"…That, indeed, would be creative. We just need to figure out *where* to drop the fire; I can only make so much." Eledine started scratching a rough map of the camp in the dirt.

Xeldia held out her hand. "Give me the spyglass." I did so, and Xeldia spent a few minutes studying the camp's layout. "Hmm… standard doctrine. Peri, see those tents? There, there, and there?" She pointed them out, and I carefully followed her gestures. "Those will be the supply tents. Target them. That should buy the Triune time enough for us to build our own armies."

Eledine took out her alchemy equipment. "Well, I suppose it's time for me to get brewing. Could the rest of you gather some of those blue-tinted mosses? That should make this mixture burn a little hotter."

Cosma's nose turned out to be pretty good at sniffing out alchemical reagents, and soon enough, we had plenty for Eledine. We found an obscured gully, and Eledine cooked up a nice, big batch of alchemical fire. I packed a dozen vials and flew into the sky.

It turned out that hitting a tent with a vial of alchemical fire dropped from beyond a crossbow's range was actually pretty tricky, and the wind knocked the first couple of vials off course, causing them to land on the grassy plains. But I managed to get the hang of it with just enough munitions to spare.

I was interrupted by the screeching of eagles. I turned to the source to see a dozen giant eagles approaching me at speed, each with a halfling on their back spinning up a sling. I gulped; there was no way I was going to be able to aim my shots with this lot harrying me. I spun around and flew back towards where my companions were waiting.

The first shots were cast, and I focused my power into my magical shielding. It held but strained against the bombardment— the eagle riders were crack shots, and their bullets had some basic enchantments on them. I spun around, flying backwards as I harried them with blasts of starlight. It didn't take them out of the fight, but it held them off, more than long enough for me to get back to my companions.

I didn't need to give any signals. As soon as I was in range, one of the riders was shot clean off their mount by Eledine. Kurra went for a bold move, leaping on top of one of the approaching eagles. The eagle in question might have been perfectly happy to carry a small halfling and a few sling bullets, but a large, heavily armed orc was a different matter entirely, and the eagle screeched in protest, bucking both Kurra and its rider. Both hit the ground hard. Kurra was the only one to get up.

My magic meant I was slower but more manoeuvrable than the eagle riders, so I kept close to the ground, taking full advantage of the rocks as cover. Now with the advantage, I turned to more offensive spells, hoping to blast the enemy out of the sky. Xeldia and Kurra had switched to their own bows, and between the four of us, we managed to drive the eagle riders off.

But we could hear signal horns from the camp below. The enemy army was scrambling to respond to us. And there was, indeed, an *army*. The remaining eagle riders retreating gave us a second to assess the situation, but that situation was one that was deteriorating quickly.

Xeldia sighed. "Well. That didn't go as planned. Time to leave."

We rushed back up the mountain, quickly putting ground between us and the church's forces. Kurra covered our tracks, and we found a sheltered gully to hole up in.

We huddled close, closer than was perhaps necessary, catching our breaths. I gave my report. "Hit three, four tents? Aiming was hard."

Eledine gave me a reassuring smile. "Well, it's not a stratagem many have tried before. But perhaps a more…subtle approach is called for? Xeldia, what kind of security will the remaining supply tents have?"

"Tighter now that some have been burned, but not impregnable; the church leaves its strongest security measures for command centres. In addition to the perimeter patrols, you'll be facing sentries and regular mage checks."

"Regular?" Eledine grinned. "Fools. Regular means predictable. I've been thinking, and with a little time, I should be able to cook up an additive to the enemy rations, something that will mean their soldiers will be spending too much time on the latrine to fight. Peri's proven her skill at stealth, and I'm not half-bad either. In fact, with a disguise, I could walk straight through the camp without raising an alarm. A few years in legal teaches you how to shut people down."

Kurra chuckled. "Enemy uniform can be arranged. So long as we clean off blood."

Xeldia added, "I'll tell you everything I know about church procedures that you'll need to know."

Eledine pulled out a parchment and quill. "Excellent. I'll start work on our poison. Let's start with gathering the materials…"

It was late evening by the time we were prepared—all the better for our infiltration. Kurra managed to take one of the scouts alive, and Xeldia talked him into giving up the passwords to access the camp. Eledine dressed in the scout's armour, and I cast my invisibility and followed her into the camp. I kept close, trusting in her presence to mask the non-visual signs of my own. The passwords worked, and we entered the camp.

Despite the late hour, the camp had no small amount of activity. Scouts were leaving and returning, supplies were being moved this way and that, and messengers were running to and fro. The bulk of the soldiers were taking one of the ever-rare opportunities to relax with games of dice, wagering rations. The camp was well illuminated with torches and campfires. No one looked at Eledine twice as she made her way to the supply tents.

We reached the first. I tapped her boot to get her attention. She knelt, acting as if she were adjusting her bootlaces.

I whispered, "You distract the guards. I'll do the poisoning."

Eledine surreptitiously nodded before standing and approaching the guards. "Hey. My quiver's got a hole in it, and the captain's being a bastard about the requisition form…"

As she and the guards got into an argument about procedure, I slipped inside. While the tent itself was surrounded by guards, the interior was mostly empty, so it was simple to open the boxes of sausages and dried vegetables and drizzle them with Eledine's concoction. I slipped out with no one the wiser, giving Eledine another tap to signal that I was done.

The next couple of supply tents went much the same. Then, we encountered one that just so happened to be next to where the church's war dogs were all based; my invisibility wouldn't fool a canine nose.

I whispered, "You do the poisoning this time?"

"Understood. I'll watch and wait."

I scanned the area, looking for a chance to cause a ruckus. I'd spent the bulk of my life trying to keep as far away from chaos as I could (the last couple of months notwithstanding), so causing it wasn't really my thing. But I then realised I was travelling with a very mischievous fox. I knelt and whispered, "Cosma, go."

She didn't need any further motivation. She scampered up to the war dogs and swiped some of their dinner. They were understandably upset. Within a second, they were barking their heads off, straining against their chains to get at Cosma, who taunted them from just beyond their reach. Of course, the guards gathered to see what the fuss was about.

One of them muttered, "Oh for the love of…come here, you little—"

Cosma nipped him on the hand before bolting.

The guard swore loudly. "Alright, you little shit, let's go!"

The guard released a few of the hounds, which leapt after a laughing Cosma. Perhaps an ordinary fox would have been caught quickly, but Cosma was anything but ordinary. She dashed between their legs, slipping between gaps in crates, dancing close to cookfires, and giggling all the while. More of the soldiers stood to see what was going on—Cosma was causing such a fuss that they nearly raised the alarm.

I kept track of Eledine as Cosma raised a commotion. It wasn't long before I saw her leave the supply tent, walking casually as if she had every right to be there. Calling on the link between master and familiar, I called Cosma back to me. She quickly scurried to my side, and I sheltered her under my invisibility field. We slunk away as the dogs sniffed around, Cosma's scent obscured by my own.

The rest of the raid proceeded as planned, and in time enough, Eledine and I calmly walked out of the camp as if nothing had happened. We returned to where Xeldia and Kurra were camped, both visibly anxious. The pair sighed in relief as Eledine came into view.

Xeldia said, "There you are! We saw a commotion and nearly intervened. Are you alright?"

Eledine smiled. "Everything went to plan. That commotion was just Cosma creating a distraction. Very well done, my fluffy friend."

Cosma yapped happily as I dismissed my invisibility, scampering up to accept some pets from Eledine.

With the church's forces hopefully held at bay, we headed to Ealshaver. Our camps were set up that little bit quicker, now that the four of us had started sharing a tent.

One night, as we roasted a boar that had wandered across Kurra's path, Eledine said, "I've had a thought. We might want to go to Avvenar first."

The town was farther than Ealshaver, so we all gave her quizzical looks.

She elaborated. "Simply because Ealshaver is an obvious move. We've taken out two colonies already. By now, they'll be ready for a third, especially if they know we're in the area. Avvenar gives us a larger force and a greater chance for success. I think that's worth a little extra travel time."

Kurra shrugged, turning the boar on the spit. "What more can they do? Post guards? Can handle them."

Xeldia gazed at the fire for a while. "Eledine's right. The revolts were messy even when the guards weren't ready. And Countess Narrisai will be no small aid in taking Ealshaver. We go to Avvenar. Unless you have any objections, Peri?"

I shook my head.

So, a few days later, we reached Avvenar. It was a small but prosperous town, though a number of its people had been mustered for war. We moved through town and quickly reached Narrisai's estate, a small manor enclosed with a large, well-kept garden. We calmly approached a guard stationed at the estate's front.

Xeldia, as usual, did the talking. "Hail. I have urgent news for Countess Narrisai."

The guard sighed in frustration. "Too late. She's been summoned to Heartshold. Ain't expected back for at least a week, maybe two."

"How long ago was this?" Xeldia asked.

"She left a couple of days back. You could leave a message." The guard casually leaned on his spear.

"Er, no. We will try again another day. Thank you." She turned and led us away. The second she was out of earshot, she muttered, "We need to reach Narrisai before she reaches the Heartshold."

Eledine seemed calm, but I could see a focus in her eyes. "She has a day head start. We need to do something clever," she said.

Kurra clenched her fists. "Let me go. Give me scroll. Will take it to her, alone. Will run from dawn to dusk. Will overtake her, in time."

"Kurra, trying to maintain that pace is dangerous. Not to mention that you're running headlong into the inquisition's territory." Eledine's voice wavered, just a little.

Kurra gritted her teeth. "Have any better ideas? We *need* Narrisai's help."

We paused, looking at each other.

Eventually, Eledine sighed. "Alright. I'll brew some speed-enhancing elixirs. Give me some time."

Xeldia turned back to the manor. "I'll see if I can talk them into giving her route."

Luckily, the guards couldn't tell the difference between a loyalist and a rebellious paladin of Raiya; they might not have even been informed that the latter existed. As such, Xeldia was able to leverage the church's weight into getting Kurra the information she needed. I did some quick shopping to get Eledine the materials she needed, and she was able to cook a few vials of fluid. She handed them to Kurra.

"Drink one at midday each day, no more," Eledine said.

"Once at noon each day, understood." Kurra pocketed the vials.

Xeldia handed Kurra the scroll. "While you do this, we'll go to Ealshaver."

Kurra snorted. "And I miss out on glory? Hah, very well. Good luck, my friends."

"Raiya guide you, Kurra." We gave each other a series of goodbye kisses.

Chapter 27

When we approached Ealshaver, we expected something not unlike Kessedarn, a large fort built into the mountains. But all we could see was the heavily guarded entrance to a tunnel.

I suggested, "Maybe the entire colony's underground?"

Some more scouting supported the idea: We found a number of windows dug into the mountainside, through which were offices and barracks for the colony's guards. We also found one or two large vents towards the top, from which the sounds of labour could be heard. The three of us regrouped to make a plan.

Xeldia's mood was grim. "Tight tunnels will rob us of any advantage in numbers. One of the few things we have going for us."

I recalled a time when a miner spent a long time whining in my parents' bar. "We could collapse the tunnels? The ones near the barracks?"

Eledine nodded. "Not a bad plan. I could make some explosives. The tricky part will be figuring out where to place them."

One of our followers, a one-handed orc named Kern, approached. "M'ladies, if I may?" We gestured for him to continue. "I used to work in the Hezerr mines. I know a thing or two about caves. You need a collapse. I can help."

"Glad to hear it. Come." Eledine beckoned him closer.

He sat down next to us. "Right, first thing I'll need is a good, solid map. As accurate as you can get it."

Xeldia said, "They will have one in the command centre. It will just be a matter of retrieving it."

I held up Cosma. She wagged her tail excitedly.

Eledine smirked. "Well, there's our thief. Now, we just need to find the command centre."

That proved easier than expected; Xeldia knew it would be somewhere towards the top of the colony, and we guessed that it would be one of the rooms with a window. We guessed right, and a little invisible scouting managed to find it. The map had been spread out on a large table, so we simply waited until the room was unattended before deploying Cosma. She tore the map pretty badly when dragging it out of the room, but it was still very much readable. With our prize, we slunk back to where we were camped.

What followed was a lengthy strategic discussion about tactics, stealth, and engineering. Only Eledine and I were remotely stealthy enough to infiltrate the colony to plant the explosives (and Cosma,,but planting the explosives would require opposable thumbs). So, we needed to cause enough damage to cripple the enemy force with only two blasts. This was a difficult problem, as the colony's engineers were competent enough to ensure their tunnels were resilient.

As Eledine and Xeldia started bickering over distances and positioning, I had an idea. I called upon the power of starlight and summoned a translucent image of the map, copying it exactly. Then, slowly and carefully, I rearranged it so that the model was three-dimensional.

Xeldia smiled warmly. "Very helpful, Peri. Good thinking. Anyway, my point is—"

Before the pair could resume their argument, Kern held up a hand to stop them. He leaned forward, peering carefully at the diagram. "…That room, there. What is it?"

Xeldia said, "The armoury. But as I said, destroying it alone will still leave us with every guard on duty."

"But here: You blast that column there, the earth will collapse into that cavern there. That'll leave an open path. It'll be a bit of a squeeze, but then the prisoners could grab the weapons themselves." Kern gestured to the various parts of my magical diagram.

Xeldia followed his gestures. "That just might work. We'd have to quickly barricade the door to bide time for the prisoners to arm themselves, but we could do it. And if we're able to collapse that corridor there, then the enemy force will be cut in half."

"Hmm…to do that, you'd have to knock out both these walls at once. It'd have to be a pretty big blast. You sure your explosives are up to it?" Kern asked Eledine.

"…Does it have to be *at once*? Peri should be able to ignite the charges from a distance with her starlight blasts. She can stand at that corner there." Eledine pointed out the location.

Kern did some internal calculations. "Hmm…you'd want to do it pretty quickly for maximum damage, but yeah, it'd work."

After finishing the remainder of our plan, we got to work. The first stage of the plan was much like Sunebarn Island; I slunk in through a large vent in the top of the colony and started gathering support for the upcoming riot. It was much easier than Sunebarn, thanks not only to my increased powers, but also to the web of small cracks and shadows, as well as the ever-present clatter of picks hitting rocks echoing throughout the tunnels, making stealth almost simple. My ability to fly made getting out just as easy as getting in.

Just like last time, the guards quickly worked out that something was amiss and started sending out search parties for me. But I could squeeze into some pretty tight cracks, so even magic-detecting mages weren't able to find me. Within a couple of days, I had a riot brewing. Eledine had spent that time brewing all the explosive charges we'd need, so we were ready to kick things off.

The tricky part was that while I could turn myself invisible, Eledine didn't have the same ability. A light step, lithe figure, and dark cloak got pretty close, especially in the dark of the tunnels, but it would still be much more difficult. The lack of an ability to fly also necessitated that she rappel down the vent, which was more exposed. Her problems were ones solved with the occasional distraction, courtesy of a cunning witch and her mischievous fox.

Once Eledine was on her way to placing her charges, I slipped through the tunnels to place my own. I kept a quick pace; I had to detonate the charges soon after Eledine detonated hers. I wove to the hidden alcove where the first of the charges was to be placed. There, I saw four guards playing a game of cards away from the watchful eyes of their superiors. I gulped; while they were clearly doing something they weren't supposed to, I wasn't willing to gamble that they'd simply let me plant a whole cluster of alchemical explosives.

I slunk down an adjacent corridor to plant the other charges I'd need to detonate; thankfully, that proceeded without issue. But there was still half a squad of guards where I'd need to cause a pretty big explosion. My magical powers had increased to the point where I could probably take them out myself, but doing so without raising an alarm was another matter entirely.

As I worked on a solution to that problem, the situation shifted: I heard the thunderous blast that could only be Eledine making her move. The guards were stunned for a second but swiftly set their game aside when Xeldia's howl echoed throughout the colony. The chaos had granted me the opening I needed, but it meant that more guards would be able to respond to the riot than we'd hoped. I rushed to plant the charges, hoping to still mitigate the damage.

I was keenly aware of every second passing as I took position, crouched behind a rock, and fired a pair of starlight blasts at the charges. The blasts were both deafening, and even from a distance and behind cover, I got a face full of dust and debris. I heard another deafening rumble as the cave shifted. I quickly shook the dust off myself and headed to the fight.

Xeldia wasn't hard to find; both the sounds of battle and the bright glow of her holy aura could be perceived from a great distance, even through the maze of tunnels. She'd successfully led a band of prisoners into the armoury through the hole Eledine had made, and they'd both armed themselves and barricaded the door against the guards. But the guards had arrived in force and had the rioting prisoners hemmed in.

It was time for some more stellar power. The first squad of guards had their backs to me, so I decided to forgo my more defensive spells, instead blasting them with the void's chill. They were dispatched before they even realised that I was there. A few more noticed me, but they made the mistake of coming at me piecemeal, meaning it was simple for me to blast them one by one.

I fought my way back to where Xeldia and Eledine were holding the line. The prisoners, one on one, were outmatched, but

Xeldia rushed to where they faltered, and in her presence, they redoubled her presence, and the guards fell back. Eledine kept up a steady fire rate of arrows, coupled with the occasional bomb, where the guards massed.

After a moment, enough guards had rallied and organised for a more sophisticated strategy. They formed into shield walls, advancing slowly and carefully, with crossbows fired over the formations. Casting my darkness slowed them, but there were too many for me to hold them all.

Xeldia shouted orders while covering behind her shield. "Get down! Take cover! Wait for gaps to appear in their formations! Peri, Eledine, I need some gaps!"

Eledine was happy to provide. She tossed another bomb, carefully aiming it to land under the advancing shield walls. It found its mark, making a bloody mess of the tightly packed formation. The prisoners, drunk on rage and newfound power, were all too happy to take advantage.

I couldn't lob my magic the same way Eledine could. My first approach was to just try blasting through the shield wall with raw power. I had enough that it eventually worked, but it took valuable time and cost me a few cuts from barely deflected bolts. When I shifted to the next formation, I came up with a new tactic. I obscured their eyes with darkness, then sent Cosma to slip between their legs. I channelled my power through the connection we shared, blasting them from behind. They turned to respond to the new threat. Cosma quickly fled, but she had broken the formation for the one critical moment the prisoners needed.

After another minute of exhausting battle, Eledine called, "I see the enemy captain!"

Xeldia charged, crashing into the enemy, shouting, "Cover my flank!"

The bulk of the remaining guards formed up, trying to hold off Xeldia. I wove my magic around her, granting her a speed to match their number. She spun like a whirlwind, her blessed sword carving clean through the enemy's armour. I followed behind her. It wasn't long before she had cut her way to the enemy captain. A stellar light show kept the remaining guards blinded long enough for Xeldia to have a one-on-one fight, which she soundly won, a straight hit caving in the captain's helmet.

The guards were disciplined enough to not surrender straight away. This was only a small problem to Xeldia, who rallied the remaining prisoners around her and started pressing the advantage. With a greater ability to coordinate her forces, she drove the remaining guards out.

Again, we had staged a successful prison riot. Again, we needed to restrain the freed prisoners from going too far in their revenge. Again, Xeldia got to work building a new government. It at least went smoother, Xeldia having learned lessons from the previous two riots and boasting an increasingly commanding presence thanks to the Triune's blessings.

Chapter 28

The next day, my party prepared to return to Avvenar, hoping that Kurra had succeeded in reaching Countess Narrisai before the inquisition.

But as we were preparing to leave, one of the ex-prisoners hurried up to us. "Oi! Might need a bit more help. Church courier just showed up. Had this." He handed Xeldia a letter.

Xeldia scanned it, deeply concerned. "The enemy has reinforcements inbound. Numerous reinforcements. If they don't know that we've revolted, they'll figure it out soon enough."

Eledine asked, "Will they attack, though? This place is a fortress, and we have supplies. If they were planning to just reinforce an existing garrison, they might be reluctant to attack."

"Perhaps. But we have no guarantees. You and Peri, scout the enemy reinforcements. I'll stay here and prepare defences."

Eledine and I nodded in agreement, so we set out. Before the day had ended, we found a large church camp. A little invisibility got me to their command centre. They had a mage watching the entrance, but not the surrounding area, so I was able to at least listen in.

I guessed a lieutenant was giving a report. "...says he fled the attack. Cunning bastards caused a cave-in in the barracks and tunnelled their way into the armoury. Had a damn army before anyone knew what was happening."

Another voice, grim and determined: "It's them."

A third voice, I guessed a higher-ranking general or commander: "Agreed. Send for Retten." I heard a messenger saluting and hurrying off, then the same voice: "We need to squash this rebellion, and we need to do so *now*. I want an assault plan."

A fourth voice: "A suggestion, sir? The colony is too well-fortified for an assault, but the terrain would make it easy to siege. With so many people, and without supply from Avvenar, they'll run out of food quickly."

The commander hummed. "Agreed. But that leaves the problem of what to do if they counterattack. And if Xeldia really is with them, they'll be able to come up with a sophisticated strategy."

"Could we let Retten deal with her first?"

"No, he works too slowly. We'll have to dig in, plan our deployments carefully. I want fortifications here, here, here, and here. We place our cavalry here, to cover this region…"

As he spoke, I noticed someone else approaching the command centre. The subtle darkening of the air around him marked him as bearing magical power. As he approached, he paused, looking straight at me.

He said to a nearby soldier, "Found the slip." He pulled out a longbow.

I dove for cover behind a nearby crate. The impact of the arrow sent a hail of splinters at me—no ordinary longbow. As the soldiers raised the alarm, I decided it was time to leave. I cast my flight spell but didn't go straight up; I would have been too exposed to the archer's fire. Instead, I flew to the side, weaving between tents and crates. It wasn't enough. An arrow landed in my arm, and it took all the wards on my robes to stop it from going clean through me. I cried out in pain. A kick of adrenaline kept me flying.

Explosions rocked the camp. The guards scrambled to respond. I kept flying. I recognised a smoke cloud belonging to one of Eledine's smoke bombs and flew towards it. Another bow shot sliced my leg open as I entered it. Tears stinging my eyes, I banked quickly, trying to lose the archer's attention. I emerged from the other side and quickly flew outside of the camp and behind a rock.

Eledine was beside me in another second. Her eyes widened with worry, but she forced calm into her voice. "Alright, Peri, I've got you. I've got you…" She immediately covered my wounds with some medicinal salve. As the guards started sweeping the area, she hissed in anger. "Damn, we need to leave."

Glancing around, she picked me up and hurried off into the night. The second she was confident we had lost the enemy, she set me back down. Despite visibly straining for breath, she held her hands perfectly steady as she tended my wounds.

We returned to Ealshaver and told Xeldia about all that had happened. She frowned as she examined the maps in the colony's command centre. "If you were detected, we have to assume they know you eavesdropped on their plans and will change details accordingly. But they are right in that a siege is the correct move. And this Retten…they would not send him against us unless they thought he had a chance. He must be very dangerous. We need a plan."

The three of us stared at the maps for a while. Eledine was the next to speak. "It's time to face facts: The prisoners could certainly cause damage, but practically, we can't survive an open-field battle *or* a siege."

"Then our only option is an ambush. In this gully here, that's our best bet." Xeldia started moving pieces on the map.

"That will be an expected move. There are only so many places we can hide, and it won't be hard for scouts to spot us."

Something clicked in my mind—this was a *mining* colony. We had plenty of picks, shovels, and explosives. "Cause a landslide?"

Eledine and Xeldia looked at me, then at each other, and nodded.

Staging a landslide turned out to be a pretty complicated endeavour, but the prisoners were outright eager to help, eager for the spectacle of burying their oppressors. Once the work was started, and Eledine was cooking up the extra explosives we'd need, Xeldia started building a force and working to manoeuvre the enemy into the trap. I kept myself and Cosma busy by keeping an eye on the church's movements.

With some alarm, I noticed that the church had deployed some light infantry climbing up our east flank, to a position where they'd be above the landslide. The difficult ridge there lessened the extent of the threat, but it'd be something we'd have to deal with. Once I felt like I was out of time, I flew back to the others.

I found Xeldia bloodied, in her wolf form, being hurriedly carried to Eledine by the liberated colonists.

One of the prisoners explained, "Someone got her! Some sneaky cloaked bastard. She chased him off, but I think she's poisoned!"

Eledine hurried to her side, studying her carefully. "I think you're right. Alright, help me—"

She was interrupted by signal whistles in the distance— the enemy was about to attack.

"Dammit! Help me move her to cover. We need to deploy the reserve force to the east. Everyone else, stick to the plan!"

The colonists rushed into position. I flew to the east flank; if the landslide plan worked, then they'd be the biggest remaining threat. The terrain was rocky and littered with crags, the very reason we were willing to bet the enemy wouldn't move a large force through it. I flew between the rocks and crags, blasting the enemy with stellar light and cosmic darkness before ducking back into cover. My empowered magic could reach far, and I was able to cause the force no small amount of trouble and damage as they advanced.

I could hear the rumble of the land as the prisoners sprung their trap. I didn't have time to watch—the reserves had engaged, and the colonists would need all the help they could get to overpower the better-trained and equipped soldiers. I had plenty of help to give. My magic blinded the enemy, leaving them wide open for the colonists' attacks.

Then, I came under fire from a barrage of arrows. I ducked down into cover. Then, I peered my head out to see what had happened. The sight made my heart sink: The landslide had gone off prematurely, and well over half of the attacking force was still at full strength and was quickly overpowering the scattered colonists. With the battle on the east flank swung in our favour, I hurriedly flew towards the front lines.

Again, I turned my magic towards the fight. My spells were powerful and far-reaching, and around me, the colonists were able to fight back. But for all my power, I was just one woman. My allies and I were swiftly surrounded, and a barrage of arrows fired from behind the enemy ranks forced me on the defensive. I gritted my teeth and kept fighting; the fate of the world was resting on my shoulders.

I heard a screech from above. I looked up and felt terror: The enemy, already having taken the advantage, had a whole flock of eagle riders advancing on our position. But I could feel my star's power coursing through me. I wasn't ready to give up, not yet. At least, I could make sure the church bled for this. I flew upwards.

An arrow wedged itself in my foot—one woven with spell-disrupting patterns. Gravity reasserted itself, and I was falling towards a thicket of spears. I managed to restore the spell just enough to stop the fall from being lethal, but I still hit the ground hard, surrounded by enemy soldiers.

As I tried to scamper away, a boot firmly pinned me to the ground. "Gotcha, slip."

It was the magical archer who had shot me in the camp. I tried casting a spell, but he deftly flicked a knife into my wrist. I cried out in pain. I struggled in vain as he dragged me deeper behind enemy lines.

I heard a familiar roar of rage, and the archer dodged just quick enough to turn a lethal strike into one that just cost him half of his arm. Kurra landed on the ground next to me. She spun like a whirlwind, her every movement carving bloody arcs through the air. Within a second, every soldier within reach was dead, and those outside were hesitating. Kurra didn't hesitate. Quickly grabbing me with one arm, she lunged into battle with the other, carving a swath through the enemy force. I was worried about the threat from above until one of the eagles swooped down on the other church forces. For reasons I didn't know, they were on our side, and I certainly wasn't about to complain.

Between Kurra and the eagle riders, the enemy force was quickly routed. The second she must have realised the enemy had got the message, Kurra turned back and rushed towards the prisoners. "Where's Eledine?" When they looked at each other, uncertain, she shouted, "The elf doctor! Now!"

Cowed, they pointed in her direction, and Kurra sprinted off. Eledine had established an impromptu medical tent, staffed with those prisoners with medical knowledge or healing magics (not many, but more than I expected), currently flooded with the wounded.

Kurra sprinted up to Eledine. "Peri's hurt!"

Eledine's eyes widened in surprise. "Kurra?" She forced her focus back on topic, examining me quickly. "Okay, do everything you can to staunch the bleeding, then put her in the mid-priority area there." She quickly got back to tending to her current patient.

Kurra wasn't Eledine, but she knew enough about medicine to stop me from bleeding out while the healers worked through the innumerable casualties.

They were eventually joined by Xeldia, looking exhausted, but otherwise recovered from the poison. As she started using her healing powers on the wounded, she was approached by Kurra, along with two others. One was a tall, regal woman who wore her hair in elaborate braids, the other a tanned halfling in colourful clothes.

"Xeldia," Kurra said. "Countess Narraisai and Chieftain Kali."

Xeldia bowed. "Well met. Your arrival could not have come at a better time."

Narraisai bowed in turn. "Nor could Kurra's. She found us just as the inquisition levelled their blades at our necks."

Kali added, "She told us about Viola's treason and your little rebellion. I mustered my tribe to help. Our shamans are currently working on our own wounded, but we'll send them over as soon as they're finished."

That night, after we patched up our wounds, we shared our stories over dinner. We were all glad to be back, together, in friendly territory, not immediately threatened. Narraisai had reinforcements coming, and, like Xeldia, she was shocked to discover the true conditions in the Reborn Colonies. She was happy to establish trade with the new settlement. She and Kali were also marshalling their forces for the coming war. Neither were entirely happy about simply being the distraction, but they acknowledged that we couldn't hope to win a conventional war.

Once everyone was brought up to speed, Kurra asked, "So, what next?"

Eledine answered, "We get some rest. Just a bit, no more than a day, but we all direly need it."

"Will Viola be resting?" Kurra grumbled.

"Maybe not, but we need to. Kurra, you've been running flat-out on alchemical stimulants for days straight, and both Peri and Xeldia have serious wounds. Healing magics have accelerated the healing all they can—if we don't rest, we're going to regret it." Eledine said, matter-of-fact.

I nodded. "Yes. Rest. Please." My foot was still aching from the hit I took the previous day.

Xeldia seemed to debate internally for a moment before saying, "Agreed."

Chapter 29

The four of us spent most of the next day sleeping (and cuddling). By the next morning, I felt like I had an entire load taken off my back. We then got to planning the next stage of our war: inspiring the oppressed to revolt. To do that, they'd just need some coordination and support. Narraisai sent some of her own agents to gather the support of scattered orc and goblin communities in the rural areas, so the four of us, more experienced with staging insurrections, decided to work on spearing a bigger fish: Hannadar, the second biggest city in the region to Ansiel itself. If we could take control, the church would lose a lot of industry.

We started our march. After spending time in the cool mountains, we enjoyed the late summer days. Word had spread of the building war, but by this time our force was visibly strong enough to deter the bandits seeking to take advantage of the chaos.

As we walked, I could faintly hear a pained grunt from Kurra. I whispered, "You alright?"

"Fine! Just tightness in the chest. Probably something I ate," she said dismissively.

Eledine frowned. "A tightness in the chest? Let me have a look. Take off your chest plate."

Kurra grumbled but did so.

Eledine held some fingers to her chest and to a vein on the neck. "Hmm…as I thought, your body is feeling the aftereffects of pushing it so far past its limits. The good news is, I think that day off has saved you from a heart attack. Let's keep going until we find a shaded spot, then have a short rest. That should be plenty for your heart to get itself back in order."

Kurra's ache vanished completely after a few minutes' rest, and we were back on our way soon enough. Within a few days, we reached Hannadar. The city was large and impressive, with large carts laden with goods travelling to and fro, buildings reaching into the sky, and the sounds of labour from every corner.

We spent some time scoping the city. At first, we were worried that our plans were drawn on poor information; the oppressed underbelly wasn't swift to show itself. But digging just beneath the calm facade built by the church, we found what we were looking for. Goblin families were crammed into side streets and alleys, workers grumbled about poor conditions when their supervisors weren't in earshot, and the aggrieved whispered about loved ones sent to the colonies. We also managed to infiltrate the guards' headquarters and gain some information about known dissidents. The impending war had both benefits and complications: On the one hand, the bulk of the city's fighting force had been sent to the front lines, and the Heartshold's increased demand for resources further strained the city's workers. On the other hand, the church's preaching of a demon invasion had proven to be an effective call for unity.

While doing a little scouting after dark, I saw a band of goblins scurrying through an alley. I stealthily followed. They headed to an abandoned barn on the edge of town, where some other of the city's disenfranchised had gathered. Flying up to the rafters, I observed. All gathered were in poor condition, ranging from unbathed to deathly ill. Most were lounging on packs of hay, listless. A few, wearing patchwork robes, had drawn a large circle of runes on the ground that I couldn't identify.

One, wearing some sort of pendant of strange black stone, called those assembled to attention. "Servants of Kaissa! I know why you're all here. First, what offerings do you grant our lady?"

The answer turned out to be mostly loose change, though one or two had brought out larger amounts of money or jewellery. The robed fellows started invoking some sort of blessing on those assembled, with more sophisticated blessings for those who brought greater offerings.

Then, another person came in, a dishevelled orc woman carrying a fussing baby. "Here! Here! Is this an offering? Is it?"

The apparent leader grinned. "An offering most grand! A very life and soul for Kaissa! Come, let us invoke her grandest of blessings!" He pulled out a ceremonial dagger.

I'd seen enough. I blinded the assembled cultists with a flash of starlight, swooped in, grabbed the kid, and flew back into the night before any had the faintest idea what had happened. I then realised I had an entire baby in my arms and no real idea of what to do with it. Not trusting the guards, I settled on a local hospital, leaving it there with a note explaining that she'd been rescued from a human sacrifice. I would have to hope they'd figure something out for the poor thing. If the Triune's plans were fulfilled, then countless desperate folk like them would benefit.

When I regrouped with the others in a dingy tavern, I explained what had happened.

Xeldia scowled. "Kaissa, one of the Grand Demons. She promises drug-like highs to those who offer her sacrifices. Offering human sacrifices is nothing new for those wretches. We should slaughter them."

Kurra frowned. "Aren't downtrodden and desperate where we seek allies?"

"It's more than desperation, to worship a Grand Demon! It's here where we and the church have a common enemy." Xeldia clenched her fist.

Eledine looked thoughtful. "…Maybe it *is* just desperation. I read a report in the university suggesting that addictions may have a medical aspect, which matches my experience; I met one or two alcoholics in legal circles, and they say trying to abstain from drink causes unbearable pain. It's possible that Kaissa is taking advantage of this phenomenon."

Xeldia opened her mouth to object. She then considered the idea. "…Maybe. Could they be healed? The church has never attempted it."

"I'd have to find the papers again, but I know a mechanism was suggested. I could try to engineer a cure. Luckily, the university has a campus here—that should give me all the resources I need."

Xeldia said, "Very well. In the meantime, I will start to rally a movement. We will make demands for acceptance and equality, and seize infrastructure if—well, when—those demands aren't met."

Eledine's part of the plan proceeded remarkably quickly; in a stroke of good fortune, there was another alchemist already in the city working on that very problem, and she was eager for Eledine's help. Ynnelia's blessing had also somehow enhanced Eledine's insight, and she worked quickly, synthesising information and drawing out new properties from reagents previously unknown. I helped; all I knew about alchemy was what little Eledine had taught me, but hard experience growing up in a tavern had taught me a thing or two about alcoholics.

After a day or two of that, Eledine and I returned to the tavern.

Finding it covered in blood.

Civilians were cowering behind tables and benches, barely daring to peer out. The sounds of battle could be heard from upstairs. Eledine and I rushed up, weapons ready.

We arrived just in time to see Kurra cleave a cloaked figure in half. She looked at us, tense and looking for targets, but her gaze quickly darted to the rest of the halls. After a moment, she relaxed. "Hah! You come just as we finish last of them!"

Eledine stowed her bow. "Are you alright? Where's Xeldia?"

From a nearby room, Xeldia called, "Here!"

We entered to find Xeldia tying up one of the assailants. She explained, "Inquisitors, no doubt. They must have noticed our activities."

Eledine frowned. "Then they're on to us. We'll have to move quickly."

Xeldia wiped some blood off her armour. "We're a step ahead, for now. But you're right. Fear not, I have our next move planned already."

Like any Triune-worshipping city, Hannadar had plenty of churches, but the bulk of its paladins were focused on the Temple of Raiya's Golden Heart in the centre of the city. It was a large and imposing fortress-cathedral, with grand statues of the Triune and their saints watching over from turrets. A grand gate opened into an immense hall, gleaming with sunlight cast through stained-glass windows, echoing with prayers.

Between our rebellion-building efforts and linking up with a cell of Triune loyalists, we'd gathered a small militia of men-at-arms, and they followed a few paces behind us, who followed a few paces behind Xeldia. She strode into the hall, her holy aura at its brightest. She'd gone without a gauntlet to show everyone the gleaming mark of the chosen.

The prayer stopped at the sight of Xeldia. Every gaze in the room was fixed on her.

The high stone roofs echoed with her voice. "Faithful of the Triune, hear me! Since I was but a girl, I have served the Triune with all my soul, as have countless of you. And like you, I have had questions. Why do we kill for a thousand different crimes, when Raiya says justice must be tempered with mercy? Why do we hate those across our borders, when Ynnelia says to embrace our differences? Why do we leave countless in slums, when Etunae says to love all? Why do we claim to serve the Triune when ignoring all they say? My brethren in faith, I have spoken with the Triune themselves—it is they that blessed me and my companions with these marks, they who chose us! And they told me the truth. The truth is"—she held up the scroll—"the Heartshold turned against the Triune's light centuries ago. Viola Senredia turned against their light—"

One of the paladins nearby stood, drawing her sword. "Heretic!" She swung at Xeldia. Her holy shield flashed with light, sending the paladin sprawling.

"The so-called Herald is the heretic! For five hundred years, she has been using the Triune's name for her own selfish ends! And all have suffered for it." Xeldia focused for a moment and shifted, to the further shock of all assembled. "All my life, I have hidden this part of myself, for the fear of others. Not once has the church offered me justice, or curiosity, or love. I say, to all of you, to all of *us*: Enough! It is time for the dawn of a new realm. A realm where righteousness, discovery, and beauty are not just words, but ideals! Ideals we live up to, not just for a handful of nobles, but for everyone! Each and every one of us!"

The priestess at the altar snarled in rage. "Traitor! Warriors of—"

She was interrupted by an adjacent paladin putting a sword against her throat. "No. She is right." Then, the paladin bloomed with golden light.

Xeldia called, "See, now! Raiya sees your faith—not in the church's doctrine, but her cause! And she rewards you! Faithful, stand with us now!"

The hall echoed with the sounds of warriors leaping to their feet and weapons being drawn. Some joined Xeldia's side, some turned weapons towards them, some turned weapons towards those in turn, and before long, it was very difficult to tell who was on which side. Thankfully, my allegiance was obvious, so all I had to do was fight the people trying to kill me.

I'd never be able to figure out exactly what happened in the whirlwind of steel that followed. But, when the cacophony of battle finally died down, and the last warrior lowered their weapon, Xeldia was still standing, the rest of us around her.

She strode to the altar, stepping over the bodies of her enemies. "My fellow faithful! The rebellion against the so-called Herald's heresy is finally at hand. This was just one of a great many victories. The rebellions in the Reborn Colonies—those, too, are steps towards our cause! Now, we take Hannadar, or failing that, deny the enemy its forges. Let us start by driving the heretics from this place; from here is where we will strike."

She quickly took charge, arranging the clearing of the dead and the detaining of surrendered enemies. She also made sure the entrances to the cathedral were guarded and fortified, as she expected the local guards would prepare a counterattack as soon as they learned what had happened. She was proved right, with the guards laying siege to the building mere moments after our followers had taken their positions. Fortunately, an outright attack was unlikely, and the cathedral was built to withstand a siege, with defensible entrances and plenty of supplies. Furthermore, we weren't planning on dragging this out.

Quick scouting showed that the city guards expected that the only threats were inside the temple and had set up their perimeter accordingly, with their rear entirely exposed. We would show them their folly. Kurra and Xeldia were a little too high profile to leave the temple, so it was up to Eledine and me to muster the mob we'd been gathering.

While we'd been laying the groundwork for a few days, it still proved far easier than we expected—soon, there was a veritable army of those with not all that much to lose, happy to grab something sharp and, as soon as we gave the signal, stick it in the guards who had been giving them all the trouble. Getting them sharp things to stick was also surprisingly easy, thanks to a few blacksmiths disgruntled with the Heartshold's ever-increasing demands. For the signal, the presence of stray dogs in the city made howling not feasible, but the temple had plenty of signal horns.

Chapter 30

That night, Eledine and I headed to the abandoned barn that the cult of Kaissa was based out of. Through a gap in the door, we saw the cult leader briefing her congregation. "Faithful! I bring word from Kaissa herself! The greatest of her enemies has returned, and she promises eternal bliss for those who bring her the souls of her enemies!"

Eledine flung open the doors, striding into the open. "You all know damn well that none of you have a chance."

"Infid—" the leader started to scream, but I silenced her with the quiet of the void. I walked behind Eledine, making obvious my magical power.

Eledine held out a series of vials. "I know why you're all doing this—because the cheap highs Kaissa offers are the only reason you have to get up in the morning. Well, I'm here to offer you a better reason. Decent jobs, comfortable beds, filling meals—"

One of the cultists rushed at Eledine, quickly meeting their end on her rapier.

"—and being able to go through a whole day without risking getting stabbed."

One of the addicts stood, pulling out a shiv. "Let me have my damn blessings, knife-ear!"

Eledine was unperturbed. "If it's easing the cravings you want, I have a solution to that as well. These are experimental addiction suppressants—not the intense high you may be hoping for, but you'll feel better over a longer period. And the rebellion is willing to offer a steady supply, so long as you stay clear of the demon cults."

One of the addicts slowly got to their feet. "Fuck it, I'm in. Hate this bitch anyway."

One of the cultists shouted, "Traitors! Get 'em!" Half of the cult stood, drawing weapons.

They didn't fare well. Once the cult leader and ranking cultists were dead, the surviving addicts quickly surrendered. While I dismantled all the magical constructs the cult had established to minimise the chance of demon incursions, Eledine handed out the addiction suppressants.

She explained, "Now, we're having some trouble distributing this stuff with the guards barricading the temple, but that's something you can help with…"

A slight wrinkle in our plan was revealed when the next day came, and the various mobs preparing to attack turned out to be kind of obvious, enough so that some of the guards turned their attention to them. Still, we had them surrounded and badly outnumbered, so we kept up with the plan. The faithful paladins mustered, visibly getting ready for battle. We waited just a moment for the guards to turn their attention towards the most obvious threat. Then, the temple blew three short blasts.

An enthusiastic roar came up from the crowd. They charged. They crashed onto the guards like a tidal wave. The guards hurried to respond, forming into disciplined shield walls and levelling crossbows at the mobs. Eledine and I weren't sitting around to just let that happen; with alchemical smoke and starlight, we blinded the guards, robbing them of the advantage of ranged weapons. This proved even worse for them when the temple revealed they still had their own missiles, opening fire from a vantage point. Seeing the chance to catch the guards between hammer and anvil, Xeldia ordered the faithful to charge. With a massive mob on one side and elite soldiers on the other, the guards stood no chance.

When the last of the guards threw down their weapons, Xeldia took position atop one of the barricades, wearing her beast form. "True faithful! Now is the time to cast down the lords that have shoved us into alleys and sewers for all these years! We march on the mayor's estate and install one that cares for the people!"

A triumphant roar came up from the assembled mob. Xeldia's holy aura was a fine standard to rally behind, and she led her army towards the mayor's estate. Mayors in cities like these were democratically elected in theory, but it was very difficult to gain the right to vote, and very easy to lose it, leaving the people who needed it most without a voice. A problem that Xeldia was hoping to solve.

We arrived at the mayor's estate—a grand, gilded manor—currently in the process of being hastily fortified by the city's remaining soldiers. As the mob approached, a hail of arrows was fired from the manor's upper levels. The rioters fell in dozens.

Xeldia called, "Take cover! Paladins, shield wall, wide and high! Everyone else, take cover behind them!"

The tactic worked, allowing a slow but steady advance on the manor. Still, we weren't in the best position.

Xeldia waved her sword in a gesture to gather. "Eledine! Kurra! Peri! With me! We finish this!"

We rallied behind her. Eledine tossed another smoke bomb in front of the manor's entrance to cover our advance, and Kurra charged, the rest of us right behind her. Xeldia's holy shield absorbed what arrows found us through the smoke, and Kurra's might crashed clean through the manor's doors.

The squad of guards behind it made a good effort to stop her, a strong shield wall delaying her attacks and spears scoring some hits. Eledine answered with some explosives to scatter their formations, which left them wide open. We kept fighting through the manor—these guards were the more elite soldiers—and we occasionally needed each other's help to get through, but get through we did.

We reached the mayor's office. Kurra kicked down the door. On the other side stood the mayor, a tall, imperious man surrounded by aides and guards. He already had a spell in his hand and sent it at Kurra in the form of an immense fireball. Xeldia's holy shield and Kurra's dragonbone plate absorbed the worst of the damage, but it delayed us for a second.

In that second, large statues of warriors around the office animated, turning towards us. Their weapons couldn't have been sharp, but they didn't need to be to be deadly. They quickly positioned themselves between us and our target. Kurra recovered and stepped forward, quickly reducing one to rubble, but two more took its place, forcing her on the defensive. The mayor and his aides blanketed us with spells and crossbow bolts, forcing us into cover.

Covering behind the wall, I ducked out to blast the enemy with starlight. The spell didn't find much purchase on the animated statues, but it did at least slow the barrage of projectiles, giving Kurra and Xeldia some much-needed breathing space.

Eledine, covering behind me, was coating an arrow in poison. "Peri! I need a clear shot at the mayor. Cover me!"

I stepped out into the open, closer to Xeldia to ensure I benefited from her holy protections and started spellcasting even more aggressively. The mayor took the bait—concentrating a large amount of magical power, he fired a blast of force that sent me flying out of a window. I managed to cast my flight spell a split second before a very painful landing.

I flew back into the fight. The mayor had ducked for cover behind his desk, while Kurra and Xeldia remained in a pitched battle against the statues and remaining guards.

Xeldia was having difficulties. "I can't hack through all this stone!"

Eledine whistled for Cosma, handing her a flask. "Give this to Xeldia! Hurry!"

Cosma yipped affirmatively, hurrying over to Xeldia. One of the nearby guards had forced her arm into an awkward position, and a statue strike had knocked the shield off her arm. It might have been bad, had it not left that arm free to quickly grab the elixir. She quickly downed it before switching to a two-handed grip on her sword. The elixir worked quickly; a few seconds later, she'd managed to hack the statue into pieces.

Kurra had managed to take out the other statue and most of the guards, and the remaining combatants surrendered. We approached the mayor, still slumped behind the desk.

Eledine smiled in satisfaction. "A mix of sventar root and powdered boar tusk—it severely hinders one's ability to focus. Not fun for anyone, but for spellcasters, it's a particular pain." She helped Kurra bind the mayor.

With the bulk of the guards killed or routed, the city was very much in the Triune's hands. Eledine handed the faithful paladins the recipe for her addiction suppressant, and they promised to hand it to all who needed it. Furthermore, an angelic messenger arrived—the rebellion in the north was in full swing. While the Heartshold had won a number of battles, they had been forced to commit the bulk of their forces to the mountainous terrain, including multiple of the Anointed. After discussing the news, my companions and I agreed: It was time to move on to Ansiel itself.

This, of course, raised the question of how to get into the city while being the inquisition's most wanted. We found the solution to that problem inside the Temple of Raiya's Golden Heart: They'd captured a smuggler some weeks ago. Not a saint, but Eledine examined the records of her cargo and found it was mostly drugs that, while illegal, weren't seriously harmful, so Xeldia was willing to strike a deal: the smuggler's freedom for access to the city.

Chapter 31

That's how we found ourselves crammed into crates in the hold of a river barge. It was more comfortable than some of our previous tightly crammed arrangements, thanks to our romantic tension being mostly resolved, but it still wasn't exactly *comfortable* being crammed into a small crate with a human, an elf, and a *massive* orc. It was only for an hour or two while the barge passed the checkpoints, but it was a long couple of hours. Especially since the smugglers warded off curious guards with an adjacent crate of rotten fish.

After a while, we heard the beat of armoured boots on the deck and chatter between the guards and the smugglers. We tensed. Voices steadily raised.

Eledine placed a hand on her rapier. "Something's wrong."

The voices grew loud enough for me to pick up words like "smugglers," "old tricks," and "criminals." Then, the armoured boots left the hold. We gave barely muffled sighs of relief.

Then came shouts of alarm. Something thumped loudly on the top deck of the barge. We paused, unsure what to do.

Eledine whispered, "… I think I hear fire."

I cracked open the crate a tiny bit. "Cosma, scout." She scurried off.

She returned a second later, screaming in alarm.

Kurra grumbled, "Guess we're made."

We left the crate, weapons ready. Fire could be seen from the upper decks.

One of the smugglers staggered down the steps, multiple arrows embedded in him. "They…didn't want…to take chances…"

Eledine rushed up to him. "I'll try to stabilise him! Peri, see if you can slow that fire. Kurra, Xeldia, get the rest of our luggage."

It was a sound enough plan, and now wasn't the time to seek better than "sound enough." I stood at the base of the stairs, calling the cold of the void, sapping the heat the fire needed to live. I managed to clear an area at the top of the stairs, but in the meantime, the rest of the top deck had caught ablaze. The walls around us were starting to ignite, and what wasn't on fire was taking on water. On the bright side, Kurra and Xeldia were quick to gather our things, and Eledine managed to heal the smuggler of the worst of their injuries. She took an arm around her shoulder and helped him up.

"We need to get out of here, now!" Eledine said.

We rushed up what remained of the stairs.

Which then turned to "nothing" as a barrage of fireballs hit it.

We rolled back onto the lower deck, our enchanted armour and the moisture in the room saving us from all but a light singe. The barge swayed underneath us, and water began pooling, high enough that I needed to engage my flight to avoid being completely submerged.

Xeldia called, "Eledine! Hand Peri some smoke bombs! She'll have to cover our escape! Peri—good luck."

I gulped; I never enjoyed being the centre of attention, especially if most of that attention was coming in the form of hostiles with magic and crossbows. But my crowd control spells did make me the best option for this situation, and besides, Cosma had taught me a new spell that I'd been looking to put through its paces. So, I covered my advance with the smoke bombs and rose into the air.

There were cries of panic and rage all around. We were in the grand canal that flowed through the centre of the city, surrounded by a host of guards, including a few wizards and a squad of church-aligned paladins, all of whom were barraging the sinking barge with fire. Between Eledine's smoke bombs and my small size, I had an opening enough to cast a spell. I focused on the invocations.

I turned my very body into a gate for my patron's power and flung it wide open. My body burst with stellar fire. It wreathed around me, through me. It empowered me. I swelled with the immense power I was channelling, morphing into an avatar of stellar power.

That certainly got the guards' attention. They turned their fire onto me. I flared with cosmic fires, incinerating bolts in flight and shattering spell constructs. Seeking a more efficient defence, I flew down to the nearby rooftops for cover, returning fire as I did so. My battle form didn't have the fine control of magic needed for my more complex spells, but I didn't need them—my power was enough to beat back the bulk of the guards, and my gleaming form kept the attention of those that remained.

A blast of necrotic energies scored a direct hit, and I felt my heart skip a beat, my cosmic fire flickering. Turning towards the source, I saw another wizard, this one floating, surrounded by a dozen runes. I returned fire with starlight. He took it on a magical shield of power and sophistication I'd never seen before. I narrowly dodged his next attack, slipping behind a church's steeple for cover, and continued the fight.

After he blew the steeple to pieces with a single fireball, one with enough force left over to send me flying, I realised that, even in my battle form, he had me outmatched. Considering all the power that my star had granted me, I came to the conclusion that either this was a venerable archmage, and/or one of the Anointed. Worse, I was struggling to maintain my form for so long. But I felt like I could hold it for at least a few seconds more, and my companions would need every second they could get. I needed to stall the wizard a little longer.

I decided on an abrupt change of tactics, suddenly rushing at the wizard with a blast of fire. Unfortunately, I hadn't accounted for how my form had drastically increased my size, and the wizard scored a direct hit with a blast of force that sent me colliding into a wall. The hit was so hard that I wasn't able to maintain my battle form for any longer, reverting to normal. I coughed up blood.

I'd bought all the time I could. I cast my invisibility spell. I abruptly remembered how unreliable that was against other spellcasters when the wizard cast a detection spell. I assumed it was effective and ran. He flung another massive fireball at me, a wise move, giving me a nasty burn even through my magical wards, as well as incinerating most of the street. I turned and cast darkness at his eyes. He countered the spell and unleashed another wave of force. It sent me flying, and I landed awkwardly on my arm. There was a sickening crack and a swell of pain.

I heard Kurra roar in rage. She leapt from a nearby rooftop, tackling the wizard, repeatedly headbutting him as the two crashed to the ground. He blasted her at point-blank range, but she barely seemed to register the hit, simply continuing to hit him as the two fell out of my sight. I gritted my teeth, and my eyes stung with tears. I forced myself to my feet. This was getting out of hand—Kurra might need my help.

The clanging of armoured boots from up the street drew my attention. Peering out, I saw a figure in the robes of a high-ranking priest, surrounded by figures in gleaming armour with elaborate headdresses. I recognised the regalia of the Herald's Guard: elite warriors hand-picked by the Herald herself. I gulped, thinking about ways to get out of sight. If the priest also had powerful magic, I couldn't rely on invisibility.

But I could rely on my own small size. The fight had left plenty of debris and covered me in a layer of ash that would serve as fine camouflage. I slipped beneath a fallen beam—a tight squeeze even for me, and I doubted most of the guards would even be able to fit more than an arm in. It worked, the guard and their leader not looking twice at my hiding place.

They marched towards where I could hear the sounds of battle. The others were still unaccounted for, and I wasn't keen on their chances against an entire company of the Herald's Guard, with likely spellcaster or even Anointed support. My love pushed me through my fear and pain. I crept out of my hiding place and towards the sounds of fighting.

All I found was a thick wall of smoke, likely from one of Eledine's smoke bombs. The church's forces had the place surrounded and were sweeping it carefully, a few venturing into the smoke to seek their quarry. I thought about sending Cosma scouting, but if she were detected, she wouldn't last long on her own. My arm being broken seriously hampered my ability to fight and cast spells. On top of my already drained magic, there wasn't much more I could do. I slunk back into cover, praying to the Triune that my loves were alright.

Time passed slowly. I couldn't tell what was worse—the pain from my innumerable wounds or not knowing where the others were. The guards swept the area for hours. Eventually, the bulk of them left or took up more stationary positions. I slipped out of cover, restored my invisibility, and slunk past the cordon they'd set up.

I needed to find the others. But there was no way of signalling them without drawing the church's attention, and I wasn't in any condition to fight. Cosma's ability to track scent wouldn't be enough; all the foot traffic would trample over any scent. I needed to find some shelter or ally in the city.

My first guess was Lady Berrisen, but when I arrived at her manor, I'd discovered she'd "disappeared"—she must have overreached herself pursuing vengeance for her son. I then remembered another—the goblin "squatters" we helped with a housing problem. Despite it feeling like years ago, it was only a month or two. Hopefully, they were still there and would be willing to return the aid. Even better, they knew Eledine and Kurra. Quickly changing my clothes and disguising most of my traits and injuries, I made my way through the city to their house.

It was evening by the time I arrived, shed my disguise, and knocked on the door. The goblin who answered gave me a suspicious look. I whispered, "I need help."

The goblin, thankfully, recognised me and quickly ushered me inside. Thankfully, their family included one that was inducted into ancient shamanic magics banned by the church that were enough to ease my wounds. As they worked, I explained everything: what I'd been up to, the growing rebellion, and being separated from my companions. Not exactly in that order, as between the complex situation, my own disorientation, and the goblins' short attention spans, we ended up bouncing between topics. But I eventually managed to convey the important information. The goblins happily promised to look for the others (assuring me that Kurra wouldn't be hard to find) and let me spend the night. The downside was that the goblin's house was an absolute mess, but I wasn't in any position to complain. I managed to find a relatively clear spot on the floor to set up my bedroll and get some sleep.

When I awoke, I got some good news—multiple vagrants had sighted the others slipping past the guards in the city's foundry district, and a woman fitting Xeldia's description had been putting out feelers looking for me. I headed to the foundry district straight away.

I never liked Ansiel's constant bustle, and being actively hunted only made it worse. My small size again turned into a useful asset; I could easily be lost among a handful of other halflings, let alone the thick crowds of the city. I managed to get to the foundry district without entering a guard's line of sight once.

When I arrived, I again pondered the problem of how to signal the others without alerting any guards. Not coming up with anything, I started looking through those areas where they'd been seen. While passing some of the debris from yesterday's fight, a scent caught Cosma's attention. Tail wagging, she followed it through a tight alley. When it emerged onto another street, she suddenly bolted through a crowd.

I followed her. Through a forest of legs, I managed to find her in another alley, in which I was swept up by a very relieved Kurra.

"Peri! We were so worried!"

I hugged her back. "Me, too."

Eledine and Xeldia were with her, both just as relieved. Eledine started to ask, "Where have you—" She peered out into the street. "We can talk later. We've managed to find something of a safe house. Come on."

We slipped through the backstreets into an abandoned guildhouse—not exactly structurally sound, but it would be shelter while we planned our next move. We took a moment to catch each other up. Apparently, the others had managed to kill the Anointed wizard before making their escape, hiding among some of the workers in the seedier parts of the foundry district. They'd forgotten about the goblins and had anticipated I'd be in the rough vicinity of the fight at the canal—and so had been searching there.

Eledine had also quickly cased the Heartshold and confirmed what we had feared: What little forces the church hadn't sent to battle, the growing rebellion had dug into the Heartshold. Entire platoons were stationed at the main entrance, and every possible access point was guarded, on top of an existing layer of magical wards. Worse, it seemed the Herald was starting to wise up to our tactics and had prepared defences to counter rioting mobs, including several stacks of alchemical charges and fortified barricades; trying to break through the sheer number would result in a bloodbath.

So: How to penetrate the most heavily defended fortress on the continent? We spent a long time thinking about that problem. Some of that time was, admittedly, just resting after the intense battles of the previous day. Some of that was also just coping with the weight of the task laid on us. I wondered how things might have been different had I been able to break the curse on that sword myself.

Kurra said, "Make her think she's outmanoeuvred us." When we all looked at her, she elaborated. "She knows we're coming for her. We have to. So why send out any force from her fortress? Because she thinks she can end war. That is chance to find opening."

Eledine peered out from our shelter, scanning the area for anyone listening, before ducking her head back in. "It'll have to be a tempting target, then. And one heavily fortified enough to warrant sending a significant force, and one brief enough to deny her waiting for reinforcements."

I whispered, "Us."

Xeldia nodded. "We're the chosen. If we overextend ourselves, she'll have the chance to neutralise the greatest threat to her reign."

Eledine fidgeted with an arrow. "But that brings us to an incredibly thorny problem: How do we get her to think she's outmanoeuvred us? With our feats, she'll be careful to not underestimate us."

"What about snitches? Every time we stage a rebellion, someone leaks our plans to the guards. I'm willing to count on it." Xeldia snorted. "Some scum looking to save their own skin, giving us the edge…ironic."

"An idea. But our plan will have to be sophisticated enough to sabotage, but not so sophisticated as to make it strange when we leak it." Eledine furrowed her brow.

Kurra shrugged. "Just need target. Valuable, but something we might think we can take. She'll come up with likely attack plans herself."

Everyone took another few moments to think before Xeldia snapped her fingers. "The Villa Wards. The noble residences walled off from the rest of the city. A big enough riot there, and Viola starts losing support from the few people who actually like her. And, once we're past the walls, it's poorly defended; she'll have to divert the bulk of her forces to hold it."

Xeldia had started sketching a map of the region on the nearby wall when a strange tingle ran up my spine. A wave of potent magic had washed over the area, and something within us echoed in response.

I whispered, "Something's wrong. Someone cast a big spell." Everyone else looked at me expectantly. I only shrugged in response. "It was quick. Can't figure out what it did."

"I'm afraid we can't do much on 'someone cast a spell,' my love. Anyway, the bulk of the guards are headquartered in the eastern gatehouse, here. Since it has access to the walls, it's the most high-value target. Something worth us going personally." Xeldia started talking about the surrounding fortifications and their defences, and potential routes.

Then, a sickly orc rushed in. "Oi! Guards are comin'! Time to scrat!"

I put a few things together. "The spell must have detected us."

We rushed out of a back door into the street, bolting into a nearby alley. A voice called from behind us, "There! After them!"

Kurra growled, drawing her axe.

Eledine called, "Kurra! Keep running! We can't afford a pitched battle!"

Kurra grumbled but ducked back into the maze of streets. Noticing I was lagging, she picked me up as she passed.

We wove between streets and crowds, slipping under carts and behind stalls, trying to stop the guards from getting a good look at us. Every time we slipped into cover, we could hear the beat of boots on the street just behind us, driving us farther. Every minute, another squad of guards joined the pursuit. We could hear orders being barked, orders to man chokepoints and cut off pathways.

Desperate, we jumped down a grate, into what we expected to be a sewer. What we found was…indeed a sewer, but much more. An entire shanty town had been jammed beneath the city, all the city's undesirables seeking what little shelter they could amidst the city's actual refuse. Not taking our chances, we kept running through the maze, eventually hitting a dead end.

Seeing no other recourse, I slipped into the dingiest, most foul-smelling tent I could see, shoving a fistful of coins into the palm of the gap-toothed woman crouched outside. "We're not here!" My companions and I hurriedly piled in.

We kept a tight grip on our weapons as the clatter of arms and armour could be heard approaching. We heard the woman moan a slew of obscenities at the guards. It was abruptly cut short. One of the guards muttered something about wretches as they left.

Eledine carefully peered outside the tent. She slunk outside, her medical equipment in hand. Peering after her, I saw her quietly tending to the woman's wounds as the guards marched away, pointedly avoiding eye contact with any of the vagrants scattered around. We exited the tent, sighing in relief.

Sheltering among vagrants and cast-outs wasn't exactly a pleasant experience, but one got used to it, especially since we were all well-armed enough to deter any aggression. Eledine and Xeldia managed to garner some goodwill among the (understandably suspicious) undercity dwellers by providing some healing. After a little exploring and a skirmish with some slimes, we managed to find a quiet enough spot to resume our plotting.

Xeldia started. "One problem that's occurred to me will be making it look like we're in one location while striking another. Especially convincingly enough to keep the Heartshold's attention."

Eledine asked, "What about illusion magic? My sister did a thesis on the subject. Cosma, could you and Peri work that out?" Cosma yipped affirmatively. Eledine sighed. "Then, we have a plan. We…Kurra, Xeldia, and I strike the Heartshold, while…"

Kurra scowled. "We leave Peri on her own? Against everything the Heartshold has?"

I whispered, "And I don't want you fighting the Herald alone."

Eledine chuckled sadly. "I hate this plan almost as much as you do. But we need a plan, and we don't have any other options. Though that's one statement I am eager for you to prove wrong."

There was a pause, brows furrowed all around. I thought back to my meeting with my patron. "…Teleportation."

Chapter 32

We got to work on our plan. My companions started laying the groundwork for a riot that would raze the Villa Ward to the ground and demand a response from the Heartshold. Meanwhile, I got to work on a more interesting problem. My study into the stars had unlocked strange secrets about space and time and how both could be twisted at my will. Outright teleportation was a very complex and power-intensive spell, so Cosma and I spent a long time developing the magic.

Once or twice a day, I'd detect another magical pulse, and we'd have to move position. This gave me an idea: If Viola wasn't expecting teleportation, and if we struck right after a pulse, we'd have her completely off guard. The tricky thing was that the Heartshold was heavily warded against such things, so we'd only be able to get so close, but it would be enough to outmanoeuvre the bulk of the guards.

Once I had mastered the spell, I started snooping around for a good destination. Sweeping the undercity showed me more routes than I thought. I hired a local to show me around. To my surprise, we managed to get to the very edge of the Heartshold's foundations, and there, I even found a weak wall! After crafting a magical beacon with which to target the teleportation, I told the others of the weakness. Eledine immediately started brewing some explosives with which to take advantage of that particular weakness.

After a week of careful planning and constant games of cat-and-mouse with the inquisition, we finally agreed we were ready. We'd stoked the fires of unrest, and the guards had plenty on their plates keeping even a semblance of order. The conspiracy of the true faithful had granted us the aid of a few agents, and they gathered at our command, ready to lead the incoming mobs of vagrants. We found an inconspicuous spot near the Villa Ward's eastern district, and we waited.

Once again, I felt the magical pulse. We waited. We watched guards gather. Soon, one of the Anointed, a dour woman marked with resplendent robes, flanked by a squad of the Herald's Guard, approached us. "You, heretics and traitors. You will come to answer for your crimes!"

We looked at each other and nodded.

Xeldia stood, shifting, letting her holy aura bloom. "Crimes will be answered for, today. The Herald's." She howled.

There was a cry of exultant rage. From every hidden corner, from every abandoned ruin, from every ignored slum, came the outcast and the oppressed, crashing onto the guards like an avalanche. The Herald's Guards spun around to respond, leaving them wide open for Kurra to start cutting through.

Xeldia charged the Anointed. She slipped under Xeldia's strike, casting a spell that called a pillar of light from the heavens, which slammed down on her with immaterial force. I didn't let the Anointed press the advantage, warping time around her, slowing her a few crucial seconds, seconds which Xeldia spent getting up, her holy gifts sealing fractured bone.

Eledine and Kurra concentrated on the Herald's guard. Each was elite, but not quite *Kurra* elite, and the mob swarming around them divided their attention that little bit. With Kurra's might and Eledine's drug-enhanced sharpshooting, gaps in their defences were found and exploited. One by one, they fell.

The Anointed cast another spell and flew to the rooftops, firing blasts of light as she fell back. Xeldia's protections and armour took the worst of the hits, though she did suffer one or two nasty burns. I returned fire. The Anointed shifted tactics, casting a new spell that stilled all the mana in the area, denying Xeldia and me our magics. I dove for stronger cover.

This didn't stop Kurra. Her athletics were an easy match for the Anointed's flight, and she quickly caught up, bearing down on her with her primordial axe, quickly drawing blood. The Anointed hurried to cast a blast of force that knocked Kurra flying, only to be left wide open for a telling shot from Eledine.

Meanwhile, Xeldia turned her attention towards the lower-ranking guards, and I slipped out of the magical null zone, just in time for a whole company of Heartshold paladins to come marching down the street. I ducked into the chaos for cover before leaping out with a blinding flash of starlight. The confused and scattered paladins bumped into each other in their tight formation, buying our side a few precious seconds.

Eledine's longbow was just out of range of the Anointed's spells, and Kurra had the idea of using the buildings for cover. With her powers no longer helpful, the Anointed used the last of her strength holding off another volley before Kurra leapt at her, slaying her with a swift swing. Kurra didn't waste any more time there, turning back to us to regroup.

Something caught Kurra's attention, and she redoubled her sprint. "It's time!"

I was about to ask if we wanted to draw in a few more of the Heartshold's forces when a mountain of a man, clad head to toe in rune-inscribed golden armour, came crashing into the ground like a meteor, crushing a pair of rebels and scattering a dozen more with the shockwave. His insignia was much the same as that of the Herald's Guard, but he was obviously high-ranking, perhaps their captain. He immediately sprinted at Xeldia with impossible speed, and it was all she could do to hold him off.

I regrouped with the others—thankfully, the magical null zone had faded, leaving me free to cast the teleportation spell. It was dangerous focusing on such a complex spell in the midst of a hundred people trying to kill me, but I trusted my lovers. As the battle raged, my companions forming a defensive circle around me, I called upon my star's power. It flowed through me, and I shaped it with rune and incantation. I wove it into the space around me. The magic built. The spell construct was finished. I cast.

There was a flash, a surge of air pressure; reality itself shifted and warped around us. And we were back in the undercity, just the four of us. Well, I did inadvertently bring along a single unfortunate guard, but Kurra quickly knocked him out before he realised what was going on. We panted in exhaustion.

Eledine relaxed her bow. "Alright, does anyone need medical attention before we proceed?"

Most of us did, so we took a minute to patch our wounds and catch our breaths. The hard stone walls of the undercity easily carried echoes, and they were carrying the sounds of the battles above. It wasn't easy to rest knowing that our chance was being bought with the blood of our followers. It was unspoken, but clear, that we couldn't—*wouldn't*—let the sacrifice be in vain. When we were ready, we gave Eledine the nod. We ducked into cover, and she lit the fuse.

The blast left our ears ringing for at least a minute, a minute we didn't want to spare, so Xeldia charged forward into the breach, waving her sword in a gesture for us to follow, and follow we did. We emerged into what seemed to be a little-used storeroom, some poor servant or other looking at us, terrified. We ignored them.

The distraction had worked—only a handful of guards were still in the upper layers of the Heartshold, all of whom swiftly fell or fled. We kept up a swift pace, Xeldia leading us through the countless corridors and halls into the deepest parts of the Heartshold.

She soon led us down a disused tunnel into a stony lower level. "Here," she said. "The inner sanctums; only the Herald and her Anointed are allowed in here. If the engines are anywhere, they're here."

We swept room after room. There were a few offices, one or two rooms full of sensitive records, and some quarters. But no sign of the engines.

Kurra began to grumble. "Taking too much time! Reinforcements on their way!"

I piped up. "Hold on!" I sent out a magical pulse, feeling how mana flowed around me. I was about to call the effort fruitless, but at the very edge of my senses, I found something. It was indistinct, but undoubtedly powerful. I followed it, my companions following me.

We came out into the grand hall, where the Herald would give her grandest sermons to her most devout followers. It was an immense space; my family's entire inn could fit inside half a dozen times! The stained-glass windows left rainbow lights twinkling on the walls, and our footsteps echoed on the marble.

Eledine adjusted her glasses. "Well, if it *is* here, it's well hidden."

I led the party to a grand dais at one end of the hall, where a large altar sat, and behind that, a gilded throne. I tapped it curiously. "...Secret tunnel."

Eledine knelt next to it, examining an armrest. "Hmm… you're right. There's a keyhole here, one rune inlaid. Peri, you know a thing or two about locks. Any ideas?"

I took out my tools and started carefully examining the lock. It was remarkably sophisticated, with both mechanical and arcane parts, as well as mechanisms and defences I hadn't encountered before. I gently prodded it, considering how I'd bypass the mechanism.

Kurra roared in frustration, cutting the throne in half with a massive strike from her axe. She ripped the ruins away, revealing a passageway beneath it. She grunted. "Too much time."

I was about to argue the point when the double doors on the other side of the hall flung open, revealing a squad of Herald's Guard and no small number of reinforcements. I turned and bolted down the passageway, my companions swiftly catching up and running past me. We didn't go far before encountering a massive door of celestial metal, the emblem of the Triune emblazoned upon it. Xeldia rested a hand upon it. The emblem of Raiya on her hand glowed, as did the section representing the goddesses on the door's symbol. Kurra and Eledine followed suit, and the whole symbol gleamed before the door slowly opened.

We rushed inside as the clatter of a dozen charging boots could be heard from up the passageway. Eledine whirled around and slammed the door shut. A moment later, we heard banging on the other side as the guards tried to open the door, to no avail.

Eledine slumped against the door, panting hard. "Well. We're here."

Xeldia took a few breaths. "We are. But that was too easy. Viola must have one last line of defence."

Kurra hefted her axe. "Then let's find it and break it!"

We marched deeper down into darkness, our way lit by a small orb of starlight in my hand. We reached another set of doors and heaved them open.

Light streamed out. Beyond an immense, circular chamber, the size of Ansiel's coliseum, gold and silver rings orbited around a central platform forged from aurora. A bridge led us to a central dais.

Atop, a woman. Clad in grand, gilded robes, wielding a staff that churned with impossible mechanisms. But beneath it all, she seemed…strangely ordinary. She was studying an altar in the centre of the room. "…I must admit, blowing your way through a storage room was the one stratagem I didn't anticipate. Slippery devils."

Xeldia growled, canine teeth bared. "You. You, who dare continue to use the name of Herald! You, who dare invoke the name of the Triune!"

"The Triune betrayed *us*," Viola hissed, turning towards us. "We had something beautiful. Something peaceful. And then they started taking the side of you *wretches*."

I looked at my lovers. "Wretches?"

"Slips. Greenskins. Beasts. Deviants." She spat at each of us in turn. "You saw the city I had outside. Peaceful. Comfortable. I even carved out a place for you ungrateful scum, and this is how you repay me?"

Something clicked. "All this…five hundred years…wars, murder, conspiracy…because you're racist?" I burst into bitter laughter.

Eledine shared the chuckle. "I must admit, I was imagining something grander, some elaborate speech about psychology or philosophy to justify your actions. But you're over five hundred years old, and you can't tolerate orcs? That's just pathetic."

Viola brandished her staff. "Pathetic!? Five hundred years, and I have only seen bloodshed from the greenskin!"

Kurra scoffed. "Have you considered that we're violent because we deal with you?"

"I have never been anything less than fair and reasonable! All I have ever asked is for things to be *normal*!" Viola slammed her staff on the ground.

Xeldia took a step forward. "You started a war, you lied to the world for centuries, you built immense slave camps and cast in the vulnerable, and you call yourself fair and reasonable!?"

"Is it so unreasonable to cast out the violent and the lazy!? To drive them out!? To enforce some level of sanity in our world!?" Viola roared.

I cocked my head. "Do you…really think that?"

"Of course I do. Have you seen the greenskins? The wretches I have sent to the colonies? Of course you have. And you'd allow my society to be overrun with them." She snarled. "No."

We raised our weapons. Xeldia snorted. "All this time…I never saw how utterly pathetic you are. All of this because you can't stand to see someone acting strange. But justice must come, to great and small—a verse you drilled into me many a time. Come then. Face it."

We charged as Viola raised her staff. An immense pulse of force emanated from her, sending Eledine, Kurra, and me flying. Eledine deftly rolled into the landing, Kurra simply leapt back to her feet, and I took flight to save myself the fall. Xeldia had deflected the blast with her holy power and was continuing the charge.

She met Viola in melee combat. While Xeldia's arms were perhaps better suited, Viola was lightning-fast and impossibly skilled, swiftly knocking Xeldia back with a heavy strike. Viola raised her staff again, and a dozen phantom blades formed, flying at each of us. We all fell on the defensive.

I ducked and weaved between the blades, my arcane defences catching one or two strikes I was too slow to evade. As Viola readied another spell, I realised we needed to shift back to the offensive, and soon. I knew that casting my speed spells would grant us the extra time we needed, but doing so would take my focus away from my arcane shields and no doubt cost me some nasty cuts.

But the women I loved were in mortal danger, and a few cuts were nothing compared to that. I called upon my stellar power, again shifting the currents of space and time, forcing them to flow in our favour. The blades sliced into me, slashing skin. I kept my focus. One cut deep into my stomach. Through tears of pain, I kept casting. I finished my spell, and the cosmos answered my call.

Together, Kurra and Xeldia rushed Viola. Viola drew her magic into herself, abandoning her phantasmal blades, veins flaring with magical fire as she met the pair in a deadly dance, her faux-holy power granting her enhanced speed to match theirs. Her staff struck with lightning speed, parrying and striking. But Kurra and Xeldia had fought together a dozen times, and each played off openings the other left, slowly forcing Viola to give ground.

My blood oozing onto the floor, I flew to Eledine's side. I squeaked "Help!"

We needed no more words. The enhanced speed meant it took Eledine only a second to smear my wound with some stinging ointment that quickly hardened over the wound. I quickly flew back into the fray.

Kurra overreached by the tiniest amount, and Viola slipped under her guard, landing a flurry of strikes that sent her sprawling. Blasting Xeldia back with magical force, she advanced on Kurra for a killing blow. I charged forward, bathing her in the void's darkness. Her eyes flared with light, piercing through as she pressed her staff to Kurra's neck. A shot from Eledine found her robes. They had clearly been given powerful enchantments, as the arrow didn't penetrate, but the impact shifted her weight just enough for Kurra to add to the momentum, flinging Viola across the room.

Kurra pressed the advantage with a charge, reaching Viola before she could stand. A heavy strike landed on a magical shield, which cracked and fractured under the pressure. Xeldia had caught up and took advantage of the gap with a thrust. Viola twisted just in time to turn a lethal stab through the skull into a cut across the nose. She hissed in rage and pain.

She fired a blast of fire directly at Kurra, point blank, full force, the intense magic penetrating even Kurra's dragonbone plate. The room filled with the horrid scent of burning flesh. I flew to Kurra's side as Xeldia forced Viola back with a shield bash. I grabbed Kurra and, with all my strength, pulled her to Eledine's side. My adventuring career had improved my strength no small amount, and Eledine was quickly tending to Kurra's wound.

I turned my magic towards unravelling Viola's. It was of a potency I'd never encountered before, but her capacity to channel it seemed to be a little bit limited; I managed to divert some of the power's flow. Only a portion of her power, but it drained her strikes that small amount, enough to turn what could have been a decisive blow to the head into something that just drew blood. Xeldia snarled, taking advantage of Viola's grip on her staff to bite hard into her hand.

Viola roared, using her other hand to cast a spell and blasting Xeldia with fire. Her holy defences held, at least enough to keep her in the fight, though she was forced to retreat behind her shield. With a moment's breathing room, Viola slammed her staff into the ground, and a magical force field surrounded her and Xeldia, cutting her off. She then bore down onto Xeldia. The barrier cut off magical flows, meaning I couldn't drain power from Viola directly. I blasted the barrier with full force, but it held.

Eledine grimaced as she finished tending Kurra's burns. She jammed another elixir into Kurra's mouth. "Strength enhancer, experimental recipe! Hit her with everything you've got!"

She didn't need any more encouragement. As Viola blasted Xeldia's shield away, Kurra charged the force field, putting all her momentum and strength into a single strike. The axe, forged from the most primal metals, cracked the force field, a crack just large enough for me to fire through. Viola was caught off guard, my strike landing a serious burn across her face.

She roared, "Enough!" She slammed her staff on the ground, sending out a shockwave that again forced us back. Face contorted in anger, she spread her arms wide, the divine mechanisms around the room whirring, glowing brighter and brighter as she called more power into herself. She rose into the air, an immense, translucent avatar of herself forming around her, five times human size. She spoke, and her avatar echoed her voice with deafening volume. "Burn, wretches!" She emitted a colossal wave of fire.

I quickly flew above it, but even then, the heat was painful. Xeldia quickly recovered her shield and focused on her holy aura, Kurra covering behind her to absorb the hit. Eledine rolled off the platform, evading the hit but falling against the room's outer walls and colliding with a spinning ring with an impact that had to be dangerous. Hoping Kurra and Xeldia could hold Viola's attention, I flew to Eledine's side.

As the ring rotated, threatening Eledine with another painful drop, I hurriedly picked her up. It was difficult to get enough leverage with my small size, but somehow, I managed it, at least for long enough for me to carry her behind a slight rise in the floor, one that would provide better cover than nothing.

Eledine handed me another vial with gritted teeth. "Try throwing this at that… *bitch's* face."

I didn't need any further instruction. As Kurra and Xeldia dodged colossal staff strikes, I flew towards the head of Viola's avatar and threw. I hit my target, but she barely seemed to notice, the avatar only slightly flickering as alchemical flames seared at it.

Worse, I'd given away my position. Viola glared at me, her avatar holding up a hand. I pushed my flight spell to its limits, barely dodging a volley of divine fire, which still managed to singe my boots. Kurra and Xeldia reached the avatar's feet, but she simply leapt out of their reach.

At least forcing her back won me a few precious seconds with which to assess the situation. The avatar was larger and faster than any of us, and it would take a massive hit to break through to Viola herself. Since she could outpace us, it'd have to be a ranged attack. I saw the avatar flicker, ever so slightly, where Eledine's flames were burning. A plan took shape in my mind; a frankly insane plan, but the situation being what it was, an insane plan was warranted.

I flew over to where Eledine was slumped on the ground, hurriedly tending to her arm. I whispered, "Concentrate fire on a single point, front of the neck, where the fire's burning! Have a plan!"

She glanced between me and her arm. Then, she downed the last of her elixirs. Grimacing in pain, she picked up her longbow and opened fire. Her shots landed, and the magic holding the avatar together, ever so slightly, began to strain.

Viola saw the new threat and answered. She held up a hand and called a pillar of light down on Eledine. I managed to push her just far enough out of the way so, instead of being entirely crushed, she just broke her leg. She kept firing.

I called, "Xeldia! Cover Eledine!"

Xeldia didn't need any more encouragement, turning back to Eledine and sheltering her with shields, both physical and magical.

Viola shifted tactics, concentrating her attacks on Kurra. Kurra's immense strength was nonetheless starting to fail, and she was crucial for the final stage of my plan.

I glanced at the avatar; a weak spot was appearing, but not quite large enough yet. I needed just a few more seconds. "Cosma! I need a distraction!"

Despite the dangers, the fox was happy to be a nuisance. She leapt from my shoulder and rushed around the avatar's feet. With her own magical power, she started interfering with the avatar's magic. It worked. Viola growled in anger, stomping hard. The shockwave sent Cosma careening. Her yelp hurt more than a broken bone. But I had a plan, and the fate of the world rested on it.

Cosma had won me those few precious seconds, and the avatar's neck began to crackle, its magic losing stability. Viola noticed, placing her staff between it and Eledine. But that would be her last mistake.

I flew to Kurra's side. "Throw me at her neck, that weak point. Hard!"

Fortunately, Kurra seemed perfectly accepting of entirely insane plans. She grabbed me, and with her colossal, alchemy-enhanced strength, she propelled me at a projectile's speed towards our target. Mid-flight, I embraced cosmic power, entering my star-empowered battle form. I collided, the cosmic fires crashing through the avatar. The pain of the impact was drowned out by the elation of a plan working. I quickly changed course, crashing down on where Viola was floating, in the avatar's torso.

She dismissed her avatar, trying to shift power to oppose me, but she was too late. I struck her with flaming fists again and again. My rage at her atrocities, my own pain, my desire to protect my loves, I channelled it all into power. I slammed her into the ground. She flinched, and her staff rolled away from her. As she reached for it, I seized her hand. I ignited her with cosmic fires. She screamed as she turned to ash.

It was over.

Centuries of conspiracy, beaten.

It seemed…unreal. My mind simply could not process the implications, not when we were all injured and exhausted. I dismissed my battle form and collapsed, panting.

I heard Kurra stand with a groan. "Cosma…?"

I was too exhausted to move, but I saw Kurra walk over and pick up Cosma where she lay. With sagging strength, she staggered over to Eledine, tears welling in her eyes. "Is she…?"

Eledine looked to be even worse off than Kurra, but she did her best to examine Cosma. "…She's not dead, but she's in critical condition, and I'm out of elixirs. Xeldia?"

Xeldia tried laying a hand on Cosma. She shook her head. "I'm spent."

I looked over at the staff. How hard could controlling a divine engine be? The answer was no doubt *very*, but there was no way I wasn't going to try everything to save Cosma. With what little strength I'd recovered, I stood, taking the staff. I opened the magical passages inside my mind, bridging it and me.

Within was…

Everything.

The light from the tiniest window into the engines was nearly blinding. I gritted my teeth and focused. Inside were innumerable forces flowing within and around each other in impossibly complex patterns. I carefully examined them, one by one. I ever-so-gently prodded, trying to unravel their mysteries.

There was so much. Viola had five centuries, and I doubted she could have possibly unlocked all the engine's secrets. There was no way I could unlock its power in the few minutes Cosma still had. But I made a connection in my mind: If the Triune was right, they and the engines operated under similar principles.

Leaning heavily on the staff, I walked over to Xeldia's side. I examined the pit in her soul formed from magic overspent. And, as I moved, I felt something else shift inside the staff—or rather, something shift from the staff's perspective. I found that pit in Xeldia's soul and the tiniest dregs of Raiya's power. Fumbling around its functions for even rudimentary control, I found some way to pull those divine strings. I did my best to mimic Raiya's power and pushed some into Xeldia.

She suddenly yelped in pain. "Peri! What did you do?"

"Tried to give you more power." I squirmed guiltily, worried I'd inadvertently hurt her.

Xeldia blinked a moment, then she examined her hand. It glowed with a faint, golden light. She laid it on Cosma. Cosma stirred. Weakly, but stirred, nonetheless.

Eledine laughed with relief. "It worked! She won't be running around for a while, but she'll live." She grunted. "I don't think any of us will be doing much for a while."

Xeldia panted. "Perhaps. My apologies, Peri, but that burned. Badly. Perhaps we save any more of…whatever you did, unless any of us is also in mortal need?"

Eledine looked at her arm. "That…well, I'm not in *mortal* need, but I may have permanently warped my arm pushing it like that."

I hummed uncertainly. "I…don't know how to use this."

"I suppose we don't want to risk anything more today." She lay back. "Okay, next thing: finding a place for some goddamned *rest*."

Kurra fished a bedroll out of her pack. "This place is as good as any."

Not having the spare energy to take out my own bedroll, I snuggled into hers. Xeldia chuckled as she got out her own and laid it beside Eledine. The four of us spent a length of time we had no way of measuring simply lying there together, panting in exhaustion, hoping the pain of our injuries would fade swiftly. Our embrace was soothing.

Chapter 33

I managed to work out just enough of the divine engine's mechanisms to dispel some of the Herald's active magical defences around the Heartshold. Meanwhile, a few hours of rest were enough for Xeldia and me to recharge some of our magics, but all of us were still in pretty rough condition, Eledine in particular; pushing her broken arm so hard, especially with alchemical enhancements, left it gruesomely warped. Our gear was also worse for wear. We'd finished our objective, killing Viola and seizing the engines, so we agreed that we'd done enough for now.

We left the Herald's staff and regalia where they lay—with Viola dead, only we could access the engines now, and we didn't want to risk any piece of the engines falling back into enemy hands. Kurra, Xeldia, and I were ready to throw the last of our strength into a fight out of the Heartshold, but in a stroke of luck, by the time we exited the underground chambers, it was night, with only a pair of the Herald's Guard stationed in the underground chamber. We swiftly detained them before they could raise the alarm, and we were able to sneak out of the Heartshold. From there, we made our way out of the city. And from there, we, or at least I, headed back home.

It was late evening when I headed through the back entrance to the tavern. Mum and Ori were busy with the post-dinner clean-up.

Ori looked up. "Hey, you're…" Her eyes bulged. "Peri!"

The sight of my family was a welcome balm after so long, and so much. "Hi!" I ran up and hugged her.

Mum was nearly crying with joy. "Peri! Look at you! Have you been doing more magic? Oh, you'll have to tell us everything!"

My other friends entered behind me. Xeldia bowed politely. "Our apologies for our sudden arrival; matters have only escalated, and we've had to operate with a level of secrecy. We were hoping you would be kind enough to shelter us for a while; we were severely wounded in battle."

Mum smiled. "Of course, of course! We'll always find room for you, never fear!"

We were soon all crouched in my old room; a little tight for my taller companions, but they didn't mind being closer to me, or each other. Mum hurried to serve up some classic home cooking for dinner. We proceeded to bring my family up to speed on all that had happened since we last visited. They were just shy of awestruck at how I'd met the Triune themselves and slew the traitorous Herald!

Before retiring for the night, I decided to spend a little more time stargazing in the fields. The others decided to join me, and I was happy for the company. Taking a break from studying the secrets of stars and void, the four of us (five if you counted Cosma) simply sat, leaning on each other, staring at the stars as they whirled overhead.

Kurra pondered, "Wonder if any realise Herald is dead."

Xeldia hummed. "Among the Anointed? They will have to at least suspect by now. But they will suppress that information as long as they can, and that may be some time. Though not forever; people will wonder why she isn't making public appearances."

Eledine asked, "Who will take charge in her place?"

"Renneth, most likely. One of the Anointed, and from what I can tell, she was Viola's second-in-command. Though with the Herald's fate uncertain, there will be a question as to how much authority she can wield," Xeldia explained.

Kurra grinned. "Doubt Herald was planning for own death. Confusion in Heartshold should be enough for Triune to turn tide."

Eledine hummed. "I hope so. But I doubt the Anointed will let their authority go without a fight. Things will get messier before they get better."

I whispered, "But they'll get better."

Xeldia smiled. "Yes. They will."

Also from Lina Hailings:

Veronica Wainwright is the greatest soldier humanity has ever forged. And Sarah Torren, a small, dorky, and otherwise average mage, has somehow won her heart.

The supernatural community trembles in fear as demon attacks rise, and even the mundane world struggles under the steadily growing darkness. Veronica, champion of an ancient order of monster hunters, is on the front lines of the war for humanity. Sarah is struggling to earn a living in the old and crumbling Circle of Magi. But amidst these struggles, they find time to be together, times they can enjoy.

When the pair inadvertently trigger the apocalypse, Veronica must fight battle after battle to safeguard humanity, while Sarah must work to survive in the ashes of society. As moments together grow ever more rare, they learn to treasure them ever more, moments when they can remind themselves why they survive in a dark world.

The Moments Between The Apocalypse: An urban fantasy sapphic romance about finding moments of light in the darkest of times

The Moments Between the Apocalypse
By Lina Hailings
← SHELTER

A Moments Between The Apocalypse Story

I might have been a mage, but unlike many of my kind, I preferred to live among modern society. As such, I'd picked up some modern hobbies, and some ordinary friends (none of which knew I was a mage, of course). One of those hobbies was tabletop roleplaying, and I had found a good group. There were five of us: Abby, Pat, Ryan, Veronica, and myself. I was friendly with all of them, but I was secretly nursing a crush on Veronica: a huge, muscle-bound woman peppered with badass scars and tattoos.

On this particular weekend, there was a big gaming convention being hosted, and that meant games, and more hard-to-find books than the game store would stock in a year. It was in another city, so it also meant transport and accommodation. To save money, my TTRPG group decided to all go together. The logistics weren't easy, but we managed to find a motel that could accommodate the five of us between two rooms at a reasonable rate, and found a timetable that allowed all of us a good deal of time.

We arrived at the motel, a clean but not nearly upscale place with bare concrete walkways connecting brick rooms. We took a look at the rooms we'd been given, plotting who would stay in each. We found the first room, with three beds, a bit cramped, so we were considering drawing straws over who'd get the second when we arrived at it. We opened the door, and it was more spacious, but with one caveat:

There was only one bed.

A double bed, yes, but only one. The five of us stared at it, not sure what to say. Pat stepped forward. "Ah, relax, these places usually just jam two beds together." He examined the bed closer. "Er. No. Not this one."

Abby piped up. "Hold on, there might have been a mix-up. Let me check." She scurried off in the direction of the lobby. The remaining four of us stood around awkwardly for a minute before she returned. "No luck, they're packed to the brim."

Ryan asked "Could we find somewhere else?"

"During this convention? I doubt it." Abby scoffed. "I guess a couple of us will have to share." We all froze, looking between each other. Friendships were being tested today. I deliberately stopped myself from looking at Veronica; too close of a gaze could reveal my feelings. Abby continued "Well, it makes sense for the biggest to share with the smallest, right?"

Veronica and I. The mathematical part of my brain pointed out it would actually make more sense for the two smallest to share. The rest of my brain told that part to shut the fuck up. "Um, okay, that could work…"

Veronica shook her head. "Nah, I can take a couch. I'm used to sleeping rough."

"No, no, it's fine! You need your sleep! Hey, if anyone's taking a couch, it's me. I'd probably fit." I hurriedly said.

Veronica turned stern. "Absolutely not. You're not taking a couch if I have anything to say about it."

Abby seemed outright excited by the situation. "Then it's settled! Sarah and Veronica will share."

There was a long pause, everyone keenly aware that this situation was awkward, but no-one offering any other ideas. Eventually, Pat scurried off to the other room, followed by Ryan and Abby, leaving Veronica and I standing outside the door to our room. We stared at each other for a long while. Eventually, Veronica took a deep breath, and entered. I followed behind. The room was more spacious, but still pretty cramped. Veronica set down her olive-green travel bag. "Look, I really don't want to make you uncomfortable, so I'll still gladly take the couch—"

"No, no! It's fine, it's fine!" I could feel my heart race. Was this really happening? Awkwardly, I set my suitcase nearby, and started unpacking. Veronica started doing the same. We both moved to bring things into the bathroom at the same time, which lead to a brief traffic jam as she took up almost the entire space with her mountainous size. She simply deposited her washkit quickly (a surprising amount of floral products, including that lavender perfume I loved!) before leaving with an apologetic look.

After I left my own things there, I started to feel the exhaustion of the day's journey. We'd left late in the day to account for our group's professional lives, and it was late night at this point. "Think I might turn in for the night."

Veronica said "Sure. I'm going to have a shower. Then I'll probably join—" you, she was about to say. "—I'll probably turn in as well."

She headed into the bathroom. I simply stood there as I heard the shower turn on. A small part of my mind happily informed me that Veronica was no doubt naked in there. I shoved the lecherous thoughts aside and started changing into my pyjamas, but it wasn't long before they returned. I managed to not get completely lost in them, but they were oh so appealing.

I finished getting changed in spite of my treacherous libido, turned off the light, and crawled into bed. Not wanting to make Veronica uncomfortable, I curled up in one corner, leaving as much room as possible for her. But now there was nothing else to draw my attention to, my thoughts fixated entirely on Veronica. The thought entered my mind that if I repositioned just so, I'd be taking up more space, and that could mean physical contact with Veronica. I shoved the idea out of my mind. If I couldn't get my mind off of Veronica, the least I could do was keep my thoughts to myself. I curled myself up as tight as I could.

It wasn't long before Veronica was finished in the shower. I heard her exit. I did my best to pretend to be asleep. I heard Veronica getting changed, before feeling the bed shift as she lay down beside me. I could, just barely, feel her warmth. Then, I could feel her hand ever-so-slightly brush my hair. My heart leapt. Veronica then turned away from me. She started softly snoring soon after.

I remained awake for a long while. Veronica Wainwright, the burliest woman I'd ever seen, confident, powerful, was sleeping in the same bed as me. I could roll over, and we'd be touching. I'd be touching—cuddling—the most breathtaking woman I've ever met. It was all I could do to not give in to that temptation. It was the warmest ache of my life.

I was woken by a shout, and movement beside me. I quickly sat up. It was night, but the motel room was faintly illuminated by the never-sleeping lights of the city. I looked at Veronica. She twisted and turned, thrashing and shouting, deep in the throes of what must have been a terrifying nightmare. I stared at her, paralysed by uncertainty. What was I supposed to do in this situation? One thing was certain: I couldn't do nothing. Something was seriously getting to Veronica. Not knowing what else to do, I gently shook her awake. "Veronica?"

A rush of movement, and Veronica was pinning me to the bed, hand tight around my throat. I was simultaneously terrified and intensely aroused. My heart thundered in my chest as I struggled to breathe. Just as the room began to spin, Veronica suddenly pulled her hand back. "Oh—Shit! Shit, I'm sorry, I'm sorry." She hurried off the bed, standing as I worked to catch my breath. Veronica kept profusely apologising. "I'm sorry, I was—I was having a nightmare, and I was fighting, and you were right there, and..."

I flicked on a nearby lamp. I'd regained enough breath to speak. "It's okay…" I slowly sat up, rubbing my neck. "Do you—" I took another breath to calm my racing heart and strained lungs "—want to talk about it?"

"Me? You're the one I nearly killed!" She exclaimed, loud enough that I was a little worried about waking the neighbours.

I couldn't think of a polite way of phrasing actually, that was a massive turn-on, so I instead said "I'm fine. Bit of a shock, that's all."

Veronica seemed to calm down. "Alright, I…" She sat down on the side of the bed.

I moved until I was sitting beside her. "Are you alright?"

She sighed. "Yeah. Just a rough night." The two of us sat in silence for a while. Then, she said "I've lived a… pretty violent life. Grew up in a hick town with a lot of boys that thought they could do whatever they wanted, and a lot of dads that let them. Never could stand a bully. And there are a lot of bullies in the world. I've spent pretty much my entire life getting into fights. And it ain't fun. I just…" She trailed off.

I had absolutely no idea what to say, but I could think of something to do. I gently wrapped an arm around her. I could feel her warmth, the build of her muscles, and the texture of an old scar. I could also feel her relax, just a little. We sat there like that, listening to the faint hum of the city outside. After a while, Veronica said "Thanks for showing me this group, by the way. Haven't had much to do, outside of work. It's nice being able to, you know, relax."

"I know the feeling. I've always found it kind of hard to make friends."

Something about my words seemed to amuse Veronica, but she didn't comment on it. After a moment longer, I asked "Feeling better?"

"Yeah." She stood, and stretched. "Come on, lets try to grab what more sleep we can." She lay back down, lying straight against the edge of the bed, giving me as much room as she could. I returned the favour, curling up on the other side. I turned off the light. We lay there in silence. I thought more of what had just happened. She didn't want to speak of it, and I didn't want to pry, but I could tell something had scarred Veronica deeply. I gently reached an arm out towards her, careful to stop halfway, just in case she wanted to take it.

She did.

A minute later, she whispered "Thanks, by the way."

"Any time."

I was warm when I woke up. I could feel Veronica's warmth all around me, her arm laid over me. I felt a deep sense of safety. Then, suddenly, she was gone, abruptly withdrawing from me and getting out of bed. The parts of my brain that were supposed to process the reasons for that were still booting up, so all I could feel was cold.

A moment later, I was awake enough to realise what had just happened: Veronica was cuddling me. My brain reached the junction of "If she didn't want to cuddle, then maybe she doesn't like me" and "Of course she suddenly pulled away, this would be incredibly awkward since we're just friends!" At which point it completely failed to choose a direction and crashed headlong into the retaining wall. By the time I got my train of thought back on track, Veronica had already cleaned up in the bathroom, and headed outside. Eventually, I got up and got dressed. My group were planning on getting breakfast together at a nearby fast food joint, and I was feeling pretty hungry. Between the hunger, the tangled state of my emotions, and the fact that my neck was still kind of sore from last night, I couldn't bother making myself look good, I could duck back in to handle all that when we packed up.

I left the room to see Abby and Veronica leaning on the railing, talking. When Abby saw me, her eyes lit up, and strangely, she blushed. "Oh, uh, hey Sarah. So… what did you two get up to last night?"

I looked at her, confused. "Um, nothing?"

Ryan exited the adjacent room. "What's going—" He looked at me, and his eyes bulged. "Oh…"

Veronica snapped "I was having a nightmare, she tried to wake me up, and panicked and nearly killed her, alright!?"

Abby and Ryan shared a look that said they didn't believe her. I was looking between the three, confused. "What are you—?" Something clicked. I took out my phone, and switched to the front-facing camera.

There was a visible bruise around my neck.

It wasn't hard to guess the conclusion that the others had drawn. I was wishing I'd studied earth magic, so I could command the ground to swallow me whole. When Abby and Ryan were unable to stifle giggles, I fled back into the hotel room, rushing for the bathroom. I felt like I'd implode. As much as I hated those two being wrong, there was a part of me that lamented that they weren't right.

I managed to get a grip on myself, and covered up the bruise with some foundation. I returned to the rest to find Pat had joined them. Veronica was wearing a scowl, and the other three "Who, me?" looks. There was an awkward silence as we headed down to get something to eat. Veronica was pointedly not looking at anyone else. The others kept looking between her and me. The night's events would be on my mind every day for weeks.

www.ingramcontent.com/pod-product-compliance
Lightning Source LLC
Chambersburg PA
CBHW030527190726
48283CB00006B/1807